FROZEN TIDES

FROZEN TIDES

BOOK **4** IN THE

FALLING KINGDOMS

SERIES

MORGAN RHODES

RAZORBILL

An Imprint of Penguin Random House

RAZORBILL

An Imprint of Penguin Random House
Penguin.com

ISBN: 978-1-59514-708-0

Printed in the United States of America

3 5 7 9 10 8 6 4

KRAESHIAN
EMPIRE

JEWEL
OF THE
EMPIRE

THE

AMARANTH

SEA

KRAESHIAN
EMPIRE

THE NORTHERN SEA

Mytica

THE
TINGUE
SEA

THE

SILVER

SEA

LIMEROS

Ravencrest

Castle
Damora

The Temple
of Valoria

The Iron Coast

The Granite Coast

The Emerald Forest

BLACK HARBOR

PAELSIA

Basilius's
Compound

Forbidden Mountains

TRADER'S
HARBOR

THE WILDLANDS

KING'S
HARBOR

The Temple
of Cleiona

AURANOS

Castle Bellos/
City of Gold

Hawk's
Brow

Elder's
Pitch

The Radiant Coast

ISLE
OF
LUKAS

VENEAS

TERREA

RAZORE
STRAITS

CAST OF CHARACTERS

Limeros

MAGNUS LUKAS DAMORA	Prince
LUCIA EVA DAMORA	Princess and sorceress
GAIUS DAMORA	The king of Mytica
FELIX GAEBRAS	Assassin
GARETH CIRELLO	Grand kingsliege
KURTIS CIRELLO	Lord Gareth's son
LORD FRANCUS	Royal council member
LORD LOGGIS	Royal council member
HIGH PRIEST DANUS	Royal council member
MILO IAGARIS	Palace guard
ENZO	Palace guard

Paelsia

JONAS AGALLON	Rebel leader
LYSANDRA BARBAS	Rebel
OLIVIA	Witch
LAELIA	Tavern dancer

Auranos

CLEIONA (CLEO) AURORA BELLOS	Princess of Auranos
NICOLO (NIC) CASSIAN	Cleo's best friend
NERISSA FLORENS	Cleo's attendant
GALYN	Tavern owner
BRUNO	Galyn's father

Kraeshia

CYRUS CORTAS	Emperor
DASTAN	Prince—first born
ELAN	Prince—second born
ASHUR CORTAS	Prince—third born
AMARA CORTAS	Princess—fourth born
NEELA	Amara's grandmother
MIKAH KASRO	Kraeshian guard
TARAN	Revolutionary

The Sanctuary

TIMOTHEUS	Elder Watcher
KYAN	Fire Kindred

PROLOGUE

35 Years Ago

The pitch-black monster reached toward the young boy with horrible, long-fingered hands, pressing him down into his bed, smothering him. It did this every night. And every night, the boy was terrified.

"No," he whispered. "It's not a monster, it's just the darkness. It's just the darkness!"

He wasn't a baby anymore, afraid of the dark. He was nearly eight years old, and he swore to the goddess he wouldn't cry out for his mother this time.

But this resolve lasted only a few more moments, until he couldn't hold back his fear any longer. "Mother!" he called, and, as she always did, she came to him immediately and sat on the edge of his bed.

"My darling." She gathered him into her arms and, clutching her tightly and feeling like a weak little fool, he let out a shuddery sob against her shoulder. "It's all right. I'm here now."

Light swelled as she lit the candle next to his bed. Though her beautiful face was cast in shadows, he could see anger in it, but he could tell it was not directed at him. "I've told them again and again to always have a candle burning in your room at night."

"The breeze may have put it out," he reasoned, not wanting to get any of his nursemaids in trouble.

"Perhaps." She pressed her hand to his cheek. "Do you feel better now?"

Now with the light returned and his mother here he only felt foolish. "I'm sorry. I should have been braver."

"Many fear the darkness, for very good reason," she told him. "You're not the only one who sees in it a horrible monster. But the only way to defeat the monster is . . . how?"

"By making friends with it."

"That's right." She waved a hand at the lantern on the wall, lighting it with her fire magic. He watched her with awe, as he always did when she wielded *elementia*. She raised a brow at his reaction. "You don't think *I'm* a monster, do you?"

"Of course not," he said, shaking his head. His mother was a witch—a secret she'd shared only with him. She'd told him that some people were afraid of witches and thought them to be evil, but they were wrong. "Tell me the story again," the boy said.

"Which one?"

"The one about the Kindred." It was his favorite story, and it always helped him fall asleep on troubled nights.

"Very well." She smiled as she took her son's small hand in hers. "There were once four crystal orbs that were carefully guarded by the immortals. Each orb contained pure elemental magic—the magic that makes life itself possible. It was said that their magic could be seen swirling, endlessly, inside, and that you could feel their power when you held them in your hand. In the amber orb was fire magic. In the aquamarine, water. In the moonstone, air. And the darkest obsidian orb held earth magic. When the immortal goddesses Valoria and Cleiona fled their enemies in their world and came here to ours, they each brought with them two orbs that

2

gave them incredible powers. Which ones did Valoria possess and protect, my darling?"

"Earth and Water."

"And Cleiona?"

"Fire and Air."

"Yes. But soon the goddesses were not satisfied to possess only half of the *elementia* each. Each wanted more, so she could rule the world without anyone else standing in her way." Whenever his mother told these stories, she would get a dreamy, faraway look in her eyes. "Alas, this lust for power transformed these two immortals, who were once sisters, into the fiercest of enemies. They fought a great and terrible war against each other. In the end, neither was victorious. They were both destroyed and the crystals were lost. Ever since, magic has been fading in this world—and it will continue to fade until someone finds the crystals again and unlocks their magic.

"An ancient prophecy states that one day, a mortal child will be born with the power of a sorceress, who will be able to command all four elements with a strength unseen in a thousand years." There was no way a witch like his mother could do that. She had some fire magic abilities, enough to light candles, and a little earth magic that helped heal his cuts and scrapes, but that was all. "This prophesized child will be the key to finding the Kindred—and unlocking the magic within them." Her face had flushed with excitement. "Of course, many believe this is only a legend."

"But you believe it's real."

"With all my heart and all my soul." She squeezed his hand. "And I also believe that you will be the one to find this important, magical child, and that you will claim this treasure for yourself. I knew it from the very moment you were born."

He felt very special whenever she told him this, but it was never long until doubt set in and that feeling fled.

As if sensing his uncertainty, she cupped his face in her hands and stared deeply into his eyes. "You will not always be afraid of the dark. One day you will be strong and brave, growing more and more so with each year to come. Darkness will not scare you. *Nothing* will scare you. And without fear holding you back, you'll take your place upon the throne and achieve your destiny."

"Like Father?"

Her expression shadowed. "No. You will be much stronger than he could ever hope to be."

Her vision for him sounded so incredible that he wanted it to be true right now. "When will I change?"

She kissed his forehead. "The most important changes take time and patience. But I have faith in you—more than anyone else in the whole world. You are destined for greatness, Gaius Damora. And I swear—no matter what I must do to ensure it—that greatness will be yours."

CHAPTER 1

MAGNUS

LIMEROS

"*All women are deceptive, dangerous creatures. Each a spider poisonous enough to kill with a single bite. Remember that.*"

The advice Magnus's father once gave him echoed in his memory as he stood on the Ravencrest docks and watched the Kraeshian ship disappear into the darkness. The King of Blood had never fully trusted a woman. Not his queen, not his former mistress and advisor, not even an immortal who whispered secrets to him in his dreams. Magnus usually ignored most of what his ruthless father said, but now he knew who was the most dangerous and deceptive of all.

Amara Cortas had stolen the Kindred, an aquamarine orb which contained the essence of water magic, leaving blood and destruction in her wake.

The driving snow bit into his skin, helping to numb the pain of his broken arm. Dawn was still hours off and the night was frigid enough to steal his life if he was careless.

Still, he found it impossible to do anything but stare out at the black waters and the stolen treasure that was supposed to be *his*.

"Now what?" Cleo's voice finally interrupted his dark thoughts. For a moment, he'd forgotten that he wasn't alone.

"*Now what,* princess?" he hissed, frozen clouds forming before his mouth with each word he spoke. "Well, I suppose we should enjoy the short time we have left before my father's men arrive to execute us on sight."

The penalty for treason was death, even for the heir to the throne. And he had, most certainly, committed treason when he helped the princess currently standing behind him escape execution.

Next it was Nic's voice that sliced through the cold night. "I have a suggestion, your highness," he said. "If you're finished inspecting the water for clues, why don't you jump in and swim after that murderous bitch's ship?"

As usual, Cleo's favorite minion spoke to Magnus with unvarnished contempt. "If I thought I could catch her, I would," he replied with matching venom.

"We'll get the water Kindred back," Cleo said. "And Amara will pay for what she's done."

"I'm not sure I share your confidence," Magnus said. Finally, he glanced at her over his shoulder: Princess Cleiona Bellos, her familiar beauty lit only by the moon and a few lanterns set along the docks.

He had yet to think of her as a Damora. She had once asked to keep her family name, as she was the last in her line, and he'd agreed. The king had chastised him for allowing her, a princess forced into an arranged marriage to help make the conquering royals more palatable to the conquered kingdom and hopefully stifle an immediate rebellion amongst the Auranian people, any liberties at all.

Despite the fur-lined cloak that she'd pulled over her head to shield her long golden hair from the snow, Cleo shivered. Her face was pale and she wrapped her arms tightly around herself.

She hadn't complained about the cold, not once on their swift journey from the Temple of Valoria to the city. They'd barely exchanged a single word until now.

Then again, far too many words had been exchanged between them the previous night, before chaos had descended.

"Give me one good reason why you wouldn't let Cronus kill me," she'd demanded when she'd finally cornered him, alone, at Lady Sophia's villa.

And instead of continuing to ignore or deny what he'd done—slaying the guard who'd been given the king's command to end the imprisoned princess's life—he'd given her an answer, the words tearing painfully from his throat as if he had no control over them.

"You are the only light I can see anymore," he'd whispered. *"And, whatever the cost, I refuse to let that light be extinguished."*

Magnus knew he'd given Cleo far too much power over him in that moment. He felt that weakness now—compounded by everything that had happened the night before, beginning with the earth-shattering kiss that had followed his foolish confession of her growing importance to him.

Thankfully that kiss had been interrupted before he'd lost himself completely.

"Magnus? Are you all right?" Cleo touched his arm, but he stiffened and pulled away from her, as if he'd been burned. Confusion fought with concern in her blue-green eyes.

"I'm fine," he said.

"But your arm—"

"I'm fine," he repeated, more firmly.

She pressed her lips together, her gaze hardening. "Good."

"We need a plan," Nic snapped. "And we need one now before we freeze to death out here."

His tone tore Magnus's attention away from the princess and straight to the red-headed, freckle-faced boy who'd always seemed weak and useless . . . at least until tonight.

"You want a plan?" Magnus growled. "Here's my plan. Take your precious princess and leave. Board a ship for Auranos. Hike down to Paelsia. I don't care. I'll tell my father you're both dead. The only way you'll remain alive and well is if you go into exile."

Nic's eyes flashed with surprise, as if this were the last thing he'd expected Magnus to say. "You mean it? We can go?"

"Yes, go." It was the best decision for everyone. Cleo had become a dangerous distraction, and Nic was at best an annoyance and at worst a threat. "That is an order."

He looked up at Cleo, expecting to see relief in the princess's eyes.

Instead, all he saw was outrage.

"An order, is it?" she hissed. "I'm sure it would make things much easier for you if we weren't around, yes? Much easier to find your sorceress sister and get your hands on the remaining crystals."

The reminder of Lucia, who had eloped to Limeros with Alexius, her Watcher tutor, was an unexpected blow. There had been blood on the floor when they'd arrived at the temple—and it could have very well been Lucia's.

She has to be alive. He refused to think any other way. She was alive, and when he found her he was going to kill Alexius.

"Think whatever you like, princess," he said, returning to the more immediate issue. Of course he wanted the Kindred for himself. Did she expect he'd want to share it with the girl who, since nearly the moment they met, has been waiting for any opportunity to reclaim her throne? The Kindred would give her the power to claim not just Auranos, but any other throne she wanted.

He needed that power in his hands—no one else's—and then finally he would have absolute control over his life and his future with no one to fear and no one to answer to.

Not even whatever it was that had happened between them earlier could change that. They were two people on opposite sides who both wanted the same thing, but only one could succeed. He wouldn't give up everything he'd ever wanted—not for anyone.

A flush of color had returned to the princess's cheeks, and her eyes flashed with frustration. "I'm not going anywhere. You and I will go to the palace together. And we will search for Lucia together. And when your father comes for us, we will face his wrath *together*."

He glared down at the angry princess. She stared back up at him, without intimidation. Her shoulders back, her chin up, she was a burning torch in the middle of the cold, endless night.

How he wished he was strong enough to hate her.

"Very well," he said through clenched teeth. "But remember, this decision was yours alone."

The carriage reached the Limerian palace grounds and passed through the guarded checkpoint shortly after the sun had risen. Perched on the edge of a cliff overlooking the Silver Sea, the black castle was in stark contrast to its pristinely white surroundings. Its obsidian towers rose up into the morning sky like the claws of a dark and powerful god.

Many found this to be an intimidating sight, but to Magnus, it was home. An odd flutter of nostalgia rushed through him; memories of simpler times, of riding and swordsmanship classes with the sons of local nobles. Of roaming the grounds with Lucia at his side, a book always in her hands. Of the queen, venturing outside wrapped in furs to welcome important guests arriving for a banquet. Of his father returning with the fruits of a successful hunt, greeting his young son with a rare smile.

Everywhere he looked, there were ghosts of the past.

He exited the carriage and walked up the dozens of steps leading to the tall and heavy main doors, their ebony surface emblazoned with the Limerian cobra signet and the credo "Strength, Faith, Wisdom." He could hear Cleo and Nic whisper conspiratorially to each other as they trailed behind him.

He'd given them ample chance to leave and face no consequences, and instead they had chosen to come here with him. They had only themselves to blame for whatever happened next.

Two guards stood before the entry doors, dressed in the stiff, red Limerian guard's uniforms with heavy black cloaks to help block out the cold. Magnus knew he needed no introduction. The guards bowed in unison.

"Your highness!" exclaimed one, before casting a look of surprise at Cleo and Nic. "*Highnesses*," he clarified. "Are you well?"

With an awkwardly held broken arm, a bruised and bloodied face, and an overall disheveled appearance, Magnus wasn't surprised the guard had taken notice of this. "Well enough," he said. "Open the doors."

He didn't need to explain to a lowly guard why he had unexpectedly arrived in such a state. This was his home, and he had every right to be there whenever he wished, especially after barely escaping death at the hands of Amara's henchmen.

Still, he couldn't ignore the looming possibility that a message demanding his arrest had been sent to the castle by raven. But when the guards opened the doors without any argument, he let out the breath he hadn't realized he'd been holding.

He took a moment to compose himself as he entered the grand foyer, sweeping his gaze around and settling on the spiral stairway chiseled into the stone walls, as if checking for flaws. "Who is in command here with Lord Gareth still in Auranos? I assume he hasn't yet returned from his daughter's wedding celebration."

"Lord Gareth isn't expected to return for several weeks. In his absence, Lord Kurtis was appointed grand kingsliege."

Magnus found he did not have an immediate reply, and that perhaps he'd misheard the guard. "Lord Kurtis Cirillo has been appointed grand kingsliege?" he said after a moment.

"Yes, your highness."

Kurtis Cirillo, Lord Gareth's eldest son, was currently in charge of Limeros. This came as a great surprise, as Magnus had heard a rumor several months ago that Kurtis had drowned while traveling abroad.

He was disappointed to learn that that rumor had now been proven false.

"I met you during my last visit here," Cleo said to the guard as she pushed back the hood of her cloak. "Enzo, isn't it?"

"That's right." The guard eyed with distress her ripped cloak and the dried blood staining her blond hair. "Your highness, do you need me to summon the palace physician?"

She absently touched the small but angry wound on her forehead, given to her by one of Amara's guards. "No, that's not necessary. Thank you." She smiled, brightening her features. "You're very kind. I remember that from last time."

Enzo's face quickly turned as red as his uniform. "You make it very easy to be kind, your grace."

Magnus fought the urge to roll his eyes. It seemed that the princess had captured another hapless fly in her web.

"Enzo," he said, voice low and commanding. The guard's gaze

immediately snapped to his. "Have Lord Kurtis meet me in the throne room immediately."

Another bow. "Yes, your highness." He scurried away without another word.

"Come," Magnus said to Cleo and Nic, then turned on his boot heels and followed the familiar route through the castle to his destination.

"*Come*," Nic sneered. "He orders us about like we're trained dogs."

"I'm not sure the prince was ever taught the polite way to speak to people," Cleo replied.

"And yet," Magnus said, "you're still following me, aren't you?"

"For now. But you should remember that charm opens far more doors than harsh words do."

"And a sharp ax will open every door."

The entrance to the throne room was also stationed with several guards who bowed at the sight of Magnus. No ax was required as they pushed open the doors so quickly that he didn't even have to slow down.

Once inside, he scanned the cavernous room. His father's black throne of iron and leather sat at the top of a dais on one end, a long wooden table and chairs for council meetings at the other. The walls were draped in Limerian tapestries and banners, and several torches peppered the molding, bringing some light to the corners of the room where the sun shining through the large windows didn't reach.

The throne room was host to many official gatherings. It was where the king would grant audience to Limerian citizens and their various requests for financial assistance or justice against wrongdoings. It was where he would sentence prisoners for their crimes and perform ceremonies during which both the worthy and unworthy were given official titles such as Grand Kingsliege.

From the corner of his eye, Magnus noticed that Cleo had moved closer to him.

"You're already acquainted with Lord Kurtis," Cleo said. "Aren't you?"

Magnus kept his gaze fixed on the throne. "I am."

"And you don't like him."

"I don't like anyone, princess."

Nic snorted.

They fell into silence as Magnus considered how best to handle the complicated mess his life had become. He felt backed into a corner: injured, weaponless, and far too vulnerable. His broken arm throbbed, but instead of ignoring the pain he focused on it, to help clear his mind of the constant buzz of confusion and chaos.

It had been six years since he'd last seen Kurtis Cirillo, yet he remembered it as clearly as if it had been yesterday.

The sun had shone bright and warm that day, and the snow had melted so much that ice lilies pushed up through the frosty ground. A rare summer butterfly, its golden wings speckled with blue and purple dots, came to rest on one of these flowers in the garden near the cliff's edge. In Limeros, it's said to be good luck to see a summer butterfly, for they only live a single day.

Magnus reached toward it and, to his amazement, it climbed onto his right knuckle, tickling his skin. It was so beautiful up close that it almost seemed magical.

"Is that a butterfly?"

A shiver zipped down his spine at the sound of Kurtis's cold voice. Kurtis was fourteen years of age to his twelve, and the king insisted that Magnus be friendly with him during Lord Gareth's visits. It was difficult to be friendly with the horrible boy since being within ten paces of him made Magnus's skin crawl.

"Yes," Magnus replied reluctantly.

Kurtis came closer. He was a full head taller than Magnus. "You should kill it."

Magnus frowned. "What?"

"Anything stupid enough to just sit there on your pale little hand deserves to die. Kill it."

"No."

"You're heir to the throne. You're going to have to grow up some day, you know. You're going to have to kill people and not cry about it afterward. Your father would crush that thing in a second. So would I. Don't be so weak."

Magnus already knew that Kurtis liked to hurt animals. During his last visit, Kurtis had butchered a stray cat and left its twitching remains in a corridor where he knew Lucia would happen upon them. She'd cried for days.

"I'm not weak!" Magnus said through gritted teeth.

Kurtis grinned. "Let's put it to the test, then. Either you kill that thing right now, before it flies away, or I promise, the next time I'm here . . ." He leaned in close enough to whisper. "I'll chop off your sister's little finger."

Magnus stared at him, horrified. "I'll tell my father you said that. You'll never be allowed here again."

"Go ahead and tell him. I'll just deny it. Who'll believe you?" He laughed. "Now choose. That butterfly, or your sister's finger. I'll cut really slowly, and tell her you told me to do it."

He wanted to call Kurtis's bluff, but the memory of that cat forced his throat closed.

Magnus knew he had no choice. He clasped his left hand down on the right, feeling the tender collapse of the soft wings as he crushed the beautiful, peaceful creature.

Kurtis smirked. "Oh, Magnus. Don't you know it's bad luck to kill a summer butterfly?"

"Prince Magnus, you look as if you've just returned from a war." Once again, Kurtis's voice wrenched Magnus out of the horrible memory.

Quickly, Magnus composed himself, setting a pleasant enough look on his face as he turned around. Kurtis was still incredibly tall—even taller than Magnus by an inch or two. His reddish-brown hair, muddy-green eyes, and pointed features had always reminded Magnus of a weasel.

"Not a war, precisely. But the past several days have been challenging."

"I can tell. Your arm—"

"I'll have it tended to very soon, once I get a bit of business out of the way. I'm so pleased to see you're well, Kurtis. I'd heard a horrible rumor that you weren't."

Kurtis smiled that familiar, greasy smile of his and waved his hand dismissively. "Ah, yes, the rumors of my death. I sent along that preposterous story as a hoax to a gullible friend, and he spread the word very quickly. But as you can see, I'm very much alive and well." Kurtis's curious gaze shifted to Cleo standing next to Magnus, and then Nic, who had remained near the door next to three guards.

Clearly, he awaited introductions.

Magnus chose to play along for now. "Princess Cleiona Bellos, this is Lord Kurtis Cirillo, Grand Kingsliege of Limeros."

Cleo nodded as Kurtis took her hand and kissed it. "It's an honor to meet you," she said.

"The honor is mine," answered Kurtis. "I've been told of your beauty, but you've far exceeded my greatest expectations."

"You're much too kind, given the way I must look this morning."

"Not at all. You are luminous. But you must assure me you're not in any pain."

Her smile remained. "I'm not."

"I'm very glad to hear that."

Every muscle in Magnus's body had grown tense at the sound of the "kingsliege's" voice. "And this is Nicolo Cassian, who is the princess's . . ." How best to explain the boy's identity and presence here? ". . . *attendant*."

Kurtis's brows shot up. "A *male* attendant? How unusual."

"Not in the south." To Nic's credit, he took the introduction in stride. "It's fine, upstanding, manly work down there."

"I'm sure it is."

Magnus had had enough forced pleasantries. It was time to move this along.

"I suppose you wonder why my wife and I are here, in Limeros, and not with my father in Auranos," Magnus said. "Or have you been alerted about our current situation?"

"I have not. This is an unexpected, but very welcome, surprise."

Some of the tension in Magnus's shoulders eased. "Then I'll let you in on a closely guarded secret: We're in Limeros to search for my sister, who has eloped with her tutor. We need to stop her from making this mistake . . . and any further ones."

"Oh, my." Kurtis clasped his hands behind his back. "Lucia has always been full of surprises, hasn't she?"

You have no idea, Magnus thought. "She has indeed."

Nodding, Kurtis ascended the stairs leading to the king's throne and took a seat upon it. Magnus watched him with sheer disbelief, but decided to hold his tongue.

"I will make a dozen guards available to you for this important search," Kurtis said. He then addressed one of the guards at the entrance. "Organize this immediately and return here."

The guard bowed. "Yes, your grace."

Magnus watched the guard leave. "They obey your orders with much ease."

"They do. It's all in their training. Limerian guards will take any official order and fulfill it to the letter at once."

Magnus nodded. "My father wouldn't have it any other way. Those who show any sign of defiance are . . . disciplined." It was a rather light word for the punishments Magnus had seen inflicted on palace guards who didn't give themselves over—body, mind, and soul—to their duties to the kingdom.

"As they should be," said Kurtis. "Now, I will arrange accommodations for you, your beautiful wife, and her attendant."

"Yes. I will take my regular chambers. The princess will need separate chambers befitting her position. And Nic can be given . . ." He eyed the boy. ". . . servants' quarters. Perhaps one of the slightly larger rooms."

"You're too kind," Nic said darkly.

"*Separate* chambers for husband and wife?" Kurtis said, frowning.

"That is what I said," Magnus said, a moment before it occurred to him that this might seem a strange request for husband and wife.

"Magnus is kind enough to ask this on my behalf," Cleo spoke up to ease Kurtis's confusion. "It's a long-standing tradition in my family to retain separate chambers for the first year of marriage, both for luck, and also to make our time spent together all the more . . . exciting and unpredictable." She blushed and cast her gaze downward, as if embarrassed by the admission. "It's a silly tradition, I know."

"Not at all," Magnus said, impressed by the princess's ready lie.

Kurtis nodded, seemingly satisfied by this explanation. "Very well. I'll ensure that you're given exactly what you require."

"Good." Magnus returned his attention to the "kingsliege." "I also need to send some men to the Temple of Valoria immediately. There was a violent, isolated ice storm there last night that killed many. The victims should be buried by midday and the temple restored to its former glory as quickly as possible."

According to Limerian religious customs, the bodies of the dead must be buried in earth sprinkled with water blessed by a priest within twelve hours of death.

He couldn't help but glance then at Nic, whose expression had grown pained at the mention of the bodies at the temple. One of those bodies had been that of Prince Ashur—Amara's brother. Nic and the prince had become close friends before his murder at his devious sister's hands.

"An ice storm?" Kurtis's brow was now raised to its highest. "No wonder you all look so disheveled. I'm very grateful to the goddess that you and your wife were spared. You must need rest after enduring such an experience."

"Rest can wait."

"Very well." Kurtis gripped the arms of the throne. "How long do you anticipate we'll have the honor of your presence before you return to Auranos?"

A dozen guards entered the throne room, momentarily stealing Magnus's attention. No matter how duty-bound and driven to please Limerian guards were, twelve weren't nearly enough to make up a search team for his sister.

"I don't intend to return to Auranos," Magnus said, turning back to Kurtis.

Kurtis cocked his head. "I don't quite follow you."

"This is my home, my palace, my kingdom. And in the absence of my father, that throne upon which you've seated yourself is rightfully mine."

Kurtis stared at him for a moment before a smile split his lips. "I completely understand. However, the king himself appointed me to this throne for the time being. I have undertaken these duties gladly—and successfully—in his and my father's absence. The council's grown quite accustomed to following my lead."

"Then they'll have to get accustomed to following *my* lead now that I'm here."

Kurtis's smile slipped. He pressed back into the throne, but didn't make a move to stand. "Magnus—"

"It's *Prince* Magnus. Or *your highness*," he corrected. Even from the bottom of the stairs, Magnus could see the flicker of anger behind Kurtis's green eyes.

"My apologies, *Prince* Magnus, but without any prior notice from King Gaius, I will have to protest such a sudden change. Perhaps you should—"

"Guards," Magnus said, without turning around. "I understand you've been taking Lord Kurtis's orders in recent weeks, as very well you should have been. But I am your prince, the heir to my father's throne, and now that I'm here you're at my command alone." His gaze was hard as he stared into the eyes he'd loathed since boyhood. "The grand kingsliege has insulted me with his protests. Remove him from my throne and cut his throat on my order."

The hot outrage in Kurtis's countenance quickly turned to cold fear as the guards approached, four of them moving swiftly up the stairs before he could make a single move. They wrenched him from the throne and dragged him down the stairs, where they forced him to his knees. Magnus took his place on top of the dais.

This cold, hard, unforgiving throne held many memories for Magnus, but he had never sat on it before today.

It was far more comfortable than he'd ever expected.

The troop of red-uniformed guards stood before him, all looking up at him without question or concern. Cleo clutched Nic's arm, her face pale and her expression uncertain.

Kneeling before Magnus was Kurtis, his eyes wild, face sweaty, and the edge of a guard's sword now at his throat.

"Your highness," he sputtered. "Any trespass you feel I've made against you was not my intention."

"That may be so." Magnus leaned forward and considered him for a long moment. "Beg me to spare your life and perhaps I'll only cut off your little finger."

First confusion, then understanding, flickered in Kurtis's eyes. *That's right*, Magnus thought. *It's different between us now, isn't it?*

"Please," Kurtis hissed. "Please, your highness, spare my life. I beg you. Please, I'll do anything to prove my worth and earn your forgiveness for having insulted you."

A rush of sheer power flowed over and within Magnus. He smiled, a genuine one, at the sniveling weasel.

"Say 'please' one more time." When there was no immediate reply, Magnus nodded at the guard, who pressed his sword even closer against Kurtis's pale throat, drawing a thin trickle of blood.

"Pleasssse," Kurtis managed.

Magnus flicked his hand and the guard removed and sheathed his blade. "See? Don't you feel better now?"

Kurtis heaved and trembled. Perhaps, unlike Magnus, he'd never before been physically reprimanded for his missteps.

He bowed his head. "Thank you, your highness. I am at your service."

"Happy to hear," said Magnus. "Now, I need a message sent to my father immediately. I want him to know what I'm up to here in the north. Wouldn't want him worrying about me."

"Of course not, your highness."

"Be a good grand kingsliege and fetch me some ink and parchment, would you?"

Kurtis's expression darkened a shade, but he quickly composed himself. "Yes, your highness."

Magnus noticed Cleo watching as Kurtis left the room, but she said nothing and neither did Nic. When her gaze returned to Magnus, he saw nothing but accusation in her eyes. Perhaps she didn't agree with the way Magnus reduced that young man into a cowering peon for what may have seemed, to her, like a minor transgression.

Yes, princess, Magnus thought. *I am the son of Gaius Damora, the King of Blood. And it's time I started acting like it.*

CHAPTER 2

JONAS

AURANOS

After a long day working in the Paelsian vineyard, Jonas's best friend had always preferred ale over wine when relaxing at the local tavern. Judging by the three empty tankards next to Brion, tonight appeared to be no different. Jonas approached cautiously, sitting in the seat opposite him, next to the fire.

"Good evening," Brion said with a sloppy smile.

Jonas didn't smile back. Instead, he stared at his friend, feeling uncertain and wary. "What does this mean?"

"Sorry?"

"Am I . . . dead? Or am I dreaming?"

Brion laughed and drained his fourth ale. "What's your guess?"

"Dreaming, likely. This scene is far too pleasant to be unfolding in the darklands."

"So serious tonight." Brion jutted out his bottom lip and gave Jonas a pointed look. "Hard day on the job?"

A dream. Only a dream. Still, Jonas tried to enjoy being in the presence of Brion Radenos again. He'd been a friend as close as a brother to him, whose death he'd barely had time to mourn. "You could say that."

"Need some advice?" Brion asked as he signaled the barmaid for more ale.

"Actually, I wouldn't mind a little."

"All right, here it is. You should give up."

Jonas frowned. "What?"

Brion's gaze returned to Jonas's, and that familiar edge of humor vanished. "Give up. Anything more you think you can do now? Forget it. You've failed as a rebel and a leader, time and time again. I'm dead because of your stupid, stubborn decisions. And so are others—dozens have died because of you."

Jonas winced as if he'd been struck. He looked down and studied the wooden floorboards. "I tried my best."

"Don't you get it? Your best isn't good enough. All those who've put their trust in you have died in agony. You're pathetic. You'd be doing everyone a favor if you surrendered to the king and joined me on the other side of death."

This was no dream. It was a nightmare.

But something had changed—during his tirade, Brion's voice had shifted. Jonas glanced up to look at him and found that he was staring into his own eyes.

"That's right," the other Jonas snapped. "You're worthless. You failed Tomas, you failed Brion, you failed your rebel comrades. And Princess Cleo? She was counting on you to bring her that magic rock and save her from the Damoras. Now, for all you know, she's dead too. Felix shouldn't have stopped at wounding you. He should have killed you and put you out of your misery."

The words were blows, each one a fist striking his gut. Of course he already knew all of this, and now his every failure and mistake rose up before him in a mountain of pain, so high he couldn't see past it.

But with each failure, he had learned. He had grown. He wasn't the same person he'd been when he'd foolishly followed Chief Basilius and the King of Blood into a war of lies and deceit, in which he and his fellow Paelsians had been used as nothing more than pawns. He had stormed into battle when neither he nor his rebels had been fully prepared. Now he bore the battle scars in both mind and body, each deeper and bloodier than the last.

"No," Jonas whispered.

The other Jonas cocked his head. "What did you say?"

"No," he said, louder. "It can be different. *I* can be different."

"Impossible."

"Nothing is impossible." He raised his gaze and glared directly into his own brown eyes. "Now leave me the hell alone so I can do what I have to do."

His mirror image smirked and gave him a shallow nod of approval before disappearing into thin air.

Jonas woke up on a cot, drenched in sweat, and stared up at a black ceiling. The moment he tried to move, his left shoulder screamed with pain.

Beneath the tight bandages covering his wound lay a layer of grayish-green mud. Galyn, the owner of the Silver Toad Tavern and Inn, had put it there, telling Jonas that a witch had once stayed there and his grandfather Bruno had accepted the healing substance as payment.

His feverish body ached as he forced himself out of bed and slowly made his way down the hall, past doorways emanating with both silence and snores. He carefully descended the rickety wooden steps leading down to the tavern. He didn't know the time, but it was still dark, still night, and the only things keeping him from stumbling were a couple of lit wall sconces. His legs were weak and nausea had fully settled into his stomach, but all he knew for sure was that he couldn't stay in bed. There was far too much to do.

He would start by getting something to drink; his mouth was as dry as the wastelands of Eastern Paelsia.

He came to a stop when he heard hushed voices within the dark tavern.

"Not a chance. He doesn't need to know," said a female voice.

"The message was for him, not you," her male companion replied.

"True. But he's in no shape for any of this."

"Perhaps not. But he'll be furious when he finds out."

"So let him be furious. You want him to go rushing out in his condition and get himself killed? There's no chance he's strong enough for this right now."

Jonas rounded the corner and leaned against the wall until he was in full view of Lysandra and Galyn.

"Oh, Lys," he drawled. "I do appreciate your endless faith in my abilities."

Lysandra Barbas, his friend and last remaining fellow rebel, grimaced as she turned toward him, twisting a finger through her dark, curly hair. "You're awake."

"Yes. And shamelessly spying on the two friends I have left talking about me like I'm a sick child." He rubbed his forehead. "How long have I been out?"

"Three days."

He gaped at her. *Three whole days?*

Three days since Felix had sliced that dagger through his shoulder, pinning him to the floor of the tavern.

And earlier, when Jonas had kissed Lysandra for the first time.

Two memories—one bad, one good—forever burned into his brain.

Galyn, tall and heavyset and in his mid-twenties, raised a bushy blond eyebrow. "How's that healing balm working?"

Jonas forced a smile. "Like magic," he lied.

In his entire life, he'd never believed in magic. But that stance had been irrevocably changed when he'd been brought back from the brink of death by powerful earth magic. But this so-called healing balm . . . well, he wasn't convinced that it was anything more than common mud.

Jonas's smile fell when he registered Lysandra's garb. She was dressed in trousers and leathers, and had a canvas satchel slung over one shoulder, her bow and quiver of arrows over the other.

"Where are you going at this hour?" he demanded.

She pressed her lips together and didn't reply, instead shooting him a defiant glare.

"Fine, go ahead and be stubborn." He turned to regard Galyn instead. "What message was meant for me and who sent it?"

"Don't answer," Lys hissed.

Galyn looked between the two uncertainly, his arms crossed over his chest. Finally, he sighed and turned to Jonas apologetically. "Nerissa. She stopped by yesterday."

Over the recent months, Nerissa Florens had proven herself a valuable rebel spy. She held a position at the Auranian palace, and possessed a rare skill for getting important information exactly when it was needed.

"What was her message?"

"Galyn . . ." Lys growled.

He grimaced. "Sorry, Lys. You know I have to tell him." Galyn turned his patient face to Jonas once again. "Jonas, the king is having a ship prepared. Nerissa doesn't know exactly when he's leaving, but it's certainly only a matter of days."

A king preparing to travel wouldn't usually qualify as important news. But King Gaius had sequestered himself in the palace for months, not setting foot outside the walls since the disastrous wedding between Cleo and Magnus. It was said he feared another rebel attack, and Jonas wasn't sure if this made him cowardly or smart.

So if the King of Blood was not only leaving the palace, but leaving it for a long journey by ship, it was *huge* news.

Jonas's heart began to race. "Did she say where he's going? Back to Limeros?" The northern kingdom could be reached by land, but it was much more comfortable—and *royal*—to take a ship along the western coastline.

"No. All she knows is that he's preparing to sail somewhere, and that no one knows where or when."

Jonas glanced again at Lys, whose eyes were still trained on Galyn, her face now red with anger.

"Don't look at him like that," Jonas said. "You should have told me all this yourself."

"When? You've been unconscious for days."

"Yes, but now I'm awake and feeling much better." It was a lie. He felt weak and unsteady, but he didn't want her to know. "So, what? Your plan is to go out on your own and assassinate the king as soon as he sticks his nose out into the fresh air?"

"That was the general idea, yes."

"It's a stupid plan." Frustrated fury rose within him, blocking out the pain in his shoulder. "You'd do that, wouldn't you? Run off and get yourself killed trying to vanquish the King of Blood."

"Perhaps I would. Or perhaps I'd succeed and get him right

between the eyes with an arrow, and put an end to him once and for all!"

Jonas glared at her, fists clenched, livid that she'd willingly put herself into danger like this with no one to back her up. "Why would you do this? Go off all by yourself?"

Eyes blazing, she dropped her satchel, bow, and quiver to the floor. She moved toward Jonas so quickly he was certain she meant to hit him. Instead, she stopped just short of touching him, and her gaze softened.

"I thought you were dead," she said. "When I saw you there, pinned to the floor with that dagger . . ." Her words faded as her dark eyes filled with tears and she rubbed at them angrily. "Damn you, Jonas. First my parents, then Brion and my brother, and . . . and then I thought I'd lost you too. And then even when I knew Felix hadn't killed you, you were still so sick. Your fever was so high . . . I—I didn't know what to do. I felt helpless, and I *hate* feeling helpless. But now, with this news of the king's departure . . . I have a chance to do something, to make a difference. To . . ." Her voice caught. "To protect you."

He tried to search for words but found he didn't have an immediate reply. He hadn't known Lysandra all that long—at least not compared to how long he'd known Brion. Brion had immediately fallen for her, hard, even with that abrasive attitude that she used as self-defense. It had taken Jonas a little longer to warm up to her, but he finally did, and now . . .

"I don't want to lose you either," he managed.

"Really?"

"Don't sound so surprised." He brought his gaze up from the floor and their eyes met. "And you should know that, one of these days, I do plan to kiss you again."

Her cheeks flushed once more, and this time Jonas didn't think it was from anger.

"Should I leave you two alone?" Galyn said.

"No," Lys said quickly, clearing her throat. "Um. Anyway, speaking of Felix—"

Jonas winced at the name. "What about him?"

"He's gone. There's been no news of him, not from Nerissa nor anyone else," Lys said. "But if I see him again, I'll put an arrow in him, too, for what he did to you."

"He could have killed me. He didn't."

"Are you making excuses for him? Do I have to remind you that he also stole the air Kindred from us?"

"And we'll get it back." Jonas still had the earth Kindred safely hidden away in his room. Not that he knew what to do with it. For a shiny rock that allegedly held enough godlike powers to shake the world, it hadn't proven all that useful yet. But it wasn't meant for him, it was promised to another. "Galyn, did Nerissa say anything else? Anything . . . about the princess? Has she been found?"

Galyn shook his head. "No. Princess Cleiona's still missing, along with Prince Magnus. There is a rumor going through the village, though, that Princess Lucia ran off and eloped with her tutor. Perhaps they're all together somewhere."

"Forget the princess," Lys said, the sharp edge returned to her voice. "What does it matter if she's alive or dead?"

Jonas clenched his jaw. "She was counting on me to bring her the crystal. She trusted me."

Lys groaned. "I have absolutely no time to listen to this. I need to be on my way." She picked up her gear. "Go back to bed, Jonas. Heal. We can deal with your golden princess's whereabouts later."

"Wait."

"What? We can't ignore this chance to put an end to the King of Blood. Are you really going to try to stop me?"

He regarded her for a moment in silence. "No. I'm coming with you."

She frowned and brought her concerned gaze down to his wound.

"I can manage," Jonas said. "You're not talking me out of this."

He was ready for her to put up a fight—a fight he knew he probably wasn't strong enough for. All he could do was try to look as strong and determined as possible.

Finally, instead of resisting, she merely sighed with resignation. "Fine. But there's no way you can go anywhere looking like *that*."

"Like what? Do I look that sick?"

"No, it's just . . ." She glanced at Galyn.

"Everyone knows who you are," Galyn said, gesturing at Jonas with both hands. "Your face is famous around here, remember?"

Of course. The posters plastered all around Mytica, offering a handsome reward for the capture of Jonas Agallon, rebel leader and (falsely accused) murderer of Queen Althea Damora, had ensured that. He'd been recognized several times in recent weeks, especially in Auranos.

"Fine. I need a disguise," he said, raising a brow at Lysandra. "But so do you. A huge audience got a nice, long glimpse of you at your interrupted execution."

She dropped her gear again. "You may be right."

Jonas touched his dark brown hair, long enough to curl around his ears and drop down in front of his eyes if he didn't constantly push it back. "I'll cut my hair."

"That's a start," Galyn said. "And you're in luck. I have an eye patch you can use. Got stung by a needle-bug a few years ago and had to wear it for a month."

An eye patch? He tried not to grimace at the thought of losing half his vision, even temporarily. "Yeah . . . that sounds, uh, great. I guess. Thanks."

Lysandra pulled a dagger out of her canvas bag. "I'll cut your hair as soon as I've done my own."

She raised the blade to one of her long, curly locks, but Jonas caught her hand. "You're not cutting your hair."

She frowned as he quickly disarmed her. "And why not?"

He couldn't help but grin. "Because I like your hair exactly as it is. Gorgeous and impossible to control, just like you."

Her hands were on her hips, and he could tell she was fighting a smile. "Then what kind of a disguise do you suggest for me?"

His smile grew. "Simple. A gown."

Lysandra's eyes widened. "A *gown*?"

"A pretty one. Silk, if possible. Galyn? Do you have anything lying around here that a guest might have left behind?"

The innkeeper chuckled. "Actually, I think I have one of my mother's old gowns around here somewhere."

"Good," Jonas said, deeply amused at the outraged look on Lys's face. "It seems we'll be ready and unrecognizable in no time. Let's get going."

CHAPTER 3

CLEO

LIMEROS

Her sister, Emilia, once said that she could tell Cleo's mood by the state of her left thumbnail. Whenever Cleo was stressed or upset, she chewed it down to the quick. According to her nursemaid, she'd also sucked her thumb many years longer than the average child, so Cleo supposed that her nail-biting habit was a natural evolution.

A quick, sharp pain tugged at Cleo's scalp. "Ouch!" she exclaimed, pulling her sore thumb away from her mouth.

She saw her attendant Petrina's eyes widen in the mirror. The girl held a small swath of Cleo's long blond hair. "Oh, your grace, I apologize! I didn't intend to . . . I've never attempted this sort of style before."

"Ripping my hair out by its roots is not the best way to learn," Cleo said, her scalp still throbbing. She willed herself to be patient with Petrina, even though she was certain that even Nic could do a better job plaiting her hair.

How she wished Nerissa were here in Limeros, rather than being at the Auranian palace. Nerissa wasn't just a good friend

32

and Cleo's main connection to Jonas Agallon, but she was also an incredibly skilled attendant.

"I don't know what to say, your highness. The prince will be furious if he learns I'm inept. He'll have me punished!"

"The prince won't punish you," Cleo assured her, patting her hand. "I won't let him."

The girl looked at the princess with awe. "You must be the bravest person in the world if you can stand up to someone as strong and . . . determined as him. I admire you more than you know."

Perhaps Petrina wasn't so stupid after all. She seemed a very good judge of character. For a Limerian.

"We should stand up to brutish boys whenever we can," Cleo said. "They need to learn they don't hold all the power, no matter who they are. Or *think* they are."

"Prince Magnus scares me. He reminds me so much of the king." Petrina shivered, then bit her bottom lip. "Apologies. It's inappropriate of me to admit these thoughts to you."

"Nonsense. You absolutely must feel free to speak your mind around me. I insist." Even though Cleo wouldn't keep this uncoordinated girl as her attendant, she knew it was best to make friends wherever she could find them. "In fact, if you ever hear any news or information around the palace that you think I should know about, come to me immediately. I promise to keep every secret."

Petrina's face whitened. "Are you asking me to spy for you, your grace?"

"No!" Cleo covered her immediate alarm with a bright smile. Nerissa was always happy to spy—she took to it as naturally as breathing. "Of course not. What a silly suggestion."

"The king has always dealt harshly with spies. It's said he cuts their eyes out and feeds them to his dogs."

Nausea rose within Cleo and she fought to hold on to her

pleasant expression. "I'm sure that's only a rumor. Anyway, you may be excused now."

"But your hair—"

"It's fine as it is. Really. Thank you."

Petrina curtseyed and left without further protest. Alone now in front of the mirror, Cleo studied her reflection, dismayed to see that her hair was a mess of half-finished braids and tangles at the back of her head. After working on it unsuccessfully for a few moments with the brush, she gave up.

"I need Nerissa," she said aloud to herself.

Not only for her skills as an attendant, but also because Cleo needed to know if she'd received any word from Jonas. In Cleo's last correspondence with the rebel, she'd given him secret information on how to claim three of the Kindred orbs. However, since then she'd heard nothing from him.

For all she knew, Jonas had failed. Or, worse, he'd succeeded and sold the crystals to the highest bidder. Or, much worse than that . . . he was dead.

"Yes, Nerissa," she said again, nodding to herself. "I desperately need Nerissa."

But how could she convince Magnus to send for her?

Well, she would simply have to *demand* it, of course. She would not cower before the prince, not today and not ever. Though, truthfully, she'd been deeply appalled and confused by the dramatic display she'd witnessed with Lord Kurtis. It was as if Magnus had been possessed by the spirit of King Gaius, turning him cruel and heartless; into something everyone within a ten-mile radius should fear.

She narrowed her eyes at her reflection. "Clearly," she said to herself, "you're forgetting that he *is* cruel and heartless. What happened in Ravencrest doesn't change that. For all you know, he was trying to manipulate you. Why do you constantly make excuses for his foul behavior? Are you that much of a fool, to let a few pretty words and a regrettable kiss change your mind?"

Magnus had saved her from certain death in the Auranian dungeon, that was undeniable. But there were many reasons why he would have done it beyond her being . . . being . . .

How exactly had he put it?

"As if you've forgotten a single word he said," she whispered.

But Cleo wasn't a romantic fool, a silly girl who believed a villain could become a shining hero overnight, even if he had saved her life once. She was a queen, who would reclaim her throne and destroy her enemies—*all* of them—once she possessed the magic and power she needed.

With one or more Kindred in hand, she would get justice. For her father. For Emilia. For Theon. For Mira. And for the Auranian people.

She jabbed her finger at the mirror. "Don't ever forget it."

Her resolve was back in place and so was her courage.

She needed to see Magnus. She needed to know how safe they were at the palace while the king remained in Auranos, and if there was any news about the missing water Kindred. She needed to make sure he made immediate arrangements for Nerissa's travel. And she refused to remain in her chambers waiting for him to come to her.

While the Auranian palace was huge—so enormous that it was easy for even the most seasoned servants to become lost in its labyrinthine hallways—at least it had been filled with light and life. Bright paintings and tapestries adorned the walls, the hallways were well-lit with lanterns and torches, and its many windows looked out on the beautiful City of Gold. Cleo had always felt safe and happy there—until the day they were attacked and conquered.

In the Limerian palace, however, everything seemed dark and

dreary, with barely any artwork—cheerful or otherwise—to adorn the walls. The stonework was dull and unpolished, the edges rough and sharp. The only warmth seemed to come from the many fireplaces, vital to a castle built in a kingdom of constant winter.

Her steps slowed as she came across a hall of portraits. The paintings reminded her so much of the Bellos family collection that once graced the Auranian palace walls, it was as if they were rendered by the same artist.

Each Damora she passed held a stern expression and a serious gaze. King Gaius, keen-eyed and ruthlessly handsome; Queen Althea, regal and proper; Princess Lucia, solemnly beautiful with dark hair and sky-blue eyes.

She paused before Magnus's portrait. When he sat for it, he was much more of a boy than the man he'd recently become, so similar in appearance to his father. But the boy in the painting still bore that familiar scar on his right cheek—a scar his cruel father had given him as punishment for something trivial.

That scar was physical proof that the prince didn't always obey the king's command.

"Princess Cleiona." A voice greeted her from around the next corner. "How lovely to see you today."

It was Lord Kurtis, now standing before her, stunningly tall. He was even taller than Magnus, but with a more slender build with narrow shoulders and thin arms: traits of one who'd spent his life in leisure. His smile was amiable, and his green eyes reminded her of the olive trees in the courtyard back at her home.

"It's lovely to see you too," she said.

"I'm glad our paths have crossed today." His brows drew together. "I wanted to personally apologize for disrespecting your husband in front of you. It was incredibly rude of me and I'm deeply ashamed."

Cleo tried to think of the best way to reply, and made a quick decision to speak her mind as bluntly as a Kraeshian would. "Perhaps you could have acted more diplomatically, but I think the prince's behavior was overly rude and uncalled for. Please accept my apology for your embarrassment."

"I'd say embarrassment took second place to the fear that he'd actually have my throat cut, your grace. But thank you."

"You were only standing up for what you believed was your duty."

"Yes, but I should have known to show more care in my words and actions when it comes to the prince. After all, I already know . . ."

"Go on," she prompted. "What do you know?"

He shook his head and lowered his gaze. "I shouldn't say any more."

"No, you absolutely should."

Kurtis looked concerned, as if he were wrestling with whether or not to speak, which only made Cleo more eager to hear it. "Please," she said. "Tell me."

"Well . . . when the prince and I were children, we didn't get along very well. My father would bring me here with him when he had business with the king, and Magnus and I were expected to spend time together, to become friends. It didn't take long for me to learn that the prince is not one to have close friends. He's . . . forgive me, your grace, but he was a rather sadistic bully of a boy. And I'm very sorry to see that little has changed over the years."

A sadistic bully of a boy. It sounded right on target for the son of King Gaius.

"I can only hope . . ." Kurtis trailed off again.

"What?"

He blinked. "I just hope that he hasn't been overly cruel to you."

Cleo reached out and squeezed Kurtis's hand. "Thank you. But I assure you, when it comes to the prince, I can handle myself."

"I don't doubt it for a moment. You're so much like your sister." He smiled, but it quickly faded at the edges. "My deepest condolences on her loss, your grace. She was truly remarkable."

Cleo tried to ignore the jolt of pain that came from being reminded of her sister, and regarded Kurtis with new interest. "You were a friend of Emilia's?"

"Acquainted, but I'm not sure I'd say that we were friends. We were rivals, really." He raised a brow at Cleo's look of curiosity. "We met several years ago in Auranos, where we competed against each other in an archery tournament held in her honor. She was so talented, and she insisted that boys and girls should compete in the same matches."

Cleo couldn't help but laugh at the memory of the festivals and competitions once held in the City of Gold. "Yes, Emilia was an incredible archer. I envied her. But, then again, it takes years of practice to hone a skill like that, and back then I preferred activities that were much less athletic."

Attending parties. Drinking wine. Exploring markets. Having her hair braided and styled by skilled attendants. Being fitted for extravagant gowns. Spending time with good friends—not that any of them had sent a single letter or condolence since the deaths of her father and sister.

Kurtis nodded. "It was unusual for a princess of her status—not to mention an heiress to the throne—to take up such a hobby, but she deeply impressed me. And I was even more impressed when she became the champion of our match."

Emilia must have loved that, Cleo thought. To have beaten the boys at their own game. "Please don't tell me you *let* her win."

"Far from it. I tried my very best and came in second place . . .

a very *close* second place. I would have loved the glory of the win, especially at that young and vulnerable age. I'd always hoped for a rematch, but some dreams aren't meant to come true."

"No, they're not," Cleo mused. Her sister had practiced with her bow and arrow every day until she fell ill with the disease that stole her life. Cleo used to joke that Emilia could bring back enough venison for a whole year after just one afternoon hunting trip. Or, perhaps, defend the palace with the rest of the guards if they were ever attacked.

Cleo had no such skills with weaponry. She'd been able to defend herself so far with a sharp dagger and a great deal of luck. Otherwise, she was dependent on others to protect her from danger.

"Lord Kurtis . . ." she began, an idea suddenly brewing in her mind.

"Please, princess. It's just Kurtis. My friends needn't use my title to address me."

"Kurtis," she repeated with a smile. "You should feel free to call me Cleo."

His olive-green eyes sparkled. "With pleasure, *Princess* Cleo."

"Close enough." She laughed. "Tell me, Kurtis, now that you've been relieved of many of your duties around the palace, you must have a great deal of time on your hands, yes?"

"I suppose I do. Although, I hope to be invited to future council meetings, at Prince Magnus's discretion of course. I believe I could still be of help."

She wondered how likely it was that Magnus would agree to that. "Well, you've just reminded me of something my sister loved and did very well. I would like to take archery lessons to honor her memory, and it seems that you would make an excellent tutor."

"It might seem vain to agree with you, your grace, but I would. And I'd be honored to be your tutor."

"That's wonderful news, thank you. Can we meet every day?" she asked eagerly. "I tend to get bored with new hobbies unless I fully immerse myself in them."

Kurtis nodded. "Every day it is. I'll try my very best to teach you well, princess."

"Teach her well?" Magnus's deep voice cut between them. "Teach her *what*, might I ask?"

Cleo thought it best not to act guilty. After all, they were speaking plainly in a hallway, not whispering in an alcove or guarding the conversation from potential eavesdroppers. Further, she had nothing to be guilty of, and so she turned to the prince without hesitation.

"Archery," Cleo said. "Lord Kurtis is a skilled archer and he's agreed to tutor me."

"How very kind of him." Magnus studied Kurtis with a sharp, even glare, as a bird of prey might study a small rabbit, right before tearing off its head.

"Yes. Very kind." Her heart sped up again, but she couldn't falter now. "Magnus, I need to speak with you."

"So speak."

"In private."

Kurtis bowed his head. "I'll leave you alone. Princess, perhaps we can have our first lesson tomorrow at midday?"

"Perfect."

"Until then. Your highness, your grace." Another bow and Kurtis turned on his heels and walked down the hallway.

"My deepest apologies for interrupting," Magnus said, his tone free of sincerity. "So. Archery?"

Cleo waved her hand dismissively. "A simple hobby to help pass the days here."

"Correct me if I'm wrong, but don't you already have a hobby?

Yes, I believe you've previously spent your free time plotting vengeance on me and my entire family?"

"I have many hobbies," she countered.

"Indeed. Now, what is it you wish to speak to me about?"

"I said I'd prefer to talk in private."

He cast a glance around the hallway, where servants bustled and several guards were stationed. "This is private enough."

"Is it?" she said. "Then perhaps we can start by discussing what happened at Lady Sophia's villa and why you seem to be trying your very hardest to forget all about it?"

His smile fell, and he hissed out a breath as he took Cleo firmly by her upper arm, directing her toward the nearest exit to a balcony. Suddenly she was out in the cold air without a cloak to keep her warm, her breath forming frozen clouds before her.

Magnus extended his arms in presentation. "Privacy. Just as the princess wishes. I hope it's not too cold out here for you. For me, this temperature is refreshing after so many months trapped in the hellish heat of Auranos."

How she wished she could read minds, to know exactly what was going on behind his dark brown eyes. Magnus had a rather enviable talent for stripping his expression of any telltale emotion. There was once a time when Cleo believed she had cracked the code, had learned how to see past this mask, but now she doubted herself, just as she doubted everything else.

All she knew for sure was that, by deciding to accompany him here to the palace rather than going into exile with Nic, she had put her immediate future in the prince's hands. But that was a small price to pay to ensure she'd live to see the *distant* future.

"If you're afraid that *I* want to discuss what happened at Lady Sophia's—"

"Afraid?" he interjected. "I'm not afraid of anything."

"—then allow me to put your mind at ease." She'd rehearsed this speech over and over in her mind since she'd left her chambers. "Emotions were running high that night and our thoughts were cloudy. Anything that either of us may have said should not be taken seriously."

He studied her for a long moment in silence, his brow drawn together. "I must admit," he said finally, "the details of what happened before we arrived at the temple are rather hazy for me. But what I can say is this: In the harsh light of day, confusing events seem much clearer, don't they? Moments of regrettable foolishness that seem like they'll carry grave consequences become entirely irrelevant."

"My thoughts exactly." The look of relief in his eyes should have felt freeing for her, but instead she felt a heavy weight bearing down on her chest.

Stop, Cleo, she chastised herself. *You hate him and you always will. Hold on to that hate and let it make you stronger. You are his pawn in his battle against his father. That is all.*

Even if Magnus had defied the king to save her, he was still his father's heir. That meant that she remained his enemy, and that he might choose to dispose of her at any moment if it served his purpose. This had never felt more possible, now that he'd shown his true face while dealing with a minor inconvenience like Kurtis.

She swore she wouldn't let her guard down around him again, as she had that fateful night.

"Yes, well, I'm very glad we could have this private talk," said Magnus, moving toward the doors leading back into the palace. "Now, if we're finished . . . ?"

"Actually, that wasn't the primary reason I wanted to speak with you." She straightened her shoulders and adjusted her own invisible mask. "I need you to send for my attendant, Nerissa Florens."

He regarded her for a moment in silence. "Do you?"

"Yes." She raised her chin higher. "And any answer besides 'yes' is unacceptable. As . . . delightful as the attendants are here in Limeros, I've grown accustomed to Nerissa and find her grooming and domestic skills to be incomparable."

"Limerian attendants are delightful, are they?" Magnus reached toward Cleo. She froze, and he hesitated before taking a long lock of tangled, half-braided hair in hand. "Did you ask your handmaiden to transform your hair into a bird's nest today?"

He was standing far too close to her now. Close enough that she knew from his scent that he'd been out riding today. She picked up the familiar aromas of worn leather and warm sandalwood.

She stepped back from him, knowing she would think much clearer with some space between them. Her hair slipped from his fingers. "You smell like a horse."

"I suppose there are worse things to smell like." He raised a brow before narrowing his gaze. "Very well, I'll send for Nerissa if you feel she's so valuable."

Cleo regarded him with surprise. "Just like that? No argument?"

"Would you prefer I argue?"

"No, but I . . ." *When one has gotten what they want, one should stop speaking.* Cleo's father used to say that to her whenever she'd continue to make her case for something he'd already relented to. "Thank you," she said now, as sweetly as she could.

"Now if you'll excuse me, I must wash the scent of horses from myself. Wouldn't want to offend anyone else with my stench." Again, he turned toward the door.

Stop being a weak little fool, she told herself. "I'm not finished."

His shoulders tensed. "Oh?"

Her teeth had begun to chatter from the cold, but she refused to go back inside yet. "The message you sent to your father. What did it say? You didn't tell me."

He blinked. "Should I have?"

"It concerns me as well, doesn't it? I'm the one whom you helped escape execution. So, yes, you should have told me. What are his plans? Will he come here? Are we safe?"

He leaned against the balcony doors and crossed his arms. "*We*, princess, are mostly certainly *not* safe. I told my father that I'd learned you had specific information on Lucia's whereabouts. I wrote that Cronus was so steadfastly loyal to the king's commands that he refused to delay your execution until after I could get this information out of you. So I took matters into my own hands."

Cleo exhaled the breath she was holding during this entire speech. "And has he replied?"

A shallow nod. "I received a new message this morning. Apparently he's traveling abroad, and he looks forward to seeing me again upon his return."

"That's it? So he believes you?"

"I wouldn't say that. His reply could mean anything—or nothing. After all, he knows that messages sent by raven aren't exactly guaranteed to stay private. But I plan to stick to the story I've told until my last breath. If I can convince him that I only acted out of love for my sister, he may be lenient with me."

"And with me?"

"That remains to be seen."

Cleo hadn't expected him to make any promises to keep her safe and alive, so she wasn't surprised when he didn't. His silence was just more proof that the boy she'd seen intimidating and humiliating Kurtis was the real Magnus.

"Now, let me ask *you* a question, princess," Magnus said, locking gazes with her. He drew so close to her that they were nearly touching and she moved backward until her spine was pressed up against the balcony railing.

"What?" She tried to inject the single word with as much defiance as possible.

"Have you managed to send word to Jonas Agallon and his trusty rebels informing him of your current whereabouts? Perhaps he can chase after Amara and bring you back the water Kindred."

The name Jonas Agallon was a sharp slap back to cold reality.

Cleo pressed her hands against Magnus's chest and pushed. "Step away from me," she hissed.

"Did I strike a nerve? Apologies, but some subjects need to be addressed—even if they prove unpleasant to you."

"I've already told you that I don't and have never had anything to do with Jonas Agallon and his followers." The belief that she'd colluded with rebels was what had led to her imprisonment and the king's command for her immediate execution.

But it was the truth of course—she *had* conspired with him. But she'd never admit that out loud. Especially not to Magnus.

"Well, regardless, might I suggest Jonas as an archery tutor instead of Kurtis? Kurtis is skilled in the sport, I suppose, but Jonas—now there's someone who's killed Auranians *and* Limerians alike with his arrows, while Kurtis has only aimed at painted targets."

"Kurtis will do nicely, but thank you for your opinion." She shoved past him, then glanced over her shoulder as she left the balcony. "Good day, Magnus."

He watched her leave the balcony with narrowed eyes. "Good day, princess."

CHAPTER 4

LUCIA

PAELSIA

He'd asked her to call him Kyan.

He didn't look much older than twenty years of age. He had dark blond hair, sparkling amber eyes, and was taller than any man Lucia had ever known.

Immortal and indestructible. Omnipotent and fearsome. Able to end a mortal's life in a flash of fire and pain with a mere thought. He was the elemental god of fire, previously imprisoned within an orb of amber for countless centuries.

And now he sat right across from her, slurping barley soup in a small public house in northern Paelsia.

"This," Kyan said as he signaled to the barmaid for another bowl, "is absolutely delicious."

Lucia regarded him with disbelief. "It's just soup."

"You say that as if this isn't a miracle contained within a wooden bowl. This is sustenance that feeds both the body and the soul. Mortals could live off unseasoned meat and plucked grass and yet they choose to make concoctions that smell and taste divine. If only they applied their minds to everything in this manner, rather than wasting their time squabbling about mundane topics and killing each other for petty reasons."

When they'd first met, she'd expected him to lay waste to Mytica immediately in his quest to assassinate his enemy—a Watcher named Timotheus who, according to Kyan, was the only remaining immortal who had the power to imprison him again.

At the time, she'd been so numb with grief she hadn't been able to think straight. Her pain was so great that it was the only thing she'd wanted to share with the world.

Lucia wondered what her father and brother might say if they could see her now, sitting in a tavern, across from the soup-eating fire Kindred. The thought almost made her smile.

"Eat." Kyan pointed to Lucia's bowl.

"I'm not hungry."

"Do you want to wither away and die?" He raised a pale brow. "Is that what you're doing? Starving yourself so you can be reunited with your beloved Watcher?"

Whenever Kyan said the word *Watcher*, his expression darkened and his amber eyes flashed bright blue.

Anger. Hatred. The need for vengeance. They simmered just beneath the otherwise genteel exterior of this powerful being.

It was much the same whenever Lucia heard Alexius's name. The pain of having learned that he, too, had used her for his own gain had faded in the days since she'd lost him. The scar tissue that wound had left behind had grown thicker, tougher, as protective as a plate of armor.

No one would ever use her like that again.

"No," she replied. "Believe me, I want to live."

"I'm very glad to hear that."

Lucia stared down at her bowl and brought a spoonful of soup to her lips. "This is watery and tasteless."

Kyan reached over and took some for himself to sample. "To you, perhaps. But that doesn't make it less of a miracle."

The miracle Lucia wanted to come upon most of all was a witch—the older and more knowledgeable the better. They needed one who knew where to find a very special kind of stone wheel used as a magical porthole leading directly to the Sanctuary, the legendary world of the immortals, where the Watchers had stood guard over the Kindred in their crystal prisons for millennia.

Lucia had wanted to know why neither she nor Kyan—as powerful as they both were—could sense this magic without outside help. He explained that there was no magic to sense, that such magic had been hidden to protect the Sanctuary from outside threats.

Therefore, they didn't need a witch's *magic* to find these stone wheels, they needed a witch who'd seen one with her own eyes and knew what it was.

Once they found one, only then could Lucia use her magic to yank Timotheus right out of his safe haven.

Lucia realized Kyan was watching her and she looked up from her bowl.

"You still want to help me, don't you?" he asked, his voice softer now.

She nodded. "Of course. I hate Watchers as much as you do."

"I highly doubt that. But I'm sure there's no love lost between you after all that's happened." He sighed. Suddenly, he looked very mortal to Lucia. Very vulnerable, and very tired. "Once Timotheus is dead, perhaps I can finally find peace."

"As soon as he's dead, we'll find your family, and *then* you can find peace," she replied. "And anyone who gets in our way will be very, very sorry."

"My fierce little sorceress." He grinned at her. "You remind me so much of Eva. She protected us, too. She was the only one who understood what we wanted—what we needed—more than anything else."

"To be free, and to be a real family."

"Yes."

It wasn't common knowledge that the Kindred weren't just magical forces trapped within crystals. They were elemental *beings*, with hopes and dreams and goals. Yet all who believed in their existence, including Lucia's adoptive father, King Gaius, thought them to be nothing more than shiny treasures that would bring ultimate power to their possessors.

Once she and Kyan had summoned Timotheus from the Sanctuary, she would drain the Watcher of his magic until he became mortal.

And then Lucia would kill him, just as she had Melenia.

She had taken such pleasure in the death of that beautiful immortal—a woman who'd corrupted Alexius to the point he'd nearly murdered Lucia. She'd used Lucia's blood to escape her own prison and awaken Kyan, her former lover.

But the pain in Melenia's eyes, just before her death, when she'd realized Kyan had never loved her back . . .

Such sweet, sweet vengeance.

"What if we find a witch and she refuses to help us?" Lucia asked. "Will we have to torture her?"

"Torture?" He frowned. "I don't think that'll be necessary. Your magic will be sufficient to help get us what we need."

She knew her magic was more powerful than a common witch's, but she'd only started to scratch the surface. She yearned to know more. "What do you mean?"

"Eva had a golden dagger, which she would use to carve symbols into people's flesh—both immortal and mortal alike. The wounds would ensure obedience and truthfulness in any subject she chose."

This dagger had to have been what Melenia had used on Alexius to manipulate his mind, force him to do her bidding, and try to kill Lucia. Her greedy act should have ended with Lucia's death, but instead, Alexius had taken his own life.

Lucia wanted so badly to forgive him, knowing that he'd been manipulated. But so much damage had already been done, and she didn't have the strength to muster up any more compassion.

"So Eva had a fancy magical dagger," she said now, shrugging. "How does that story help me?"

"Eva could compel truth and obedience from mortals even without the dagger. It was a combination of all of her magic, blending the elements together to create something new—something beyond what anyone else could do. Manipulating one's very will and molding it into a different shape. Drawing truth from a reluctant tongue. The same magic that the dagger had been infused with at its creation was the magic she possessed naturally. You possess it, too, little sorceress."

Lucia regarded him with awe at the sheer number of possibilities this presented. "Honestly, I've never experienced anything like that. It sounds far too good to be true. I mean, I have Eva's magic, but I'm not immortal like her."

"Mortality has nothing to do with it, really." Kyan polished off what was left of his third bowl of soup. "However, you are correct that you're sixteen years old and Eva was ancient and ageless. You'll need a lot of practice before you'll be ready to wield this power without any serious difficulties."

She frowned. "Difficulties? Like what?"

"Best to show rather than tell." He nodded at the approaching barmaid. "Try this new gift on her. Capture her gaze. Will your deepest magic into her as if it's a substance she will breathe in, and have her tell you a guarded truth."

"That's about as clear as mud."

He spread his hands. "I can't do it, myself. I've only seen it done. But I know it's within you. You should be able to feel it rise up and flow through your every pore."

"Well . . . I can light candles by just looking at them."

"Like that simple magic, yes. But more. Deeper. Bigger. More epic."

More epic? She rolled her eyes, equally exasperated and fascinated by everything he said. "Fine. I'll try."

The ability to pull the truth from anyone's lips was a skill far too tempting to ignore. It would be so useful in countless ways.

The barmaid arrived at their table and slid another steaming bowl of soup in front of Kyan. "There you go, handsome. Can I bring you anything else?"

"Not for me. But my friend has a question for you."

The barmaid looked to Lucia. "What is it?"

Lucia took a deep breath and locked eyes with the woman. It had become effortless to use the magic she'd grown accustomed to, but this had to be different.

Show me the way, Eva, she thought. *Let me be like you.*

While the amethyst ring she now wore on the middle finger of her right hand helped control the more beastly and uncontrollable parts of her *elementia*, she still felt that swirl of darkness down deep inside of her. An endless, bottomless ocean of magic, all contained within her. It was as if she could see that magic—a magic whose surface she'd only skimmed.

Awakening the Kindred had meant tapping into this swirling ocean. Lucia had dove into it so deeply she'd nearly drowned.

She needed to go there again, to that deep, dangerous place.

This was not lighting a wick with a flame. This was not levitating a flower or healing a scratch or turning water to ice.

The deep, dark magic within her blended together and formed into the shape of a dagger. Lucia envisioned pressing this black dagger to the barmaid's throat.

"Tell me your darkest secret—the one you've never told anyone else." Lucia spoke the words, a whir of echoes all around her, and forced them into the woman's mind.

"I . . . uh . . . what?" the barmaid sputtered.

Lucia inhaled deeply and pressed that invisible dagger closer to the woman's throat. "Your darkest secret, speak it now. Don't resist."

A violent shudder shot through the barmaid, and blood began to trickle from her nose. "I . . . I killed my baby sister when I was five years old. I smothered her with a blanket."

Stunned, Lucia fought to hold on to her concentration. "Why would you do that?"

"She . . . she was sickly. My mother spent all her time with her and none with me. I was ignored. So I got rid of her. I hated her and never regretted what I did."

Lucia finally broke eye contact with the barmaid, disgusted by the confession. "Leave us."

The woman absently wiped her bloody nose, then turned and quickly scurried away without another word.

"Well done." Kyan nodded. "I knew you could do it."

"The magic causes *them* pain," Lucia observed. "Not me."

"Only if they try to resist. Eva had such great control over the power that no one resisted, and no one was harmed. You'll grow stronger in time."

A little blood wasn't anything to get squeamish about. This ability was worth the price that had to be paid, but Lucia decided right then that she'd use her truth powers sparingly. Some truths were not meant to be known.

But some most certainly were.

"What she confessed to us," Lucia said, her thoughts swirling. "It reminded me of a secret of my own."

"What?"

"When I was a baby, I was stolen from my cradle by a witch working for King Gaius. I know my birth mother was killed, but I know nothing about my real father." She hesitated. "If he's still alive, I want to find him. And I want to know if I have any sisters or brothers."

Just considering the possibilities of having her real family back gave her new life, and an oddly giddy sense of hope.

Finished with his meal, Kyan stood up from the table and offered Lucia his hand. "I will help you find your family. I promise I will."

Her heart skipped a beat, and she couldn't stop the smile that began to stretch across her face. "Thank you."

"It's truly the least I can do for you, my little sorceress, after all you've already done for me."

Lucia reached into her cloak, pulled out a bag of coins, and placed a silver one on the table to pay for their meal, her mind still reeling from this new and powerful discovery.

A bald man with a short black beard approached their table, smiling. "Good evening to you both."

"Good evening," Kyan replied.

He rested the edge of his dagger on the table. "I'm not one for formal introductions, so let me get right to the point. I'm very interested in that pretty bag of coins you were just waving about. How about you give it to me, and then all of us can leave this public house unharmed?"

Lucia regarded him with disbelief. "How dare you insult me," she hissed, lurching up to her feet.

He laughed. "Sit down, little girl. And you too," he said, looking fiercely at Kyan.

"Lucia," Kyan said calmly, taking a seat again. "It's fine."

"No, it's not." In the space of a heartbeat, Lucia had grown ready to peel the skin from this loathsome thief one inch at a time for this insult.

"Oh, you've got some fire in you, don't you?" The thief's loathsome gaze slid over her open cloak as he nodded with leering approval. "I like pretty young girls with fight in them. Makes it more interesting."

"Kyan," Lucia snarled. "Can I kill him?"

"Not quite yet." Kyan leaned back in his chair and pressed his palms down against the table, looking completely at ease. "See, Lucia? This is a perfect example of what I was talking about before. Mortals have so much potential, but they lust after such base, unimportant things. A few pieces of gold or silver, meaningless sex. Small symbols of power or momentary pleasure. Immortals aren't any better. It disgusts me." He looked up at the thief and shook his head. "If you'd only ask for help, we'd give it to you. Are you hungry? Let us buy a meal. I do recommend the barley soup they have here."

The thief eyed him. "As if you'd actually help a stranger."

Kyan nodded. "If every mortal looked at others as their friends, not as their enemies, the world would be a much better place, wouldn't it?"

Lucia regarded Kyan with total bemusement. He sounded like the Limerian priest who used to give long sermons about the goddess Valoria and her virtues.

Trust strangers. Give of yourself. Be kind.

She'd once believed in such nonsense.

"That's so incredibly kind of you, *friend*," the thief said, smiling. Then he raised his dagger and stabbed it down, hard, pinning Kyan's left hand to the table. "But I'd really prefer to get what I asked for. Give me that bag of coins now, or I'll stick my dagger in your eye next."

Lucia stared at Kyan with shock as the fire god calmly studied his impaled hand. "I offered to help you, and this is what you do?" he asked, dismayed.

"I didn't ask for your help. Only asked for your gold."

Kyan slowly pulled his hand toward himself, forcing the blade to slice between his fingers.

The thief grimaced and nearly gagged. "What the—?"

Now free from the dagger, Kyan rose to his feet, his previously peaceful expression only a memory. His eyes had shifted from amber to blue, so bright that they glowed in the dimly lit tavern.

"Your weakness disgusts me," he said. "I need to cleanse it from this world."

The thief took a step backward, raising his hands in surrender. "Look, I don't want any trouble."

"Really? You could have fooled me," Lucia said, her skin still crawling from the lecherous way the man had looked at her. "Kill this pathetic mortal, Kyan, or I'll do it myself."

She felt the heat before she saw the fire. A narrow whip of flames snaked toward the man, licking his boot and slowly winding up his ankle, calf, and thigh like a vine of fire. Every patron in the tavern took notice as chairs skidded against the wooden floor and men and women collectively rose to their feet with alarm.

Lucia watched fear flicker in their eyes as they watched the strange fire entangle the thief.

The thief stared at Kyan with wide eyes. "No! Don't—whatever you're doing—don't do this!"

"It's already done," Kyan replied simply.

"You—what are you? You're a demon! An evil beast from the darklands!"

The flames engulfed his mouth and face until his entire body, head to toe, became a torch. Then, suddenly, the fire turned from deep amber to brilliant blue—just as Kyan's eyes had.

The thief screamed. The shrieking sound reminded Lucia of a frightened rabbit caught in the jaws of an ice wolf.

The crowd around them scrambled, tripping over each other in their rush to get outside. The thief continued to burn, and the fire caught hold of the dry wooden chairs, wooden tables, wooden floor. Soon the entire tavern was ablaze.

"He deserved to die," Kyan said, calmly.

Lucia nodded. "I agree."

Still, Lucia felt shaky as she followed him through the flames— flames that didn't burn or even touch her. She glanced over her shoulder as the screaming finally stopped and watched as the thief's body shattered like a blue crystal statue hitting a marble floor.

Once outside, Lucia took one more look at the burning tavern.

There was no one in this world who could stop them from reaching their goal. A god and a sorceress—they were the perfect match.

Lucia glanced down at Kyan's hand.

His wound had healed so perfectly, it was as if it had never been there in the first place.

CHAPTER 5

FELIX

AURANOS

It was fun being one of the bad guys again.

No remorse, no conscience. Free to be cruel and uncaring. Creating chaos and instilling fear wherever he went with a song in his heart.

Good times.

Felix had just spent three very enjoyable days in shiny and extravagant Hawk's Brow, the largest city in Auranos. First, he'd beaten up a man for no particular reason and then stolen his clothes, only to find that his fine leather shoes were disappointingly tight. He'd bedded two gorgeous blondes—identical twins, in fact—and hadn't even bothered to learn their names. And then he'd robbed a busy tavern of nearly two hundred centimos while the barkeep had his back turned.

Felix Gaebras, a highly valued assassin for the Clan of the Cobra before his short leave of absence, had returned to the life he was meant for.

He tossed his Kindred crystal up into the air and caught it, enjoying the familiar weight of it in his grip.

"Where to?" he asked the air magic swirling inside the orb of moonstone, then held it to his ear. "To the City of Gold, you say? What an excellent idea. Let's you and I pay a visit to the king."

The last time he'd seen the king, he'd been given a very special assignment: find Jonas Agallon and infiltrate his band of rebels, learn as much as he could about their plans, kill Jonas, and then swiftly return to report his findings to the king.

Instead, Felix had decided that this would be the perfect time to redeem himself for his past wrongdoings and become a good, upstanding citizen rather than a cold-blooded killer working for the King of Blood.

What a laugh.

Hopefully, despite the unexpected delay in his travels, the king would welcome him back into the fold with open arms. He'd be back to cutting throats and burning villages by the following week.

Felix was passing through a small village nestled in a forest when he heard someone call out to him.

"Young man! Young man! Please, I need your help!"

Ignore her, Felix told himself. *You don't help people, you kill them. Even helpless old ladies if they're foolish enough to get in your way.*

"Young man!" The old woman scurried up to him and grabbed hold of his shirt sleeve. "Goodness, child, didn't you hear me? Where are you off to in such a hurry?"

He pocketed the air Kindred. "First of all, lady, I am not a child. And, secondly, where I'm going is none of your concern."

She put her hands on her hips and looked up at him. "Well, never mind then. All I know is I need help, and you're tall and you look strong enough."

"Strong enough for what?"

She pointed at a nearby tree. "Up there!"

Felix frowned and peered up into the thick tree, heavy with leaves. Perched precariously on a branch high above their heads was a small gray-and-white kitten.

"Somehow my darling little kitty got herself up there," the old woman explained, wringing her hands, "and now she can't get back down. She's so very frightened, can't you see? And so am I. She's going to fall or get snatched up by a hawk!"

"You really do have to be watchful for hawks," he said, then snorted. The woman stared at him blankly. *"Watchful. Hawks.* Get it?"

She pointed again, more frantically this time. "You must climb up the tree and save my kitty before it's too late!" The kitten let out a tiny but plaintive *mew,* as if to emphasize the dilemma.

It was rather unfortunate for this woman that Felix had happened along in her time of need. Had he been Jonas Agallon, he'd likely have already rescued the cat, and would now be busy milking a goat for its dinner.

Even just that brief thought of the failed rebel leader had managed to darken Felix's mood.

"I don't save kittens, lady," he growled.

Her eyes brimmed with tears. "Oh, please. There's no one else around to help right now. *Please* do this, in Goddess Cleiona's name. She loved animals—all animals, big and small."

"Yeah, well, I'm Limerian and our Goddess Valoria only liked animals if they ate kittens for breakfast."

A hawk passed overhead, its shadow crossing Felix's path. The woman shielded her eyes from the bright sun as she looked up at it with panic.

Felix wasn't sure if it was a real hawk or a Watcher, but it did look rather hungry for small felines.

Cruel and uncaring, remember?

He glanced at the woman who looked up with him with such hope that he might help her.

Damn it.

It didn't take very long at all to climb the tree, grab the cat, and return to the ground.

"Take it," he said gruffly, shoving the furry handful away.

"Oh, thank you!" She gratefully took the kitten into her arms and kissed it multiple times. Then she grabbed Felix's face and noisily kissed both his cheeks. "You are a hero!"

He just glared at her. "I am most definitely not a hero. Now, do *me* a favor and forget you ever saw me."

Without another word, he began walking away from the old woman, her cat, and the stupid tree of shame.

He reached the city late that afternoon, when the sun had begun to slip behind the horizon, painting the sky with streaks of red and orange.

Felix took a deep breath as he approached the first palace entrance. Two guards crossed their sharp spears in front of him, stopping him from taking another step. He sized them up. Both massive men made Felix's own tall and muscular frame look puny in comparison.

"Greetings, friends," he began with a grin. "Lovely day, isn't it?"

"Go away," the mountainous guard on the left said.

"Don't you want to know who I am and what business I have here?"

"No."

"Well, I'm going to tell you anyway. The name's Felix Gaebras, and I'm here to see his majesty, the king. No appointment necessary. He's not expecting me, but I assure you he'll know who I am and want to speak with me personally."

Two spears now pointed directly at his throat. "And why's that?" the smaller guard snapped.

He cleared his throat, determined to hold fast to his courage. "Because of this."

Without making any sudden moves to provoke them to put their spears to use, Felix pulled up his sleeve to show the snake tattoo on his forearm that marked him as a full member of the Clan of the Cobra.

"And?" The guard didn't seem to know the importance of what he was looking at.

"You might not personally know what this mark means, but believe me when I say that the king will be *very* angry if he were to find out you turned me away. I'm one of his favorite and most accomplished assassins. I know you wouldn't want to make the king angry, would you? You both seem like men who value having all of their limbs intact."

The large guard's eyes narrowed as he peered at the tattoo again, his lips thin. After a rather torturous silence with the pointy end of both spears still pointed at Felix, the guard nodded once.

"Follow me," he said.

Felix was ushered into a dark salon off the main foyer. The little room was decked out with a mosaic floor of silver and bronze and massive tapestries on every wall. Hanging front and center was the Auranian crest, which featured a hawk and the credo OUR TRUE GOLD IS OUR PEOPLE.

Felix guessed this room must not be used often since it still displayed a relic of the former royal family.

After what felt like a small eternity, a man came to the archway and peered in at him. He had a sharp nose and black hair that was graying at the temples.

"You are the one who has asked for an audience with his majesty?"

Felix straightened his shoulders and tried to look all official. "I am."

"And you say you are . . ." He looked down at a piece of parchment in his hands. "Felix Gaebras."

"That's right."

The man pursed his lips. "What business do you have with the king?"

"That's something I need to address privately, with only him." He crossed his arms. "Who are you? His valet?"

At this, he received a rather unpleasant smile. "I am Lord Gareth Cirillo, grand kingsliege and high advisor to the king."

Felix whistled. "That sounds fancy."

He'd never personally met Lord Gareth before, but he was well aware of his name, and that he was the wealthiest man in Limeros, apart from the king himself.

Lord Gareth blinked slowly. "Guards, take this boy into custody immediately."

"Wait . . . what?" Felix was barely able to move a muscle before several guards approached from behind the archway and grabbed hold of him.

"There is a warrant out for your arrest."

"What? On what charges?"

"Murder. And treason. It was so kind of you to turn yourself in today." Lord Gareth gestured toward the archway. "Take him to the dungeon."

Felix refused to walk at the guards' violent prompting, so they dragged him. His stolen shoes squeaked and scraped against the decadent floor.

"Treason? No, wait! I have to see the king. He—he'll want to

see me. I have something he wants. Something of great value."
Felix hesitated, not wanting to show his hand so soon but finding
he had no other choice. "I have a piece of the Kindred."

Lord Gareth halted the guards and regarded Felix for a moment
of contemplative silence. Then he began to laugh. "The Kindred is
only a legend."

"Are you sure about that? If I'm lying, I'll end up in the dungeon anyway. But if I'm telling the truth, and you don't inform
the king about it, you'll end up holding your own severed head in
your hands."

"If you are lying," Lord Gareth said, narrowing his gaze, "you
won't even make it to the dungeon."

With a nod from the grand kingsliege, a guard brought the
heavy hilt of his sword down against Felix's head, and everything
went black.

When Felix came to, he had only one thought: The dungeon didn't
smell nearly as bad as he would have expected it to. As he pried
open his eyes, he realized that was for a very good reason. He
wasn't in the dungeon.

He was in the throne room, lying flat on his back at the bottom
of the stairs, looking up at the royal dais. And there was the king
seated upon the golden throne he'd stolen.

Or won, depending on what side one was on.

This throne room was nearly identical to the one in the north,
only where the Limerian one was dark and gray and hard, this one
was gold and bright and . . . hard.

Felix pushed himself up to his feet and bowed deeply, ignoring
the pounding pain in his head.

"Your majesty."

Standing to the right of King Gaius was Lord Gareth. His arms were crossed, and his lined expression was dour as he peered down his sharp nose at Felix.

"Felix Gaebras," the king addressed him. "I've been very disappointed not to receive word from you in all this time. Many believed you to be dead, which would have been a loss for both the Clan and for Limeros. But here you are, alive and well."

Felix spread his hands. "Allow me to explain my lengthy silence, your majesty."

"The only reason you're still breathing," the king said, leaning forward on his throne, "is because I very much would like an explanation. And make it a good one. I've been disappointed many times by those I formerly held in high estimation in recent months. I cannot tell you how much I despise being disappointed."

Lord Gareth's expression darkened. "Your majesty, I don't understand why you've chosen to give this stupid, insolent boy even a moment of your valuable time. He's committed treason, and treason is punishable by death."

"At what time did I commit treason, might I ask?" Felix ventured. "I don't seem to recall."

The king's attention remained firmly on Felix, his gaze sharp and assessing. "You don't seem to recall assisting Jonas Agallon in freeing two rebel prisoners I'd chosen to execute? You have no memory of being responsible for the explosions that caused the deaths of many loyal citizens?"

Felix blinked. "I have no idea what you're talking about, your majesty."

Lord Gareth let out an exasperated huff. "You were seen, you stupid boy. The guards' uniforms you and the rebel stole didn't cover your faces."

Oh, shit.

"I can explain," he began.

"Save your breath," the king hissed. "I had given you the task of getting close to the rebel, not to assist him in opposing me."

Had Felix honestly thought it would be so easy to stroll into the palace and go back to life as usual after all he'd done?

His mouth had gone dry, but he tried to find the words to speak. To explain. "I served you and the Clan very well for many years, your highness. I gave my life over to the kingdom and I learned how to survive, how to thrive in that environment, and how to kill in your name without question. I was only eleven when the Clan took me in."

"Eleven, yes." The king nodded. "I remember you, Felix, more clearly than any of the others. When you were brought before me—a boy only a year older than my own son, who had seen his family killed, his village destroyed—you did not look at me with fear. You met my eyes with defiance and strength. Eleven years old. I knew there was something special within you. A rough spirit that I could harness to create greatness. I thought I had succeeded. Clearly, given your recent choices, I was wrong. Admit to your crimes, boy, and then let's be done with this foolishness."

There was once a member of the Clan of the Cobra, an old man who'd served as the group's wise guardian. When he was on his deathbed, he'd said that, in life, a man only comes to a few cross-roads that can shape his future for good or for bad. Sometimes one recognized these crossroads, and could stop and think about the right decision. But other times, the choice could only be seen with the clarity that came afterward.

This crossroad was well-lit and impossible for Felix to miss.

While Felix considered himself a skilled liar, he knew that the king might be the one person able to see right through him to the truth.

Felix took a deep breath and gathered every last ounce of

courage and bravado he had left. "It's true, I helped Jonas save his friends, and in doing so I committed treason against you, your majesty. Abandoning the Clan wasn't a plan I'd had in the works for ages, but it happened. I made a mistake. I came to trust the wrong people—to believe I had a choice in how my future could unfold. But I was wrong. I am exactly what you see before you, your loyal servant who regrets his recent actions and wishes to beg for your forgiveness."

"I see." The king pursed his lips. "And where is Jonas Agallon now?"

Felix hesitated. "I don't know. All I know is that he's an unlucky, untrained fool who runs headfirst into danger without thinking. That he's managed to live this long is a miracle in itself. He is no threat to you, your majesty. And his only remaining follower is one equally foolish girl."

He didn't like to think about Lysandra. From the moment he'd helped rescue her from execution, they'd argued and squabbled about anything and everything, and he'd enjoyed every moment of it. The girl was a handful and had an attitude harsh enough to reduce any normal boy to a sniveling wimp. But Felix was no normal boy.

And he'd rapidly been falling for Lysandra, with no idea whether she realized it or not.

But at the very first moment of doubt, she'd sided with Jonas. The girl was in love with him, which was too bad for her, since Jonas was already in love with Princess Cleo.

"In summation, your majesty, I have learned now without question that I wasn't meant for any different life. I'd already been leading the life I was meant to, and had a job I was skilled at. I stand before you today as your loyal servant, with renewed commitment to you, the Clan, and my duties. And I have brought with me absolute proof of that loyalty, something I wouldn't have if not for my short-term association with the rebel."

He reached for the air Kindred in his pocket, but found it was empty.

"Are you looking for this?"

Felix shot his gaze up to the throne to see King Gaius, holding the moonstone orb in the palm of his hand.

"Uh, yes. That's exactly what I was looking for." Felix was astounded by his own stupidity. Of course Lord Gareth would have him searched him after he'd claimed to have the Kindred.

"Do you even know what this is?" the king asked.

"I do." Felix nodded. "Do you?"

"Speak to the king with respect," Lord Gareth snapped.

"Lord Gareth," King Gaius said evenly, "perhaps you should leave us to speak in private."

The kingsliege frowned. "I meant no disrespect, your highness. *He* is the one who's being disrespectful."

"My son is currently seated upon my throne in Limeros, but only after having to explain his rightful place to your disrespectful son. If you want to remain in my good graces, Lord Gareth, then do as I say. I won't ask again."

Without another word, Lord Gareth descended the steps and slunk out of the throne room.

Felix watched this exchange with a heady combination of interest and fear.

The king rose from his throne and descended the stairs. He stopped and stood just inches away from Felix and raised the moonstone orb to eye level.

"This, Felix, is something I have desired my entire life. But it is a great surprise, to say the very least, to have it delivered to me in this manner. How did you come to acquire it?"

"Jonas received a message containing its location and instructions for its retrieval. We were successful in our search, and then I stole it from him."

He wasn't going to admit that he and Jonas had also uncovered the earth Kindred, and that the message was from Princess Cleo. It wasn't as if he was trying to protect anyone—and he certainly wasn't trying to protect Princess Cleo, whom he didn't know from a blond hole in the ground. But he'd rather not give away *all* his valuable secrets to this powerful man all at once.

The king stared at the air Kindred as if it were a long-lost love that had finally returned. He was so engrossed by it that Felix figured he could slip out of the room without him noticing—if there weren't a dozen guards behind him, that was.

"There's only one *little* problem," Felix admitted. "I have no idea how to make it, uh . . . work. As far as I'm concerned, all it is is a pretty rock with a swirly thing inside of it."

"Yes. There is that swirly thing." A corner of the king's mouth quirked up. "It's fine, Felix. I am one of very few mortals who know how to access its magic."

Felix's brow shot up. "How?"

The king laughed. "Never mind how. The important thing is that I have it now, and I have you to thank for that."

"You don't doubt its authenticity?"

"Not for a moment. I know it's real. I can *feel* it." The king's dark eyes glittered. "Does Agallon know where to find the other three?"

"Not that I'm aware of." With this outright lie spoken, Felix held his breath.

But the king only nodded, his attention still fixed on the orb.

"Guards, bring the other prisoner in," he called, then turned back to take his seat upon the throne.

Felix waited silently as the guards brought in another man, dirty and in chains. Despite the prisoner's thick, matted beard and the wild look in his eyes, Felix recognized him as a fellow Cobra.

"Felix . . . is that you?" the man snarled. "You *are* alive. You little bastard!"

"Wonderful to see you too, Aeson. How have you been?"

Felix was never very close with Aeson, but he knew him enough to know that he was one of the most brutal and effective assassins he'd ever met.

"I see you remember each other," the king said. "Well, you might be happy to learn that the two of you have something in common: You both abandoned your duties to the Clan for a time. Aeson has been in the dungeons awaiting his execution for . . . how long is it now, Aeson?"

"Three very long weeks," he sputtered.

Felix cast a wary glance at the king. "So, what? I'm going to be his new cell mate?"

"No, I have something much more interesting in mind." He nodded at the guards. "Unchain Aeson and give him a weapon."

Bewildered, Felix eyed the guards as they swiftly carried out the king's orders. Now free from his chains, Aeson rubbed his raw wrists and snatched the broadsword from the guard offering it to him.

"I've listened to your explanation," King Gaius said. "I've received your gift of this orb. Now, Aeson is going to try to kill you. If he succeeds, he will be freed. If he fails, I may choose to pardon you for your momentary alliance with the Paelsian."

Felix was certain the roof had caved in on top of his head. He scrambled for words in the stunned silence of the throne room. "But, but . . . wait. Where's *my* weapon?"

The king responded with a patient smile. "You don't get one. Consider this a test of your abilities and your desire to survive."

Aeson didn't waste a moment. He lunged, closing the distance between them, and brought the blade down hard. Felix felt the cool breeze brought by the sword as he barely stepped out of its way in time.

No weapon to defend himself, only his bare hands.

This was a test he was meant to fail.

"Last I heard, everyone thought you were dead," Aeson snarled. "But I knew you'd gone off of your own free will. I could see it in your eyes, it was always there—that wanderlust."

"You've really got me figured out. So what's your excuse?" Felix walked a careful circle around Aeson, watching his every move, then ducked under the next side-swiping swing.

"I realized that it's much more profitable to be a mercenary than to kill for the kingdom." Aeson grinned, revealing a row of broken, yellowed teeth. "Do you happen to know how much certain individuals are willing to pay to have the King of Blood killed?"

"Plenty, I'm sure," Felix replied tightly.

"A small fortune, actually. I also learned a lot in the dungeons . . . tasty rumors of all kinds." His glittering eyes narrowed, and he flicked the barest of glimpses toward the king. "Is it true your son recently committed treason, your highness? That he freed a prisoner you'd condemned to death and then they both fled to Limeros? Perhaps you're losing your grip on your kingdom after all this time. I assure you, it's a long fall for someone like you."

"The rumors of the condemned," the king's words weren't much more than an icy hiss. "Sad, really."

Aeson gave Felix one last crazed smirk, then turned and stormed toward the dais, slicing his sword through two guards, one after the other, who stood in his way.

Felix was after him in an instant. He snatched the sword off one of the fallen guards and took leaping steps toward his enemy, who was fast approaching the king. Then, in a single, instinct-driven motion, he thrust his blade clean through Aeson's chest. The man's borrowed sword clattered to the floor.

Felix pulled his blade free. Aeson's lifeless body fell backward down the steps, landing in a broken heap on the floor.

The remaining guards swarmed Felix. One of them pressed a blade to his throat, hard enough to break the skin and send a trickle of warm blood down his neck, while another disarmed him and a third dragged him back down the steps.

The king was still up on the dais but was now on his feet, clutching the moonstone.

"Release him," he commanded.

The guards obeyed, but kept their heated glares fixed on Felix.

King Gaius silently regarded Felix for a long, tense moment. He looked perfectly calm for man who'd just been seconds away from being assassinated.

"Well done, Felix. I knew Aeson would use this opportunity to make an attempt on my life."

"And so you just sat there?" Felix sputtered.

"I was more than ready to defend myself," said the king, pulling a dagger from his leather surcoat. "But you acted swiftly, and chose to protect me. You passed my test."

The realization of what the king said slowly sank in. "Well, good then. So . . . now what? What does this mean? Will you pardon me?"

The king re-sheathed his dagger and slipped the orb into his coat. "I'm leaving Auranos's shores tomorrow at dawn to set out on an important journey. You will accompany me as my bodyguard."

This unexpected pronouncement stunned Felix every bit as much as a slap would. He grappled to find his voice. "Where are we going?"

The king smiled, but his eyes remained cold. "Kraeshia."

CHAPTER 6

AMARA

KRAESHIA

"*I will find you . . .*"

This is what Ashur snarled in every nightmare she'd had since leaving the shores of Limeros.

"*And when I do, I will tear you apart for your betrayal. I will make you scream for mercy, but no one will hear you.*"

She woke with a start, frantically reminding herself that no, her brother *wouldn't* find her. Not ever again. She tried to focus on pushing away any remaining doubts she had about her new responsibilities, and what still needed to be done to fulfill them. Nothing else mattered.

Finally, her ship passed through the sea gates and docked at port. She'd returned to the Jewel of the Empire, the capital of Kraeshia.

"Welcome home, princess," said a familiar voice. Mikah, a palace bodyguard, waited for her at the end of the gangplank. Like all Kraeshian guards, Mikah started his training at the age of twelve—after having been sold to the emperor by his parents—and had now been stationed at the royal residence for a decade. In a way, he and Amara had grown up together.

She raised her chin and did not smile in greeting. "Take me to my father."

Mikah bowed. "Yes, princess."

The following journey to the palace went by like a blur. She didn't bother to gaze at the sights her carriage passed—she'd seen them a million times before, and even her long stay in Mytica hadn't done much to erase them from her memory. One could get bored even with beauty when one was constantly surrounded by it.

Auranians believed their City of Gold was the most beautiful place in the world, but that's only because they had never been to the Jewel. Here, it wasn't gaudy gold or cold marble, but rather the brilliant and diverse colors of nature that ruled.

It was evident everywhere one looked that Emperor Cyrus Cortas favored shades of amethyst and emerald. Huge murals depicting the emperor himself adorned the walls of every block in every neighborhood, painted predominantly in those two bold shades. The streets were paved in beautifully complicated patterns of purple and green cobblestones, and so many citizens of the Jewel daily wore purple and green robes and gowns to try to please their ruler that foreign visitors might think it was the country's official uniform.

The emperor was passionate about nature and insisted that the conditions be made such that it could always flourish, but he also insisted that every shrub, every leaf and blade of grass, was well-tended and tirelessly manicured. He imported rare plants and flowers from conquered lands. An army of gardeners was constantly trimming hedges and trees into precise geometric shapes. Landscape artists were summoned from all over the world to apply their skills to the Kraeshian canvas. The road Amara was traveling on appeared to be a seemingly endless blanket of beauty, which led straight to the royal residence: a massive green tower; an emerald spear piercing the sky. So it was fitting that the structure was known as the Emerald Spear. Most of those who'd ever seen it before called it a miracle of architecture, constructed with angles so impossible there had to have been magic involved.

But nothing was impossible if you had the resources to scout the best and the brightest, those with true vision and expertise, to do the work. The emperor found these artists and architects in kingdoms he'd not yet conquered, and paid them small fortunes for their skills. They always returned home smiling, eager and willing to come back at a moment's notice to do more. It had taken more than twenty years for the Jewel of the Empire to reach this height of beauty, but Amara's father was still not satisfied. Just as he did with everything else in his life, he always yearned for more.

After having grown up surrounded by so much manufactured beauty, Amara had come to want something different. Something that wasn't necessarily beautiful. Something imperfect, interesting, and perhaps even ugly.

But *ugly* wasn't allowed in the Jewel.

"Did you have a pleasant trip, princess?" Mikah inquired after a long stretch of silence.

"I did. And now I'm very happy to be home."

The orb of aquamarine sat heavily in the pocket of her silk cloak. She wrapped her fingers around its cool surface. For days on the ship she'd tried to unlock its secrets and learn how to harness its water magic, but each time she'd failed. Finally, she'd grown so frustrated with it that she'd nearly tossed it overboard.

Amara inhaled slowly and then let out the breath, counting to ten as she did. She needed to stay calm, to ignore all the disappointment or doubt that kept trying to creep in.

Clear mind, sharp sight. Nothing else would help her now.

The Kindred is real. And it is mine.

She repeated this mantra again and again, until the water Kindred felt fully and wholly hers. She would have preferred to stay in Mytica to find the remaining three, but one would have to do for now. All she needed to do was unlock its secrets.

"Your father has been looking forward to your return," Mikah told her.

"Really?" A smile barely touched her lips. "He missed me that much?"

He raised his dark brow.

Her smile grew, looking more genuine now. "Don't worry, Mikah. I'm only playing. I know what to expect from my father. He rarely surprises me."

Mikah had known her long enough to reply to this with only an understanding nod.

They arrived at the Emerald Spear, and Mikah led Amara to the emperor's map room.

"Wait out here," she said as Mikah pushed open the heavy door.

He bowed. "Yes, princess."

The map room was appropriately named. Underneath the vaulted ceilings and taking up the majority of the lofty space was a three-dimensional map of the ever-expanding Kraeshian Empire, which now made up a full third of the known world. Master cartographers made twice-yearly journeys to the Jewel to update the topography to include any kingdoms or tracts of land that had been newly acquired.

Standing opposite her, on the far side of the map amidst a group of guards and advisors, was Amara's father. He was engrossed in a whispered conversation with her brother Elan, four years older than Amara and at least four inches shorter. Elan was very thin and frail, and tended to cling to their father like a barnacle to a ship. So unlike her oldest brother, Dastan, the first born and heir, who was tall and handsome, who looked so much like Ashur. They could be identical twins, had they not been six years apart in age.

Amara was grateful that Dastan was currently at sea, on his way home after having successfully claimed a new swath of land for the Empire. She didn't feel ready to see anyone who reminded her so strongly of Ashur just yet.

"Father," she called out. He didn't look up from Elan, so she said it louder. "Father!"

The emperor turned his steely gaze on her. "So. You've finally returned."

"I have." Her heart pounded, so hard she could barely think. There was so much to say and even more to conceal.

The emperor's advisors eyed her appraisingly, but neither spoke nor smiled. These men always made her nervous; they were like vultures waiting to pick at the remains of the dead.

"Come here." The emperor gestured toward her. "Let me see my beautiful daughter up close."

Perhaps what she'd told Mikah about her father wasn't quite accurate—her father calling her beautiful was a great surprise indeed. He rarely acknowledged her, and especially not in this way. Amara navigated her way around the map, her left hand gliding over its smooth edge.

If only she were free to share all her accomplishments with him, if only he'd listen, she was certain he would be proud of her.

Perhaps she hadn't found all four of the Kindred, but given that they'd been lost for a millennium, it was an incredible victory to acquire even one.

"Sister," Elan said, the tone of his greeting thin and flat.

"Brother," she replied with a nod.

The emperor regarded her, his arms folded in front of his dark green robes, intricately embroidered with flecks of gold and violet dragons and phoenixes—the symbols of Kraeshia and the Cortas family. "Tell me, daughter, how was your trip to little Mytica?"

"Eventful."

"I see you've come alone. Does Ashur ever plan to return home? Or will he continue to roam the world, chasing after his magical butterflies?"

In Limeros, Amara had threatened to return to her father and accuse Magnus of slaying Ashur. In that moment of passion, it had seemed a logical choice, but now that she'd had many days to consider her options, she'd decided to hold back—for now.

She forced a smile. "Yes, my brother has a wanderer's soul. But it was lovely to be able to spend a bit of time with him. I'm sure he'll return soon, but he didn't say when."

Perhaps in his next life, Amara thought. Kraeshians believed in reincarnation; just like the phoenix that represented the empire, they too would rise again after death and begin a new life.

"I'm sure you had the chance to meet King Gaius during your stay."

She nodded. "The king was very kind to me and Ashur. He even gave us our own villa."

She didn't mention that the villa was as far away from the palace as possible. Or that the king nearly imprisoned her and Ashur to try to use them against the emperor. Or that it only took her one meeting with him to make her sure that he would have cut both of their throats without remorse if he'd felt it would serve him.

All of the rumors about Gaius Damora were true. He was a snake: cold-blooded and venomous. Of course she hadn't tolerated his attempts to make her his prey while she was in Mytica, but now, with some distance between them, she found she could actually appreciate his ruthlessness.

"And what kinds of discussions did you have with the king?" the emperor asked, absently picking up a small model ship from the shore of the map.

"Nothing of particular interest; it was all very polite." She tried to recall a single memorable conversation she'd had with the king. "He made introductions to his palace advisors, spoke a bit about the attractions in Auranos—nothing useful or enlightening. Of course that wasn't surprising. Myticans don't speak bluntly from their hearts and minds like us. It's all empty courtesy and passive-aggressive innuendo."

"No, not like us at all." The emperor cupped her face in his large hands and smiled at her.

"Definitely not like us."

"Then let me be blunt, daughter." He tightened his grip on her, the pleasant expression fading from his weathered face. "What secrets did you share with the King of Blood that might be used against me?"

Her eyes widened. "What? I told him nothing, of course."

"Really," he said, his gaze steady and unmoving. "Because I have to wonder why it is, exactly, that I've received a message from Auranos, informing me that the king is on his way here to see me. What a coincidence, don't you think, that the king has chosen to take this little trip now, so soon after your departure from Mytica?"

Deep, aching pain spread across her temples where he kept pressing harder. "Father, I assure you, I said nothing."

"Perhaps you talk in your sleep, then?" He raised an eyebrow in response to her stunned expression. "I know you don't think I pay attention to you, Amara. But I do to what they say about you. That you take to your bed any man who smiles at you. That my daughter, the princess of Kraeshia, is no better than a common whore."

"Father!" Her cheeks flared with heat and she grabbed at his hands, digging her fingernails in. "I am not a whore! And I didn't sleep with the king. Nor did I tell him anything about you or our empire. I don't even know any secrets about you. Remember, I'm not one of your sons. I'm your daughter, just a girl. I'm well aware I'm little more than window decoration to you."

He studied her for a long moment, his gray-blue eyes an exact match for her own, only his were watery and surrounded by the wrinkles consuming his leathery face. Finally, he released her. "You disappoint me at every turn, you worthless girl. If only I'd succeeded in ridding myself of you years ago."

Pain tore through Amara's chest. "Yes, well, unfortunately the ancient laws only allowed you one chance to murder an unwanted daughter, didn't they?"

She was trying to provoke him, but he didn't even flinch. "Remove yourself from my sight so I can prepare for our unwelcome guest."

"Perhaps King Gaius means to conquer you," she said under her breath.

A heavy moment of silence lingered before the emperor's booming laugh filled the large room. "I'd like to see him try."

"A pathetic little king conquer *you*, Father?" Elan joined the emperor in his boisterous amusement. "What a ludicrous thought!"

Amara turned, fists clenched, her fingernails biting into her palms, and left the map room.

Yes, how deeply ludicrous it was for anyone to think they had a chance against such a great and powerful conqueror.

"Something troubles you, princess," Mikah said as Amara hurried toward her chambers in the east wing of the Spear.

That she'd thought for even a moment that her father would be pleased to see her after her journey embarrassed her. Of course he hadn't been pleased. Why would she think that anything would have changed over the course of a few weeks when it had been like this for her entire life?

"My troubles are none of your concern," she replied curtly. Perhaps too curtly. She stopped for a moment and turned to him. "I'm fine, Mikah," she said, softer now. "Really."

"I hope so. I don't like to see you so sad."

She spared him another glance and found him studying her intently with dark eyes, curious and searching. Other servants typically kept their gazes lowered in her family's presence and didn't speak unless first spoken to.

"Why are you always so kind to me?" she asked. "No other servant cares how *I* feel."

His expression grew thoughtful. "I suppose when I see someone in pain, I want to help them."

"Some injured animals will bite the hand that tries to help."

"Then I suppose it's a good thing you're not an animal, isn't it?" He allowed himself a small smile. "One day, perhaps we'll become close enough that you'll feel free to confide in me all manner of feelings and secrets."

"And allow myself to trust a Kraeshian man?" she said, half to herself. "I'm not sure that's possible."

"Perhaps I'm different than other Kraeshian men."

"A phrase many Kraeshian men might say," she countered.

They reached her chambers and stopped in front of the entrance. She stood at the door for a moment, regarding Mikah's handsome face.

It was difficult for her to see him as more than an indentured servant, still working to pay off the fee for which his parents traded their strong, healthy son to the Empire. And even though he'd always been kind and considerate to her, Mikah *was* Kraeshian. In Kraeshia, all boys—and girls, too—were brought up believing that only men were worthy of respect and honor, while women existed as mere ornaments and playthings, with no influence on others or the world at large.

She refused to let herself fall for a Kraeshian man, only to be deceived by him.

"I need to rest after my long journey," she said. "But first, send for my grandmother. I wish to speak with her."

He bowed. "As you wish, princess."

Amara went inside, closed the door, and leaned against it. All of the roiling emotions that Amara had pushed so deep down inside herself during the journey home now came rushing to the surface. She ran to the mirror and clutched the sides.

"I'm alive," she reminded her wild-eyed reflection. "Nineteen years later and I'm still here. I can do anything I want. I can *have* anything I want."

"Yes, my sweet. You certainly can."

She spun around to see her grandmother Neela sitting by the window that overlooked the sea.

"Grandmother!" The joy of seeing her chased all of her doubts and sadness away. She loved this wrinkled, gray-haired woman, her only confidante, who still took the time to dress impeccably in her finest silks and jewels. "You were waiting for me?"

Neela nodded and rose to her feet, extending her arms. Amara rushed into a tight embrace, knowing that, despite her seemingly frail appearance, her grandmother was the strongest woman she knew.

"Is it done?" Neela whispered, patting Amara's shining hair.

"Yes."

There was a moment of silence. "Did he suffer?"

Amara swallowed the lump in her throat and stepped back from the old woman. "It was quick. Just as you suspected, he betrayed me at the first opportunity, choosing to give his trust and loyalty to a boy he barely knew rather than to his own sister. Grandmother, I know it had to be done, but I have so many doubts."

Neela nodded, her lips thin and expression plaintive. "Your brother had a good heart. But that was his fatal flaw. He trusted strangers too easily; he saw good in those who only had bad within them. He could have been a valuable ally to you, to *us*, but when it came down to the crucial moment, he didn't prove himself."

She knew Neela was right, but it didn't make any of it easier. "He spent his last moments hating me."

Neela pressed her cool, dry palm against Amara's burning cheek. "Then let that hatred make you stronger, *Dhosha*. Hatred and fear are the most powerful emotions there are. Love and compassion make you weak. Men have known this since the beginning of time, and they use this knowledge for their own gain."

Her grandmother spoke without a trace of anger or pain in her voice. Rather, she made her statement simply, as a truth handed down from a woman who'd lived her whole life under the thumbs of oppressive, controlling men.

A question Amara had locked away inside her heart her whole life burned on her tongue, brought back to the surface after having been insulted and dismissed by her father. She needed to ask it now—needed an answer that could help her make sense of so much.

"*Madhosha* . . ." It was the Kraeshian word for grandmother, just as *dhosha* was for granddaughter. As he continued to add new kingdoms to his empire over the last three decades, Emperor Cortas had allowed their language to fade away in favor of the universal dialects spoken by most of the world. Neela had always mourned the loss of her native language, and had privately taught Ashur and Amara several Kraeshian words to ensure that they would retain some of their heritage. Amara had a large Kraeshian vocabulary, but the language was complex and she wasn't nearly fluent.

"Yes?" Neela replied gently.

"I . . . I know we're not supposed to speak about the ancient laws, but . . . please, I'm nineteen and I need to know. How did I survive the ritual drowning? How is that even *possible*?"

"My sweet, it pains me greatly that you even know about that horrible day."

The memory was foggy now, as Amara was not much more than five years old, when she'd overheard her grandmother and father talking about her—her grandmother speaking softly, her father's voice booming.

"*Special, you say,*" he snarled. "*I see nothing special in her.*"

"*She is still a child,*" her grandmother replied, her voice small but calm— a tiny ship in the middle of the sea confronted by a looming hurricane. "*One day, you'll see why the gods spared her.*"

"*Bah. I have three fine sons. What use do I have for a daughter?*"

"*A daughter means a marriage to the son of a worthy king, to help political negotiations.*"

"*I've no need for negotiations when all I need is to send my armada to that worthy king's shores and take his land in the name of Kraeshia. But blood . . . I could certainly use a fitting blood sacrifice as an offering to the gods to keep my empire strong."*

"You already had your chance with Amara," Neela hissed. *"One chance and one alone. But she survived, because she is special and meant for greatness. Make any further attempt on her life and it will be a black mark against your soul. You know this to be true. Even you would not be so bold as to risk so much."*

Neela spoke with a quiet strength that not even the emperor could ignore.

When Amara had tentatively approached Neela about what she'd heard, her grandmother had bristled, sent her away at once, told her she had nothing to worry about.

"Please tell me, *Madhosha*," Amara insisted now. "Why didn't I drown? Even if I was, somehow, *special* . . . I was still just a baby. A baby is not a fish; they're not born magically knowing how to swim."

"*Magically*," Neela repeated slowly, nodding. "That is an important word, isn't it?"

Amara studied her grandmother's wise gray eyes, her heart skipping a beat. "Did magic have something to do with my survival?"

"It is time you knew the truth." Neela went to the window and gazed out at the sparkling Silver Sea. "Your mother loved you so much. She barely survived the beating she received for birthing a girl." Neela's cheek twitched, as if it pained her to recall the memory. "My daughter hated her husband, your father, from the moment she learned they were to marry. He was well-known to be especially vicious toward women who knew their own minds and argued with him. He enjoyed breaking them of this tendency until they agreed with every word he spoke. For years she tolerated his abusive ways. After you were born, she knew that he would invoke the ritual to rid himself of a female child, a symbol of his own perceived weakness. She had stopped trying to protect herself by then, but she swore to protect you at any cost. She found an apothecary from a recently conquered kingdom, who was rumored to be able to brew a very rare—and dangerous—potion, which she poured in your ear just before the ritual took place."

Amara knew next to nothing about her mother, who'd died shortly after she was born. Her father—who had yet to remarry, but kept many mistresses—refused to talk about her, and thus so did everyone else in the Spear. "The potion—that's what kept me alive?"

"Not exactly. It was a resurrection potion."

Amara regarded Neela with widening eyes.

"The potion did not keep you alive," Neela said gravely. "The potion brought you back from death."

Amara clasped her hand to her mouth to cover her shocked gasp. She always believed there had to be a simple answer to why she didn't drown—perhaps the water hadn't been deep enough. Perhaps she'd managed to float or a nursemaid had done something secretly to help her stay alive.

There were many potions that could be acquired for a variety of illnesses and uses, but Amara had never heard of anything so powerful. "What is the price of such magic?" she asked, her voice raspy.

Neela curled her gnarled fingers around the locket at her throat. "It is the most costly magic of all. A life for a life."

An icy wave of dizziness stole her breath and nearly knocked Amara to her knees. She absently grabbed for a chair behind her and sat down with a thud. "My mother gave her life for mine."

Neela turned to her granddaughter, her eyes glossy but tearless. Amara had never seen her cry, not once. "Like I said, your mother loved you, very much. She knew you would grow up to be strong and brave, like her. And you have. I can see it in your eyes, my sweet *dhosha*. This is why, from the moment you were able to speak and learn, I've taught you all the specific skills and knowledge I have. And I swear on my life, this one and the next, that I will continue to guide you to your destiny."

Neela reached for her, and Amara pushed herself up from the chair and grasped her grandmother's hand.

"Thank you, Grandmother."

This chilling revelation only made Amara more committed to her ultimate goal. Killing her traitorous brother and stealing the water Kindred had only been the first step. It didn't matter how long it took her to achieve it. No matter the cost. No matter how many lies she had to tell or how much blood she had to spill.

One day, Amara Cortas would be the first Empress of Kraeshia. And she would rule the world.

CHAPTER 7

JONAS

AURANOS

The docks of King's Harbor were swarming with activity by the time Jonas and Lysandra arrived at mid-morning. Hundreds, perhaps thousands, of men milled about, loading and unloading ships at port. Perched there on the edge of the sea was a lively village, its taverns, inns, and shops ready and waiting for the workers to finish their day.

The plan had been to get there by dawn, but Jonas was moving slower than usual, burdened by his injury.

Lysandra pressed a mug of spiced peach cider into his hand outside of a meeting house. "How are you doing?" she asked with concern.

"Fine." He forced a smile. "Just fine. For a poor half-blind guy, that is." He indicated his borrowed eye patch. "By the way, have I mentioned how lovely you look in that gown? Rose is definitely your color."

She scowled and looked down at her outfit. "Don't remind me of the fact that I'm wearing this monstrosity. I *hate* this dress. Who would ever want to wear such a fancy thing?"

"It's essentially just a cotton frock. It's not exactly all satin and frills fit for a palace ball."

"I wish I'd have just cut my hair instead," Lys said, then grimaced and nodded her chin at Jonas. "Or let you or Galyn cut it."

She was referencing Jonas's new hairstyle, which was courtesy of Lysandra and a sharp blade. His scalp was a tapestry of shaved swatches, scraped skin, and small tufts of dark hair. Thankfully he'd managed to disarm her before she'd drained him of too much blood. The girl was an excellent fighter, but a terrible hair-cutter.

"Nonsense, the gown is just fine," Jonas said. "And now we're here. Do you see anything?"

"In this crowd? No. We're going to have to split up and start asking around. Someone must know when the king's ship is scheduled to depart."

"Then let's not waste any time." He drained the cider, its sweetness giving him a little more energy. Now he only wished his shoulder wasn't on fire and that his fingers on that arm weren't going numb.

Let's worry about one thing at a time, he thought.

They made a plan to meet in an hour, then parted ways. Jonas watched Lys swish off in her rose-colored skirt. If it wasn't for the large canvas sack slung over her shoulder to conceal her bow and arrows, she'd easily be able to pass for the daughter of a wealthy Auranian.

Many of the men on the docks were bundled up in wool cloaks and heavy overcoats. Jonas knew from looking at them how chilly the morning was, but his fever made him feel as though it were the hottest point of midday. He also felt dizzy, but still he refused to go somewhere and rest while Lysandra took over. This was too important. The king would be here, out in the open. In this crowd, surely he and Lysandra could create enough chaos to distract any bodyguards, corner the king, and question him about Cleo's whereabouts before Jonas finally sliced his evil throat.

He forced his weakened body forward into the crowd, closer to the ships, stopping several men as he went and inquiring about departure times and passengers. He and Lysandra had prepared a story to tell these deckhands, that they were a couple who'd eloped and were looking for passage aboard a ship to take them overseas on a wedding journey. They thought this fib would be particularly successful in leading into a conversation about the king, since Princess Lucia was rumored to have just eloped herself.

After speaking to at least ten men, Jonas had been offered passage aboard five different ships, but no information of any use.

Feeling frustrated and faint, he took a break and stood on the creaky wooden dock, scanning the line of ships until his gaze settled on one in particular: a rickety-looking boat, half the size of all the others, painted along the sides with grapevines and the words WINE IS LIFE.

A Paelsian ship delivering wine to Auranos.

On any other day, the sight of this docking boat might have made Jonas feel nostalgic. But today, nothing but rage rose within him.

"Back to business, just like that," he muttered.

Of course, no matter what kinds of travesties and violence Jonas's homeland had just endured, Auranians wouldn't dare deprive themselves of their fine Paelsian wine, which was valued for its perfect sweetness and its total lack of any ill effects after a night of overindulging.

Drink yourself rotten and feel just fine the next day. Of course that was a promise of the utmost importance to these Auranians—still hedonistic, even under the King of Blood's rule.

Now that Jonas believed in the legends, and had witnessed firsthand the life-giving effects of Paelsian grape seeds infused with earth magic, which had brought him back from the brink of death, he was certain that Paelsian wine had *elementia* to thank for its success.

And Jonas still had Auranos to condemn for enslaving Paelsians, monopolizing their vineyards, and binding them into a contract to sell only to them.

It was a good reminder that Limerians weren't the only evil-doers in the world.

Jonas swayed on his feet as a wave of dizziness washed over him. It stank near the water—of fish, of waste thrown over the side of the docked ships, of the ripe body odor of the workers. And he could feel his fever getting worse.

Just before he was about to keel over, a hand gripped his arm, keeping him upright.

"Well, if it isn't my favorite rebel!" boomed a jolly voice. "Good morning, Jonas!"

Jonas turned toward the man, who regarded him with a wide, toothy grin. Ah, yes, it was Bruno, Galyn's grandfather. Jonas was well acquainted with the old man, who had great enthusiasm for the rebel cause, as well as a tendency to speak his thoughts and opinions aloud at high volumes.

"Bruno, please, speak softly." Jonas looked around nervously.

Bruno's smile dropped away. "My poor boy, did you lose your eye?"

"I . . . uh, no." He absently brushed his fingers over the eye patch. "It's only a disguise. I'm rather recognizable around here, in case you didn't know. So, hush."

"Well, thank the goddess for that! Two eyes are much more

useful than only one." The old man signaled toward a worker from the Paelsian ship who'd disembarked and drawn closer to them. "Good, that's good! Twenty cases, yes?"

"Yes, sir!"

Jonas eyed the ship. "You're picking up a shipment?"

Bruno nodded. "Been checking here every day for nearly a week because the ship was delayed. But I had to be diligent so someone else wouldn't sweep in and steal my order. The wine's so popular the Silver Toad would be shuttered for good without it."

If he'd been here for a week, he could be of great help to Jonas.

"Bruno . . . do you know when the king will be here? Have you heard people here talking about his departure over the past week? Nerissa told us he's taking a trip overseas."

Bruno frowned. "King Corvin? But he's dead!"

Jonas tried to keep his patience. "No, Bruno. King Gaius."

Bruno's entire face went sour. "Bah. He's an evil snake, that one! Going to take us all down in flames if we give him half a chance!"

"Agreed. But have you heard anything about his departure from Auranos?"

He shook his head. "Not a thing. However, I did see him."

Jonas blinked. "You *saw* him?"

Bruno gestured toward the flock of departing ships with his thumb. "Left earlier this morning on a big black Limerian ship with a red sail. Ugly snake crest painted on the side. How could anyone think he's trustworthy, sailing in on an evil-looking ship like that?"

"He left this morning?"

Bruno nodded. "Passed right by me while I waited in this very spot. I tried to spit on him, you know, to show my support for the rebels, but it landed on a seabird instead."

The king had already left. And it was Jonas's fault that they'd missed him. He'd been stubborn in his insistence that he come along. Had Lys left early, while Jonas was still asleep, like she'd wanted to, the king might be dead right now, instead of fleeing off on his next evil mission.

"My boy." Bruno patted his arm. "You've gone very pale. Are you all right?"

"No. I am definitely not all right." This was just another painful failure to add to his lengthy list.

Bruno sniffed the air, then cocked his head and sniffed again. "What is *that*?"

"What?"

"I smell . . . ugh, merciful goddess, it's like a cross between horse dung and rotting meat." He continued to sniff, then drew closer to Jonas.

Jonas peered at him warily. "What are you doing?"

"I'm sniffing your shoulder, of course. What does it look like I'm doing?" The man's face fell. "Oh, my. It's you."

"Me?"

Bruno nodded. "I'm afraid so. My grandson gave you some of the healing mud, didn't he?"

"He did."

"Let me see." Bruno poked his left shoulder, causing Jonas to yelp in pain. "Come on, let's see it."

Jonas tried to concentrate on something other than the stench of the docks and the sweaty bodies passing by all around him. Suddenly, he wished he'd never woken up after his injury, that he was still unconscious in his cot at the Silver Toad.

Grudgingly, he pulled his shirt to the side to give Bruno better access to the bandages.

Bruno gently unwound the bandages and peered underneath.

His expression turned squeamish. "That looks even worse than it smells."

"And it feels even worse than it looks." Jonas glanced down at it. Most of the mud had been rubbed away, exposing a raw red wound surrounded by angry purple marks like lightning bolts and green edges that oozed pus.

"You're rotting like a three-week-old melon," Bruno announced, putting the bandages back in place.

"So the healing mud isn't working at all?"

"That concoction is quite old. It did work moderately when I first received it, but it *never* would have worked for a wound as serious as this. I'm sorry, my boy, but you're going to die."

Jonas gaped at him. "What?"

Bruno frowned. "I'd suggest cutting off the arm, but unfortunately the wound isn't in the best place for that. You'd have to take the shoulder as well to clear away all the infection, and I'm afraid that just won't work. Perhaps you could find some leeches and hope for the best?"

"I'm not going to go find any leeches. And I'm *not* going to die." Still, as he said it, even he knew that he didn't sound convinced. He'd seen men in his village fall terminally ill from rotting wounds. Some of the more superstitious Paelsians believed those deaths to be punishments for speaking ill of the chieftain, but even as a child Jonas knew that couldn't be true.

"There's that fighting spirit!" Bruno now patted Jonas's head. "I think that's what I'll miss the most about you when you're dead."

"I have far too much to do before I die," Jonas growled. "I just need . . . a healer."

"Far too late for a healer."

"Then I need a witch! I need a witch who can heal through touch. Or . . . or grape seeds."

Bruno eyed him as if he'd gone mad. "Grape seeds, eh? Perhaps there are some witches who can heal a simple scrape, with magi- cal mud or, perhaps, enchanted seeds of some kind. But to heal a wound as deep and putrid as this? Not a chance."

"But I know one who . . ." He trailed off, remembering that, of course, Phaedra wasn't a common witch; she was a Watcher. And she was dead, after sacrificing her immortality to save Jonas's life.

"You might be able to find a witch with earth magic strong enough to take away your fever and give you some strength back," Bruno said. "It's unlikely, but I'd say that's your best hope."

"And where am I supposed to find someone like that?" he muttered, and then a thought occurred to him. "Do you think Nerissa might know?"

"Nerissa might, yes," Bruno said, nodding. "But she's gone, too." He gestured toward the sea. "Apparently, Prince Magnus officially requested her presence in the north. See that Auranian ship in the distance there, with the golden sails? That's her, headed off to Limeros."

"Wait. Did you just say that Magnus is in Limeros?" Jonas said, ignoring another wave of dizziness.

"Yes. On the throne, apparently, with his beautiful wife at his side. You've met the princess, haven't you? She is such a lovely young girl. Of course, I don't support the Damoras by any means, but on a purely physical level, don't you think she and the prince make a rather striking couple? And the chemistry between the two when I saw them on their wedding tour—it practically sizzled!"

Jonas now felt even more ill than before.

"I need to go, immediately. Tell Galyn . . . tell him I'll send a message as soon as I can." Before Bruno could reply, Jonas was off, his head swirling with new information, far too much to process all at once.

The king had departed, to who-knows-where.

Nerissa was gone.

Prince Magnus was on the throne in Limeros.

And Princess Cleo was with him.

The hour was up, but Lysandra wasn't at the meeting place. Suddenly, he heard a loud shriek coming from somewhere close by.

Lys.

Jonas's legs were weak but still he ran toward the sound, drawing his sword with his right hand.

"Lys!" he yelled as he reached the edge of the village, ready to protect Lysandra from attackers, to fight as hard as he had to to keep her alive.

When he turned a corner he saw her standing there, her chest heaving, her skirts dirty. Two young men lay on the ground in front of her, groaning with pain.

Lys turned to Jonas, her cheeks bright with color, her eyes wild. "This is why I don't wear gowns! It brings about the wrong sort of attention—attention I don't want!"

"I . . . uh . . ." Jonas shocked at the sight, stumbled over his words.

"This pile of dung"—she kicked the buttocks of one of the groaning men—"tried to grab my chest! And this one"—a sharp kick to the other—"laughed and cheered him on! I'm never wearing a dress again. I don't care if King Gaius himself recognizes me."

Jonas felt half-appalled, half-delighted as one of the young men looked up at him in agony. "Get her away from us," he moaned to Jonas.

"Gladly." Jonas took Lysandra's arm and pulled her back around the corner and onto a main street.

"You never fail to amaze me, you know that?" Jonas said to Lysandra as they walked. "I thought you were in serious danger."

"Insulted and annoyed, perhaps, but not—"

Jonas pulled her closer and gave her a quick, hard kiss on her lips, smiling. "You're amazing. Never forget it."

The bright color had returned to her cheeks as she touched her mouth. "You're lucky I'm all right with you, or you'd be on the ground, too, for taking me by surprise like that."

"Very lucky," he agreed, still grinning.

She bit her bottom lip. "Now, um, what's going on? I couldn't get a helpful word from anyone around here. What about you? Anything?"

"Yes, I learned plenty." He told her about Bruno, about the king's departure, and that Magnus and Cleo were in Limeros, soon to be joined by Nerissa.

Lysandra swore under her breath. "So, what now? Should we get on a ship and try to go after the king?"

He shook his head. "Too late for that. But luckily we've got something just as important to do instead."

Her gaze dropped to his shoulder. "Find someone who can heal your wound?"

Jonas knew he couldn't hide his feverish face and weakness from her, so he didn't bother trying anymore. Whether they could find someone skilled enough to help him in time, though—that was the question.

"If we can find a proper healer, then yes." He set his chin and looked into her light brown eyes with determination. "And then we're going to Limeros to rescue a princess and kill a prince."

CHAPTER 8

MAGNUS

LIMEROS

His father used to insist that Magnus sat in on royal council meetings when he was younger, although he hadn't paid much attention to them. He regretted that now as he tried very hard not to drown in a sea of complicated political dilemmas and decisions.

His first meeting had gone poorly, and the councilmen did not hesitate to show their dismay that Kurtis was no longer in command. Of course they didn't dare be rude to his face, but from Magnus's seat at the head of the long table he could sense their simmering disapproval in their rigid body language and harsh glares. Many of the current councilmen, including the wealthy and influential Lord Francus and Lord Loggis, and the High Priest Danus, had been in the king's inner circle since Magnus was a sullen boy with a habit of keeping to the shadows of the palace. Surely they hadn't seen him then as a strong and capable heir to the throne. And Magnus could tell that they still judged him that way, not knowing that he was different, much more like his father now, in many ways.

The council had unanimously requested that Lord Kurtis take a seat on the council, claiming that it was rightfully his, given all he'd been responsible for in his father's absence. Since Kurtis had committed no actual crime against the throne, and to appease the council as much as he was able, Magnus decided to grant this request.

Magnus scanned the document that had been presented to him at the beginning of today's meeting.

"It's quite a problem, isn't it, your highness?" Kurtis asked in his reedy voice.

The war against Auranos—short as it may have been—had cost Limeros a hefty fortune. This deficit was further compounded by the high cost of constructing the Imperial Road. To compensate, even the poorest citizens were now being taxed to the point of utter destitution. The kingdom hadn't yet been completely bankrupt, but it was clear that something needed to change.

"This situation is deeply troubling," Magnus said slowly. "But what troubles me more, Lord Kurtis, is that in your father's months as grand kingsliege, he was not able to come to a reasonable solution."

"My sincerest apologies, your highness, but my father wasn't granted the authority to make such sweeping changes without the permission of the king. And the king has been in Auranos, occupied with southern affairs, for so long that I daresay many of his citizens have nearly forgotten what he looks like."

A comment as insolent as that should have received dark looks from the other council members, but instead Magnus saw them nodding their heads.

A guard pushed open the doors and entered the room.

"Your highness," said the guard, bowing his head, "my apologies for interrupting, but Princess Cleiona is here."

This was the last thing he expected to hear from a guard interrupting a council meeting. "And?"

The guard frowned, then glanced at Kurtis, who stood up.

"Your highness, this is my doing. Your lovely wife expressed an interest to sit in on this council meeting during our archery lesson this morning, and I didn't dissuade her."

"I see," Magnus replied tightly.

"She's eager to learn about everything, your highness, but of course I understand if you feel that a woman has no place in such meetings."

Murmurs hummed along the council table of the old men who agreed with this statement.

Magnus thought he knew what Kurtis was trying to do. He wanted to make Magnus look like a fool before the council. Either by allowing a woman to sit in on the meeting—women were sternly forbidden from participation in any official palace affairs—or by tempting Magnus to protest his suggestion, thus risking offending the princess, which might allow Kurtis to gain more of her trust.

Magnus gestured to the guard. "Bring her in."

Cleo entered the throne room, her gaze keen and her chin raised. If she was at all nervous about being here, she didn't show it.

Her gown was blue, the color of Auranos and her favorite. Her long, golden locks hung in loose curls to her waist, free of any braids or twists.

He much preferred when she wore her hair up. It wasn't such a distraction to him then.

"Princess," he said stiffly, indicating the vacant chair to his right. Hesitating only slightly, she approached and took the seat.

During their time in Limeros, he'd of course seen Cleo at meals and other public events, but he hadn't spoken to her privately since their discussion on the balcony. He reminded himself to avoid balconies in the future—they were dangerous places to find himself alone with her.

"All of you have had the honor of meeting Princess Cleiona Bellos of Auranos." He reintroduced the members of the council, who all nodded at her in turn. "And, of course, princess, you're already well familiar with Lord Kurtis."

"Indeed. Lord Kurtis has been teaching me how to handle a bow and arrow this last week," Cleo explained to the councilmen. "He's an excellent tutor."

"And you are an excellent student," Kurtis replied. "Soon you'll be winning competitions, just as your sister did, if that's your goal."

Oh yes, Magnus thought wryly. *I'm sure that's exactly why she wants to learn how to send sharp arrows directly and precisely into a target.*

Magnus decided to imagine Kurtis's right eye socket as his own personal target.

"Your highness, perhaps it would be interesting to get the princess's take on the problem at hand?" Kurtis suggested.

This sounded very much like a challenge.

"Yes," Magnus agreed. "It would be interesting, wouldn't it?"

"How absolutely ludicrous," the high priest said under his breath.

"What was that?" Magnus asked sharply. "Did you say something?"

The priest smiled weakly. "No, your highness. I was just clearing my throat. I look forward to hearing your wife's thoughts."

Magnus slid the financial document in front of Cleo. She scanned it quickly, her expression turning serious. "This is a great deal of money," she said. "To whom is it owed?"

"King Gaius has an agreement with the moneylenders in Veneas," Kurtis replied. "They expect to be repaid without extensive delay."

"And so you're taxing all of the Limerian people to these great extents?" She looked sharply at each of the council members. "What about the rich?"

"What about them, your grace?" asked Lord Loggis.

"According to this document, these financial issues are due to the decisions of the rich. Why wouldn't they be expected to contribute the lion's share of this debt? To clean up their own mess?"

"That's quite a sentiment for an Auranian royal to have," Loggis countered. "Then again, Auranos's poor would be the equivalent of our rich, wouldn't they?"

"Thank you for your opinion about my homeland, but you didn't answer my question," Cleo said with a patient smile. "Should I take your insult to mean that you're trying to avoid this matter? Or that you're not sure why your taxes are structured as they are?"

Magnus watched her with barely concealed amusement. Cleo certainly wasn't winning many allies in this room, but he found her ability to stand up for herself deeply admirable.

Not that he'd ever admit this out loud, of course.

"Well?" Cleo prompted, glancing next at Lord Kurtis.

Kurtis spread his hands in the air before him. "We can only hope that your husband will come up with a solution that benefits everyone. He is, after all, currently in command here."

Now Magnus pictured another arrow entering Kurtis's *left* eye socket. Slowly. Again and again.

"Well," Magnus said after a tense silence, "what might you suggest, princess?"

Cleo met his gaze, the first time she'd looked at him so directly since their last private talk. "You really want to know?"

"If I didn't, I wouldn't ask."

She regarded him for another moment before speaking again. "My father never had trouble with debt."

"How lovely for your father," Lord Loggis mumbled.

She gave the lord a sharp look, then turned back to address the rest of the group. "In fact, it was just the opposite. Auranos was and is very wealthy. My father would often lend money to other kingdoms, just as those in Veneas are known to do."

"And?" Magnus prompted after the table fell silent. "How does this recollection of the past help the current situation? Auranian finances are included as part of this document—part of Mytica as a whole. And they, too, have recently been depleted in an attempt to pay off part of this debt."

Thanks to your father's lust for power were the unspoken words he was certain he saw glittering in her narrowed eyes.

Cleo cleared her throat, then softened her suddenly rigid expression with a patient smile. "Perhaps," she said. "But the problem stems from Limerian, not Auranian, origins. Limeros, to my knowledge, has never been nearly as wealthy as Auranos. There is so much that separates our people, not just Paelsian land. But within those differences, I believe an answer can be found."

Lord Francus leaned in closer and studied the princess with a peevish—yet curious—expression. "And what, precisely, is that answer, your grace?"

"In a single word?" She sent her glance around the table, resting on each councilman's face in turn. "Wine."

Magnus blinked. "*Wine.*"

"Yes, wine. Your laws prohibit inebriants of any kind, yet wine is a source of great wealth—both in sales within the kingdom and export to lands overseas. While Limerian soil is likely too cold to nurture any crops, Paelsia vineyards lie not so far away. A solid third of their land is still rich—even if its people are not. If Limerian workers and merchants were to assist Paelsians with their wine production and trade, with Auranos's help, Mytica could again become a very wealthy kingdom."

"Wine is forbidden in Limeros," the high priest pointed out sternly.

Cleo frowned. "So make it . . . *un*forbidden. This council certainly has the power to do that, right?"

"The goddess forbade it!" cried the high priest. "Only she can choose to make such a change, and I don't see her here at this table. Such a suggestion is . . ." He shook his head. "Ludicrous. And, frankly, offensive!"

Cleo glared at him with exasperation. "The suggestion to change an outdated law that is single-handedly preventing you from solving your financial crisis, that could ensure this kingdom's future if it were reversed, is *offensive*?"

"Our goddess—" he began.

"Forget your goddess," Cleo cut him off. Several council members gasped. "You need to think of your citizens—especially the poor, who are suffering right now."

Everyone began speaking at once, one argument overlapping another, creating a cacophony of grunts and chatter.

Magnus leaned back in his chair, clasped his hands on his lap, and silently observed the outrage. Cleo's cheeks were flushed red, but he knew it wasn't from embarrassment. Her heightened color was a product of sheer outrage.

"Quiet, all of you," Magnus said, but no one heard him above their own noise. He raised his voice and shouted. "Silence!"

The council finally hushed, all eyes turning to look at him expectantly.

"Princess Cleiona's suggestion is certainly"—*How best to put it?*—"Auranian."

"*Outrageous* is more like it," Loggis mumbled.

"Outrageous to us, perhaps. But that doesn't mean it has no merit. Perhaps Limeros *has* been stuck in the past for far too long. Religious tradition aside, the princess has suggested a potential solution, and I agree that it's worth more thought and discussion."

Cleo turned to him, her expression gripped with surprise.

"But the goddess—" the high priest protested once again.

Magnus held up his hand. "The goddess does not currently have a seat on this council."

"*I* represent the goddess here, lest you forget," he continued, his voice edged in fiery defiance. He sniffed as Magnus gave him a sharp glare, then lowered his gaze to the table top, his jaw clenched.

Magnus stood up and walked around the long table, considering the problem at hand. "I'll send a message to my father, presenting this proposal to him. As he has made no attempts to cease the sale and consumption of wine or ale in Auranos, I believe he may see the potential here to solve a great many problems with one bold decision." The high priest again opened his mouth, and Magnus raised his hand to stop him. "Can you swear to the goddess right now that you have never tasted a drop of wine in your entire life, High Priest Danus? I certainly can't."

"Nor I," Kurtis conceded with a nod. "The princess is as smart and innovative as she is beautiful."

"Indeed she is," Magnus agreed without thinking.

Cleo glanced at him, clearly surprised by this admission. Their gazes locked and held. He was the first to look away.

"This meeting is at an end," Magnus said, managing to find his voice again.

The council members moved to leave, but Lord Loggis raised

a finger, stopping them. "There is one last matter to discuss, your highness," he said. "The large search party of guards that has been sent out to find Princess Lucia has found nothing at all. Apologies, but to continue to have so many men focused this task seems to me a misuse of both manpower and resources."

His sister's name drew Magnus's full attention. "I disagree."

"But, your highness," Lord Loggis went on, "nothing about the current situation suggests that your sister is in any danger. Perhaps . . ." He cleared his throat. "Perhaps once the princess has had enough time to think through her recent actions, and how they might have caused some alarm, she will simply return to the palace and all will be well and forgiven."

When Magnus had tripled the number of guards assigned to scour the land for Lucia, he hadn't given them or their commanders any additional details about her disappearance. He didn't reveal that her tutor was an exiled Watcher. That Lucia was a sorceress. That the last place he knew for certain that she'd been was left with a floor splattered with blood, dead bodies outside, and an ice storm summoned by pure, unleashed elemental magic.

"Another week," Magnus said. "If the guards don't find her by then, I'll call half of them back." Lord Loggis opened his mouth to protest further, but Magnus raised his hand. "That's my final decision."

The lord nodded, his dark eyes empty of anything friendly. "Yes. Of course, your highness."

Magnus gestured to the door and the council members filed out of the room.

"Princess, wait," he said, stopping Cleo short on the threshold.

She turned to him, her face once again full of surprise, as he pushed the doors closed behind the others, leaving them alone in the cavernous throne room.

"Yes?" she said.

"Strangely, I find it necessary to thank you for your input today."

She raised her brow. "Thank me? Am I dreaming?"

"Don't worry. I'm sure it won't happen again anytime soon." Magnus drew even closer to her, and her smile faded at the edges.

"Was there something else you wanted from me?" she asked.

If only you knew, he thought. *You'd probably run away from here and never look back.*

"No," he replied.

She cleared her throat. "Nerissa arrived this morning."

"So she's the one responsible for your hair today, is she?" He wound a silky, golden lock around his finger and studied it carefully, taking in its scent, like an intoxicating, exotic flower.

"She is," Cleo said after a lengthy pause.

"In Limeros, proper women don't wear their hair loose like this. Tell her to braid it or tie it back from now on. That is, unless it's your goal to look like a courtesan."

She pulled her hair from his grip. "I should thank you too, Magnus."

"For?"

"For constantly reminding me who you really are. Sometimes, I forget."

With that, she slipped past him and left the room.

The reason, it was said, that the goddess Valoria had forbidden alcohol in her land was to ensure that her people always maintained purity, health, and clarity of mind.

But in any land where something was forbidden, there were always ways to acquire it. Magnus had heard rumors of one—and how to gain entry to it—only a couple miles away from the palace, a shabby-looking inn called the Ouroboros.

Magnus entered the inn, leaving the single guard he'd brought with him to wait outside with the horses. It was nearly empty; only a handful of patrons occupied the small eating area, none of them bothering to look up at who had entered.

Magnus scanned the room from beneath the heavy hood of his black cloak, his gaze falling on a wooden door with a bronze knocker in the shape of a snake devouring its own tail. He grasped this and knocked three times quickly, three times slowly.

The door creaked opened a moment later and he strode through into another room—much larger and busier than the one before. He scanned the ruddy faces, hands clasping tankards of ale at twenty or more tables, until he came across a face that was painfully familiar.

"Wonderful," he grumbled as he drew closer to the table in the far corner.

"Well, well!" Nic slurred and raised his tankard, causing ale to slosh over the rim. "Look who's here. Shall I make a formal announcement of your arrival?"

"I'd prefer that you didn't." Magnus swept another glance through the large room, but no one seemed to have recognized him yet.

"Come." Nic shoved the heavy wooden chair across from him with his foot. "Join me. I hate to drink alone."

Magnus gave this a moment's thought, before he did as Nic suggested. He kept his back to the rest of the room to further conceal his identity.

"Thirsty?" Nic asked, but without waiting for a reply, he gestured for the barkeep to come to their table.

The heavyset bald man with a thick, dark beard, approached confidently, but the moment Magnus glanced at him from the cowl of his cloak, his steps faltered.

"Your highness," the barkeep gasped.

"Quiet," Magnus replied. "No need to inform anyone of my presence here."

The man trembled as he bowed deeply and lowered his voice to a raspy whisper. "I beg of you, don't judge me too harshly. I don't usually serve such evil, sinful beverages here. The night is so cold and . . . well, these loyal citizens were just looking for something that might warm their bellies."

Magnus regarded the man patiently. "Is that so? In a dedicated room that requires a secret knock?"

The barkeep grimaced, his shoulders slumping. "Spare my family. Take me. Execute me. But leave them. They had nothing to do with my dark decisions."

He had no patience for sniveling martyrs tonight. "Bring me a bottle of your best Paelsian wine. No need for a goblet."

"But . . ." The barkeep blinked rapidly. "Well, your highness, Paelsian wine is only sold in Auranos. It's part of their treaty—as I'm sure you know. Even if I were allowed to serve it by law, it could not be imported here."

Magnus gave him a hard look.

"Yes, of course, very well," the barkeep sputtered. "My best bottle of Paelsian wine. Coming right up."

He disappeared into a back room, returning almost immediately with a dark green glass bottle roughly etched with the Paelsian symbol of a grapevine. As the barkeep uncorked it, Magnus spared a glance at Nic.

"That's forbidden." Nic gestured toward the bottle. "Bad Prince of Blood. Very bad!"

Magnus waved the barkeep away, then took a deep drink from the bottle and allowed himself a moment to enjoy the familiar sweetness as it slid over his tongue.

Nic snorted. "But of course, *you* can do whatever you like. As long as your daddy says it's all right."

Even though Magnus believed this boy was well overdue for a painful death, he had to admit that Nic did occasionally amuse him. "You might do well to consider the possibility that I don't care what my father says," he said, taking another swig. "Just how long have you been drinking here tonight, Cassian?"

Nic waved his hand flippantly. "Long enough not to care what happens next. I should kill you now, really. Just stab you with this dinner knife. Until you're good and dead."

"Yes, well, the feeling is mutual. Now, shall we pick something worthy to drink to tonight?"

Nic returned his attention to his ale, staring down into it as if it might tell his fortune. "To Prince Ashur."

"What?"

"Prince Ashur. Remember him?" His expression darkened. "I want to know that he was buried, and where. It's not right that he's in an unmarked grave. He was a royal, you know. His body should have been treated with more respect."

Magnus went to take another sip, but found that he'd already drained the bottle of its contents. But, mere seconds later, the nervous barkeep hurried over to replace it with another. "Just what was it between you two?" Magnus asked, his new bottle uncorked. He'd been curious about Nic and Ashur ever since the night it was revealed they were working together against Amara.

Nic didn't answer, instead continuing to stare deeply into his drink.

Now the sublime effects of the swiftly consumed wine began to take hold of Magnus, and the room began to swim and sparkle around him. The heaviness of the day finally lifted. "Oh, so now you've decided to keep your mouth shut, have you? Given the rumors I've heard about the prince, I'm not overly surprised."

Nic frowned. "What rumors?"

Magnus eyed him. "I'm sure you know my meaning."

Nic took a slurp of his ale, his knuckles white around the mug. "It's not like that. He was my friend."

"Such a short friendship, yet his death has caused such deep grief."

"I don't want to talk about this."

The boy's face had flushed. It appeared that Magnus had treaded too closely to the truth. He wanted to feel smug about this small victory, but he couldn't seem to summon such emotion. Instead, he felt—what was that?

Sympathy?

He took a deep drink of his wine. "It must be very unpleasant to feel something so . . . *undeniable* toward someone for whom you're supposed to feel nothing at all." He paused, suddenly lost in thought. "And to know such feelings are wrong."

"There was nothing *wrong* about it," Nic mumbled.

Magnus went on, ignoring Nic's argument. "Such . . . *weakness* for another can destroy you if you let it. No, it *will* destroy you. There's no other way it can end. So you need to be strong, even when all seems hopeless. When there's no way to deny that . . . that pebble stuck in your boot—annoying and painful and impossible to ignore."

Nic stared at him. "What in the goddess's nightmares are you talking about?"

Magnus drained the rest of the new bottle before speaking again. "Forget it."

"I see it, you know," Nic said, his eyes narrowing. "You can't fool me. I know why you did what you did. Why else would you save her life? You want her, don't you?"

His worst fear—that he was so transparent, even to someone as insignificant as Nicolo Cassian—dangled before him, threatening to weaken him to the point of no recovery.

He should just get up and leave without another word, but his limbs had grown heavy and his thoughts were so muddled that they anchored him in place. "This isn't about who I want," he countered. "This is about you, wanting Prince Ashur."

"Shut your mouth," Nic snapped.

Magnus pushed up from the table so he could look down his nose at the boy. "No, you shut *yours*. If there's anyone I want, it's Lucia. *Only* Lucia. I'm sure you've heard rumors that my lust for my sister controls everything I do, every decision I make."

A shadow of doubt slid behind Nic's gaze. "Perhaps I have. But rumors are rumors, and I've been watching you. The way you look at Cleo sometimes—"

In a heartbeat, Magnus pulled his sword out and pressed it to Nic's throat. "You see things that don't exist," he hissed.

Fury sparked in Nic's eyes. "Go ahead and do it. Cut my throat. You may not have known who Theon was when you killed him, but imagine how much more Cleo will hate you if you killed me too. That's why I know you won't do it. She's defended you to me again and again, but I see the truth. I don't care how many times you save her life or spare mine. What you've done, what your family is responsible for, it's unforgiveable. No matter what I have to do to protect her from you, I'll do it."

"So strong, aren't you? So brave."

"I'm stronger and braver than you might think. Mark my

words, *your highness*: I will hate you and your father for the rest of eternity. Now kill me or let me leave."

"It's only the ale that's making you brave tonight. You wouldn't say any of these things to me if you weren't already drunk."

Nic pushed the tip of Magnus's sword away from his throat. "I assure you, I would."

Nic stood, drank the rest of his tankard, and left the tavern.

CHAPTER 9

JONAS

PAELSIA

"Let me see it just once . . ."

"No, Lys," Jonas said. "Keep your hands to yourself, would you?"

"Come on, don't be shy."

"I'm not being shy." When Lys reached for Jonas's shirt again, he scooted out of her way. "Stop it."

She glared at him. "Let me see your wound, you stubborn arse."

"No." He focused on the campfire, poking at it with a stick to keep it burning.

"Damn it, Jonas. It's bad, isn't it? Worse than you're letting on."

He refused to meet her eyes, lest she see right through him to the truth. "I feel fantastic. Never better. Now, let's rest for a few hours and then we need to keep going. We have a lot of ground to cover before we get to Limeros."

"Don't you trust me?"

There was a catch in her voice that he'd never heard before, and it made his heart ache. "Of course I do." He swallowed hard, past the lump in his throat. "I trust you more than anyone else in the world."

Her bottom lip trembled. "The mud isn't working at all, is it? You're getting worse and you don't want me to know how horribly sick you are."

He tried to laugh. "Do I really look that bad?"

"Yes, actually, you do." She put her hands on either side of his face, forcing him to meet her serious gaze. "Are you dying?"

"We're all dying. We're mortal, remember?" He tried to maintain his grin, but found it took too much strength. "All I have is Bruno's assessment, which is that I don't have much longer, not that he knows anything for sure."

Her jaw tightened, and Jonas could tell she was fighting to appear resolute. "So we need to focus on finding someone to help you."

"If we happen upon someone, yes. But my first priority is to get to Limeros and kill Prince Magnus."

"And my first priority is fixing you—and it should be yours as well."

He snorted. "You really think I'm worth saving again after all the trouble I'm responsible for? Things would be a whole lot easier for you without me around."

Anger flashed through her dark eyes. "You're really this big of an idiot? Have I been traveling with a complete and utter moron all of these months?"

Her outrage was strangely endearing to him. "Gee, Lys, your honeyed words are so soothing to my—"

Before he could finish, she pulled him to her and kissed him, hard and deep. Suddenly the pain in his arm and the numbness in his hand fell away. He weaved his right hand into her mass of dark curls and pulled her closer.

"I'm in love with you, you stupid arse, and I'm not losing you. Got it?" she whispered against his lips before kissing him again.

Her confession had stolen his breath, so all he could do was nod.

"Now, once again, how do we fix you?" she asked, when they finally parted.

To be honest, he had nearly given up hope that he might find a way out of this problem. But Lysandra's stubbornness, her devotion, and her friendship had given him new determination to fight to see another day.

He took a deep breath. "We need to find a witch."

She nodded firmly. "Then we'll find a witch."

They left the campfire right away and pressed on through northern Paelsia, finally stopping at a village a few miles over the border in Limeros that had several inns and taverns at its center, surrounded by other shops and its residential area. It was the first sign of life and community the pair had seen in over a day. It had grown much colder during their journey, and the ground here was covered in a thin layer of frost and ice, a few snowflakes drifting down from the cloudy night sky.

Lysandra disappeared for a short time to scout a few cottages, returning with some warmer clothes. He noticed she'd replaced her dirty and torn rose-colored dress with a new pale yellow one.

"Where did you get all this?" he asked as she tossed him a warm leather cloak.

"The same place I got this." She pulled out a small drawstring bag and shook it so he could hear the clinking of coins.

He couldn't help but grin. "I'm impressed."

"Now let's go get you healed."

She gently took his hand and helped him into the nearest inn.

Even at this late hour, it was busy with customers eating dinner huddled by the blazing fire.

Jonas adjusted his eye patch as Lys placed a few coins on the innkeeper's counter. "What will this get us?"

The innkeeper pushed his spectacles up on his nose. "This is plenty for a night's stay in a comfortable room for you and your . . ." He frowned at the pale, sweaty Jonas.

"Husband," Lys provided.

"Husband. Yes. And you'll get a fine dinner out of this, too." He spoke pleasantly, but the innkeeper's forehead remained creased. "Young lady, pardon me for saying so, but your husband looks rather ill."

"That's because he *is* rather ill." She placed two more silver coins on the counter. "Which is why we're also looking for someone to help him. We need someone with very particular, very special abilities, and we're willing to pay very well for information."

The innkeeper raised an eyebrow. "Special abilities?"

Lys leaned closer to the man and lowered her voice. "We need a witch who is extremely skilled with earth magic."

The man stepped back, sweeping a cautious gaze over Lys and Jonas. "A witch? My dear girl, you know you're in Limeros, don't you? This isn't Auranos; our laws regarding witchcraft and dark legendry aren't so relaxed. The king imprisons—often executes—anyone accused of witchcraft, and he doesn't look fondly on anyone who helps them in any way."

Jonas turned to the dining room and noticed a few people shooting curious looks their way. He homed in on one in particular: a woman in a black satin cloak, her face concealed by shadows.

"Forget it, then. We don't want to get anyone in trouble," he said. Then Lys squeezed his hand, hard. "Ouch!"

"Sir, I understand the risks but we're willing to take them," Lys said. "You see, we're only newly married and . . . and I'm already with child." Tears brimmed in her brown eyes. "I can't lose my darling husband so soon. I need him, don't you see? I'm lost without him to protect me and care for me. Please, I'll do anything to heal him. *Anything*, you understand? Please help us."

Jonas couldn't help but be impressed by Lysandra's skill at manipulation. He decided to stay quiet and let her take the lead.

The innkeeper stared at her, his brow furrowed, until Jonas saw tears forming in his eyes. "My dear, dear girl. You are so brave . . . you're both so brave. This world needs more young people like you who are willing to take great chances. Love . . ." He shook his head slowly, "It's all that matters, isn't it?"

"Yes, it is," Lysandra agreed. "So can you help us?"

"If I could, I would. Truly. But any witches rumored to be in this area are long gone." His expression grew pensive. "However, I've heard several can be found in Ravencrest. I would strongly urge you to try to find assistance there."

Ravencrest, the capital of Limeros, was several days' journey from the border.

Jonas wasn't sure he had that much time left.

They ate, they slept, and before dawn the next morning, they left the inn, with a plan to somehow find—or steal—two horses to help speed up their journey.

Jonas tried to keep his steps steady and swift and not let Lysandra know how much weaker he'd grown since yesterday.

Suddenly, Lysandra clutched his arm. "Someone's following us," she whispered.

Jonas stopped short, his stomach plummeting. "I'm not sure if I can fight," he admitted reluctantly.

"Don't worry. I've got it."

Jonas again tried to keep his footing, but his smooth-soled boots weren't made for such icy-slick pathways. They turned a corner, then another, and then Lysandra motioned for Jonas to go ahead. He went, his staggering footsteps crunching loudly in the snow, while she waited behind the trunk of a large oak tree near a row of shops, its branches heavy with icicles.

A moment later, Jonas saw Lys lunge out from her hiding spot and grab hold of a cloaked figure. She slammed her victim against the wall, pressing the edge of Jonas's jeweled blade to the stranger's throat.

When it became clear that their stalker had been caught, Jonas drew closer and saw that the figure was about the same size and height as Lys. "Why are you following us?" she snarled.

"Your weapon isn't necessary," answered a female voice.

Jonas knew her words meant nothing to Lys, who trusted people less easily than anyone Jonas had ever met. And despite her size, Lys was as dangerous as any man when she had to be.

"I'll be the judge of that," Lys said, taking a more forceful grip on the dagger. "Who are you?" Before giving her time to answer, Lys pulled back the hood of her black satin cloak.

Jonas nearly gasped when he saw the girl's lovely face, only a few shades lighter than her dark brown hair, set with a pair of emerald green eyes that gazed calmly at them both.

"I'm a friend," the girl said. She didn't seem afraid.

"Why were you following us?" Jonas asked, stepping closer. He thought he recognized her. "You were in the inn last night, weren't you?"

"I was. Which is precisely why I know you're looking for a witch who might be able to help you."

His heart jumped at this statement. "Do you know of one?"

"I *am* one." She looked back at Lys. "Now remove your weapon, or I might change my mind."

Lys glanced at Jonas with uncertainty. He nodded, and she reluctantly sheathed the dagger.

As Lysandra stepped away, the girl's expression remained serene rather than relieved or grateful to have been set free.

"So," Jonas said, wary of this seemingly too-fortunate encounter. "What's the catch?"

"There's no catch," the girl replied evenly. "Now, I advise you to stop wasting time. By the looks of you, Jonas Agallon, you have very little of it left."

A shock of sweat trickled down Jonas's spine. "You know who I am?"

"Despite your rather weak attempt at a disguise, yes." She glanced at Lys. "And you are Lysandra Barbas, Jonas's companion and fellow rebel. Lovely gown, by the way. A simple yet effective costume for one who's clearly worn nothing but trousers all her life."

Lysandra crossed her arms in front of her chest, eyeing the girl with deep wariness and distrust. "So that's what you are, a spy? For the king, perhaps?"

"No."

"And why should we believe you?"

"I don't really care if you believe me or not."

"I think I understand," Jonas said. "You want money. How much?"

The girl sighed with impatience. "I'm really not in the mood for a debate about my intentions. It's painfully early, it's unpleasantly cold out here, and I'm only doing what I must by offering to save your life. If you don't take my help willingly, I'll have to force it upon you."

Jonas's brows shot up. For someone who claimed not to give a damn one way or another, she was very insistent.

Lysandra eyed her up and down. "What's your name?"

"Olivia."

"Jonas," Lysandra said slowly, "let's give Olivia a chance."

"But Lys—"

"No," she cut him off. "It's decided. Olivia, what do you need to begin?"

"First, I need to get out of this cold air."

Lysandra nodded and led them to the nearest building, a shop that sold candles and lanterns, that was closed at this early hour.

"Stand back," Lys said, approaching a window and preparing to break it.

"No need." Olivia grasped the handle and pushed the main door open.

"Is that the custom in Limeros, to leave doors unlocked?" Jonas said.

"No. But it's unlocked now."

Jonas and Lys shared a wary look as they followed the witch into the small, vacant shop furnished with tables heaped with wax candles in every size and shape imaginable. Lysandra immediately took a few in hand and lit them with her flint to provide additional light to the small area.

"Show me your wound," Olivia said, waving her index finger at him. "Quickly."

Jonas removed his satchel and dropped it to the floor.

Olivia sighed with impatience. "Today would be lovely. Really."

He glared at her.

He had absolutely no idea why she wanted—seemingly needed—to help him, but if anything she'd said was true he couldn't risk losing this opportunity. They were looking for a skilled witch, and—as if by magic—one had just marched right up to them and offered her services.

Now wasn't the time to question her intentions. He promised himself he'd do that later, when he didn't feel like death itself.

That was, if Olivia could do what she claimed.

Lysandra helped him untie the front of his shirt and pulled it off his left shoulder.

"Oh, Jonas!" she gasped.

Olivia scrunched her nose up at the sight of the festering and oozing wound. "That is the foulest thing I've seen in my entire life. I'm truly stunned that you're still upright and breathing."

He narrowed his eyes. "Yes, well, imagine how I feel. Now, can you help me or not?"

She rolled her eyes and glanced at Lysandra. "Is he always this belligerent?"

"Never mind him. What do you think? Can you make some fresh healing mud?"

Or perhaps she has a bag of shiny, magic grape seeds in her bag ready and waiting, Jonas thought. Then he'd know for sure he'd fallen into a fever dream and none of this was real.

"Is *that* what you originally applied to this?" Olivia gagged. "Oh, my. I think I may actually vomit."

Lys grimaced. "The mud was apparently too old to hold its magic so it did nothing at all."

"No wonder it's such a repulsive mess." Olivia shook her head. "Fine. Yes, I will make some fresh healing mud since it is a perfect substance to hold earth magic. First, I'll have to find a cow."

Jonas was too weak to fully express his impatience for her to start, but this was truly unexpected. "Why do you need a cow?"

"What do you think the mud is made from?" she asked, a

glimmer of amusement in her emerald eyes. "Cow dung is a common ingredient in many earth magic concoctions."

She left the building without waiting for a response.

Jonas stared after her, stunned. "She means to heal me with cow dung."

Lysandra patted his good arm. "And you're going to let her."

Olivia returned with a bucket of her foul-smelling findings. She ordered Jonas to take his shirt off completely and peel away all the bandages when she was ready to begin.

Lysandra peered into the bucket of brown muck. "So that's it, is it?"

"It is."

Jonas gritted his teeth. "Let's get it over with."

"Lie down." Olivia reached into the bucket and drew out a handful of the stinking mud.

Jonas lay down on the sturdy table before which he'd previously been seated. He reached for Lysandra, who took his right hand in hers. "Ready," he said.

"Think healing thoughts," Lys suggested.

"I'll try my best."

The witch began to smear the healing mud over his shoulder. Even the slightest touch was painful, but the mud felt cool against his burning skin.

"More," he said.

"Yes, you're definitely going to need all of it," she agreed.

This was very different from when Phaedra had healed Jonas with the grape seeds. Olivia's magic gave him a cool and pleasant sensation, whereas Phaedra's had felt like lava had been poured down his throat, only to go shooting through every limb.

"This feels so nice and soothing," he said. "Is that what it's supposed to feel like?"

"Soothing?" Olivia frowned. "I don't think that—"

Jonas lurched up and cried out in pain. It was as if a soldier had grabbed hold of his arm and tore it right out of its socket before setting it on fire and throwing it to the wolves. He flailed, desperately trying to wipe the burning mud off his skin.

"Hold him down," Olivia barked at Lysandra. "We can't remove any of it yet."

Lys immediately did as the witch ordered. They each took an arm and held Jonas down against the tabletop while he writhed in agony.

"She's trying to kill me!" he exclaimed. "Lys—Lys, stop her!"

"Hang on," Lys whispered. "Please, just hang on a little longer."

He felt the mud sink deeper into his skin, burning through every layer, eating right down to his muscle and bone. It sliced through his shoulder like the razor-sharp bite of a demon.

But then, as suddenly as it came on, the pain vanished completely. He felt his body grow slack again in the girls' grips, and all he could hear was the sound of his own ragged gasps.

"It's done," Olivia said, letting out a long, relieved sigh. "See? That wasn't so bad, was it?"

Bad? It was worse than bad. It was torture.

The witch disappeared into the back of the shop. Lys grabbed a cloth and shakily wiped at Jonas's shoulder.

"It worked," she said, clearly amazed. "She didn't just help you . . . she actually *healed* you."

Jonas managed to push himself up to sitting. He took the cloth from Lys, wiping the remaining mud away from his shoulder, revealing an unblemished patch of smooth skin. No wound, no infection.

But . . . how? Jonas might be a converted believer in Mytican magic, but he hadn't thought a witch could be capable of a miracle this perfect.

Bruno was the one who'd said a witch couldn't heal an injury this bad. But perhaps the old man had just never met one who could.

Lysandra grabbed him and hugged him tight. "I thought I was going to lose you. Don't scare me like that again, got it?"

"I got it," he whispered into her hair.

Olivia returned, wiping her hands on a towel. "All better?"

Lysandra rushed to Olivia and placed her hands on her shoulders. "To think, only a little while ago I didn't believe a word about witches or magic, and here you are . . . and you've done even more than I ever could have wished for. Thank you. Thank you so much!" Then Lysandra pulled the girl into a tight hug.

Olivia's brows raised with surprise and she awkwardly patted Lys's back. "I'm grateful I was able to help in time."

Despite his previous misgivings, the witch had more than proven herself to him. "My deepest gratitude to you, Olivia," Jonas said. "I owe you my life."

She gently pushed Lysandra away from her. "Yes, I suppose you do."

He waited for her to name her price, probably some outrageous request that he'd never be able to grant. "And . . . ?" he prompted.

Olivia cocked her head. "And . . . I must be on my way now. Farewell."

She turned toward the door.

"Wait!" Jonas said. "Where are you off to? Got some other random strangers to heal around town?"

"Perhaps," she allowed.

The girl was a true mystery. But, really, all Jonas needed to know about her was that she could work real magic.

"Come with us," he said.

She frowned. "Where?"

"The Limerian palace."

Olivia crossed her arms and studied him for a long, silent moment. "Jonas Agallon, a failed rebel leader whose life purpose is to destroy King Gaius and bring peace and freedom to Mytica again, wants me to join him in a journey to the Limerian palace."

"Actually, I'm going to start by destroying his son. And, yes, I do want you to join us. Lys, what do you think?"

Lysandra met his gaze. "You're right, we need her."

"Am I to become your newest rebel recruit?" Olivia asked.

"You did just save my life, knowing who I am," Jonas reasoned. "And knowing my goal."

"And you'd like me around to save it again, if need be," Olivia said.

"I won't deny that that would be a large perk. I know there's not much in it for you, but if I'm successful . . . if I can pull this off . . ." He shook his head. "Everything will be better in Mytica, for everyone who calls this place home."

Olivia turned, as if to leave, but then paused. "Fine. I will agree to accompany you on this fateful journey."

"Good," he said, a grin breaking out on his face. "Then let's be on our way."

CHAPTER 10

FELIX

KRAESHIA

Felix hung over the side of the ship, trying his best not to fall into the choppy waters below. He looked up to watch the seabirds swirling, and saw that, among their numbers, was a golden hawk.

Perhaps a Watcher was overlooking his suffering.

He felt someone slap him on his back, and he turned around to cast an unfriendly glare on the offender.

It was Milo Iagaris, a former palace guard who'd been accused of aiding the rebels, a crime for which he'd been sent to the Auranian dungeon, where he'd remained until very recently. Upon his release, Milo hadn't been told that it was Felix's fault for stealing his uniform.

It would be best that Milo never learned that little detail. Felix thought he wouldn't be nearly as forgiving as the king had been.

He'd been partnered with Felix as a bodyguard for this journey. Felix had to admit that Milo, made of muscle on top of muscle, did have the right build for the job. Also, from the conversations they'd had over their days at sea, Milo seemed more than ready to remorselessly inflict pain whenever it was necessary. And even when it wasn't.

"Still seasick?" Milo asked.

"What does it look like?"

Milo laughed. "I'll take that as a yes. I can't believe you've never been to sea before."

"Believe it. Now go away and leave me to die."

"Don't worry, it won't be much longer now. I can see land from here."

Felix managed to raise his bloodshot eyes to see that, far in the distance, across miles upon miles of churning, open sea—

His stomach flopped and gurgled.

—was the edge of land.

"Praise the goddess," Felix groaned. "I think I might stay in Kraeshia forever."

"I imagine we'll soon find out exactly why the king decided to come here," Milo said.

"You don't think it's just for the sand and sunshine?"

The two shared a droll look at the thought of the King of Blood caring about anything so mundane. But it did trouble Felix that he had no clear idea as to why the king wished to set foot in the capital of an empire that had crushed more than a third of the known kingdoms in the world.

Finally, the ship came into port and docked. Felix followed the king closely as they proceeded down the gangplank, trying not to give into the compulsion to throw himself down on the wooden dock and kiss it.

Here it was, the Kraeshian Empire. Or, more precisely, the capital of Kraeshia, known as the Jewel of the Empire, a city carved out of the natural, exotic wonders that made up this large island that was roughly the size of Auranos. Felix had heard tales of Kraeshia's beauty, but after a life spent mostly in cold, stark Limeros, no mere description could have prepared him for experiencing it in person.

The tall trees were rich with thousands of shiny thick green leaves, each the size of a man, and the sand sparkled like jewels along the shore. In the far distance, along the beach, he was certain he saw a cluster of women basking under the sun, as naked as ice-lizards.

The king had decided that, for the duration of the trip, Milo and Felix would not wear official Limerian guard's uniforms, which would have made them stand out like two red weeds in a garden of fine flowers. Instead, they wore tailored finery fit for a lord—leather trousers, bleached linen tunics, and the finest cloaks Felix had ever laid his eyes on, made of woven lamb's wool—and seemingly as light as air.

Now that he stood on solid land, Felix found that he felt more like a Cobra than ever, ready and eager to protect the king in this unfamiliar territory.

The King of Blood. One who harms the innocent, who enslaves the poor, who tortures the weak.

His cheek twitched.

Get out of my head, Jonas, Felix thought.

He saw a figure waiting for them at the end of the docks, and suddenly his steps faltered. He straightened his shoulders and held his head high as they approached a dark-haired beauty.

Felix didn't believe in love at first sight—but *lust* at first sight? That was an incredibly real concept, and one newly proven by this gorgeous creature standing before him.

"Well, do I dare believe my eyes?" King Gaius said, stopping before the beautiful girl. "Princess Amara Cortas, come to officially greet me? I admit I'm surprised to see you."

Princess Amara.

Felix had heard that Emperor Cortas's daughter and son had recently been in Auranos, as guests of the king, but he hadn't before seen this princess in person. She was as exotically beautiful as her homeland, with long jet-black hair hanging in loose waves down her back. Her lips were as red as rubies, her eyes the color of silver touched by a whisper of blue. Her flawless skin was a dark tan shade. She wore a teal-colored gown, sleeveless to show her lovely bare arms and cut with a long slit that stopped at mid-thigh. Her firm, trim belly was shielded only by a layer of diaphanous material that moved gently in the warm breeze.

She smelled of jasmine, just a hint, but combined with the sweet aroma of this lusty tropical weather, Felix found it as intoxicating as a swig of Paelsian wine.

"King Gaius, what a pleasure to see you here." She ignored his sarcastic display of surprise as she gave him a small nod and held out her hand. "Welcome to Kraeshia."

"You're even more beautiful than the last time we met." He took her hand and brushed his lips over it. "How is that possible? It's only been a matter of weeks."

Her smile tightened. "You honor me with your kind words."

"And is the emperor here as well?"

"No. He's at the palace. My eldest brother, Prince Dastan, returned only this morning from the kingdom of Castoria, our newest acquisition."

"What a great victory for him." The king furrowed his brow. "I do hope he can spare some time to meet with me today. We've traveled quite a long way."

Princess Amara nodded. "Of course, I'm sure he is eager to see you. My father is honored by your visit, and I am likewise honored to accompany you to the royal residence. Once at the Emerald

Spear, you can eat, rest, and recover from your journey. Is that acceptable to you?"

The king smiled thinly. "Of course. Much gratitude, princess."

She smiled and looked to Felix and Milo. Felix fixed a lopsided smile on his face, hoping it was as charming as the girls in Mytica usually found it.

Yes, princess, he thought. *You could make me forget all about Lysandra.*

"Princess," the king said. "Allow me to introduce you to two of my most trusted advisors, Milo Iagaris and Felix Gaebras."

Felix and Milo bowed before her.

"A pleasure," she said, giving a slight curtsey in return. "Given the looks of them, your grace, I will assume that in Mytica 'advisor' is synonymous with 'bodyguard'?"

The king laughed. "You're very perceptive. How could I have forgotten that about you, princess?"

"I haven't forgotten anything at all about you." Amara's smile remained fixed on her lovely face. "Shall we be on our way?"

In Mytica, the carriages were enclosed, with small windows, sturdy doors, and large wooden wheels designed for long journeys over icy, rocky roads. In Kraeshia, the carriages had more of a canopy design, shaded yet open to the sun. The wheels were impossibly delicate and slender, and the body was carved from pale white wood trimmed in precious metals.

Felix leaned back in his seat and closed his eyes, relishing in the warm rays on his face. Several horses with pure-white coats and fragrant flowers braided into their manes and tails pulled the carriage away from the docks, and the driver began to navigate the smooth, winding roads of the Jewel. Kraeshia was so colorful, its buildings and shops and taverns so different from what Felix was used to.

Soon Felix realized that the Jewel boasted so much more than riches. It was perfection itself. Every detail, every nook, every thoughtful inch of the city was flawless, like a pained-over detail in a painting or a sculpture. The windows sparkled. The streets shone. The sky held not a single cloud.

"Beautiful," Felix murmured.

"Yes, it is, isn't it?" responded Amara, and Felix was surprised he'd accidentally caught her attention. "My father has made physical beauty a priority in Kraeshia—especially here in the Jewel itself. He believes that beauty is power."

"What happens when something ugly pops up?" Felix asked.

Her expression grew thoughtful. "I can't think of anything here that could be described that way."

"Well, now that Milo's here, I suppose your streak is ruined."

Felix had successfully managed to summon the edge of a true smile from the princess, but with the king and Milo so close to overhearing, he knew when it was time to shut up.

The carriage passed its reflection in a gigantic, domed silver building, which Amara described as the Jewel's main temple. Felix didn't know much about Kraeshian religion, but he was certain they didn't pray to either Valoria or Cleiona.

Silence fell in the carriage for several long moments, until Amara finally spoke.

"Forgive me, King Gaius, but I must ask, as I've been so deeply curious ever since I learned of your visit. What is it that you wish to speak to my father about? What urgent matter has brought you all this way?"

"I admire your candor as much as your curiosity, princess. But I'm afraid my business here is between me and the emperor. I'm sure you understand."

"Come now. I'm sure you can give me just a little hint."

The cordial smile remained fixed on the king's lips. "Did you enjoy your visit to my kingdom, princess?"

Amara hesitated before conceding a reply to the abrupt shift in subject. "Very much so."

"I was sorry to hear that you'd set sail before I had a chance to bid you farewell."

"Yes, and I was likewise so unfortunate to miss the fleet of guards you'd sent to the villa to escort my brother and me back to your palace. My apologies for the rude departure, but it was time to go. I wouldn't have wanted to outstay my welcome in your kingdom."

On the surface, this was just a polite conversation between two royals, but Felix could have sworn he heard something darker, something entirely other than friendly, in their tone.

"What a pity," the king said. "I sent the guards because I'd managed to arrange excellent new accommodations for you, right there at the palace."

"How incredibly thoughtful."

The king watched her, his smile growing wider and his dark eyes glittering with interest. "You disappoint me, princess. The famous Kraeshian bluntness is usually not so difficult to elicit. Are we really going to play this game?"

"I only indulge in games when I know I'm going to win."

"And your brother, Prince Ashur? Does he play games as well as you do?"

"Not nearly as well, I'm afraid."

"Has he also left Mytica and returned home?"

Felix studied Amara's face, but found her expression impossible to read.

"Not yet," she replied simply.

The king went silent for a long moment as the carriage proceeded on toward the palace. "Perhaps one day you'll wish to speak your true thoughts to me rather than hold them back."

"I'm not sure you'd enjoy that day very much, King Gaius."

"Don't be so certain."

Felix felt as if he and Milo had become completely invisible, leaving only the two royals in the carriage to face off against each other.

"How is Prince Magnus?" Amara asked.

"Very well."

"Really. You've seen him recently?"

The king narrowed his gaze. "My son is traveling at the moment, but we keep in very close touch. I've just received a message from him, informing me that he's currently in Limeros."

"Oh, yes, I already knew that." She sighed. "Your darling little heir, so determined to do things his way, isn't he? So stubborn."

"I suppose stubbornness is another trait we share as father and son."

"Yes. And he's quite taken with his wife, isn't he? When I last saw them in Limeros, they couldn't keep their eyes off each other. Love's like that. It's one of the few things in life that are worth killing for, wouldn't you say? He'd likely do absolutely *anything* for her, wouldn't he? How romantic, considering she remains the greatest threat to your throne."

The king's expression was resolute and impassive, but his face had turned a shade redder.

"Apologies." Princess Amara frowned. "Did I say something to upset you?"

"Not at all," the king replied, and Felix watched him shift in his seat. "But tell me, while on your . . . impromptu trip to Limeros where you allegedly saw my son and his wife—"

"Not allegedly. I did see them . . . at the Temple of Valoria, in fact."

"Did you also happen to see my daughter, Lucia?"

"I can't say that I did. Why? Has she also fled her royal nest? Goodness, your grace, it seems that both of your children have abandoned you at such a delicate time in your rule. That must be rather disappointing."

Felix and Milo shared a confused look. What, exactly, were they witnessing here?

The king chuckled, surprising his small audience. "Princess, you are a very special young woman indeed. I promise never to underestimate you again."

"That would be wise," she said, then glanced ahead. "Oh, look. We've nearly arrived at the Emerald Spear. This was the place I missed most while I was away."

Felix turned in his seat to see the massive green palace rising high up into the sky.

"King Gaius . . . Felix, Milo . . ." Amara smiled brightly. "Welcome to my home."

CHAPTER 11

CLEO

LIMEROS

"Yes, very good, princess," Lord Kurtis said. "Focus all your energy on the very center of the target."

Cleo took her time carefully aiming her arrow, standing twenty paces from the target. It was cold, but the skies were clear and there was no snow to distract her today.

"When you're ready, release the arrow."

She let the arrow fly, feeling more confident than she had in any previous lesson.

But the arrow made it only halfway to its destination before taking a nosedive straight into the frozen ground.

This particular failure had become very familiar to her over the last week.

The sport of archery had seemed so easy from the sidelines, where she'd watched her sister compete. Now, looking down at her fingers, blistered and bleeding from daily practices, she realized how wrong her assumption had been. Every day it was the same: drawing back the bowstring, aiming, letting the arrow free. Over and over. And then failing each time, again and again.

She was further embarrassed by the fact that there were several guards posted near the archery field to witness her lack of progress, including Enzo, the friendly guard she made sure to say good morning to every day.

"Very good," Kurtis said, trying to cheer her up. "You're getting much better."

She tried not to laugh. "You lie."

"Not at all. You don't see your progress, but I do. Your aim has become excellent and your strength is improving with each session. To master a skill like this takes extreme quantities of both patience and time."

Why must everything important take so much patience and time when she had none of either left?

When she'd first met Lysandra Barbas, Cleo had been impressed by the rebel girl who had been so easily able to keep up with boys like Jonas, who could wield a bow and arrow as if she'd been born with them already in her grip. Although she'd never admit it to anyone, especially not to the belligerent Lysandra herself, Cleo had come to admire her deeply.

"I think that's enough for today," she said, putting down her bow and tucking her hands into the folds of her pale blue, fur-lined cloak.

"Very well." Kurtis ordered a guard to pick up their equipment and they began to walk slowly toward the entrance to the palace. "Your grace, may I speak frankly with you?"

"About?"

"Prince Magnus."

She glanced at him with surprise. "What about him?"

He hesitated. "Forgive me if I've misinterpreted, but I feel that you and I have become friends."

"You haven't misinterpreted at all." Cleo could use as many

friends as she could get. "Please, feel free to say whatever's on your mind."

"Thank you, your grace. The fact of the matter is . . . I'm a bit concerned for your husband. During the council meetings over which he's presided, I can't help but notice how so obviously doubtful the prince is about his abilities to lead. I fear it's only a matter of time before the rest of the council catches on and begins to believe him inept. If the council finds him unfit to rule in his father's place, they have the power to remove him from command."

"All new leaders make mistakes at first," Cleo said after a thoughtful pause. "And, as a matter of fact, I must disagree with you. When I sat in on the meeting he seemed both confident and capable."

Did I just say that aloud? she thought with dismay.

She knew how much Magnus disliked delivering public speeches, so she really had been surprised at the seemingly effortless way he took command of the council meeting. When he spoke, it was as if everyone else faded from her view.

"I've known the prince a great deal longer than you have," Kurtis replied without hesitation. "He's never shown any signs of leadership, nor any interest in learning more about what makes a great leader. Yet he suddenly shows up here out of the blue, demanding control and sowing frustration."

Cleo wasn't sure she liked the direction of this conversation but still wanted to see where Kurtis was trying to lead it. "He is heir to the throne."

"He is," Kurtis acknowledged. "As were you to the Auranian throne, if not for Magnus's father. I'm no fool. I know this marriage wasn't one you made of your own free will. Forgive me if this seems quite harsh, but it's almost as if you're less of a wife and more of a prisoner of war. Knowing what a bully he was when we were children, I greatly sympathize with your position."

He was far more perceptive than she'd given him credit for. "I'm not sure how to reply to that, Kurtis."

"You don't have to say a thing. But, know this: In my heart, I know that Magnus is not meant for that throne. It belongs to someone else. Someone who has earned it, and who is much more worthy."

She found she couldn't breathe. Was Kurtis offering his allegiance to her?

"Kurtis . . ."

"That throne is *mine*," he continued. "With both the king and my father in Auranos, *I* should be the one in power here."

She grappled to conceal her shock. "It's unfortunate, then, that the prince of Limeros disagrees with you."

"You should know that the prince has succeeded in making far more enemies than friends since his arrival," Kurtis said, his voice hushed as they drew closer to the palace. "I've become concerned about his safety."

"You believe his life's at risk?"

"I pray to the goddess it isn't, of course." He paused, his lips thinning out to nearly a grimace. "But what I know for sure is that very few in Limeros would mourn either his or his father's death."

"Why are you telling me this?"

"I hope that you might encourage your husband to step down."

"You think I have that kind of control over him?"

"You certainly seemed to have a certain sway over him at the council meeting when it came to how to handle Limeros's debt. It's clear to me that he's come to value your opinion."

"I don't think we share that clarity."

"Even so, will you consider this request, princess?"

She pushed a smile onto her lips and squeezed Kurtis's arm. "I appreciate your frankness today, Kurtis. And yes, I will consider it very carefully."

"Excellent. Then I promise not to take up any more of your time."

He bid her farewell until tomorrow's lesson and left her there at the palace entrance, lost in her thoughts.

What just happened?

Cleo's desire to reclaim what was rightfully hers had not faded at all, and Kurtis Cirillo would make for an interesting ally. If only something about his approach, his naked desire for the throne, hadn't left such a rancid taste in her mouth.

So, the council hated Magnus. And, if presented with a choice, they would side with Kurtis. If Magnus were to then put up a fight, his life would be in danger.

That had once been her goal—to see the prince dead alongside his father.

Judging by the tight, sick sensation that now roiled in the pit of her stomach, times had certainly changed.

She returned to the ice gardens later that day, pulling her cloak closer as she explored the grounds, trying to clear her head. Everything around her was covered in a coat of pure white. Even the palace, a black and ominous beast of a structure, appeared muted and gray today, frost covering nearly every inch of its surface. She walked the long icy pathway leading through the gardens, imagining that it was lined with manicured hedges and blooming rose bushes. Perhaps an ivy-covered archway. Full of color and warmth, just like home.

Cleo loved Auranos, of course. But Limeros did have its beauty, too—a cold, untouchable beauty best admired from afar.

Much like the prince himself.

Yet the prince isn't always cold and untouchable, is he? she thought.

Suddenly, something—a sensation, a small sound . . . she wasn't sure what—made her pause and turn around.

Someone walked along the pathway behind her, about a hundred paces off. She stood there, transfixed, as the figure drew closer.

Until she could finally make out who it was.

"This is impossible," she whispered.

When he was about thirty paces away, she started to walk, her legs moving of their own accord, taking her closer to him.

Theon.

Theon Ranus wore brown woolen trousers and a thick black cloak, the hood pushed back to reveal his handsome face. It was a face she'd memorized, a thousand times over. A face that had haunted her. A face she loved.

"H-how? How are you here?" she managed when she knew she was close enough from him to hear her.

He stopped, only an arm's reach away. "I told you I'd find you and I meant it, princess. I will always find you. Did you doubt me?"

She reached out to him with a trembling hand, and found him solid and warm and real. "But . . . I saw you die! That—that sword pierced straight through your heart. You were *gone!*"

He grasped her hands in his. "An exiled Watcher found me, just in time. She healed me with a grape seed concoction enchanted with earth magic, but still it took months before I was strong enough to leave. I've searched for you ever since, princess. I searched everywhere and, thank the goddess, I've finally found you."

That was why she'd been in Paelsia in the first place, to search for the mythical grape seeds rumored to bring someone back from the edge of death.

He was alive. Theon was alive! This changed everything. "I've missed you so much!"

Theon looked at her tenderly, seriously. "You've endured such horrors these last months. You've been forced to do terrible things in order to survive. But it's over now. I'm here, and I promise to keep you safe." He looked up at the façade of the black castle. "We need to leave here immediately."

"Leave? But wait . . . I have to tell Nic . . ." Her life had been filled with hope again, but everything seemed to be changing so fast that she barely had the time to process it.

"We'll send word to him so he'll know where to find us."

"My kingdom . . . Theon, I need to take it back."

"You will, but not here. Not with *him*." Theon's expression darkened. "I'm sorry I couldn't protect you from that monster, my love. But I will now. You'll never have to see him again."

He drew her into a tight embrace, but she stiffened against him.

"I can't leave," she said, her voice so quiet she barely heard it herself. "There's too much I need to do here. I'm sorry."

Theon pulled back from her and shook his head. "How can you say this to me?"

"Please, try to understand—"

"Why would you stay with him a moment longer than you have to? Don't you remember what he did to me?"

Slowly, blood began to trickle from the corner of his mouth.

She covered her mouth in horror. "Theon!"

"He murdered me, princess. That evil coward plunged a sword through my back and in return he deserves nothing but pain. You know this!"

She shook her head, her eyes stinging with tears.

Theon staggered backward and fell to his knees. He ripped open the front of his cloak to show her the bright red stain in the center of his tunic. "He stole me from you. He stole your kingdom and your family and your future. Do you forget that?"

Hot tears streamed down her cheeks. "No. You—you don't understand . . ."

"I loved you, princess. We would have been so happy together, if not for him. Why would you betray me like this?"

He fell to the ground, his accusatory eyes glassy and staring at her.

Cleo woke from the dream screaming.

She searched for Nic, but passed Magnus in the halls instead. She tried to avoid him, but he stepped directly into her path.

"Princess," he said, eyeing her cloak and gloves. "In a hurry to go somewhere?"

She had trouble meeting his gaze, so she kept her attention on the dark floor instead. "Nowhere in particular."

"I'm curious, how are your archery lessons coming along?"

Of course, today, of all days, he wanted to stop for a friendly chat. Lovely. "Couldn't be better."

"Lord Kurtis is a good instructor?"

"Very good. I—I'm actually looking for Nic. Have you seen him?"

"Not recently." Magnus blinked, then straightened his shoulders. "The last place I saw him was at a public house nearby. It seemed to me he was there to try to forget a certain Kraeshian prince. Curious, isn't it? And here I'd thought he was madly in love with you. Some people are full of secrets, aren't they?"

"Indeed. Now, if you'll excuse me."

He caught her arm as she brushed past him. "Is everything all right, princess?"

"Everything's fine."

"Look at me."

Cleo gritted her teeth before forcing herself to meet his dark gaze. As soon as she did, a thousand different emotions hit her all at once, and her eyes began to sting.

No, not here. I won't cry in front of him.

Magnus drew his brows together. "Tell me why you're so upset."

"As if you'd care." She looked down at his large hand gripping her upper arm. "You're hurting me."

He let go of her immediately, and she felt his gaze hot on her back as she walked away, trying to appear as if she wasn't in a rush.

She tried to breathe normally, tried to find a way to find her strength again, but it slipped from her grasp with every step she took.

Finally, she found Nic exiting his room in the servants' wing. There were dark circles under his eyes and his red hair was a mess.

"Remind me of something in the future, Cleo," he said. "Stick with Paelsian wine. Any other drink imbibed to excess leads to nothing but great pain and regret the next morning."

If it were any other day, she might find this humorous. "The pain you're feeling right now should be reminder enough," she said, then glanced up and down the hallway. "I need to talk to you about a private matter."

He rubbed his forehead. "Now?"

She nodded, her throat tight.

"Fine." He gestured toward his room. "Come in and experience the fine luxury I've been given by his majesty."

She chewed her lip. "No, let's go outside. I need some fresh air and . . . it will do you good."

"Excellent idea. And if I freeze to death, I'll be no further burden to you."

"Stop it, Nic. You're not a burden. I honestly don't know what I'd do without you." She grabbed him and hugged him hard.

He stiffened with surprise, but then returned her hug. "Are you all right?"

"That's a very good question. I'm not so sure anymore."

He nodded. "Then let's have that talk."

Nic grabbed his warm cloak, and Cleo led him out of the palace and into the ice gardens.

"Have you seen the labyrinth?" she asked, drawing the hood of her cloak up over her head to help block out the chill.

"Only from a distance."

She eyed the red-suited guards dotting the white landscape. "I've walked it several times and know the way through. It'll give us some privacy."

As they entered the maze, Cleo hooked her arm through Nic's for additional warmth.

"All right," he said. "What's so urgently private that we need to walk through a maze of ice on the coldest day I've ever lived?"

"Well, first I want to apologize. I feel that I've been neglecting you when you . . ." She took hold of his cold hand in her gloved one. "When you've been deeply in need of a friend."

His steps faltered and his expression grew serious. "What do you mean? I know you're my friend. I mean, you're *more* than that. You're my family now. The only family I have."

"Yes, of course. But I know you've been so troubled since the temple . . . since Prince Ashur died . . ."

His face went pale. "Is that what this talk is all about? Don't ask me about him, Cleo. Please."

"I know you're in pain, Nic. I want to help you."

"I'm working it out for myself."

"By getting drunk every night?"

"Perhaps it's not the best strategy to clear a confused mind, but it's one of the few I have available to me."

"I can tell you're confused. Talk to me about this, Nic—about *him*. I'm here for you. I mean it."

His nose had already gone red from the cold, and his freckles stood out sharply on his pale face. "All I know is I've never felt that way, ever, for . . ." His jaw tightened. "I don't know, Cleo. I can't explain it, not even to myself. I've liked girls all my life, and I know I haven't only been fooling myself. Girls are pretty and soft and . . . amazing. What I felt for you, *especially* for you . . . that wasn't fake or a lie I told myself. It was real. But with the prince . . . I don't know what to think. It's not as if I've undergone some massive change and now want to kiss every boy that crosses my path."

"But you liked him. Perhaps *more* than liked him."

He rubbed his hand through his short red hair. "I barely knew him, Cleo. But . . . what I'd begun to feel, it . . . it didn't feel wrong."

Cleo nodded. "I completely understand. What our hearts want can overtake what our minds tell us is forbidden to us. We can't control these feelings, even if we desperately wish we could."

He began to eye her with suspicion. "You understand, do you? Why? Is *your* heart currently confused as well? Are we even out here to talk about me? Or are we talking about *you*?"

Nic always saw her clearly—more than anyone else did. She would be wise to remember that now.

She closed her eyes to try to block out all of her confusion, but all she could see was the Theon from her nightmare, staring at her with pain and confusion.

"Why would you betray me like this?"

"Cleo, look at me," Nic prompted.

Reluctantly, she opened her eyes.

"Don't," he said sternly. "Just don't."

"I don't even know what you're talking about."

"Of course you do," Nic said, then groaned. "Just remember one thing: Everything the prince has done lately, he's done it for one person only—and it's not you. It's him. He is every bit as scheming and conniving and selfish as his father. You're smarter than this, Cleo. I know you are. You have to see through to the motivations behind everything he does."

His tone was free from accusation or disgust. Rather, he spoke with patience and understanding . . . and perhaps a little frustration.

"I'm not sure what to believe anymore, Nic."

"I can see that." He swept her hair back from her face and behind her shoulder. "I know you didn't come to me today to talk about love, Cleo. You came to me because you know that, whenever things get a little blurry, I can always help you see reason again. Prince Magnus is your mortal enemy, not a dark hero who will redeem himself for true love. And that's never, ever going to change."

She couldn't help but laugh, but it held no humor. "You make me sound like a complete fool."

"No, you're no fool. You're the smartest girl I've ever known." He grinned. "And the best-looking one, by far. I know you're going to do the right thing. But you have to remember who your enemy is. Remember why we came back to this palace—for more information about the Kindred. If we can get even one of them you'll have your throne back."

What was more important to her? Vengeance for her family's death, the reclaiming of her stolen throne, ensuring a future for her people that was free of the King of Blood?

Or a prince, whom she knew she could never fully trust with her heart or her life?

It all seemed so clear again. Thank the goddess she'd had that dream about Theon to remind her of what she could never forget—and that she had Nic as her voice of reason.

"You're absolutely right," Cleo managed to say after a heavy silence. Finally, she led them toward the labyrinth's exit. "Magnus is my enemy. I hate him for everything he's taken from me—from both of us—and I always will."

Nic let out what sounded like a sigh of relief. "Good to hear."

They finally exited the maze, only to be greeted by a dry, humorless voice.

"Yes, that is good to hear, isn't it? For all of us."

Magnus leaned against the frozen labyrinth wall, as if he'd been waiting there for them to emerge. Cleo's blood turned to ice at the sight of him.

"My, that must have been a fascinating conversation. I'm sorry I only caught the end of it. I wondered why you were looking so upset inside the palace, princess, so I took the liberty of following you and your best friend out here to learn why. After all, as your mortal, eternal enemy, I'm quite wary of your intentions."

The thought that he'd only heard the end of their conversation and not any hints at her internal struggle about him was the only relief she could find.

"You're not wearing a cloak," she said when she'd finally found her voice. "You'll freeze to death out here."

"Would you like that?" He wasn't shivering, but his arms were crossed tightly over his chest. "Very sorry to disappoint you, but I'll be fine. Perhaps it's my cold, black heart that makes all the difference?" He shifted his icy gaze to Nic. "And here I thought we'd somewhat bonded over our drinks and secrets last night. How disappointing." He hesitated, frowning. "Do you even hear me, Cassian?"

"Um," Nic began. "Looks like you're about to have some unexpected company today."

Cleo turned, followed Nic's line of sight, and gasped.

Heading directly toward them was Princess Lucia Damora.

CHAPTER 12

MAGNUS

LIMEROS

"Lucia . . ." Magnus moved toward her as if in a dream. Was this true? Was this actually happening? "You're here. You're safe!"

She wore a long gray cloak with a white rabbit fur trim. Her raven-black hair hung loose, a stark contrast to the snowy surroundings, as were her red lips and sky-blue eyes.

Walking next to her was a young man Magnus didn't recognize.

"Greetings, Magnus," Lucia said. "I had no idea you were back in Limeros."

She spoke so calmly, it was as if they'd seen each other only yesterday. As if he hadn't chased after her all over Mytica, trying to stop her from letting that devious Watcher ruin her life, only to find blood and death at the temple.

All he wanted was to reach forward and take her hand in his, to ensure that she was real. There was a time not so long ago when she was his only friend in the world, the one who knew him better than any other.

Cleo and her devoted minion remained standing by the exit to the ice maze, but they were close enough to overhear this conversation. The last time the two princesses had seen each other, Lucia had allegedly tried to kill Cleo. After overhearing the cold words Cleo had spoken to Nic, Magnus was more certain than ever that Lucia had ample reason to threaten the Auranian princess's life. He couldn't stop himself from glancing over his shoulder to see her reaction to his adopted sister's return. Cleo stood there, her fists clenched at her sides, with not a glimmer of fear in her eyes. No great surprise.

He frowned. "Where else would I be, Lucia? The note you left, your elopement . . ."

"I don't believe I mentioned I'd be going to Limeros."

"Remember, I do know you. Perhaps better than you realize. It was immediately clear to me where you'd want to go with your . . . *beloved.*" And then there was also the fact that, in her fit of rage, Lucia had told Cleo that the water Kindred could be claimed here. Where else would her devious Watcher want to take her?

"I'm sure you were very angry with me," said Lucia after a moment of consideration.

"I was angry," he admitted. "But not with you. I blame Alexius for everything."

"Me too."

That was a surprising admission, and one that perhaps explained Alexius's curious absence from Lucia's side. "You were there at the temple, weren't you? Before the ice storm?"

She nodded. "We were."

He'd been doing a good job of ignoring the cold, but now a chill crackled down his spine. "You *caused* the ice storm, didn't you?"

"Yes," she replied simply.

His gaze flicked again to the young man beside her, eyeing him now with intense curiosity. He was very tall, with a strong jaw, amber-colored eyes, and dark blond hair long enough to brush his shoulders. The boy eyed Magnus with interest, an eye-brow raised.

"Who are you?" Magnus asked sharply.

"I am Kyan."

"What are you doing with my sister, Kyan?"

He cocked his head. "Many things."

Kyan's short, disrespectful reply infuriated Magnus, but he held his anger tightly to his chest. "Where's your new husband, Lucia?"

"Alexius is dead."

He snapped his gaze back to her. *"What?"*

"He's dead. He and Melenia both."

Melenia. The powerful Watcher who'd visited his father's dreams, advising him to build a road that would lead him to the Kindred. Up until now, Magnus had assumed that the king was still impatiently waiting for her to contact him again.

It seemed King Gaius's days of immortal guidance were over.

"Were you the one who killed them?" Cleo asked from several paces away. Magnus tensed at the sound of her voice.

"One of them," Lucia replied calmly.

Magnus knew how powerful Lucia's *elementia* was, but he also knew that it was often uncontrollable, so much that she'd been afraid of it. She'd worried that her magic had made her evil, but he'd always reassured her that nothing about her could ever be evil.

Did he still believe that?

Lucia looked sharply to the other princess. "I'm surprised to see you here, Cleo. I was certain you'd be long dead by now."

"Alive and well, thank you," Cleo replied through gritted teeth.

"Magnus," Lucia said, turning back to him, "you should take more care in selecting your company. That girl will put a dagger in you the moment your back's turned."

"Trust me, I'm well aware of that," he said with a nod.

"And yet you let her live."

"I believe she could still prove useful to me."

"I disagree."

He ignored Cleo's soft grunt of disgust. "Why are you here, Lucia?"

She raised a dark eyebrow. "I thought you'd be happy to see me."

Her chilly demeanor, coupled with her emotionless admission that her precious golden Watcher was dead, had put him on edge. This wasn't quite the brother-sister reunion he'd imagined, nor was this the same Lucia he remembered. "You just told me you didn't know that I was here, so clearly you've come home for another reason entirely. What is it?"

"This isn't my home," Lucia said, glaring at the palace with displeasure. "It never was, not really."

"You're wrong. This is as much your home as it is mine." He eyed Kyan with wariness. "Why don't you and your new friend come inside, where it's warm?"

With his right arm still bound in a sling, he reached for her with his left hand, but Lucia stepped backward and closer to Kyan.

"Not just yet," she said.

Magnus's hand dropped back to his side.

"We've been told that, somewhere on these grounds, there's an ancient stone wheel," Kyan said. "I want to see it."

A stone wheel? Immediately, the wedding gift Lord Gareth presented to him during their royal tour came to mind. The lord had boastfully claimed that the ugly wheel carved out of seemingly ordinary rock was a valuable piece of history with ties to the Watchers.

"You must have been misinformed," Cleo spoke up before Magnus could reply.

Magnus turned and frowned at her, their gazes meeting for a

brief moment. He swore he saw a silent warning move through her cerulean eyes.

Don't tell them anything.

A glimmer of a memory flickered in his mind, a connection he hadn't made until this very moment. The Auranian library was home to a much more diverse collection of books and topics than the Limerian library. Over the centuries, ever since Valoria had ruled, Limerian kings had ordered many volumes about legends, goddesses, the history of *elementia* to be destroyed. However, various radical groups had managed to salvage an impressive number of books, sending them down to be part of Auranos's vast collection, where they would be safe.

Recently, Magnus had taken to reading everything on the subject of magic that he could find. It was the least he could do after the king had revealed the shocking truth that his mother was not Queen Althea, but his former mistress, Sabina, a scheming witch whom Lucia had killed.

If this was true, Magnus needed to know what it might mean for him, what effect this witch's blood could have on his life and his future.

Magnus had read that there once was a time when immortals were able to come and go from the Sanctuary as they pleased, in both hawk and human form. Some of those immortals carried on affairs with mortals, and some of those affairs resulted in children. Because those children, and their children's children, were the result of an immortal pairing, they all potentially held a small amount of *elementia* within them. Those who possessed those traces of magic were witches, and the vast majority of witches were female.

Too bad. A part of Magnus had been intrigued by the possibility that he might have traces of magic within him.

But this was unimportant at the moment. What was important was the memory of an illustration he'd found in an ancient book, which depicted the gateway the immortals used to enter Mytica from the otherworldly Sanctuary.

A gateway that looked a great deal like a stone wheel.

He cast another glance at Princess Cleo and narrowed his eyes. *Just how much do you know about this, princess?*

"Princess Cleo is correct," Magnus said after several moments of silence. "Your information is faulty. Don't you think you'd remember such an object if it really existed here, Lucia? You spent sixteen years wandering these grounds at my side. Remember?"

Lucia and Kyan exchanged a look, grave and filled with silent understanding. When she returned her attention to Magnus, something in her expression had softened. Her lips curved into that sweet smile he remembered so well.

"Of course I remember," she said. "We had such a wonderful childhood, didn't we?"

"The parts that included you were wonderful." He hesitated. "I know you can't forgive me for . . . many things I've done. But my only wish is for us to find a way to move past these mistakes. One day I hope you can see me again as you once saw me—as your brother and your friend."

"What an unusually sentimental thought for you, Magnus." She raised an eyebrow. "But are you certain that's all you want from me anymore? A chaste friendship between siblings and nothing more?"

His heart had begun to pound. "Lucia . . ."

She drew closer and took his face between her warm hands. "The knowledge that you loved me so deeply is the only truth I've held on to in the last weeks. I was a fool to deny my feelings for you all this time. I see that now."

"What are you saying?"

"Only this." Lucia pulled his face to hers and kissed him, making him gasp with surprise.

He'd kissed her only once before, when he foolishly chose to expose his heart and soul and tell her how he'd been secretly harboring intense feelings for her. They might have been raised together, but they weren't blood. That revelation had made it acceptable to him to want her as more than just a sibling, but it hadn't for her.

When he'd kissed her then, she'd pushed him away in disgust. But now she was the one so unexpectedly kissing him, and she just pulled him closer, her lips warm and soft against his.

How different everything would be if this were the way she'd kissed him back those many months ago.

"Magnus." Cleo grabbed hold of his arm, breaking him free from the moment.

His head swam and he felt unsteady on his feet. "Unhand me."

She did as requested, but then fixed him with a glare. Nic remained close to his princess's side, his arms crossed over his chest. "Magnus, listen to me. She's trying to manipulate you, are you too stupid to see that?"

"I supposed you know all about manipulation, don't you, princess?" he countered.

A smile played at Lucia's lips. "Why do you tolerate this fallen princess, Magnus? I should have killed her when I had the chance."

"But you didn't," Cleo said. "You stopped yourself because you knew it was wrong. Has that sane and good part of you been somehow erased?"

Lucia groaned. "I am so very weary of the sound of your voice." She flicked a finger at Cleo and a burst of air magic blew the princess backward, sending her crashing into a heap of snow.

Nic rushed to her side immediately, checking her for wounds and helping to get her upright.

Lucia looked down at Magnus's sling. "Poor brother. That looks painful. Ever since *her*, your life has been filled with so much pain. This only proves that you still need me."

"Of course I need you," he agreed.

"Shh. I need to concentrate." She placed her hands atop his damaged arm, pressed down gently, and poured healing earth magic into him.

His knees buckled in response to a sudden blaze of pain, so similar to the sensation that overcame him when he was moments from death in the Auranian battle, and he collapsed to the ground, gritting his teeth and trying not to cry out.

When the pain finally faded, he squeezed his hand and bent his elbow, barely believing that the break had been healed and his arm felt just as strong as ever. He looked up at her with awe. "Thank you, Lucia."

She slid her fingers up into his hair, tucking it behind his ears, as he pushed back up to his feet. "Now, my darling Magnus, look at me."

He smiled and did as she asked, but then—with no warning, no movement on his part—he was overcome by a sort of dizziness that pulled his mind backward into what felt like a dark and endless abyss. Suddenly, it was as if Magnus couldn't look away from her familiar bright blue eyes, even if he wanted to.

"Where is the stone wheel?" Lucia asked.

Immediately, the answer rose up painfully in his throat, summoned by the utmost need to tell her the truth, but he managed to swallow the words back down, each one as sharp as a blade.

"Don't resist," she said. "Please, Magnus, for your own good, don't resist this."

The unrelenting pressure of a thousand vises clamped down on either side of his skull. "What are you doing to me?"

"Tell us where the wheel is," she said again.

When he resisted, a thick, coppery taste flooded his mouth and he gagged.

"Lucia . . ." he sputtered, and blood spilled over his bottom lip.

"What are you doing to him?" Cleo shrieked as she drew closer again.

Lucia didn't move her gaze from Magnus. "Quiet."

"You're hurting him!"

"And if I do? What would you care? Magnus, please stop resisting my magic and tell me the truth, and this will all be over in an instant. Where is it?"

He couldn't hold back any longer; the pressure—the pain—was far too strong. The words rushed forward. "The far . . . side . . . of the labyrinth. Near the cliff's edge."

She nodded, her eyes bereft of pleasure. "Well done." She turned to Kyan. "That's only a hundred paces from here."

"Lead the way, little sorceress."

Resisting the overwhelming compulsion to speak had been torture unlike anything Magnus ever before experienced. He dropped to his knees and braced himself against the ground, his chest heaving, as drops of his blood stained the white snow.

"We'll be back shortly," Lucia promised him, before she and Kyan began moving toward the wheel.

Cleo took hold of Magnus's arm. "Get up."

"I can't," Magnus heaved through heavy breaths.

"You must. We need to follow them. If this has something to do with the Kindred, we need to know."

"Leave him," Nic said. "We can go by ourselves."

"What did you know about the wheel before today?" Magnus

snarled at Cleo, wincing at how strained and weak his voice sounded.

"Next to nothing," Cleo said. "But if a sorceress and her strange new friend want to find it badly enough that they'd resort to magical torment to wrench the truth out of you, then it has to be important." She knelt down and roughly wiped the blood off his chin with the discarded bandages from his arm. "We're not allies and we never will be, but now Lucia has shown herself to be an enemy to both of us. My ring—the ring that now sits upon your sister's finger—had a strange reaction to that wheel the last time we were here. I'm afraid of what it might do today. Now get up. If Nic and I approach her without you, I'm sure she'll kill us."

"Cleo . . ." Nic protested.

She shot him a sharp look, and he clamped his mouth shut.

The last thing Magnus wanted to admit was that Cleo was right, but it was true: The sister he'd once known would never have wanted to inflict such pain upon him, no matter what kind of truth she was seeking. What new magic was this? She'd grown so much more powerful since the last time he saw her.

The Kindred were meant to be his; they were the only way to ensure his future, and three of the crystals were still unaccounted for. He knew, now more than ever, that Lucia was the key to finding them.

He didn't doubt that her new friend Kyan knew this as well.

Magnus pushed himself up to standing and mustered all the strength and willpower he could to trudge around the side of the labyrinth with Cleo and Nic trailing closely behind him. He could see the pair; they'd reached the ancient stone wheel, half-buried in snow and taller than any man he'd ever met. He watched them inspect it together, and the anger in his heart gave him fuel to straighten up and walk faster.

Kyan's amber gaze narrowed at Magnus as he approached. "Who has visited this wheel here before us?" the angry young man demanded.

"I have no idea what you mean." Magnus came to a halt, as did Cleo, only an arm's reach away from him.

"The magic . . ." Kyan placed his palms against the rough surface and pushed. "I feel nothing, even this close."

"How strange. I, on the other hand, do feel something. I feel the very strong need to throw you in my dungeon for kidnapping and corrupting my sister."

Kyan snorted softly. "The sister you remember showed only a glimmer of what she was destined to become. Does her magnificence blind you?"

"Kyan," Lucia interrupted, coming to stand between the two. "Ignore Magnus, there's nothing he can do to us. We've found a wheel, right here in Limeros, just like that old witch promised. What's the problem?"

"Can you feel its magic? Can you summon it back?"

Lucia frowned, then pressed one hand against the frosty surface. Magnus couldn't help but notice the amethyst ring on her right index finger that Cleo once wore. "I don't feel anything."

"Any magic that previously existed within this stone has been removed." His expression darkened. "This is Timotheus's doing. He's trying to keep me away from the Sanctuary, away from his little safe haven." He shook his head. "He honestly thinks he can win this game."

"A *game*? This is a game to you?" Magnus said through gritted teeth. "Let me guess. You think Lucia is the secret weapon you'll use to help you win?"

"Magnus, be careful." Cleo took a step closer to whisper to him.

He glared at her. "Stay out of this, princess."

Cleo stared back at him, resolute. "I think it's far too late for that."

Kyan smiled at Magnus, a grin more sinister than even those he'd received from his father. "You think I'm *using* Lucia," Kyan mused. "Yet you and your entire greedy family have been using her for what she is for over sixteen years. It's only now that she's finally free from you and able to make her own choices."

"I've never used her, for anything." The thought was an insult. "Not once."

"Oh, Magnus." Lucia shook her head. "I think you actually believe that. I think you believe that lie so completely that if I magically extracted the truth you'd say the very same thing."

"Who is this creature you've become?" Magnus asked, his eyes narrowed and fraught with concern. "And what have you done with my caring, beautiful sister?"

Lucia rolled her eyes. "Your *caring, beautiful* sister died when her lover took his life on the floor of a temple, right before her eyes. The Lucia you knew was weak and pathetic. Trust me, Magnus, I'm much better now. I pursue the things I want and I get them. And nobody will ever use or manipulate me again." She hooked her arm through Kyan's. "If this wheel is useless to us, Kyan, we'll find another one."

"Whatever you're trying to do," Cleo said, "you'll fail."

"Will I?" A cool smile spread across Lucia's face. "Much gratitude for your opinion. I value it so much."

Cleo took one step closer to the sorceress. "You lost someone you loved. I know what that's like. But you can't let that grief, that unspeakable pain, turn you into something you're not."

"Are you really attempting to sympathize with me? No need, little one. Everything I've felt, all the trials and pain I've experienced, all of it was necessary to get me here. My prophecy has been fulfilled and now my future is my own." She smiled sweetly. "Cleo, let's talk about the water Kindred. I know it was claimed at the temple after I left that night. Where is it?"

Magnus watched as Cleo began to tremble, yet she still continued to stare directly into Lucia's eyes. "I . . . don't . . . know."

"Yes, you do. And, just so you're aware, while I didn't take any pleasure in causing Magnus pain, I'll take great pleasure in causing yours."

Cleo cried out, pressing her palms to her temples as blood began to trickle from her nose. Magnus watched with horror.

"Stop it!" Nic rushed at the sorceress, but at the flick of her finger he flew backward, hitting the wall of the labyrinth so hard that it knocked him out cold.

"Tell me," Lucia gritted out.

A bloody tear slid down Cleo's cheek as she continued to resist this fearsome new magic. "Princess Amara," she finally gasped. "She stole it. I'm sure she's returned to Kraeshia with it by now. You evil bitch!"

Lucia held her smile in place. "See? That wasn't so bad, was it?"

She turned toward Kyan, and Cleo fell to the ground. Magnus rushed to her side, helping her back up to her feet, and swept her golden hair away from her face.

She wiped her hand under her bloody nose. "I'll be fine."

Magnus nodded once, firmly, and then sent a dark glare at Lucia and Kyan. "When you leave here, don't ever return. Either of you."

Lucia turned to him, still calm but clearly surprised.

"And if we refuse to follow your orders?" Kyan asked lightly, as if Magnus's words were those of a court fool, there only to amuse him.

Magnus took another step forward and eyed him up and down with disdain, just as he had with Lucia's prior, unworthy suitors. He attempted to shove Kyan, but the young man didn't budge an inch.

Magnus then swung his right fist, striking Kyan squarely in his jaw.

Again, he didn't flinch, but the amusement faded from his expression. "You try my patience, boy."

"Do I? Good." Magnus struck him again, this time with his left fist. His fingers itched to wrap themselves around the hilt of a sword, to plunge it into Kyan's chest and watch the life leave his eyes.

Then, in an instant, those very eyes Magnus wished to snuff out turned from amber to a vivid, glowing blue.

Magnus took a step back, bumping into Cleo, who was now standing and waiting only a foot behind him.

"What are you?" he demanded.

His feet grew warm. He looked down, astonished to see a ring of bright, amber fire had formed around him. Cleo shrieked and leapt away from the flames.

"*What am I?*" Kyan repeated, cocking his head. "You mean, you really don't know?"

"No!" Lucia grabbed hold of the young man's arm. "Kyan, don't do this. Not to him."

"Apologies, little sorceress, but it's already done."

The flames grew higher, curling up around Magnus's legs like fiery snakes. He couldn't move, couldn't think; all he could do was watch them slither around his body. But while he could feel the warmth of the flames through the leather of his trousers, they hadn't actually touched him—hadn't burned him—yet.

But they would. Magnus knew this, without a single doubt.

"Perhaps you didn't hear me the first time, Kyan." Lucia's voice rose. "I said *no*."

A ferocious blast of air magic slammed into Magnus. He flew backward, hurtling about twenty paces, to land hard right next to

Nic's unconscious body. He looked around, stunned. His legs had been freed from the flames, which continued to burn where he'd previously stood.

Magnus quickly jumped back up to his feet, exchanging a brief, pained look with Cleo, before his gaze landed on his sister. "Lucia!"

Her arm hooked with Kyan's, and she dragged the young man away in the opposite direction. Shakily, Magnus began to run after them.

"Lucia! Stop!" he called. "I can help you!"

"Help *me*?" She gave him a bleak look. "My darling brother, it seems you can't even help yourself."

A wall of flames rose up to block his path and obliterated any sight of her.

CHAPTER 13

JONAS

LIMEROS

Finally, after a long, several-days' journey, there it was: the Limerian palace, just visible in the distance.

As big and ugly as Jonas had always heard it was.

"Your job is to get something for us to eat and find us some rooms for the night," Jonas told Lysandra and Olivia. They'd just stumbled upon a small village a little more than a mile away from the palace grounds.

"Fine," Lys said as Jonas handed his satchel to her for safe keeping. "You're still insisting that I stay behind while you go case the palace? Go ahead then, and lose your head all on your own."

"I don't know," Olivia said. "Jonas is quite notorious. After all of his alleged crimes, I believe they would throw him in the dungeon rather than kill him outright."

"Good point," Lys said flatly. "They'd want enough time to draw a crowd of spectators before removing his head."

Jonas glared at them as he adjusted his eye patch. "Thank you both for your confidence in my abilities. I'll be back as soon as I can."

He left them without another word and quickly made his way

to the palace. He'd been to Limeros before, but never to the palace itself, and he had no idea what kinds of barriers to entry awaited him there.

Unlike the Auranian palace, there was no wall surrounding the castle to separate it from the landscape. Instead, there was a tall watchtower about a quarter mile from the castle gates, along the single road leading toward the massive black granite structure. Any visitors or deliveries would first need to stop here, be questioned by the armed guards, who would log their names and purpose before giving or denying them permission to continue on.

Jonas saw just a sliver of all this from beneath a canvas tarp and between two large sacks of potatoes, in the back of the wagon he'd snuck onto.

The security here paled in comparison to that in the City of Gold. Then again, the kingdom of Limeros had not had waged a battle on its land in . . .

Jonas thought hard. His knowledge of Mytican history wasn't vast, but he couldn't think of *any* significant battle ever fought on Limerian land.

No wall, few guards, and one big ugly black castle that would be very easy to breach.

The thought made him smile.

After clearing the guards at the gate, the rickety wagon continued on. Once they'd moved closer to the palace, Jonas quietly slipped off. Scanning the area, searching for signs of any hidden red-uniformed guards and finding none, he began to explore the grounds.

The winds that raced across the snowy plains surrounding the palace were the harshest he'd ever felt, and he pulled on the thick pale gray cloak he'd stolen on their journey. It camouflaged him well in this monochromatic winterscape. He passed a small lake, completely covered by a sheet of ice punctured with a few holes for ice-fishing. Next he approached a gigantic structure made of what appeared to be chiseled ice, and when he got closer he realized it was a life-sized maze. It seemed a rather frivolous detail for a kingdom that prided itself on its austerity.

Only more proof that King Gaius was nothing more than a hypocrite.

Jonas stopped short when he heard the not-too-distant sound of voices. When he was sure they were drawing closer to him, he ducked behind the western wall of the maze.

"You've always thought the worst of me."

"You've given me no reason to think of you any other way."

Jonas didn't recognize the first male voice, but the second was one he could never forget.

Prince Magnus Damora.

Jonas peeked out from his hiding spot by the maze to watch the scuffle play out, stunned by the good luck he had today.

Just the prince he'd been looking for.

"Your highness, I am your loyal servant," the slender and tall young man said in a sniveling tone.

"Really. Is that why you'd try to turn the council against me?"

"Their opinions are their own. Why would they listen to me?"

Magnus chuckled humorlessly. "Lord Kurtis, you remind me of your father: a man who tries to expand his power by manipulation rather than by skill or intelligence."

"In case you've forgotten, I'm still Grand Kingsliege here. That title comes with power of its own, given to me by the king himself. You can't take that away from me, not even if you try to slit my throat again."

"What an excellent suggestion."

"I don't think your wife would like that very much." Lord

Kurtis paused, his eyes narrowing. "You know, Princess Cleo and I, we've become very close friends."

Jonas's heart leapt at the name.

Magnus's expression remained cold. "Let me guess. You're trying to turn her against me as well? That won't be nearly as much effort as you might think."

"I know she hates you. But I'm not so sure the feeling is mutual."

This statement had coaxed a scowl from the prince. "Trust me. It is."

A cold smile now played at Kurtis's lips. "Such a lovely, fragile creature. Have I told you how much she reminds me of a summer butterfly? So beautiful and rare—yet so easily crushed if it comes to rest on the wrong hand."

In an instant, Magnus grabbed the young man by his throat and slammed him back against the ice wall.

"Mark my words . . ." he growled as Kurtis sputtered, his face turning red in an instant. ". . . if you challenge me again, I will bury you so deeply in this frozen ground that you'll never be found. Do you understand?"

Kurtis stopped his wheezing and choking when Magnus released him. His eyes now blazed with hatred, but he nodded his head once in agreement.

"Now get out of my sight."

There was no more conversation, only the crunch of boots on snow as Lord Kurtis departed.

Once he was sure Magnus was alone, Jonas didn't hesitate another moment. He rounded the corner, drew his sword, and placed it against the neck of Prince Magnus, who shot him a rather gratifying look of shock.

"Now, where were we?" Jonas asked. "I believe the last time we saw one another, I was about to kill you when we were rudely interrupted."

"I remember. Watchers and magic and elemental wildfires."

"Indeed."

Magnus raised an eyebrow. "Nice eye patch, Agallon. And the hair . . . a very innovative look for a Paelsian. I assume that's supposed to be your masterly disguise?"

"On your knees." Jonas pressed the blade harder against the prince's flesh. "Now."

Slowly, Magnus lowered himself to the ground.

"Are you going to kill me?" Magnus asked.

"I've learned my lesson. Why hesitate when you can finish things right away?" Jonas couldn't help but revel at this incredible victory. "But first, tell me where Cleo is."

"Cleo," Magnus repeated. "Yes, of course you'd be one of the privileged few who don't address her by her royal title, being allies and all. Is she expecting your arrival today?" When Jonas didn't respond, Magnus ventured to look up, his brow raised. "Oh, please. She confessed everything. I know that she helped you and your little rebels plan the wedding-day attack. Too bad it didn't play out nearly as smoothly as you'd hoped." The prince smiled darkly at Jonas's stunned silence. "It's all right, Agallon. She's very convincing when she wants to be. Could wrap a dull-minded boy like you around her little finger as easily as she flips her golden hair."

"You don't know nearly as much as you think you do."

"Are you in love with her?" Magnus's unpleasant smile stretched wider. "Is that why you risk life and limb again and again for that girl? The type of girl who normally wouldn't give you a second glance?"

Jonas wouldn't allow himself to be insulted or intimidated by this evil, murderous snake. "Where is she?"

"Around the palace, I suppose. Doing princess things."

"If you've hurt her in any way, I swear—"

"What? You'll kill me twice?"

"I'll do everything I can to make it feel that way."

"I know we've never exactly seen eye to eye, Agallon. But before you cut my throat, I have some very valuable advice for you."

"What's that?"

"If you want to get anywhere in this kingdom—and especially with Cleo—killing me is the absolute last thing you should do."

Jonas barked out a laugh. "Is that so?"

"I know you want my father dead more than anything else. And I'll let you in on a little secret . . . so do I."

Jonas struggled to maintain his steady grip. "Liar."

"My father wanted the princess dead, but I chose to keep her alive. That's treason, Agallon. And one day very soon he'll arrive here and demand my head for defying him. Gaius Damora is still a relatively young man. He has plenty of time to spawn a new heir to take my place."

The prince's claims sounded absolutely ludicrous. Was Jonas really expected to believe that Magnus had defied his father and saved Cleo from death? "If all that's true, then why are you here at the Limerian palace, playing king on your daddy's throne?"

"I'm standing in as the man in charge, which is within my rights while my father's away. I figured this would look much better than if I were to disappear and go into hiding. So here I am, waiting for the King of Blood to return so we can finally face each other, ruthless father against disappointing son. The wait has given me a lot of time to think. And what I've realized is that my father has done many evil things—to you, to me, to virtually everyone who's crossed his path—that can never be forgiven. He deserves death, not a golden throne and a bright future."

Jonas grappled to maintain both his concentration and his grip on the sword. "Even if I believed you, which I don't, what difference does it make to me? Why should I care about any of your royal problems?"

"Because we both hate the king. And because you and I shouldn't be enemies anymore." Magnus held Jonas's gaze steadily. "We should be allies."

Now Jonas had to laugh, the suggestion was so ridiculous. "How convenient for you to make such a suggestion while I have a sword to your throat."

"You and I don't exactly get many opportunities to talk," Magnus countered. "Now put down your sword and join me inside the palace where we can discuss our plans."

Jonas was in the perfect position. He had the opportunity to kill the Prince of Blood, to strike a serious blow against King Gaius that would damage him deeply. But if Magnus was being truthful, if he'd committed treason against his father and was patiently awaiting his wrath, then if Jonas were to kill him, he'd be worse off than he was before. Then the king could easily persecute Jonas as the killer of both Prince Magnus and Queen Althea.

The bounty on his head would quadruple.

"I have friends watching," Jonas said slowly, inwardly kicking himself for leaving Lysandra and Olivia behind in the village. "If you try anything, *anything*, they'll put an arrow in you."

"Understood." Magnus held his hands out to either side of him, showing that he wasn't going to reach for any weapons. "So, what do you say? Truce?"

"I wonder, would you show me any mercy if our positions were reversed?"

"If I thought you could help me, I certainly would."

"If I find out that Cleo's been mistreated in any way, I *will* kill you."

"I assure you she's fine." Then Magnus nodded sagely. "I can see that it's true what the princess says about you, Agallon. You're a great leader who cares about others more than yourself. You've changed a lot over these last few months, haven't you?"

Had Cleo really said that about him?

"She's changed too," Jonas said, trying not to let on how flattered he was. "She's been through immeasurable pain, and has only grown stronger from it."

"Yes. She's a glowing example to us all." Magnus eyed the blade that was still at his throat. "So let's go inside and talk, then, just the three of us."

Jonas had two choices. He could assume that Magnus was a manipulator and a liar, just like his father, and follow through on his initial plan to end his life right now. Or, he could take a risk—the ultimate risk—and trust the claims of his sworn enemy in the hopes of benefiting the greater good.

He was still haunted by the pained and disappointed look on Felix's face when he'd learned that Jonas believed the worst about him despite months of loyal friendship. Of course Felix had lied about his past. He did it because he wanted a new beginning, to be free from his past mistakes.

Jonas wished he could go back to that night and make a different choice.

Forcing himself to put Felix out of his mind, he sheathed his sword and offered Magnus a hand. Magnus grabbed his wrist and got to his feet.

They eyed each other for a silent moment.

"This feels very strange," Jonas admitted.

"For us both."

Magnus led him to a palace entrance, where two guards opened the doors for their prince.

"Guards," Magnus gestured toward Jonas, "this boy here is a known rebel. Remove his weaponry and put him in chains. Then bring him to the throne room."

Jonas grabbed for his sword, but the guards slammed him to the ground before he even touched the hilt.

"And send for the princess," Magnus said. "It's time we all had a nice little chat."

Jonas wasn't sure what felt worse: losing his weapons, or losing his mind.

The latter, he thought. *Definitely the latter.*

Jonas had no one to blame but himself for believing the prince's lies. The only relief he felt came from the fact that Lys and Olivia were still safe in the village. But that bright spot was quickly snuffed out when he was brought into the throne room, in chains as requested, where he saw both Olivia and Lysandra standing helplessly with their hands bound behind their backs.

"What are you doing here?" he hissed.

Olvia shrugged. "We followed you."

"I told her we probably shouldn't," Lysandra said. "But she convinced me."

"And now . . . ?" Jonas prompted the witch, hoping she would wield her *elementia* and somehow break them free. "Can you do anything?"

"I'd rather see what happens next and take it from there."

"'See what happens next'?" he repeated, stunned.

The earth Kindred sat at the bottom of the satchel he'd given to Lysandra before trespassing on the palace grounds. Where was it now?

"Please do alert me when you're finished talking amongst yourselves." Magnus's voice drew Jonas's attention to the dais, where the prince sat upon his father's black throne.

"We're finished," Jonas snarled.

"Good." He flicked his hand at a guard. "Bring her in."

The guard opened the doors and Princess Cleo entered the throne room. For a moment, all Jonas could do was stare at her, grateful that she was every bit as beautiful—and *alive*—as the last time he'd seen her. At least the prince hadn't been lying about that.

She took three graceful strides inside before her steps faltered. Her wide-eyed gaze went from Jonas to Magnus and back again.

"What's going on?" she demanded.

"Someone dropped by for a visit," Magnus said, gesturing toward Jonas. "I thought letting him stay for a while would be the hospitable thing to do."

"This . . . this is Jonas Agallon," she said.

"Yes," Magnus said. "I'm impressed that you recognized the great rebel leader, even with his cunning disguise in place."

Her face went pale. "Why have you brought him here? To answer for his crimes?"

No, Jonas thought. *Oh, no. What have I done?*

More proof of the prince's lies. The princess had never confided in him about her role in the uprising, yet Jonas had all but confirmed that they had been allies.

Now, thanks to Jonas's persistent gullibility, he'd doomed not only himself but Cleo too.

"I met this esteemed leader outside, where he attempted to

assassinate me," Magnus said. "Clearly, he failed. But that is what they say about the rebel leader: *he fails.* Time and again."

"Do you know what they say about you, Magnus?" Jonas said, deciding there was nothing left to lose. "That you should go suck the arse end of a horse."

"Ah, just the sort of charming statement I'd expect from a Paelsian peasant."

"I will see you bleed, you son of a bitch," Lysandra hissed.

Magnus flicked his dark gaze to her. "Greetings, Lysandra. I remember you, of course."

"And I remember you."

"I'm sure you won't believe me, but I think you should know that I thought the king made an unforgivable error in the execution of your brother. He would have been much more helpful to us alive."

Lysandra drew in a shuddery breath, her eyes flashing with pain and hatred.

Cleo twisted her hands. "Magnus, why did you bring these rebels to the throne room? Why didn't you send them directly to the dungeon?"

"Why do you ask, princess? Perhaps because that would make it easier for you to help them escape?"

"Excuse me?" Her face blanched further. "What are you suggesting?"

"Enough. I know the truth, which you're certainly free to deny until your dying breath. My father was right about you and your alliance with the rebel." She grappled for words, stuttering and stumbling over false starts, but Magnus held up his hand to silence her. "Don't bother. Agallon has already confirmed it."

Jonas waited for the onslaught of shame and failure, but all he felt was rage.

Confusion slipped from Cleo's eyes, replaced by a sudden blaze of defiance. "Is that so? And you believe someone who kidnapped me twice to use for his own gain?"

Magnus laughed. "Now you're only wasting your breath. Any further lies are irrelevant to me. I'll have him put to death by sundown."

Cleo gasped. "No! You can't do that!"

"Can't I?" He studied her. "Very well. Admit to me that you and Jonas have been working together for months—that you stooped so low as to conspire on the attack of our own wedding—and I'll let him live. One word seals his fate. Will it be yes? Or no?"

A flurry of anger, doubt, and fear rushed across the princess's face, until her features settled down into pure and utter fury.

"Speak, or I'll make the decision for you. Yes or no?"

"Yes," she finally hissed.

"Well done, princess." Magnus nodded, but there was little pleasure in his expression now. Jonas watched a muscle in his scarred cheek twitch.

She glared up at the prince, her hands in fists. "And now you're going to kill him anyway, aren't you? Perhaps me too? Or would you rather I grovel some more?"

"If this is what you call 'groveling,' I'm very disappointed." Magnus gestured toward the guards. "Unchain the rebel and his friends. Take the female rebels somewhere comfortable to wait while we finish here in private. If you speak to anyone about what you witnessed here, I'll have your tongues removed."

Jonas stared at the prince, astonished, as the guards unlocked his heavy chains. Then they did the same to Lysandra and Olivia before firmly escorting them out of the throne room.

Magnus stood up and descended the stairs, then took his seat at the head of the long black table.

"Let's talk," he said, gesturing for Cleo and Jonas to join him.

Jonas sat on a carved mahogany chair and rubbed his sore wrists. "If all you wanted was to talk, why bother with the chains? The guards?"

"You had me on my knees with your sword to my throat, believing I was moments from death. This was the least I could do to keep us on even ground."

Unbelievable, Jonas thought with disbelief. This had all been a show to soothe the prince's wounded pride.

"Now, back to the business at hand," Magnus said. "My offer stands, Agallon."

"What offer?" Cleo said. Her cheeks were now flushed, her fingers gripping the edge of the table.

Magnus's jaw tensed. "I proposed a truce between me and Jonas."

Shock crossed Cleo's expression. "A truce? I . . . I find that very difficult to believe." Her gaze met Jonas's. "You agreed to this?"

He nodded reluctantly. "I agreed to discuss it."

"I don't undertand."

"While the rebel has been a painful thorn in my side, I believe he can be useful," Magnus explained. "He's agreed to kill my father so he'll no longer be a threat to me, or any of us. While Agallon has attempted this before and failed, he'll be much more successful aligned with me."

Cleo's brow creased in thought. "With your father dead, that would make you the king of Mytica—all of it."

"Yes, it would."

"Well, that's rather convenient for you, isn't it? Jonas will do the work, and you will reap all the rewards."

"I'm sure you have a point, princess."

"My point is: What happens then? If the king is dead and you have all the power? You won't need Jonas anymore . . . or me."

"I don't particularly need you now. But if you're fearful for your life, you shouldn't be. I wouldn't gain anything from your death once I have what I want."

Her cheeks reddened. "You confirmed today that I'm a liar and a former rebel aide. Why would you pardon me for that?"

He regarded her for a moment in silence, his hands pressed palms down against the table. "Why wouldn't you lie? Why wouldn't you align yourself with someone who might help set you free from your enemies? I would have done exactly same thing if I'd been in your position."

Her frown deepened. "Sometimes I think you make it your daily task to confuse me."

"The feeling is utterly mutual, princess."

They continued to glare at each other in silence as the tension in the room grew as thick as three-day-old gruel.

Jonas cleared his throat. "The princess is right. It seems as though you're asking me to do your dirty work, while you sit back and reap the lion's share of the rewards. What's in it for us?"

"Us?" Magnus repeated unpleasantly. "You mean you and the princess?"

"Sure. And Lys and Olivia. And Paelsia as a whole. It's part of your father's kingdom now. *Your* kingdom if I'm successful."

"It was my father's goal to unite all of Mytica because he thought it was the answer to finding the Kindred," Magnus said. "Chief Basilius foolishly helped him drag Paelsia into ruin. And now he's dead. When my father finally joins him in the darklands, I want to restore this country to a simpler time. Limeros is my only concern—both now and in the future. Paelsia is yours, Agallon. And Auranos will be returned to you, princess."

Jonas was certain he'd heard the prince wrong. The thought that this could be real made the world start to spin all around him. "And you expect us to believe this?"

"It can't be true," Cleo said in a tone of disbelief, shaking her head. Her face had gone very pale.

"It is true and it is my plan. It's your decision entirely if you wish to be a part of it. Disagree, or choose to doubt me further, and you can leave my palace and never return."

The first time Jonas had decided to trust Magnus's word he'd been immediately put into chains and threatened with death. And that was only moments ago.

It would be a deadly gamble to trust him again.

Still, there was too much to lose to walk away, and far too much to gain if this was real.

"Fine," Jonas said, his jaw tight. "I'm in."

"Wonderful. And you, princess? Do you agree as well?" Magnus said, turning to Cleo. "When the king is dead, your kingdom will be returned to you, and I promise you'll never have to see me again."

She was silent for so long that Jonas wondered if she'd lost her voice.

Finally, she nodded.

"I agree."

CHAPTER 14

LUCIA

LIMEROS

With the help of witches along the way, Lucia and Kyan had successfully found four of the stone gateways.

Unfortunately, all four had been stripped of their magic.

Kyan was all but certain that Timotheus had sent his minions from the Sanctuary to render each wheel dormant. With every new discovery and disappointment, Kyan became more and more irate. And Lucia knew that the more irate he became, the more people would die.

After leaving Magnus and the third wheel, they'd traveled to a broad, vacant field in central Limeros to find the fourth wheel, which was deeply embedded in snow.

"That Watcher must think quite highly of himself," Kyan growled, pacing in front of the wheel. "But he won't win."

Intense heat emanated from Kyan as he paced, until the snow around them melted and they were surrounded by a field of flames.

Lucia stood by silently as Kyan ranted about Timotheus, but her patience was growing thin. She knew Kyan had a temper, of course, but ever since their visit to the Limerian palace, she found herself questioning her kinship with him.

How could it be that this omnipotent elemental god, one whom Melenia had lusted after for millennia, was about as mature as a toddler?

But no. He wasn't omnipotent. If he were, he wouldn't need her help.

"Are you finished with your tantrum?" she asked.

He glared at her, his eyes still glowing blue. "Nearly."

"Good. Because this is growing wearisome."

"Is that so? My quest to destroy my enemy and reunite with my family is growing wearisome for you, is it?"

"No. But all of *this* certainly is." She indicated the burning field.

"I would have thought you'd enjoy a little something to warm you up on this cold day. My mistake." Suddenly, his irises shifted back to amber and the flames surrounding them vanished. He raised an eyebrow. "Better? Be sure not to smile, little sorceress. It'll ruin that stern look you've been practicing."

"I've no intention of smiling. You know I'm still furious with you for what you did to Magnus."

"Your brother disrespected me."

"He doesn't know who you are."

"Exactly."

"So instead of sparing him for his ignorance you decided to kill him?"

All the anger in Kyan's expression faded away as he gave her a charming grin. "I wouldn't say unleashing my rage upon him was a *decision,* exactly. Fire magic is who I am. *What* I am."

She crossed her arms and began walking away from him. "That's no excuse. Magnus is off-limits. If you harm him in any way, I won't help you anymore."

The fact that she'd willingly tortured Magnus with her magic until he'd spoken the truth didn't sit well with her. Still, if he hadn't resisted, she wouldn't have had to inflict so much pain.

Causing Cleo pain, however, hadn't troubled her at all.

Catching up with her, Kyan kept pace at her side. "Timotheus deserves to die."

"Then he'll die." She shook her head. "I just don't understand why you're in such a rush to tear him out of the Sanctuary. You've only just awakened. And you're just as much an immortal as he is."

"I've waited an eternity to be free, little sorceress. Why should I have to wait another day to know it will be permanent?" He grasped her arm, slowing her down and stopping her. "I know you're angry with me, and that's the last thing I want. But I think I can redeem myself."

"Really?" She eyed him skeptically. "How?"

"Let's go find your real family."

A breath caught in her chest. "Now?"

Kyan smiled. "You're right, my vengeance can wait a few days. But you've waited sixteen years to learn who you really are."

The witches who'd helped them find the wheels had also given up information about Lucia's prophecy. They'd learned that the night Lucia was born, the stars had aligned, setting many witches out on a journey to Paelsia to find her. According to one witch's rumor, two sisters with blood magic skills had succeeded.

One of those sisters was Sabina, the witch Lucia had killed many months ago in the Limerian palace when her powers were first awakening. If only she'd known enough to wait to crush Sabina's skull and set her on fire until after she'd questioned the witch about her origins.

"All right, let's go," Lucia said now, eagerness rising in her chest. "We're close to learning the truth. I can feel it."

"Then it's settled." Kyan nodded. "Tomorrow we'll set off for Paelsia."

The second she closed her eyes to sleep she was haunted by the image of Magnus on the palace grounds.

His joy and relief as she approached.

His confusion when she didn't immediately throw herself into his arms.

His uncertainty when she kissed him.

And his pain when she pulled the truth out of him, brutally and against his will.

This is who I am now, dear brother, she thought. *This is who I was always meant to be.*

With this affirmation, she was finally claimed by a sleep she prayed would be dreamless.

Unfortunately, her prayers were not answered.

In her dream, she stood in a meadow. But not any ordinary meadow. This was a meadow in the Sanctuary, the same one where she'd met Alexius, also in a dream.

Apples as shiny red as rubies hung from the surrounding trees, the sky was as bright as a sapphire, and the ever-brilliant sun shone down on the splendor all around her.

It was the last place she wanted to be.

A hawk circled high above her head, then descended and perched in a nearby tree.

It isn't Alexius.

It can't be.

Still, a small part of her heart had been holding out hope that maybe, just maybe, he could still visit her. When immortals ceased to be, their bodies returned to the elemental magic from which they'd been created. They didn't leave behind a corpse unless they'd lived as a mortal for many years.

Was it possible he could still contact her through her dreams?

She approached the bird tentatively. "Alexius?"

The hawk cocked its head, then vanished before her eyes.

"I'm very sorry to say that no, I'm not Alexius."

Lucia spun around. Standing before her in the meadow was a young man wearing white robes like those of a high priest. But most priests Lucia had ever known were old and wrinkled and ugly—not like this man, who was every bit as beautiful as Alexius had been.

"Beautiful, am I?" he said.

She gasped. "You can read minds."

"Only in dreams. Like yours right now."

"Who are you?" she demanded.

"I think you already know the answer to that question," he said, walking a slow circle around her.

"Timotheus."

He nodded, smiling slightly. "And you are Lucia Eva Damora, the princess of Limeros. The sorceress reborn. The king gave you Eva's name. How predictable."

So here he was, the creature who'd imprisoned Kyan and kept him apart from his family for countless centuries. A monster as cruel and evil as Melenia had been.

Her fists lit up with fire and she narrowed her eyes. "You made a mistake drawing me into this dream."

"Oh, don't insult me, child." He flicked his wrist and her fire went out.

She looked down at her hands and, hiding her dismay, tried to reignite her fire magic. But she couldn't even summon a spark.

"Let's take care to understand each other from the beginning," Timotheus said. "You have no power here. I am in control of this dream."

"This is *my* dream. And I want to wake up."

For a long silent moment, Timotheus said nothing, did nothing, except stand before her and watch her. Finally, in a calm, even tone, he spoke. "I never understood why Alexius was so smitten with you. So far you've done nothing to impress me. They say you're as powerful as Eva? Even if you spent the next five centuries living and breathing nothing but *elementia*, you would only be a fraction as great as she was."

She lunged forward, trying to hit him. If she couldn't use her magic she'd happily use brute force. But when she swung her fist, she hit not Timotheus, but an invisible surface, solid and hard as rock.

She cried out as unimaginable pain shot up her arm.

"How dare you!" She reached for him, fighting against futility to try to scratch and claw at his face, but the invisible, magical barrier he'd manifested prevented her from touching him.

"Stop acting like an infant."

He flicked his wrist again, sending her flying backward and slamming, hard, into a rough, thick tree trunk and knocking the breath clean out of her lungs.

"Just let me go!" she gasped. "Let me wake up! I don't want to be here with you. This meadow was for me and Alexius, and all you're doing is destroying it."

Timotheus stared down at her with his eyes like churning, molten gold, filling her with disgust. "Alexius gave up his immortality to be with *you*."

"At Melenia's request."

"You make theirs sound like a friendly partnership. Melenia used him."

"And he let her!"

"My, you're stubborn. Fine. I won't sully your memories of this imaginary location another moment." Suddenly the air began to swim and shimmer, and the scene around them began to shift and change.

Lucia stood up and found herself in the ice gardens of the Limerian palace. Standing before her was Timotheus, wearing a black cloak, leather boots, and the same hateful expression she remembered from the meadow.

"Now that I've proved I'm in control here," Timotheus said, "we can begin."

"Begin what?" she snarled.

"What has the fire Kindred told you? What does he say he wants?"

"Fire Kindred?" She offered him a thin smile. "I'm sure I've no idea what you're talking about."

"Does he think you can kill me?"

"Why would anyone want to kill you, Timotheus?" she asked. "I honestly can't imagine that, given how kindly and respectfully you've treated me so far."

"Has he told you what he plans to do after I'm dead?"

She inhaled deeply, ignoring her racing heart. "Your questions are meaningless to me and I'm not answering any of them."

"You killed Melenia," Timotheus said, not a trace of a question in his tone.

"Are you sure about that?"

He studied her, ignoring her deflections. "You drained her of her magic. Alexius taught you that trick. Very clever of him. It seems he had more control over his free will than I thought."

"How do you . . . ?" But then she stopped herself, because she suddenly realized how Timotheus knew about that night in the temple. In this dream, he could read her mind, so he could also see memories. Could all Watchers do this? Had Alexius possessed this skill as well?

"No, he didn't," Timotheus said, answering her silent question. "Though he would have been considered ancient in your world, Alexius was one of the youngest of our kind. I, however, am not so young. I am one of the first immortals created to protect the Kindred and all that lies beyond the Sanctuary."

"So was Melenia," she said.

He nodded. "There were six of us in the beginning."

"Now you're the only one left." She cocked her head. "So much for immortality."

"We are immortal. Not indestructible."

"Much gratitude for the reminder," Lucia said, her chest aching as she thought once again of Alexius.

"Kyan misleads you. He doesn't care for you. He's manipulating you to get to me."

"He's not manipulating me. I agreed to help him."

"So it seems that Lucia Damora is capable of speaking the truth." He shook his head, then looked at her with what Lucia recognized as pity. "You are filled with so much anger and pain and grief. Yet instead of letting those emotions run through you and make you stronger, you choose to unleash them on the rest of the world so that others might feel your pain as well."

"Are we done here?" Lucia snapped, trying her hardest not to think of anything truthful, lest Timotheus use it against her. "I'm getting very bored."

"You think this armor you've created will protect you, but it's only a distraction. Beneath it you're still the same spoiled and selfish girl you've always been."

Her mouth dropped open. If she could summon even a fraction of her magic, he would be engulfed in flames by now.

"Kyan's right," she snarled. "You are just like Melenia. And you deserve to be destroyed every bit as much as she did. Although, I suppose your death won't come as a surprise to you, will it?"

"Do you think I was surprised by Melenia's death, child?"

"Stop calling me 'child,'" she said through gritted teeth.

"I saw her death," he said, tapping his temple. "I saw it nearly seventeen years ago."

"You 'saw' it?" She frowned. "You're able to see the future, too?"

"On occasion."

Lucia couldn't wait to get away from this monster and return to Kyan, but now she found herself quite curious. The more she learned about him, the more power she'd have when they finally met in the flesh.

"Do all Watchers have prophetic abilities like yours?" she asked. "Melenia had my father believing she could see his future, and how powerful he'd become if he listened to her. However, she didn't see her own fate."

"Melenia didn't possess the sight. If she had, she would have been a very different Watcher."

"So you're the lucky one, are you?"

"Lucky?" Again, he didn't smile. His expression remained plaintive as he regarded her with those ancient golden eyes, set perfectly in his young golden face. "When Eva's magic was stolen from her, I became the heir to her visions. So yes, I am the only one in the Sanctuary lucky enough to see all possible futures, to have them tearing through my mind constantly and unbidden."

"*Possible* futures?" Lucia said.

His jaw tightened. "Choice, child. The freedom to choose makes all the difference. For instance, you have chosen to help the fire Kindred in his quest to destroy me. That choice determines both your fate and mine."

"Have you seen it? My future?"

"I've seen enough of it."

"Care to share any of what you've gleaned?"

"No."

She felt her whole body tense up with fury. "Then I'm sure you've seen the day when Kyan and I finally find a wheel you haven't tampered with."

"Oh, child. You are in so deep you don't even know you're drowning. You're right, I've sent my people out to slow you down. But not to stop you. Not to kill you."

She inhaled sharply, perplexed by Timotheus's confession and what it might mean if it were true.

"I've sent my people on other missions, too. Missions meant to change certain visions I find unacceptable or compromising to everything I'm here to protect. Mortals are so very fragile. They are foolish creatures who dance toward their own deaths with every idiotic decision they make. But that does not change the fact that every mortal life is precious. Some mortals simply require more protection than others."

"Mortals like me?"

"No, not mortals like you. You—you and your new friend— you're the ones from whom they'll need to be protected. Remember one thing, child."

"I told you to stop calling me 'child,'" she hissed.

"Remember. All magic comes with a price. A price that is never revealed until after the damage has been done."

"If I'm beyond saving, if I've already drowned, if I'm so

dangerous that the entire mortal world is threatened by my very existence, then what is this, Timotheus? What do you want from me?"

He took one step closer, locking his serious gaze with hers. "I need you to wake up, you stupid girl."

With a gasp, she sat up in her cot, her eyes wide open, staring wildly around at the dark, empty room.

"Thank you for introducing yourself to me, Timotheus," she whispered.

Kyan was right—that Watcher needed to die.

CHAPTER 15

AMARA

KRAESHIA

Emperor Cortas kept the king waiting two full days before he agreed to receive him. The thought of how insulted King Gaius must have been by that snub brought Amara quite a bit of amusement.

Amara's grandmother had told her that the men were meeting for a private feast in the banquet hall. The princess hadn't been invited, but that didn't stop her from going.

As Amara breezed into the room, her head held high, she felt the disapproving gaze of Dastan. Due to his nearly exact resemblance to Ashur, Amara had been avoiding her eldest brother ever since his return from sea, and Dastan hadn't gone out of his way to find her, either.

Elan, as always, stayed close to his father's side, as if the emperor had developed an Elan-shaped tumor.

Seeing Amara, the emperor narrowed his pale eyes at her uninvited presence. But before he could say a word about it, King Gaius entered the room flanked by his bodyguards, both dressed as finely as any nobleman.

A smile parted the emperor's lips, and his fine silk robes swished as he approached the king. "Ah, Gaius Damora. Finally, we're able to meet."

The king pressed his right hand against his heart and bowed shallowly from the waist—the traditional Kraeshian greeting. Amara was mildly impressed that he'd learned this custom. "Emperor Cortas, this is a pleasure beyond words. Your Jewel is just that . . . a precious treasure unlike any I've ever seen before. Stunning. I can see why it's reputed to be the most beautiful place in the known world, without competition."

"I hope it's not too vain of me to agree with you."

The emperor had prepared a table laden with Kraeshian delicacies. Vibrantly colorful fruits and vegetables grown right there in the Jewel, served with fresh kintha herbs and rich saffra oils. The Kraeshian diet eschewed all meat except for fish, and today there seemed to be no species unaccounted for—smoked salmus, red prawns, shelled lobrarus, to name but a few. An artful spread of sweets was arranged on a separate table, including indigo-berry tarts and sugar-cakes of the most intricate details and designs, and all nearly too beautiful to eat.

Amara watched the king with careful curiosity. Every gesture, every word, every sneaking glance. She had to admit his little act was quite convincing. If she didn't already know what a conniving snake he was, she'd believe he was actually enjoying the company around him. His words were smooth, his demeanor charming and polite, and he was handsome and charismatic.

Very unlike what one would expect of a man who'd earned the nickname of the King of Blood.

Amara drew closer to him, pretending to admire the dining table so she could listen in on his conversation with her father.

"These are my sons," the emperor said, placing a hand on Dastan's shoulder. "Dastan, my firstborn, undefeated in every battle he'd ever commanded . . ."

"Yes, of course. We speak of this young man's fine reputation all the way back in Mytica. Congratulations on your recent acquisition of Castoria," the king said.

Dastan pressed his hand to his heart and bowed. "Thank you. And since you're aware of my victories I suppose it's fortunate that we're meeting on friendly ground, isn't it, your grace?"

King Gaius smiled. "This couldn't be more true."

"And this is Elan," said the emperor, patting the boy's back and prompting him to perform the Kraeshian greeting. "I like to think of him as my most trusted vizier, one whose opinion is always invaluable to me. In all his twenty-three years, I don't believe he's ever told a single lie. Correct, my peach of a boy?"

"Correct," Elan agreed. He stood as if sewn to his father's sleeve, like a child afraid of getting lost.

Elan really was so sweet, so without guile, and Amara had always hoped they'd one day become close. Yet despite his gentle nature, he was still a Kraeshian male, raised not to show an iota of respect or regard to his sister or any other woman.

"Unfortunately, Ashur, my youngest son, isn't here to greet you. But I'm sure you had plenty of time to become acquainted with him during his stay in your little kingdom."

Every muscle in Amara's chest clenched up at the sound of her dead brother's name. To steady herself and keep from keeling over, she took a sip from her glass of sparkling wine.

"I did indeed," Gaius said. "Ashur is a charming boy, you must be so proud of him."

Instead of nodding proudly, as he had when introducing

Dastan and Elan, the emperor winced a bit and then pursed his lips. "Ashur reminds me of his mother in so many ways. Always gallivanting around the world, searching for treasures."

"Is he successful in his quests?"

"Not nearly often enough to justify the time and finances necessary to fund these little excursions."

With that, the emperor gestured for his guests to take their seats at the table and eat of the feast. Amara watched as Gaius's two bodyguards filled their plates with piles of food, and when Felix caught her looking, he grinned and winked at her.

She didn't find his boldness offensive, but rather took it as proof that he hadn't been to very many formal banquets before.

As the guests tucked into their meal, the emperor drove the conversation, informing Gaius about a new structure currently being built in the Jewel, an auditorium that would play host to poets, singers, and theater troupes.

"My, that sounds wonderful. Culture is so important to the vitality of civilized countries," the king said.

"I'm surprised you think so," Amara said, taking the opportunity to speak up. "Especially since artistic endeavors are discouraged in Limeros."

Gaius lifted his goblet and swirled his cider around thoughtfully. "That is true, princess. Our radiant goddess did not approve of frivolity or flights of whimsy, and if Limerians are anything it's loyal to our beloved goddess's laws. However, having lately spent so much time in Auranos, I've come to realize that the arts have the ability to elevate the spirits of citizens during difficult times. Art gives them hope. And without hope, what is there to live for?"

"Well said, Gaius," said the emperor, spearing a chunk of fried squar fish and dipping it into a spicy shanut sauce. "And please excuse my daughter's boldness; I was not aware she'd be joining us today. But, yes, hope is a beautiful thing—and I love beautiful things!"

The guests talked and ate happily straight through until dessert. When the servants had cleared all the plates away, the emperor leaned back and patted his large belly. "Now, Gaius, my friend. Tell me, why are you here?"

The king raised his brow a tiny fraction of an inch. "I'm here, your eminence, to get to know you better. To understand your intentions. I know you soon plan to conquer Mytica."

Amara stifled a gasp at the king's unexpected bluntness and gazed around the room to see the others' surprised reactions in the moment of echoing silence that followed. While the king's two guards remained as composed as the sentries they were, she did notice a momentary raise of Felix's brows.

The emperor acknowledged this with a nod. "I must confess, given its size, Mytica hasn't been a high priority for me. Your country would make for just a tiny speck of dirt on my map. But yes, Ashur's great interest in your history and legends drew my attention. Your shores are a mere leap from my Jewel, so the cost and effort to acquire the land would be minimal. And then there are your vineyards, which are reputed to produce the finest wine in the world. I think it would make a nice little addition to my empire."

"I see. And when were you and your sons planning to visit my lovely speck of dirt?"

The emperor laughed. "Let's not talk strategy, Gaius. Today we sit around this table as friends, not enemies."

"As a fellow leader I admire how confident you are that Mytica would be so easily captured."

The emperor smiled, drained his glass of wine, and signaled to a servant to pour him another. "Dastan? I believe this is your area of expertise."

"We have great reason to be confident," Dastan said, taking over for his father. "Your army is currently scattered across all of Mytica, and your coastal defenses are laughable at best. We outnumber you one hundred to one."

King Gaius nodded cordially. "You're right, of course. With those statistics on your side, Kraeshia would easily conquer Mytica."

"Good, then!" the emperor said. "We're all aware of the situation between our two lands, and it seems we've no more business to discuss." He stood up from the table and placed his hands on his hips. "Now, if you're here to surrender your country in person, you will save much gold and the lives of many of your people."

The king frowned. "Surrender? I think you may have misunderstood me. I did not come here to serve Mytica to you on a golden platter."

"Then explain it to us again," Dastan said. "What, exactly, did you come here for?"

"I came to issue you a warning. A friendly one, for now. And also to make you an offer."

The emperor's jovial expression faded, though he looked no less pompous than usual. Amara bit her bottom lip, fascinated by what might happen next.

Her father sat back down at the table. "A warning, you say."

"Yes."

"You, the king of a land as tiny as Mytica, have a warning for me, a leader who has conquered a hundred kingdoms?"

Gaius smiled calmly and allowed a moment of silence to pass before going on. "I have to assume that Prince Ashur shared some of his favorite Mytican legends with you, didn't he? Before he left for his visit?"

Elan nodded, clearly eager to contribute. "There were two legends he loved. The one of the magic of the elements trapped in rocks. And the one about immortal hawks that travel to other worlds. Rocks and hawks."

"That's correct, Elan," said King Gaius, nodding with smug satisfaction. "You're speaking of the Kindred and the Watchers—two of the most important figures in two of our most fascinating legends about the unlimited magic that can be found in my kingdom."

"Are you trying to tell us that these legends are true?" Dastan said smoothly.

"Not trying. Stating as fact."

"If that's so," the emperor spat, "then all you're doing is giving me reassurance—the reassurance Ashur has been unable to deliver—that Mytica is worth my trouble."

King Gaius went on, undeterred. "There's a prophecy tied to the legends, your eminence. It foretells of a mortal girl able to wield the *elementia* of a sorceress and light the way to the Kindred, the lost elemental crystals." He paused, taking a slow look around the table of wealthy Kraeshians. "My daughter, Lucia, is this sorceress."

Gaius's revelation was met with stark silence, broken only when the emperor let out a sharp laugh. "Your daughter is the prophesied sorceress? How terribly convenient for you."

"She's my daughter, but not by blood. I found her when she was an infant, and took her from her true parents with the aid of witches and blood magic. I waited sixteen years for her to come into her powers, but it was well worth the wait. It was her magic that allowed me overthrow the Auranian king and conquer his land in less than two days. And it's her magic that led me to the Kindred."

"Oh my, you Myticans do enjoy sharing such interesting fables! But words are but words, and only proof is proof. I doubt there's anyone—in your kingdom or mine—who has seen any real evidence that this princess is a sorceress."

"Actually, *I* have," Amara said. Every single pair of eyes at the table shot to her, and she smiled. "I befriended Lucia when I was in Mytica, and I personally witnessed her magic. I promised to keep her secret, but this seems to me a situation that requires me to go back on my word. Everything the king says about his daughter is true."

The room had settled down to an awe-filled silence, one that not even the emperor himself could have manufactured.

"You knew this?" he said, slamming his fist down on the table. "Why didn't you tell me?"

She allowed herself a moment of satisfaction that this information had stunned him. "You didn't ask."

The king nodded. "Princess Amara, perhaps you're also aware that, thanks to my daughter, I now possess all four crystals of the Kindred."

Amara had to take a sip of her wine to stop herself from replying with a laugh. "All four?" she said once she was composed. "That is rather incredible."

And a rather huge lie, she thought. After all, *she* had the water Kindred, not this deceptive king, and the other three orbs could be anywhere.

"Yes, your eminence," the king addressed the emperor again. "I have found all four Kindred. To unlock even one would make me a god."

The emperor regarded him with an expression of waning patience. "How humble of you, then, to travel here by ship instead of flying through the air."

"This is absurd, father," Dastan interjected. "These children's tales are a waste of your valuable time."

"Perhaps. But Amara claims that what the king says is true. My daughter may not approve of the life I've laid out for her in my empire, but she's never lied to me."

Amara allowed herself an internal grin. For such a cunning and powerful man, her father really was quite stupid when it came to women.

The emperor studied Gaius. "Prove your claim."

"Very well." King Gaius stood up, reached into his coat, and drew out a small milky-white sphere. Dancing inside of it was a pale, wispy shadow.

Amara gasped. "The air Kindred."

The king shot her a sharp look.

"Am I right? Ashur gave me books to read about the legends," Amara said, trying now to inject some uncertainty into her voice. "The air Kindred is said to be an orb of moonstone. Is that really it?"

"It is."

The emperor stood, strode briskly over to Gaius, and peered at the orb. "How interesting."

"I've come here to warn you," Gaius announced, pulling the orb closer to him and away from the emperor, "that if you attempt to conquer Mytica, my daughter will fight back with the power of a sorceress who can capsize entire fleets of ships. Who can freeze the Silver Sea with a single thought. Who can incinerate your soldiers into piles of ash and dust. Who, with the swipe of her little finger, can steal the breath of any enemy who dares cross her path. No army, no matter how large, can compete with the strength of her *elementia*."

The emperor's lips were thin, his gaze fierce. "And your offer?"

"I am offering you a share in my treasure. This," he said,

indicating the orb, "will be yours. Once I reveal the secret to unlocking the power within this crystal, it will give you the gift of air magic. In return, you will agree to embrace Mytica, not as a conquest but as a partner, and you will share your empire with me equally."

So *this* was why the king had come to Kraeshia. Amara was both stunned and impressed by his audacity.

The tension now hanging in the air was nearly as visible as smoke.

"Half of my empire in exchange for a polished rock?" Despite his sarcasm, there was a glimmer of worry in the emperor's expression that made Amara believe he no longer found any of this funny.

"That's right," Gaius said, calmly gazing at the crystal.

This banquet was far more exciting than Amara had anticipated. Even though she knew the king had lied and bluffed his way into this situation, he did possess at least one Kindred. And Lucia *was* the prophesied sorceress.

Her father would be wise to take the king very seriously.

"You say you know how to unlock the magic within the Kindred," Amara said. "Can you share with us how you came to know this secret?"

Gaius gripped the orb of moonstone and studied Amara for a moment. "I know this secret because my mother told it to me. She was a witch, one with vast knowledge of the immortals' world. She knew that one day I would be the one to find and possess the Kindred, so of course she told me what to do once I claimed my destiny."

Amara considered his words. "Your story is sweet, but it makes me wonder why so many accused witches in Limeros have been executed on your order over the years if your own mother was one herself. I'm sure there's a fascinating explanation there that has nothing to do with the laws of your goddess."

When he met her gaze this time, his eyes were black and cold and bottomless. "You have no idea, princess."

The emperor stepped forward, halting the conversation between Amara and the king. "What's to stop me from taking that crystal and killing you right now, Gaius?" Felix and Milo rose to their feet, and the emperor flicked his hand dismissively at them. "Unless you're a couple of sorcerers, you can't protect your king from me."

"You could kill me and take this Kindred," the king acknowledged. "But it will be useless to you if you don't know how to unlock its magic."

The emperor scoffed. "I could torture the secret out of you in minutes."

The king didn't flinch. In fact, his gaze grew hard and steely. "You would do so at your own peril. Besides, such a secret would do you no good at all, here in Kraeshia. And should you arrive in Mytica without me, my daughter will be waiting to destroy every last one of you." He pocketed the orb. "I've had my say and I've made you my offer. Surely you'll want to take some time to think about it. This meeting is over." He nodded at his guards.

Felix offered Amara a slight shrug and another small grin as he accompanied the king out of the room.

"Father?" Dastan said quietly when all had fallen silent in the hall.

"It seems I have a great deal to think about," the emperor replied.

Yes, Amara thought. *You certainly do.*

Later that evening, Amara wandered the hallways, feeling too energetic to retire to her chambers for the night. She couldn't stop thinking about the way the king had taken full command of that meeting. She'd wondered why he'd been so foolish to come here, thinking it was a mistake for anyone to try to confront her father.

She'd forgotten King Gaius's reputation.

He was ruthless, power hungry, and now claimed his mother had been a witch.

Fascinating.

Her reverie was broken when she bumped into Felix.

"Stop," she said.

"Stopping," he replied, then gestured at the doorway beside him. "Luckily, this is my room anyway."

"I know you didn't grow up in a palace, but you should at least know that it's not very smart or polite to wink at a princess, especially during a formal event," she said.

"Well, I've never been accused of being smart or polite before."

She regarded him for a silent moment. He was tall, and she liked the broadness of his shoulders. And despite the fact that he kept tugging at his collar, she also liked the way he filled out his fine tailored clothing.

"Your nose is crooked," she said.

He touched it, then frowned. "It's been broken a few times. Frankly, I'm lucky to still have a nose."

"It's quite ugly."

"Um . . ."

"I like it."

"Thanks?" He cleared his throat. "Is there something I can do for you, princess?"

"Actually, yes."

"And what's that?"

"You can take me to your bed."

Felix blinked. "I'm not sure I heard you correctly."

"You heard me just fine. After a day of being ignored while two powerful, ruthless men discuss politics and magic, I'm in need of a little attention." She slid her hands up his chest and to the nape of his neck, then pulled him closer and kissed him.

He didn't resist.

She smiled against his lips. "One night. That's all I want from you."

He pushed open the door to his room with his elbow and gave her a wicked grin. "It would be my pleasure, princess."

CHAPTER 16

CLEO

LIMEROS

"Let me try to understand this," Nic said to Cleo. He was with her in her chambers while Nerissa helped her with her hair. "Jonas Agallon storms into the palace grounds, holds a sword to the prince's throat, at which time Magnus learns you've been lying about working with Jonas for months, and, instead of killing you both, he's decided to give you your kingdom back?"

Cleo looked up at Nic's reflection in her mirror. "It does sound rather difficult to believe when the story's put like that. Do you think he's lying?"

"Apologies, but did you just ask me if I think Prince Magnus, the King of Blood's son and the brother of a power-crazed sorceress, would lie to the former princess of Auranos? Are you being serious right now?"

Nic's smugness had a way of annoying Cleo to no end—especially because he was often right to be smug and suspicious. And right now, she wanted to hold on to the belief that Magnus was being sincere. After all, if Magnus did want his father dead, he'd need Jonas's help to carry that through. And if he cared only for Limeros, and didn't want the trouble that came with controlling all three kingdoms, then all of this really did make sense.

Luckily, Nic wasn't the only person whose opinion she trusted.

It was so wonderful to have Nerissa, the pretty girl with short dark hair and more wisdom in her eyes than any eighteen-year-old she'd ever seen, back with her. For the seemingly small favor of bringing Nerissa up north from Auranos, Cleo was grateful to Magnus without reservation. He could have easily denied her request.

Not that Cleo would have accepted that response as final.

Cleo grasped the girl's hand. "Nerissa, what do you think?"

Nerissa placed an opal-handled hairbrush down on the vanity table and looked back at Cleo's reflection. "You say you've already agreed to go along with this new plan," she said, "so I think you should stay true to that agreement. At this stage in the prince's scheme, there's very little to do with you, and much more to do with Jonas. Nothing has really changed, it seems. Except, perhaps, your ongoing question of whether the prince is capable of being honest about his true agenda."

"I suppose you're right," Cleo said.

"You said he's forgiven you for conspiring with Jonas."

"He says he understands why I did what I did."

Nic let out an exasperated groan. "How have you two not figured this out yet? If the prince's mouth is moving, he's lying."

Cleo's eyes flashed with frustration. "And what if he isn't lying this time? We just give up the first chance we've had in months to reclaim our kingdom?"

"But what if he is, once again, misleading you? Cleo, damn it," he swore under his breath, "I can't lose you, too. Got it?" His tone was fierce, but his eyes had grown glossy. He rubbed at them and turned away from her. "I need some air, even if it might turn my lungs to ice."

He left the room, and Cleo rose to her feet to go after him.

"Let him clear his head," Nerissa said, placing her hand on the princess's shoulder. "It'll give you the time to do the same."

"Nerissa . . . I don't know what to believe an used to be so clear and now . . . I'm just so co caught. "I haven't even had a chance to speak to

Magnus had put the rebel and his friends the far side of the castle, but Cleo didn't know the prince made it clear he wasn't going to tell

"Yes, of course you need to talk to him," Ner you need to talk to the prince. If you peel back mosity and suspicion and . . . confusion you feel, perhaps your sense of clarity isn't as marred as you think it is."

The thought of talking to Magnus after all that had unfolded in the throne room sent a shiver running through her.

No. She wouldn't allow herself to fear him. Hate him? Loathe him? Distrust him? Yes. But never fear. She'd decided that long ago.

Still, Cleo shook her head. "It's the Limerian day of silence. I wouldn't even know where to find him." Cleo had never experienced a single day of silence at the Auranian palace, and to witness such quiet in a place as stark as this northern castle was about as jarring as she could imagine.

"This day of worship will only make it much easier to find and speak to him in peace," Nerissa reasoned. "Everyone in Limeros has gathered in the temples and village centers to worship their goddess. And I happen to know exactly where the prince has gone to do his worshipping."

"Where?"

"He's right here in the palace, spending the day in the royal temple." Cleo gave her a look of surprise—she hadn't even known there was a royal temple on the palace grounds—and Nerissa smiled. "I've made very good friends with Enzo, the young palace guard. He's full of useful information. Much gratitude for introducing us, princess."

"*Very* good friends, are you?" Cleo knew all about Nerissa's proficiency with manipulating willing and gullible men and couldn't help but be amused. "I'm glad to see you're already having fun so soon after your arrival."

"Limeros is far more enticing than I'd previously guessed. And, frankly, so is Enzo."

"Well, I'm just glad that one of is happy here."

Nerissa's smile widened. "Go and have that talk with the prince. I have great faith that you—more than anyone else—can summon words from Prince Magnus today."

Cleo walked to the west side of the castle, flush against the high cliffs. She came to the end of a corridor and pushed open two tall ebony doors engraved with a twisting maze of snakes. Inside, she'd expected to find a small replica of the central temple near Ravencrest—dark and foreboding, so unlike the temples devoted to Cleo's namesake goddess, which were adorned with mosaics, gold, and jewels.

Instead, while this small palace temple did have black stone floors and hard wooden pews in front of an obsidian altar, it had another feature so surprising to Cleo that she couldn't hold back a gasp. Across the temple from its entrance were three floor-to-ceiling windows that looked out on the Silver Sea, giving her a full view of the setting sun, the sky alive with colors—red, orange, purple, and indigo.

She managed to tear her gaze away from the stunning sight,

then scanned the room for worshippers. She saw only one figure, Prince Magnus, seated at the front, facing the windows with his back to her.

She walked slowly down the aisle and sat in a pew directly behind the prince.

"This view," Cleo said after a few moments. "I can see why you'd choose to spend the day here. So beautiful—and, I must admit, so unexpected in a place like this."

He didn't reply, but Cleo wasn't discouraged. She scooted over and leaned forward against the back of his pew. His dark brown hair had grown quite long in the last months, and he hadn't bothered to trim it. He didn't smell of warm leather, as he did when he went riding. Today, he smelled only of sandalwood, as usual, and of citrus. Was that a hint of lemon she caught?

Lemons were a delicacy here in frozen Limeros, very expensive to import.

"Do you put sugar on your lemons?" she asked. "I've never been able to eat them without sugar. I've always preferred to have my lemons squeezed and made into a sweet drink."

Again, Magnus didn't reply, but if nothing else, this was much more pleasant than arguing.

Her gaze settled on his scar—a jagged line that stretched from the top of his right ear to the corner of his mouth. The king had done this to Magnus, sliced his cheek for trying to steal a pretty dagger during a visit to the Auranian palace.

He'd been seven years old. To receive such a violent punishment at such a young age . . .

"Why are you here?" he finally asked, his deep voice just above a whisper.

The sound of his broken silence jarred her from her thoughts. "He speaks."

"Only to ask why you've interrupted me at such an obviously inappropriate time."

"I know about the traditions of the day, but even so, you spend far too much time alone, thinking. So much solitude isn't good for the soul." She glanced down and saw a leather-bound book balancing on his lap. "Are you doing some more research on magic?"

"How wonderful that you've chosen to be so talkative today, of all days." He gripped the edges of the book, whose cover was stamped in gold with the name LUKAS and an outline of what looked like a small country or island.

"Lukas. Your middle name," she said.

"Very good, princess. You've been paying attention." He traced his index finger over the letters. "And this is where that name comes from. The Isle of Lukas."

That's right. The isle was familiar to her, a fifty-mile journey from the southwest tip of Auranos, but she hadn't thought of it in ages. "I've heard of it. I wanted to visit some summers ago, but at the time my father was furious at me for sneaking some friends of mine into a royal ball and refused to send me as punishment." She frowned. "They teach art lessons there, don't they?"

"Among other things."

She saw now that the book did not come from the library, but rather was a sketchbook, similar to the one her sister used to have. Emilia had attended art lessons on the island, the same summer she'd discovered that her archery skills far surpassed her talent for drawing trees and flowers. Cleo's mother had also been a student there long ago. Elena Bellos's sketchbook was one of the only mementos that Cleo had of the mother who'd tragically died giving birth to her.

"You were named after an island?" Cleo asked.

"The queen wanted to use my grandfather's name, Davidus, as

she believed I'd one day become a great king, like he had been. It was my father who insisted upon Lukas. He spent a season on the isle when he was young, just as I did only three summers ago. I suppose the fact that he named me after the place suggests that he valued his time there. Or perhaps he hated it and wanted a constant reminder. He's never bothered to explain to me his reasons."

Cleo couldn't help but laugh. "You're saying that both you and King Gaius are former fine arts pupils? Don't Limerians frown upon such frivolous pursuits?"

"There's something honorable in learning how to perfectly render something's likeness—the kind of honor that makes my father think art can sometimes be a worthy pastime."

"*Perfectly*, you say. Let me see for myself, then, how well you can render." He remained still, his hands still grasping the sketchbook, so she leaned farther over the bench. "Come on, don't be bashful."

Feeling bold, she reached out and took it out of his hands, and he didn't stop her.

Cleo expected to flip through the book and find nothing more than half-filled pages of abandoned, uninspired sketches from Magnus's bored summer on Lukas. Instead, she found that the entire sketchbook was full, from beginning to end, with dozens of beautiful drawings, each one different and more impressive than the next. "These are incredible," she said, unable to look away from her most surprising discovery yet.

The first half of the book was filled with drawings depicting various glimpses of the Isle of Lukas, from sprawling landscapes, to intricately detailed close-ups of small rodents with bushy tails, to portraits of young people Cleo assumed to be Magnus's classmates. But when Cleo reached the second half, she noticed an abrupt change in subject matter. The rest of the sketchbook contained only portraits, and they were all of Lucia.

Lucia gazing out of a window, Lucia walking through the gardens, Lucia holding a flower, Lucia smiling, Lucia laughing.

Each one depicted her perfect likeness, no detail left uncared for. Only the portrait on the final page was unfinished. The only thing Magnus had sketched were two eyes that were unmistakably Lucia's—drawn so vividly they seemed to pierce right through Cleo.

He'll always be mine, Lucia seemed to be saying to her. *This is the only proof you need.*

Magnus pulled the book away from her and glanced down at the final picture of his adopted sister.

Cleo's mouth had gone dry. "This is why you came here today, why you wanted to be alone. Not to honor this day of worship, but to look at your sketches. You're worried about her, aren't you?"

Magnus didn't respond, but his jaw tightened. She moved to sit right next to him, and when she placed her hand on top of his, he tensed, but didn't pull away.

"You love her," she said.

"More than anything."

She'd always known this to be true, no matter what had happened between her and Magnus. Still, something inside Cleo twisted unpleasantly at his easy admission. She pushed past it. "And she loves you too," she said. "But she's not herself right now. That man, Kyan . . . he's manipulating her."

"The man of fire. I've heard rumors of him in recent months. I used to think that's all they were: rumors." He looked down at Cleo's hand. "You know, it doesn't feel like all that long ago that we were sitting in a different temple, having another grave conversation."

She remembered that night in the City of Gold far too clearly. Her need to align with him was so strong that she thought it might actually be a possibility.

"*Rather than always fighting,*" she'd said to him, "*we could find a way to help each other.*"

Since then, Cleo had learned a great deal about the dangers of just letting her true thoughts pour right out of her mouth. Those were the kinds of thoughts that could later be used against her as weapons. "You were drunk that night," she said, trying to put on a dismissive tone.

"I was. Far too drunk. That was also the night I took Amara to my bed. I found I needed to be with someone much less . . . belligerent than you. It was refreshing, for a while."

She tried not to react with any of the displeasure she felt about this subject. "We all make harsh errors in judgment."

"Indeed." For the first time since she'd entered the temple, his flat, dark eyes met hers directly. "It's too bad, really. We made an incredible match, Amara and I. Her skills as a lover are beyond compare—even to those of the most coveted courtesan. Perhaps if she'd confided the true reason of her visit to me, I would have shared the Kindred with her."

Cleo withdrew her hand from his, her blood turning to acid. "I don't believe you."

"Really? Is that any less believable than a secret union between you and Jonas Agallon?"

She'd been wrong. His eyes weren't flat and emotionless; they were full of simmering outrage. "I thought you said you understand why I did that."

"Understand? Yes. Approve of? No. You have a stunning talent for concealing the truth. I rarely meet a liar as skilled as you are. Congratulations, princess."

How had it taken her this long to realize that he was furious with her?

"So what?" she said, abandoning all hope of staying diplomatic and diving right into interrogation. "Were *you* lying too? About this new alliance? About what will happen afterward?"

"Finally, the princess reveals her true intentions, the real reason you've come up to me on this day of worship. You've no interest in the details of my past at all."

"Can't it be both? Why can't I want information about my future and be curious about your past as well?"

"We're done here." He stood up and walked toward the exit, and she hurried after him to block his path.

"No, we're *not* done here," she hissed.

"Answer me this, princess. What exactly is there between you and Agallon? Is it more than a friendly alliance between a princess and a rebel?"

"What do you mean?"

He glared at her as if she were a child purposely avoiding an answer. "Are you in love with him?"

Her mouth dropped open. *"What?"*

"Under any other circumstances I wouldn't care, of course. But if the two of you were in love, it would make it much more complicated for the three of us to go forward."

"You're insane."

"A yes or a no would suffice. I'll take your response as a . . . probably. Good to know, princess. Much gratitude."

She grabbed his arm and held on tightly.

He glared down his nose at her. "Let go of me."

"Not yet. I need you to hear what I have to say to you."

Cleo sought to hold his gaze, trying to see past the anger and uncertainty in his eyes. Was there anything else there? The new mask he wore was marvelous, thicker and stronger than ever, covering every emotion but anger.

But every mask could be cracked.

"What do you need to say to me?" he finally prompted.

She took a deep breath and stood as tall as she could. "I did fall in love with someone. Someone whom many would say was completely wrong for me. But I didn't care."

He now studied her for a long, heavy moment. "Did you, princess? And who was that?"

Boldly, she placed her hand over his heart to feel its swift pace.

He looked down at it, his brows drawing together as he met her eyes.

"Do you really want to know?" she asked, her voice now soft.

He was silent so long that she wasn't sure he'd ever speak again. Then, finally he nodded once. "Yes."

He watched her with a darkening gaze as she bit her bottom lip. She'd seen that darkness in his eyes before, and she knew it didn't come from anger.

"Princess," he urged. "Tell me."

She met his eyes directly. "His name was Theon Ranus," she said. "And you murdered him."

Magnus pulled away from her, the growing tenderness in his expression slamming shut like an iron door.

"Sometimes I forget about that day." She tried to ignore the pain in her heart as she spoke. "But something always ends up reminding me. Good evening, Magnus."

Cleo left the temple and didn't look back.

There was a message waiting for Cleo when she returned to her chambers.

Meet me in my room.—Nerissa

Cleo rushed to the servants' wing and knocked on Nerissa's door.

"Good, you're here," Nerissa said, opening the door immediately and grabbing Cleo's wrist to pull her inside. She peeked out the door, glanced up and down the hallway, then turned around to grin at the princess. "I'll leave you two alone to talk. But please, don't be long."

"Nerissa, what are you—?"

But before Cleo could finish her sentence Nerissa slipped out of the room and closed the door behind her.

"Well, your highness. After a small eternity it seems we're finally alone again."

Cleo spun on her heels, eyes wide, and found herself face-to-face with Jonas. The rebel was no longer wearing his ridiculous eye patch today, which was a relief—especially since, when she'd first seen him, she'd thought he'd had a horrible accident. Or that Magnus had done it to him.

Cleo met Jonas's greeting with stunned silence, and then his pleased expression turned tentative. "I'm sorry for the manner in which I arrived. It was not my intention to implicate you . . . for that I want to kick myself. Trust me, Lys has promised to throttle me at her earliest opportunity for nearly getting us all killed. I was stupid and irresponsible, but I assure you that I—"

Cleo ran across the room and threw herself into his arms. "I was so worried about you!"

"Oh." He stiffened, then gave a little laugh and pulled her closer. "And here I was expecting a painful slap. I like this much better."

"Why did you come here? You must have known how much danger you'd be putting yourself in."

"Why?" He brushed her hair back from her face. "To save you, of course. And to kill the prince. In that order."

"I don't need to be saved."

"Yes, well, how was I supposed to know that? You disappeared from Auranos. You could have been dead for all I knew. You didn't send me any messages to let me know you were safe."

"And where should I have sent them? To some tree house in the Wildlands? Or should I have sent them through Nerissa and put her in further danger?"

"If there's anyone who can handle herself, it's Nerissa."

"So can I."

"Yes, I see that now. It seems you've managed to tame the darkest of beasts." He tried to smile, but Cleo saw that his expression was strained. "And here I thought you loathed each other."

"We do. *I* do." Enough of this, she didn't have much time with him, and she wanted to spend it discussing more important matters. "Jonas, I know you received my most recent message. The instructions to go to the Temple of Cleiona . . ."

"I did. And I followed them, exactly. In fact, we were still there when you and your entourage arrived."

"You . . . what?"

That mischievous look had reappeared, and his grin seemed much less strained than before. "I know it was risky to stay behind, but I couldn't resist the chance to see the disappointment on the prince's face when he realized someone had gotten there before him to claim the earth Kindred. Priceless."

A wave of relief fluttered in her chest, and she ignored the dig against Magnus. "So you have it."

"Oh, yes." He reached into his pocket and pulled out an obsidian orb small enough to sit on his palm.

Somehow, she'd forgotten how to breathe. "That's it," she managed to get out. She reached for the orb with a trembling hand. "The earth Kindred! It's real!"

"And it's yours." He took her hand and placed the crystal in her palm. "I've been keeping it safe for you. And warm. So warm I thought it might hatch."

This reality was more than she could have hoped for—more than she was *letting* herself hope for. The earth Kindred, right here, endless earth magic at her fingertips. With this in her possession, she could easily take her throne back. She felt the tingle of magic run up her arm as she stared at its glossy surface, and she was certain she saw an ebony shadow swirling within the orb.

She was breathless. "Jonas. . . . Thank you. I promise to reward you handsomely when this is all over—you'll have riches beyond your wildest dreams. And what about the air and fire Kindred? Did you claim them, too?"

"Well, princess, we did travel to both of the locations you described, drew the symbols on the ground in blood just like you said . . . but it didn't work. Not like it did with the earth Kindred. This is the only one I have. I'm sorry."

"No, Jonas, please don't be sorry. Finding just one is miracle enough. This is wonderful." She squeezed the orb, finding that the mere weight of it in her palm gave her strength. "Now, how does it work?"

Jonas's brow wrinkled up with uncertainty. "I have absolutely no idea. You had such clear instructions for how to find it . . . don't you know how to use it, as well?"

She stared at him for several stunned moments, then started to laugh. "I have absolutely no idea either!"

"That is unfortunate. I was completely prepared for you to transform into an all-powerful earth goddess tonight and vanquish us all."

Though Cleo was disappointed that, after all this, she still didn't have access to all the secrets and powers of the Kindred, she also felt a large wave of relief. If she didn't know how to unlock the earth Kindred's power, that meant Amara probably didn't know how to unlock the water Kindred either.

"Princess, I have a plan," Jonas said in an unusually serious tone. "I believe I've now proven myself worthy of your trust, so I do hope you'll listen with care."

Cleo shook her head. "I've never doubted you."

"Never? Really?"

She felt her cheeks grow warm. "Well, after you kidnapped me—*twice*—and tried to kill me, we did eventually come to a mutual understanding."

"I'd feel so much better about things if you could forget about the kidnappings. At least the first one."

She raised her brow. "Those days I spent trapped in your sister's shed were very unpleasant for me."

"I dug you a very nice makeshift chamber pot. I wouldn't do that for just any royal hostage, you know."

She grimaced. "Thanks for providing that memory. I *do* want to forget that."

"I knew you'd come around."

Cleo smiled and looked back at the orb, her thoughts swirling in time with the shadow of magic trapped deep inside of it. "So, what's your plan?"

"I don't trust the prince. Not for a moment."

"No? You seemed to have trusted him well enough when you agreed to help kill his father—before and after he put you in chains."

"Yes, well, luckily I've had time to think about it since. I've proven my trustworthiness to you, to many people over these last months, but he hasn't. I'm not willing to take any more risks when it comes to him. Lys, Olivia, and I are leaving—and you're coming with us. We can figure out how to get that magic rock to work and get our land back all on our own once we're far away from here."

Cleo had had many opportunities to simply walk away from the Limerian palace ever since that very first night when they'd arrived at the docks of Ravencrest. But she hadn't. She felt she had more to learn here, more to gain, and that running away would only keep her in the same place she was now. "I know the prince is a brute with morals that can only kindly be described as questionable. I don't want to be around him any more than you do. But I need to stay here a while longer. I need to know where the king is and what he's planning."

"We can track the king from anywhere."

She shook her head. "That won't be nearly as easy to do without the resources and intelligence in Limeros. Jonas, I also have a plan, and I hope you'll be willing to help me with it."

Jonas opened his mouth, as if ready to argue with her decision. But then he nodded. "Very well. Tell me."

"We have a crystal, but we don't know how to unlock its magic. However, I believe a Watcher would know this secret."

"Well, then let me just snap my fingers and transport us to the Sanctuary to find one," Jonas said, a sarcastic edge in his voice.

"Please, just listen to me. I know an exiled Watcher who lives in Paelsia. She spoke to me of legends, told me stories I'd never read or even heard of anywhere else. Real accounts of Eva, the original sorceress, and her love affair with a mortal hunter. Eva gave birth to his baby before the goddesses killed her for the Kindred." Cleo paused to take a deep breath, then steadied her gaze on Jonas's again.

His expression grew more rigid with every word. She could see the patience feuding with skepticism in his brown eyes. "Go on."

"I need you and your friends to visit this exiled Watcher and find out if she knows how to unlock this magic. Nic can go with you; he'll know where to find her."

He raised a brow. "You're suggesting that Nic, Lys, Olivia, and I just run off and leave you here, all alone with a prince who could very well be plotting your demise?"

"I'll be fine. I can take care of myself."

"Yes, you've proven that very well." He rubbed his chin and frowned. "I will say this much: Your plan is much more intriguing than mine."

She tried not to smile at this. "High praise, rebel."

"You really think the prince will just let us leave the palace so easily?"

"Your own plan was to leave, wasn't it?"

"Yes, but that was with the certainty we wouldn't ever return. The security here isn't as impenetrable as it is in Auranos, but it's still a palace, and there are still numerous sentries who keep watch over all who enter or leave these grounds."

The rebel had made an excellent point. And even if Magnus hadn't officially announced to everyone here that the Paelsian rebel leader was currently a "guest" at the castle, he would have many questions if, suddenly, Jonas and his friends were to wander off unexpectedly.

"I'll speak with Magnus and give him an excellent reason for your temporary leave," she said with a confident nod. "I'll keep the earth Kindred here with me. That exiled Watcher may have been very kind and wise, but I'm not sure I trust even her with it."

Jonas crossed his arms and studied her. "And it'll be just that easy, will it? He'll simply take your word without question?"

"He'll have to. Otherwise my plan won't work."

"No, princess. Let me handle it. If I'm to agree to this, I don't want you tangled up in it at all. When he asks about me, you will simply say you have no idea where we went, that I left without saying a word. I'll deal with the ramifications when I return."

Her heart lifted. "So you're saying you'll do this? You'll go?"

Jonas paced to the other side of the small room, his arms still folded tightly over his chest.

She held her breath as she waited for his answer.

Finally, Jonas turned to face her again and gave her a grin. "It would be my honor, your highness. But when I come back, surely successful and impossibly heroic, I will ask for something in return. Something I haven't had in far too long."

Her heart leapt. "Anything. What is it?"

His smile grew. "A kiss from a princess."

CHAPTER 17

LUCIA

PAELSIA

If Kyan learned about Lucia's dream visit with Timotheus, he'd be furious. And since Lucia had quickly learned during their travels that the best kind of fire god was a calm fire god, she'd chosen not to speak a word of it to him.

Still, the dream had troubled—not to mention annoyed—her. Timotheus's goal had been to dissuade her from helping Kyan, but his abrasive manner and disrespectful words had only succeeded in renewing her commitment to the fire god's cause. Had Alexius been even half as unpleasant as his elder, Lucia wouldn't have bothered with him at all.

In hindsight, that would have been much better for everyone.

She put that hateful encounter with Timotheus out of her head and focused on her current quest: finding her true family.

Lucia and Kyan had been working together to pull information out of various Mytican witches through a combination of fire storms and truth extraction, and finally they had a solid lead to follow.

This lead took them to the village of Basilia near Trader's Harbor in Paelsia. The village was surrounded by vineyards, and thus its citizens subsisted on profits made from visiting ships and wine exports to Auranos. Thanks to its prime port location and never-ending cycle of visitors and merchants, Basilia was the most affluent and luxurious village in all of Paelsia, with comfortable inns for weary travelers, busy taverns serving libations imported from all around the world, and plenty of brothels for sailors.

They entered a tavern called The Purple Vine, already buzzing with patrons despite the fact that it was only midday.

The first thing Lucia noticed was that she was one of only five women there, and that the vast majority of the male patrons were loud and big and lewd, yelling and slamming their tables and call-ing out for more food and drink. And the smells—every odor from burnt goat's meat to the sour stench of unwashed armpits—had Lucia wanting to turn right around and go back outside, promis-ing lead be damned.

"This is fascinating," Kyan said, smiling as he scanned the crowd. "Mortals at play."

She could barely hear him over the vile din. Taking hold of Kyan's arm, she threaded her way through the crowd toward a vacant table next to a small wooden stage across the room. It was impossible to get to the table without brushing against the men, and Lucia cringed at each point of contact.

One large, hairy brute whistled at her through his teeth. "Pretty girl, come here and sit on my knee!"

She sent a whisper of air magic toward him, which tipped his large tankard of ale right into his lap. He swore loudly and jumped to his feet, and Lucia turned her head to hide her sly smile.

Sick of the groping she had to endure just to get to the stage, she stopped in front of a table several paces away from her original goal. It was already occupied.

"I want to sit here," she said to the gruff-looking patron seated there.

"Go away, girl." The man flicked a dismissive hand at her. "And fetch me some lamb stew . . . and some bread to go along with it."

Kyan watched Lucia with a smile, his arms crossed over his chest. "Well? Are you going to get him the stew? I wouldn't mind trying some myself."

Lucia leaned closer to the man and, ignoring the rotten stench of his breath, met his watery gaze. "I said, I want to sit here. Remove yourself from my sight."

The man's cheek twitched, and he sputtered out a mix of spittle and ale. Immediately, Lucia thought of Magnus's pained reaction to her magic, and her stomach clenched.

The man grabbed his bowl of stew and vacated the table without further argument—and thankfully before she could inflict any real suffering.

"Well done," Kyan said, reaching for man's newly vacant chair. "You're getting so much better at that."

"Weaker minds do make things easier—for them and for me. Sit."

As they sat down, Lucia gestured for the barmaid and asked for two apple ciders and a bowl of lamb stew for Kyan.

"No wine?" the barmaid asked, a hand on her plump hip. "Most fine ladies like yourself can only tolerate a place like this with some wine in their bellies."

"I don't indulge in wine."

"No wine?" The barmaid snorted. "What are you, a Limerian?" She turned around without waiting for a reply, and Lucia followed her with a narrowed gaze until she disappeared into the crowd.

In the far corner of the tavern, a trio of flutists started up with a song, and the room began to quiet down.

The show was beginning.

Lucia was here to find a dancer known as the Goddess of Serpents, and now she knew that she was in the right place. As the trio's melody hit its first crescendo, a young woman emerged from behind the stage. Her arms, legs, and face were streaked with golden paint, and her raven-black hair was long, falling nearly to her knees, with slender braids scattered around her face. Her blue eyes were heavily outlined with kohl. She wore an ornate jeweled mask that covered half of her face, and all that covered her lithe, tanned body was a costume of diaphanous scarves and veils. Such an outfit wouldn't have turned a single head in a more exotic locale, like Kraeshia, but here it was a shocking sight, at least to Lucia. But the most shocking aspect of the girl's appearance was not her revealing outfit; rather, it was the large, snow-white boa constrictor draped over her shoulders.

The crowd roared with approval as the Goddess of Serpents danced and swayed her hips to the music, as her pet snake's tongue shot out every few seconds, as if searching for its next meal.

When the dance ended, the crowd cheered for more, and the snake goddess blew them all kisses, promising to return later that afternoon.

She was about to retreat backstage when Lucia reached into her drawstring purse and pulled out a handful of coins, setting them on the table before her. Lucia watched the dancer stop, raise a curious brow at the clank and sparkle of silver, then turn around and walk over to the table. She stood before Lucia and Kyan, offering them both a big smile.

"Welcome to The Purple Vine, friends," she purred as she stroked the head of the white snake still wrapped over her shoulders like a scaly shawl.

Lucia pushed the coins toward her. "Sit with us for a moment."

There was only a slight hesitation before the dancer snatched up the coins, wrapped them up in one of her scarves, and took a seat.

Suddenly, Lucia found that she was nervous, and it had very little to do with the serpent. How ridiculous. She was the one in control here. Silver would buy her the answers she needed, and if it didn't, her magic would.

The barmaid returned with their ciders and Kyan's stew. Lucia waited for her to leave before she spoke another word.

"The Goddess of Serpents is such a lovely name," Lucia said, willing her voice to stay calm and even. "But what's your real one?"

The girl smiled. "Laelia."

"I see. And I take it you're not an actual goddess."

"That is a matter of opinion." She smiled and slid a hand up Lucia's arm as her pet wound closer around its mistress's body. "For a few more coins I would be happy to make you and your handsome friend feel like a god and goddess tonight. This is a special offer, one I only rarely make, and only to those special souls to whom I take an immediate liking."

Lucia shot Laelia a sharp, withering look, and the dancer withdrew her hand, as if burned. "Apologies," she said, clearly frightened. "Perhaps I misinterpreted your intentions...."

"You certainly did."

"Another time perhaps." Laelia composed herself, leaning back leisurely in her seat and placing a fresh smile on her red lips. "So. Why, then, did you lure me over to your table with a gift of more coin than I can earn here in a month?"

Kyan remained silent and focused on his meal, letting Lucia take the lead.

"I was told you might know something about a prophecy," Lucia said.

Laelia's smile wavered. "A prophecy?"

"Yes," Lucia said, humoring the girl's feigned ignorance but growing impatient. "A prophecy about a child said to wield the magic of a sorceress. When this prophecy came to fruition, two witches stole that baby from her cradle and murdered the mother. This happened somewhere in Paelsia, nearly seventeen years ago."

"What a tragic story," Laelia said, the skin above her mask now nearly as pale as her cold-blooded companion. "But I'm sorry, I don't know how I can be helpful to you."

"How old are you?" Lucia said. The girl was obviously lying. "Nineteen? Twenty? You would've been very young at the time, but I imagine a tale like that—of murder and kidnapping all in the same night—would have been passed around Paelsian villages for many years. I know you know the story I speak of."

Laelia stood up, her breath quickening. "Why are you asking me these questions?"

"Because I'm the child from the prophecy," Lucia said, her eyes steady on the girl's.

"What?" Laelia dropped back down in her seat, then stared at Lucia for several moments. "*You're* the stolen child?"

Lucia nodded in silence, waiting for Laelia to put together the pieces and say more.

Finally, Laelia spoke again, her voice raspy. "When I was three years old . . . my mother was murdered right after two thieves stole my baby sister from her cradle in the night. My father searched everywhere, but no one knew anything—or else, they chose not to say what they knew. Soon after, he married again, and it was as if he forgot all about it, as if the loss of his daughter and wife no longer mattered to him." Her expression grew haunted. "But that prophecy . . . it wasn't about my sister. It was about my father.

That's what he always told us. He believed he was a sorcerer, and that one day he would save Paelsia from its dark curse. He believed that to be true his whole life, right up until the day he died."

Lucia's chest tightened with every word Laelia spoke. "Who is . . . who *was* your father?"

The girl scanned the tavern, as if suddenly afraid they might be overheard. "I try not to talk about him anymore. I don't want anyone to blame me for all the things he did. That's why I wear this mask when I dance."

Lucia squeezed Laelia's hand, hard, forcing her to snap her eyes back to hers. Eyes, she now realized, that were the exact same color as her own.

"*Who was he?*" she pressed.

Lines of pained concentration settled into Laelia's face as Lucia forcibly pressed for the truth with her magic. "The former chieftain of Paelsia. Hugo Basilius."

A stab of shock sliced through Lucia. She released the girl's hand.

Chief Basilius. A foolish, ignorant man who taxed his people to death while he lived like a king. Murdered by King Gaius after being tricked into helping him conquer Auranos.

His people had believed he was a sorcerer. They'd believed he was a living god, when he was nothing but a fraud. A selfish, delusional, lying fraud.

Laelia's snake slithered, wrapping itself tighter around her neck, as if trying to give its mistress a reassuring hug.

"You're my sister," Laelia said, her voice barely above a whisper.

Lucia stood up. "I must leave. Now."

Laelia grabbed her hand, stopping her. "No, please. Please stay. We need to speak further. You're my sister—and you have money. You need to help me."

Lucia shut her eyes and summoned fire magic to her hand. Laelia gasped and yanked her hand back, her skin red and blistering. "Stay away from me," Lucia hissed. "I want nothing to do with you."

Finally, Lucia had the answer she'd been seeking for so long. And it only made her feel emptier than she ever had before.

She had no real family. And she never would.

Kyan followed her outside. "Lucia, stop."

"It's funny, really." Lucia laughed, but it sounded as humorless as it felt. A storm was brewing inside of her, one she couldn't wait to unleash. "What was I expecting? To discover a nice, normal family, with a mother and father and siblings who would be happy to have found me again? How ridiculous."

Kyan took her by her shoulders. "I know your frustration and disappointment very well. You need to use it to make you stronger. Use everything you feel—both the good and the bad—to give you power."

"I'm utterly alone. In a world that I hate. I hate it so much."

"You're not alone, little sorceress. You have me."

Her eyes stung, but she refused to cry. Instead, she looked up into his face. "I do?"

"Of course you do. You think you and I are so different, but we're exactly the same. I want all the same things you do—a family, a home. A real, passionate life. But those things are always just out of reach for us. And because of that, we both harbor an uncontrollable rage that needs to be released. And when we release that rage, others join in our suffering. Do you know what that means?"

She neither nodded nor shook her head, instead keeping her gaze on him steady and resolute. "What?"

"It means *we're* family."

He said it with such certainty, such confidence, that she knew he meant it. The heavy weight that had settled on her heart lifted just a little. "You and I. Family."

Kyan smiled. "Yes. And once we reunite with my siblings, we'll be a fearsome sight for these flawed, lowly mortals."

"But I'm a mortal."

"Oh, that's nothing but a bit of a hindrance, a small dose of fragility that we needn't think about just yet." He stroked her dark hair, tucking it behind her ears. "Now, I'm going to go see a witch about a wheel. You stay here and explore the market. Clear your mind. Enjoy yourself until I return."

"My mother used to do that—go to the market to make herself feel better." Lucia frowned. "The queen, I mean. Not my mother. The queen used to take me to Ravencrest to buy me things she thought a proper Limerian princess should wear. Dresses, slippers, jewelry. But all I wanted was books."

Kyan smiled and nodded toward the busy market. "I'm sure there are all sort of books over there. Go. Buy whatever pleases you. And I'll see you soon, all right?"

"All right." He leaned forward and kissed her forehead, and the unexpected gesture made her smile.

Lucia walked to the market in the center of the village, immersing herself into the crowd buzzing around hundreds of vendors selling their wares from colorfully painted stalls and tents. Anything she could have wanted—wine, vegetables, dried meats, beaded jewelry, embroidered gowns, beautiful quilts—was available to buy.

A man seated behind an easel called out to her. "Lovely young lady! Please do me the favor of allowing me to draw you. It would be my pleasure. Only five silver centimos."

"I have only limmeas."

"Very well. A portrait for only ten silver limmeas, then."

"You would ask for twice the price in Limerian currency? That doesn't make any sense. I've used my coins in Paelsia without problem up until now."

The man spread his hands, as if to suggest he had no control over his prices. "Centimos are accepted everywhere in Mytica without question, but limmeas are not. That is just the way it is. But all right, how about eight silver limmeas?"

"Your work is not worth that price," she scoffed. She continued on, leaving the foolish artist behind. What a lowly, peasant-like thing to do—bargain with customers to make a sale.

Next she passed a stall strung up with small, skinned animal carcasses hanging. The seller waved at her. "Come, sample my spiced warlag shavings on some freshly baked bread. Or perhaps some chaeva seeds, just the thing to relieve one's dreaded monthly cramps?"

Lucia caught a whiff of the strongly spiced warlag, a common animal native to Paelsia that looked like a cross between a rabbit and a rat. Her stomach lurched.

"No, thank you." She quickly passed the stall.

Having escaped the vendor and the overpowering warlag odor, she came to a stall adorned with scarves, all hand stitched with elaborate floral patterns. She stopped to run her hand along a pretty blue and violet one.

"Yes, lovely choice. That would go very well with your eyes." The old vendor smiled, stretching her gaunt, lined face and revealing several missing teeth.

"It's beautiful," Lucia acknowledged.

The woman took the scarf and draped it around Lucia's

shoulders. "I knew it. This was made for you. You were meant to have it, no one else."

The sumptuous material alone was worth far more than any quickly sketched portrait, let alone the time and skill that went into the tailoring and intricate embroidery. She reached into her bag of coins. "How much is it?" she asked. "Fair warning, I have only limmeas with me."

The vendor nodded. "Two silver limmeas, then."

Lucia's brows shot up. "So little?"

"It would be my pleasure to know my creation will be worn and appreciated by a lovely girl like you."

Lucia handed the woman three gold coins instead. "Take these and know I will wear it with pride."

All the old woman could do was stare after her, a gleam of delighted surprise shining in her eyes, as Lucia continued on in her new purchase.

Next, she lingered at a busy stall displaying beaded tunics, all of them far too eye-catching and colorful for anyone in Limeros to wear in public. Still, she found herself drawn to one in particular, soft and tailored to look like a hawk's silhouette, and ran her fingers along the seam.

Someone bumped into her, and she turned to see a handsome young man with wide shoulders and sparkling eyes. "Oh, apologies," he said.

She tried to ignore him, turning back to the hawk tunic.

"Lovely shirt," he said. "Don't you think? A bit too Auranian for my tastes, though."

"I don't much feel like conversation today. You can be on your way."

"Oh, come on. It's a beautiful day . . . not as beautiful as you, of course."

"Leave me alone."

"Very well, as you wish. But before I go, I need something from you."

She turned to glare at his smiling face. "What?"

He nodded at her drawstring purse. "That."

She sighed, feeling sorry for the aspiring thief who chose to bother with her today. "You definitely need to—"

But before she could finish, the man yanked the purse right out of her hand with nearly painful force. She gasped, and he covered her face with his hand and shoved her backward, sending her crashing into the tunic stall.

Then a familiar shroud of darkness descended over her.

She looked up to see the sky quickly clouding over as she rose to her feet, then scanned the crowd for the thief, ready to light him on fire and watch him burn.

He thought he could steal from her?

He would never steal from anyone else ever again.

She had him clearly in her sights, but before she could unleash her magic, the thief tripped and fell, hard, to the ground. Lucia rushed over and joined the crowd forming around him.

A young man wearing a black eye patch stood over the thief, the sole of his boot pressing against the man's chest. "You know," he said, leaning over to snatch the purse from the thief's grip, "you're the sort of scum who gives all of us Paelsians a bad reputation."

Lucia's purse in hand, the young man lifted his boot from the thief's chest.

"You should learn to mind your own business," the thief growled as he scrambled to his feet.

"I've always been terrible at that. Now go. Before I change my mind." He removed a dagger with a jeweled hilt from a sheath on his waist and showily spun it around on his hand.

The thief took one brief look at the knife before running off in the other direction.

Lightning crackled in the darkening skies.

The young man with the eye patch looked up then brought his gaze down to Lucia, who drew closer to him. "Seems we're due for a storm," he said to her. "You can never tell here in Paelsia. They always come upon us without warning, as if by magic."

He was young, not much older than her, with dark hair like Magnus's, though much shorter than her brother's. His skin was deeply tanned, and his visible eye was a cinnamon shade of brown.

"Are you all right?" he asked, frowning at her silence.

The darkness within her continued to swell, still craving a release.

"Here." He handed her the drawstring purse, and she hesitated only a moment before taking it from him and tucking it beneath her cloak.

"I suppose you want a reward," she said.

"Of course not. Assisting a lovely young lady such as yourself is reward enough." He gave her a toothsome grin.

And then it hit her like a thunderbolt. She knew exactly who he was.

"You're Jonas Agallon."

He blinked. "Sorry, what—?"

"You're Jonas Agallon. The rebel leader wanted for the murder of Queen Althea." She'd seen his wanted posters, heard rumors about his crimes, though she couldn't recall ever seeing him in person before. Surely, she would have remembered. "Apologies, but your disguise is a disgrace."

"Oh, you mean this?" He pointed at his eye patch. "An accident involving a pitchfork. Very gruesome. And sorry to disappoint, but I'm not this Jonas Agallon person."

His attempts at denial were very nearly comical. "Don't worry, I won't turn you in. I'm grateful for all you've done in your fight against the king. Why did you stop?"

The boy glanced up at the sky again. "Seems the skies are clearing. No storm after all."

"Very well. Can I ask you a question that perhaps you *will* answer?" Lucia said, her tone free from anger.

"You can certainly try."

She fixed a steady smile on her lips. "Where is the earth Kindred?"

The stunned look on his face confirmed Lucia's long-running suspicion: Cleo had fed this rebel information about the crystals, allowing him to claim it first.

That lying princess did deserve death.

Lucia was suddenly distracted by the sight of someone striding through the crowd, shoving people out of her way, heading right for Lucia. The strange girl, who had dark, curly hair, and wore a very ugly yellow dress, came to stand next to Jonas. She held a bow and readied it with an arrow, pointing it directly at Lucia's face.

Jonas eyed the girl with alarm. "Put that down, Lys. You're going to hurt somebody."

"Shut up," the girl hissed. "Have you completely lost your mind? Do you have any idea who this is?"

Jonas turned away from the wild girl and looked again at Lucia.

"Of course I do," he said, his voice hard. "She's Princess Lucia Damora."

CHAPTER 18

JONAS

PAELSIA

Before today, Jonas had seen Princess Lucia from a distance on three separate occasions: on a horse, regally riding next to her father and brother into Auranos; at the Temple of Cleiona, just after he'd claimed the earth Kindred; and on the royal dais at Lysandra's scheduled execution.

It had taken him a moment to recognize her, what with her plain frock and her hair worn as loose and free as a Paelsian girl's, but as soon as he saw those piercing blue eyes and their knowing gaze, he was reminded of exactly how unforgettable the beautiful princess was. However, the busy Basilia market was the last place he'd ever have expected to spot her.

Nic and Olivia caught up with them, and now stood next to Jonas and Lys. After Lys drew her bow and arrow, the rest of the crowd had backed away, and now the five of them stood, isolated in the middle of the market, as a hundred vendors and customers looked on with both interest and wariness.

"Be careful, princess," Nic said to Lucia. "I've seen what Lys can do with that thing."

"Nicolo, isn't it?" Lucia said. "Of course I remember you. Cleo's little trained pet she keeps around to amuse her. What did you think of the entertainment my friend and I provided during my recent visit to the palace?"

Nic just scoffed, eyeing Lucia with a mixture of hatred and fear. This was a rare moment, seeing Nic at a loss for words. Nic's talent for talking was what had gotten them past the guards manning the gates at the Limerian palace. He'd insisted, as the princess's closest confidant, that he and his friends had every right to leave the grounds to go to Ravencrest to find a gift for Cleo's upcoming birthday. Jonas had been rather impressed when the guards had then readily stepped aside without further questioning.

Lucia sighed, then fearlessly shifted her gaze to face the sharp arrow again. "And you are . . . Lys?"

"Lysandra," she hissed.

"Lysandra, darling, I strongly suggest you stop pointing that weapon at me. It's very rude."

"Put it down, Lys," Olivia gritted out through clenched teeth.

"Why should I?" Lysandra snarled. "This is the same snotty royal who looked on, as if watching a puppet show rather than an execution, while my head was about to be chopped off."

"Ah, yes. Of course," Lucia said, her tone calm and even somewhat sweet. "I know you. You're the savage little rebel girl who slipped away from the execution stage, as free as a bird. I really must congratulate you. Do you know you're one of a very small group of prisoners who've managed to escape King Gaius's punishment?"

"My, what confidence you have. Even right before I kill you."

"Confidence is a virtue I lacked in the past. But now I find I'm overflowing with it." Lucia took her eyes off Lysandra and addressed the rest of Jonas's group. "Now, enough of this. You're boring our audience. They'd much prefer to see a little action, don't you think? Let's start with some dust."

Lucia flicked her wrist, and Lysandra's bow and arrow disintegrated into a pile of sawdust and ashes, drawing gasps from the crowd.

"She's a witch!" someone yelled. "An evil witch!" The mass of people rose up in murmurs and yells, and then a rock came hurtling toward Lucia's head.

She held up her hand, palm forward. The rock froze midair, less than a foot from her face. Another flick of her wrist and it, too, was transformed to a fluttering of dust.

"Now," she said, turning back to Jonas, "about that earth Kindred you stole from me."

Jonas had heard all about Lucia's visit to Limeros, and he didn't underestimate the sorceress for a moment. "Sorry," he said, "but I don't have it."

"Oh, please, Jonas. Do you really think you can fool me so easily? Let's try again."

"Princess Lucia . . ." he began, but then he was interrupted by a sudden crackling of lightning above. The storm had begun to gather again. A sickening feeling seeped into his stomach. This storm was made from magic, he realized. Summoned by a sorceress who could conjure darkness and evil without even a single crack to her calm, collected exterior.

"Yes, Jonas?" Lucia replied, a menacing smile creeping over her beautiful face.

"You want the earth Kindred?" His mouth was dry, his heart was pounding, but he tried to keep his voice steady and confident.

"Obviously."

"Then I propose a partnership."

She raised a brow. "And I propose that you hand over the Kindred before I light you and your friends on fire."

"All right, all right." He held up his hands, wracking his mind for the right way to deal with this dangerous girl. "Not the time to consider a partnership. Understood."

"Trust me on this, rebel. You have no idea what you've stolen."

"Kill her!" came a shout from the crowd. "The King of Blood's daughter deserves to die!" A chorus of cheers and cries for justice followed, and Jonas turned to scowl at his unwanted and vastly unhelpful audience.

This was all his fault. He'd just *had* to intervene when he saw that thief snatch a bag of coins from a pretty girl.

Good deeds had never served him well.

Jonas looked up again at the roiling storm clouds above. "Princess, listen to me," he said. "I am not your enemy."

A roll of thunder rumbled. *"Everyone* is my enemy."

"I want you to know that I wasn't the one who killed the queen."

"I'm disappointed to hear that," she said. "That was the single thing I liked about you before now."

"Enough talk," Lysandra growled. "My parents are dead because of your father. Because of your father, my village was enslaved. Because of your father, my brother was executed right in front of me!"

"I am sorry for your loss, Lysandra. Truly. But King Gaius is not my real father. Queen Althea was not my real mother. I hate the Damoras every bit as much as you do."

Surprised by this sudden admission, Jonas sent a furtive glance at Olivia. Could she help if this got out of control?

Most likely she would only prove herself to be nothing more than a common witch, powerless against a prophesied sorceress with her heart set on vengeance.

But he knew there had to be a way to resolve this without any-one getting hurt.

"If that's true, then I have an excellent suggestion for you," Jonas said slowly, evenly. "You should become a rebel."

Amusement flickered in the princess's sky-blue eyes. "And bumble along with the lot of you, failing at every turn? What a brilliant suggestion."

Jonas ignored the bite in her words. "Well, why not? By joining us you could help bring peace back to Mytica, end the suffering of its people."

"And how do you think you're going to do all that? By using me and my magic to achieve your goals? Apologies, rebel, but my charitable days are over."

Jonas had to bite back the snarky, smug responses to this incredibly abrasive girl as they shot through his mind. He took a deep breath. "If King Gaius's daughter were to stand up in defi-ance against him, everyone all over Mytica will wake up and begin to see through his lies. Not only would even more Auranians and Paelsians band together and rise up against him, but Limerians, too. It's Limeros that's been trapped under his thumb for all these years, and it's those citizens who would benefit most from the demise of his regime. It will be a revolution of both body and spirit, and your magic would have very little to do with it."

"Jonas," Nic growled. "Look at her. She's clearly not interested in listening to reason."

"Now, now, Nicolo, be nice," Lucia said. "I'm perfectly capable of thinking and answering for myself." She turned back to Jonas. "You make excellent points, Jonas. But you mistake me for some-one who cares about peace or ending the suffering of common citizens. Don't look so surprised. After all, even if I don't share their blood, I *was* raised a Damora."

Jonas searched her expression for a hint of something soft, something other than vengeance. But all he found was rage, and suddenly he felt pity for her. "What happened to you to make you so angry? So bitter?"

"Perhaps I was born this way."

Jonas shook his head. "I doubt it. No one is born with such hatred in their hearts."

"How dare you presume to know anything about me, Jonas Agallon."

"I know more than you might think, and I have a very reliable gut. You're a good person, princess. You could improve so many lives with your magic. You could change the world. Make it better, brighter, happier. Don't you see that?"

"I don't care about any of that. All I want right now is for you to hand over the earth Kindred."

Jonas was about to respond when a voice cut through the conversation, interrupting them. "What was that?" A young, fair-haired man approached Lucia, his expression fearless and quizzical. "Did I hear you say something about the earth Kindred?"

Lucia pursed her lips and glanced at him. "I didn't expect you back from your errand so soon."

"I move quickly." The man looked at Jonas, his brow furrowed. "Am I to understand that you are in possession of the obsidian orb?"

"Jonas," Nic whispered in a warning tone. "That's the man who was at the palace with Lucia. He nearly killed Prince Magnus. Say nothing."

"Let me handle him on my own, Kyan," Lucia said.

Kyan kept staring at Jonas. "You're wrong," he said to Lucia, his eyes still on Jonas. "He doesn't have the orb. I know I'd be able to feel its magic if it were really this close."

"Perhaps not on him, but he did claim it," Lucia pressed. "Where is it, Jonas?"

"No idea," Jonas said evenly. "Sorry I couldn't be more help."

The young man narrowed his eyes, and in a sudden flash of light and heat, a ring of flames shot up from the ground, enclosing them in its circle. Jonas started and heard the crowd beyond the fire scream and scatter, abandoning the market.

Jonas shot a tense glance at his friends. "Olivia, tell me you can do something."

Her eyes were wide and staring, filled with fear he'd never seen from this brave witch. "Oh, no," she whispered. "Not now. Not here."

"What are you talking about?" The heat from the flames grew ever more intense around Jonas.

"It—it's too soon," she said, clearly stunned and in a daze. "I'm not ready. I'm not strong enough."

"Do what you can, then!" Jonas urged. "We'll help!" He looked back to Kyan. "*What* are you?"

"You people keep asking me that. You weak, ignorant mortals. Born with so much potential, yet you are always falling short, failing at every turn. Sickening."

"Kyan . . ." Lucia said, an edge of warning in her voice.

"Except you, little sorceress. You're completely exempt from the failings of the rest of your kind. You are a perfect specimen, an example of what humans *should* be. What they *will* be."

Jonas glanced nervously at the flames, the hellish cage trapping them there with a sorceress and this man—someone far more dangerous than any simple magic-wielder.

Kyan took a step closer, his fists clenched at his sides.

"Stay away from Jonas, you freak," Lys snarled, stepping forward resolutely and fearlessly, then she gave Jonas a sidelong glance. "We can handle this, you and me. We've handled worse."

Jonas's heart swelled. He suddenly couldn't take his gaze off her, this fierce, stunning warrior who'd stood by him every step of the way. This remarkable girl who'd told him she loved him.

But then his heavy heart ached when he thought of how he'd forgotten all about her the moment he'd seen Cleo, how he'd practically fallen at the golden princess's feet as he'd begged for a kiss.

He'd been too blind to see that he'd already won the greatest treasure of all.

Jonas turned to face Kyan, staring him right in his amber eyes. "You heard Lys. Back off. I don't have your orb, but if I did, I'd happily shove it right up your arse."

Kyan regarded him with a chilling smile. "You're either exceedingly brave or utterly stupid, boy."

Jonas eyed Kyan and Lucia in turn. "Enough of this. Go play with your magic somewhere else. I can't help you." He sent a withering glare to Lucia. "And clearly you can't help me either."

Kyan continued to stare at Jonas so intently that he thought the man might be trying to read his mind. But then his expression slackened just a touch, and he frowned and cocked his head. "I do sense other magic here," he said. "Undiluted elemental magic."

Kyan snapped his gaze to Olivia and in the beat of a hawk's wing, his amber eyes shifted to a vivid shade of blue. "*Watcher.*"

Olivia staggered back a step, shaking her head. "Stay away from me."

"You dare to oppose me?" Flames rolled down Kyan's arms, billowing with rage as bright as his eyes. "Did you really think you could conceal your true identity? What has Timotheus told you to do? Take me by surprise? Fool me? Trap me?"

Olivia turned to meet Jonas's stunned gaze.

"Is that true?" he asked. "Are you a Watcher?"

"I'm so sorry, Jonas. I can't . . ." Her voice trembled, she continued to shake her head. "Timotheus was wrong to send me."

The circle of fire blazed brighter, rose higher, as tall as the oldest trees in Mytica.

"You wish to help your elder imprison me?" Kyan snarled. "You will fail, and I will gladly watch you burn."

Jonas could barely think; the roaring heat was becoming too much to bear. "Olivia, tell me what's going on!" he demanded. "Who is he?"

Olivia's tawny complexion had grown dead and ashen. "I'm sorry. I'm so sorry I'm not as strong as Phaedra was."

Jonas was about to respond when suddenly the outline of Olivia's form began to shimmer, and the air before her shifted. Her clothes dropped away, crumpling to the ground, and from them sprung a golden hawk, spreading its wings and flying up past the ring of fire, into the sky.

"Coward!" Kyan roared after her.

"Kyan," Lucia said softly, placing her hands on his burning arm. "We need to leave. She's gone, and the rebel doesn't have the Kindred. We'll keep looking."

But he wasn't listening, didn't even look at her. Instead, Kyan pulled his gaze from the sky and sent Jonas a look so fierce that he staggered back a step.

Beside Jonas, Nic frantically scanned the circle of fire. "We have to get out of here," he said.

Lys nodded, her expression grim. "There must be a way."

"You've been assisting an immortal in her quest," Kyan snarled at Jonas, pulling away from Lucia. "You wish to see me trapped again? Tortured by my eternal imprisonment so lowly mortals won't need to fear my wrath?"

"I have no fight with you, whoever you are." Jonas held his

hands up in a gesture of surrender, feeling the heat of the fire grow more intense behind him. "Honestly. I didn't know what she—"

"More lies!" Kyan thrust his hands out and, with a violent push, sent a blast of fire magic searing directly toward Jonas.

"No!" Lysandra screamed, and she shoved Jonas out of the way, knocking him to the ground. On her way down after him, she was struck in the heart by the spear of flames.

And then it disappeared.

She gasped and collapsed to her knees.

Jonas grabbed her, searching her for signs of damage. "Lys! Are you all right? Lys, please! Answer me!"

Her face was damp with perspiration, her breath coming in small, rattling gasps, but still she managed to grin up at him.

"You were in my way, you arse."

A wave of both blind fury and pure relief overcame him, and Jonas smiled back at her. "Do you have any idea how much I love you, Lysandra Barbas?"

"What?" She blinked. "You love me?"

"Yes."

"And what about Cleo?"

He grinned. "Cleo who?"

"Nicolo." Lucia's voice was quiet but firm as she interrupted the tender aftermath of Kyan's rage. "Get Jonas away from her before it's too late."

Jonas glared up at her. "You and your friend need to leave. Now. Hear me? Come any closer and I swear I'll kill both of you."

All the fight that had been glimmering in Lucia's eyes was gone, leaving only a sad, bleak expression. "I didn't mean for this to happen. I know you won't believe me, but I'm sorry. Nicolo, do it now!"

Without a word, Nic grabbed Jonas and yanked him away from Lysandra.

Jonas tried to break free. "What are you doing? Let go of me!"

"Jonas?" Lys reached out toward him, a smile playing at her lips. "I love—"

Her sweet words were snapped into silence as a nest of flames burst up and blossomed from her chest, flowing over every inch of her body like lava.

"No!" Jonas shoved Nic away and scrambled to get to Lysandra, whose form had been transformed in an instant into a blazing column of amber fire.

The flames rose up and up, and with a violent lick they shifted from deep orange and amber to bright blue—the same shade as Kyan's eyes.

The sound of Lysandra's screams sliced through Jonas's very soul, and in one heartbreaking instant, the flames themselves shattered like glass, sending shards of blue crystal flying and falling all around them.

Leaving nothing behind.

With a breathless wail, Jonas crumpled in a hard heap to the ground, staring at the empty space where Lysandra had been only moments ago.

He stayed like that, motionless, tears burning in his eyes, for some time, and he didn't notice when the circle of fire disappeared, or watch as Lucia and Kyan left the abandoned market, leaving Jonas and Nic there all alone.

CHAPTER 19

FELIX

KRAESHIA

Felix woke up with the urgent knowledge that something was terribly wrong. If only he had any idea what it was.

He tried to ignore it, though, because life had never been better for him. He'd earned back King Gaius's trust. He'd traveled beyond the shores of Mytica for the first time ever, to the beautiful empire of Kraeshia. And a gorgeous princess had invited him to share her bed for not one, but seven nights.

Seven. In a *row.*

Felix's life had become so shiny and bright, so why did everything suddenly feel so damningly dark?

He crawled out of Princess Amara's huge feather bed, draped with green silks and diaphanous veils of pale gold, and hastily got dressed.

His stomach grumbled. Perhaps he could attribute this dark feeling to hunger—ever since his arrival in Kraeshia, he'd consumed too many fruits and vegetables and not nearly enough red meat.

"Felix, my pretty beast . . ." Amara said sleepily. She wrapped her arms around his waist as he sat on the side of the bed to put on his boots. "Leaving me so soon?"

"Duty calls."

She slid her hands down his bare chest. "But I don't want you to go yet."

"The king might disagree."

"Let him." Amara pulled his face to hers and kissed him. "Who cares what the king thinks, anyway?"

"Well, me for one. I work for him. And he's very strict."

"Leave him and work for me."

"And be what? One of your lowly manservants?" He was surprised by the amount of poison in his voice. Where had that come from?

He knew theirs wasn't a relationship with any potential or future. Amara was a princess with a large appetite and a short attention span—nearly as short as his own. But of course he wasn't complaining. Amara was beautiful. Willing. Enthusiastic. Double-jointed.

So what the hell was wrong with him today that he wasn't thanking the goddess for his enviable current situation?

He cast a wary look at her as he stood up and her hands dropped away from his body.

"Oh, dear," she said. "My pretty beast is grumpy this morning."

He wasn't sure he liked that nickname, but knew enough not to correct her. "You know I'm not the grumpy sort."

Amara leaned back against the pillows and watched him put on yesterday's shirt and coat. "Tell me," she said, her tone less playful now, "what will happen if my father refuses the king's offer?"

They hadn't spoken a word about politics all week, which was fine with Felix. He wasn't the king's advisor or confidant, nor did he have any interest in being anything more than his muscle and brawn.

"Don't know," he said. "You think he'll refuse?"

Amara raised an eyebrow. "Do I think my father will refuse to hand over half his empire for a shiny bauble and a threat of magic?"

When he'd watched King Gaius wave the air Kindred under the emperor's nose, Felix had been certain the Silver Sea had risen up and crashed over him right there at the banquet. It had taken every last sliver of his strength to keep his expression neutral. "It does sound pretty crazy, doesn't it?"

Felix didn't know much about the crystal, but he knew enough to be sure that it didn't belong with an emperor who would use it to conquer the world.

Amara draped her long dark hair over her shoulder, absently twirling a tendril of it around her finger, as if lost in thought. "Is it true that King Gaius is in possession of all four Kindred?"

"He says he is, so he must be," Felix lied. "But I've only seen the moonstone."

"I wish the king had offered it to me." Amara smiled conspiratorially. "Then perhaps you and I could rule the world together."

"You and me, huh?"

"Can't you imagine how incredible that would be?"

"Look, princess, you don't have to say these kinds of things to me. You don't have to make me any promises. I'm perfectly happy with our arrangement, just as it is, for as long as you need me. However, with respect, my days belong to the king."

Without giving her the chance to change his mind, he left her room. Once outside the door, he leaned against the hallway wall, letting out a heavy sigh.

"Is that a sigh of sadness or relief?"

Felix looked up to see Mikah, a palace guard he'd met upon his arrival.

"Look at you, just lingering out here in the hallway," Felix said with displeasure. "You weren't listening in, were you?"

Mikah cocked his head. "Why? If I were, would I have heard anything other than sighs and heavy breathing? I'm quite accustomed to the princess's casual dalliances."

"Happy to hear the two of you are so close," Felix said with narrowed eyes as he started to walk away. "Now, if you'll excuse me—" Mikah grabbed Felix's arm, his grip tight enough to hurt. "Let go of me," Felix growled.

Mikah didn't smile, didn't flinch. "Tell me," he said, "have you fallen in love with her yet?"

Felix blinked. "What?"

"Answer the question."

"Ah, I get it. You're a former *dalliance*, are you? A jealous one? Don't worry, there's nothing permanent between us. I'll be moving along soon so you can continue to moon over her. Now let go of me, or we're going to have a problem."

Mikah studied him intently for another long moment, then released him roughly. "Good. Wouldn't want to see you get hurt."

"I can take care of myself, but much gratitude for your concern."

"The king wants you to go check on the ship," Milo told Felix later that day. "Ensure it's suitable for departure at a moment's notice."

"And he sent you to give me the order?" Felix eyed the other guard skeptically.

Milo shrugged. "Just passing along information. The king is busy."

"His majesty wants a swift escape, does he?" he said aloud.

Milo nodded, his expression pinched. "The swifter the better, it would seem."

The two hadn't discussed the king's offer—or, rather, *ultimatum*—to the emperor, but they'd most certainly exchanged worried glances during the banquet. After all, they were the ones responsible for saving the king's neck, even when he'd willingly bared it to a known enemy's blade.

Felix lowered his voice. "Does King Gaius really think the emperor will simply let us sail away without consequence?"

A muscle in Milo's left cheek twitched. "I'm not aware of the king's thoughts. . . ."

"Nor am I."

"But if I were . . ." Milo continued, his expression as grim as Felix had seen it since their first meeting, when they set sail from Auranos, "I would start to prepare for a very hasty departure."

What would the king expect his bodyguards to do if the emperor chose to answer with wrath rather than agreement?

Assassinate the most powerful leader in the known world in his very home and expect to walk away unscathed?

Finally, he nodded with a firm jerk of his head. "I'll check on the ship immediately."

It seemed that Felix had fooled himself into smelling nothing but roses upon gaining the king's favor once again, but this was, truly, the deepest and foulest pile of dung he'd ever waded into.

As he walked along the main dock under the intense heat of the mid-day sun after checking on the Limerian ship, an image slid through his mind. Jonas, pinned to the floor by the dagger. The rebel had stared up at him, pain and accusation in his eyes, as Felix pocketed the air Kindred.

"Yeah, well, he deserved it," he mumbled to himself.

Had he? Had Jonas really deserved to be so abused by someone he'd previously trusted? Jonas, who had done nothing but continue to try to do what was right and good, despite failure after failure?

Perhaps they could have made peace if Felix hadn't been such an impatient, rage-filled arse who solved all of his problems with his fists.

He'd been with the Clan for eight years. Eight years as an assassin before he tried to choose a different path.

He'd been nothing more than an innocent kid when he was first recruited. An innocent kid chosen and plucked up by the king, who gave him no choice but to become a murderer.

He stopped at the storage house at the far end of the dock and smashed his fist into the glittering stonework. He'd always found that physical pain helped clear his head and chase away ugly memories.

Bad things happened when he thought too deeply about the past.

"Stop this," he gritted out. "Life is good. The future is bright. And I'm going to—"

Felix lurched back as someone grabbed his arm and shoved him backward. He hit the wall of the storage house hard, his vision swimming.

He blinked back his focus just in time to see a fist heading directly for his jaw. He caught it, thrusting forward so the blow landed across his assailant's face instead.

"Don't try me today," Felix growled. "I'm not in a forgiving mood."

"Funny. Neither am I," Felix's attacker said, rubbing his jaw and grinning. The young man had bronze shoulder-length hair that was tied at the nape of his neck. "Impressive maneuver. Did your Cobra friends teach you that?"

So this attacker knew exactly who he was. That wasn't good.

He eyed their surroundings to find that the large building shielded them from the view of the people on the busy docks. Only the scent of salty water-weed and the squawk of seabirds populated this isolated patch of the shoreline.

"As a matter of fact, they did. And this, too." He swung his fist, but the assailant ducked, then punched Felix in the gut. He doubled over, giving his attacker ripe opportunity to bring his arm up in an uppercut, hitting Felix right under his jaw. Felix wheezed out a breath and dropped to the ground like a bag of hammers.

"That felt quite good," the long-haired young man said. "I've been itching for a fight for some time."

As he sat, gasping for breath, on the ground, Felix heard someone else approaching from the far side of the storage building. "That's enough for today," said a voice that Felix recognized.

Felix looked up to see Mikah, standing next to the brute and looking calm as ever. "Following me, are you?" Felix said. "I'd take it as a compliment, but you're not really my type."

"On your feet," Mikah commanded.

"I don't take orders from you."

"Fine, then sit there. I don't care. This won't take long anyway."

"Are you here to kill me? Or try to?"

Mikah leaned over until he was eye level with Felix. "You have a death wish—I can see it in your eyes. I'm sorry to say I won't help you with that today."

"Oh, my. You can read minds, too?" Felix pushed himself to his feet. Surely these two figured his new injuries made him an easy target. But that was exactly what he wanted them to think. It was all part of the game he'd learned from the Clan: Keep the target guessing; let them get in a couple of hits and, just when they think they've won, go in for the kill.

Felix knew he could take on this pair if he had to. But first he needed to know what they wanted with him.

"Are you here to harass me about Princess Amara again?" Felix rolled his eyes. "Jealousy really doesn't suit you, friend."

"This has nothing to do with the princess."

"Good. You'd hate to have me as a romantic rival. Now tell me what you want."

"I don't like this one," the long-haired young man said, his arms crossed over his broad chest.

"You don't have to," Mikah replied.

"You trust him?"

"Of course not. He's a Limerian."

"You do know I'm still standing right here?" Felix reminded them. "And I can hear you loud and clear. Now, I'll ask you one more time: What does a Kraeshian guard and his little minion want with me, a common thug working for the king of Mytica?"

Mikah regarded him skeptically for a long moment, while his friend stood by holding eager fists at his sides. "I wear this uniform, but I'm not really a guard. And though you're dressed in finery that hides the mark of the Cobra I know you have on your arm, I don't believe for one moment that you're a servant to the king or a common thug." A sly smile spread across Mikah's face, which only piqued Felix's curiosity more. Mikah went on. "I'm here, in this uniform, because I'm a revolutionary. I've earned this position at the palace to gain information about the royal family." He nodded at his friend. "This is Taran. He's not originally from Kraeshia, but he's joined our worthy fight to rid the empire of the Cortas regime."

This, he didn't expect. It seemed he couldn't wash his hair of all the rebels all over the world. "Well. That . . . sounds like a rather lofty goal. I wish you the best of luck. But what does it have to do with me?"

"We want your help."

Felix had to laugh. "And why would I help you?"

Taran stepped forward, his posture softer now, but his brown eyes still full of anger. "If you only saw the truth here in Kraeshia. If you knew what the emperor does to anything and anyone that doesn't meet his standards . . . you wouldn't hesitate to join us." Taran's expression darkened. "The man is a monster. He sends his armies off to invade and conquer every chartered land out there, picking and choosing at random what he wants to keep, and then discarding and destroying the rest—and, yes, that includes citizens as well as property and possessions."

"Yours is a country constantly at war. People die in wars," Felix reasoned. "Often people who don't deserve to."

Mikah shook his head. "This is not an ideology I'll ever accept. Brute force—relentless greed—is not right, and I'll do anything I can to stop it."

"So it's just the two of you, huh? And you're looking for new recruits?"

Mikah smirked. "There are thousands of us, all organized in factions and stationed across the empire, readying ourselves to rise up and fight."

"Thousands of you." Felix raised his brow. "Well, that does sound more intimidating than the duo standing before me. Still, yours is only a small army compared to what the emperor has to protect him."

"That's why we want your help."

Felix snorted.

"I heard what you said to the princess this morning. I was listening in on you."

"I knew you were a pervert."

"Shut up and listen to me. Princess Amara mentioned the Kindred—that your king has access to one. That their powers are real. If all of that is true, then we need to get that crystal from the king."

Felix nearly laughed. "Oh, is that all? Then you should ask the king for it. I'm sure he'd be happy to help you out."

Without warning, Taran smashed his fist into Felix's face.

Swearing, Felix clamped his hand down over his nose, which was gushing blood. "You broke it. Congratulations. You've just given me my sixth broken nose, and now I'm going to kill you."

"Try it. I dare you." Taran pulled back his cloak to reveal the gleaming blade of a dagger. "Or instead, you could shut your mouth and take us seriously. Because we are very serious."

"Apologies, Felix," Mikah said, glaring at Taran. "My friend here is a bit of a . . . free spirit. Probably due to his Auranian heritage."

Auranian? Felix knew there was a reason he'd taken an immediate dislike to Taran. "So you're the leader of this revolution, are you, Mikah?"

"Here in the Jewel, yes. I've been at the palace for ten years preparing for this revolution, following in my father's footsteps."

"Ten years?"

Mikah nodded. "Our battle will be a long one, and it has taken us two generations to prepare. But we will fight to end the emperor's rule and free our people from his cruelty and greed, no matter how long it takes."

It certainly sounded like a worthy fight. Most definitely doomed, but worthy.

"You're going to fail, and you're all going to die," Felix said. "You must know that, right?"

He was expecting Taran to attempt another strike, but instead the two revolutionaries only looked at him solemnly. "Perhaps," Mikah said.

"So why go through with it?"

"Because if you don't choose to fight against the wrong in the world, then you *are* the wrong in the world."

This guy had devoted his entire life to this rebellion, and it hadn't even begun yet. A rebellion Mikah knew they'd probably lose.

But he wanted to try anyway.

That sick, twisting slice of darkness that had stayed inside of Felix ever since he'd left Jonas and Lysandra and aligned with the King of Blood now grew tighter and darker within him. How could he be a rebel? He was nothing but a killer.

Before today, Felix hadn't believed he had any real choice about that.

"I might have an idea that could help," Felix finally said.

Mikah eyed him. "What is it?"

"I'm going to need to send a message to Prince Magnus Damora."

"What? The King of Blood's little heir?" Taran spat out, eyeing Felix with both disgust and wariness, as if to question his sanity.

"Yup. The same little heir who's rumored to have killed a palace guard in order to rescue an enemy of his father. And now, in King Gaius's absence, he has has taken over the throne in Limeros."

"Rumors aren't facts," Taran scoffed.

"No. But, apologies, they're still about a thousand times more potentially useful to your revolution than anything you've told me today."

Mikah studied him, his brow furrowed in thought. "If these rumors do prove true, it sounds as if Prince Magnus might be staging a rebellion of his own."

"I'm sure it's more complicated than that. But if father and son are currently at odds, the prince will want to know the king's plans—including that the king now has a shiny Kindred in his possession—and he could possibly become an ally."

"Possibly," Taran repeated. "But not definitely. That doesn't sound like much of a plan to me. In fact, it sounds outright reckless."

"It would be a risk, sure. But I'm the one putting my neck on the line."

"Why would you do this?" Mikah asked, his tone thick with suspicion. "Why would you help us? Just a moment ago you were threatening to kill us."

"Hey, you came to *me* for help, remember? Help you wanted so bad I now have a broken nose to show for it. And you're complaining that I'm willing to give that help to you?"

"That doesn't answer my question. Tell me why you've changed your mind."

Felix went silent for a moment as he sorted through his jumbled thoughts. "Perhaps I've finally chosen once and for all to fight for the right things." He absently scratched his arm. His clan tattoo had started to itch, as if to protest his decision.

Mikah grinned. "Welcome to the revolution, Felix."

"Happy to be here."

Taran's expression remained rigid, his eyes narrowing on Felix.

"You're still officially with the Clan of the Cobra," Taran said. "Mikah here might believe you when you say your loyalties have shifted, but how would you convince someone like the prince?"

Now, that was an excellent question. What could he possibly write in that message, sent from his current station as the king's bodyguard, that might gain the prince's trust?

Felix scratched his itch again, then pulled up his sleeve to look down at his snake tattoo. The physical evidence of his oath to the Clan and to the King of Blood, etched into his very skin.

"I think I know a way," he said.

CHAPTER 20

MAGNUS

LIMEROS

The princess wore blue.

The princess *always* wore blue.

Magnus leaned against a palace wall, watching Cleo and Lord Kurtis as they began her archery lesson for the day. It was the first time he'd gone out to watch her practice, but after Nic and all of Cleo's little rebel friends vanished from the palace in the dead of night without permission—allegedly to buy a gift for the princess in celebration of her seventeenth birthday—he'd decided to keep a closer eye on the deceitful princess.

His fury at learning that his new "allies" had disappeared with all of the information he'd revealed to them had since calmed into a seething, but controllable anger. The princess had not accompanied them. If she had, he would be scouring the land for all of them and would show no mercy when they were found.

Nic, he knew, would return. He would never abandon his precious princess so easily.

And, so, Magnus waited.

Since then, he'd grown much more curious about Cleo and her progress with a bow and arrow.

She wore a cloak of robin's-egg blue, which she'd purchased in Ravencrest a few days ago. She'd taken Nerissa with her, and after a day of shopping, they'd stopped in at Lady Sophia's villa.

Lady Sophia's villa. A place that would forever hold unavoidable memories for Magnus. And none of them had anything to do with Lady Sophia herself.

Magnus narrowed his eyes as he watched Kurtis place his gloved hand upon Cleo's shoulder and whisper something in her ear. A small fleet of guards that Magnus had appointed—more to protect Cleo from Kurtis than from any outside threats—stood rigidly a few paces beyond them.

Now the kingsliege motioned toward a target twenty paces in front of them. Cleo nodded with confidence before expertly notching an arrow in her bow.

She drew back the string, aimed, and—

Magnus held his breath.

—the arrow flew straight up into the sky, as if she'd been targeting a cloud. It landed only a few paces away from her, burying itself in the snowy ground.

Hmm.

Kurtis edged closer to Cleo and gave her an encouraging smile as he handed her a new arrow to try again. She nodded firmly, then put the arrow into place, pulled back, aimed, and . . .

Magnus watched Kurtis shield his eyes from the sun as he followed the arrow's upward path. Then, suddenly, he started and leapt out of the way to avoid being hit as it came back down.

Magnus covered his mouth to conceal his grin.

Oh, princess. You're absolutely dreadful at this, aren't you?

She tried twice more, with the same results, then threw the

bow to the ground, stomped her foot, and gestured angrily at the target.

"Now, now," Magnus said under his breath. "Don't be a sore loser."

Then, as if somehow she could hear him across such a distance, she turned in his direction. Their eyes met.

He froze, instantly remembering the painful animosity of their last confrontation and the fresh hatred that blazed in her eyes when she'd mentioned Theon.

But instead of turning away, he began to clap. "Oh, well done, princess. You've a natural gift."

Cleo narrowed her eyes and frowned, then headed straight for the palace gate closest to Magnus, leaving Kurtis behind without a farewell. Magnus gave him a dark look, then strode over and met Cleo at the entrance.

She pulled off her gloves. "You can make fun of me all you want, I don't care. You weren't invited to watch."

"This is my home, my palace. I can do anything I want, including watch you practice your incredible weaponry skills." As much fun as it sometimes was to taunt her, he had more important matters on his mind. "Tell me, princess. When will your friends be returning?"

"I've already told you, Magnus, I have absolutely no idea. I'm quite sure that they would never have predicted you would be so upset by their absence. I'm certain that they'll be back soon."

"How can you be certain of that if you've no idea where or why they've gone?"

She smiled brightly. "Don't you have a council meeting to go to?"

Avoiding the subject, princess? he thought. *I'd expect no less.* "They can wait."

"Are you sure? If I were you, I wouldn't want to do anything that might make them any unhappier than they already are."

What very little patience he had left was waning. "Luckily, you're not me."

He knew Kurtis continued to fill the council's ears with all kinds of tales of his ineptitude, telling them he's a fool who makes poor decisions, who didn't know how to lead. That rooster could crow all he wanted—it wouldn't make any difference. Magnus knew he was a worthy leader. And, unlike both the council and his father, he actually cared about the lives of Limerians.

He sighed aloud. "Why do I bother to speak with you at all? We'll never see eye to eye on any subject."

"Perhaps it's because you have no one else to talk to?"

The insult landed with a sting that he didn't expect. A muscle in his scarred right cheek twitched. "How true. No one knows me like you do, princess."

She looked at him with a furrowed brow. "That was unkind of me to say."

"The truth is never unkind, princess. It's liberating. Now, if you'll excuse me." Magnus turned and walked away from her before she could reply.

Several days later, Enzo arrived at his door. "They're ready, your highness."

Magnus nodded at the guard and rose from the table piled high with parchment. He was grateful for the chance to have a bit of respite from the monotony of staring at endless lines of small, cramped cursive for hours, by candlelight, trying to master each and every detail of each and every law of his land.

Enzo escorted him to the northwest tower, where the king kept cold quarters for high-profile prisoners who were too valuable to throw in the dungeon with the common thieves and criminals. The walls were coated with a thin layer of ice, but the guards were under orders to ensure that the temperature stayed bearable.

At the top of the narrow spiral staircase, Magnus stepped into a small, circular room to greet the tower's two newest inhabitants.

"Welcome back."

Two pairs of eyes stared back at him, one flashing with hatred, the other with pure emptiness. There was Nic, straining against the chains that held his arms above his head. Locked up right across from him was Jonas, who hung slack in his shackles.

"Why do you have us chained up like thieves?" snarled Nic. "Where is Cleo? I want to see Cleo!"

Magnus moved closer to him. "You're chained up like a thief, dear Nicolo, because when I pledge a partnership with someone, I assume a certain level of trust going forward. I don't leave in the night, without any word or hint at where I'm going. What you did is unacceptable. As far as I knew, you were off gathering an army to help overthrow me."

"What an inspired idea. Wish I'd thought of it myself."

"You still don't think very much of me, do you, Cassian?" Magnus smiled and patted Nic's cheek.

"You don't want to know what I think of you." Nic growled. "I need to see Cleo."

"And I need you to tell me what you've been up to this last week so that we can all be friends again. Then again, it has been a while since I've seen an execution. That last one was quite entertaining. Remember, Agallon? It was very . . . explosive, no?"

Jonas neither responded nor moved.

Given the rebel's usual defiance, his silence was unnerving to Magnus.

"We were acquiring a gift for the princess," Nic said. "It takes time and effort to find something worthy."

"I'd rather hear it from Agallon." Magnus grasped the rebel's chin and raised his face up, expecting Jonas to spit in his face. Instead, Jonas simply stared straight forward, his eyes glazed over and dull.

"What's wrong with you?" Magnus frowned and flicked a glance at Nic. "Is he drunk?"

Nic's expression had grown haunted. "No."

Magnus let go of Jonas and walked a slow circle around the two prisoners. "Leave us," he said to the guards.

The guards bowed and left, closing the door behind them.

"Where are the two girls you were traveling with? Lysandra and Olivia?" Magnus asked. Jonas and Nic had returned to the palace grounds alone.

"Olivia's gone. And Lys . . ." Nic swallowed hard. "Lysandra's dead."

Jonas flinched, as if someone had cracked a whip against his back.

Magnus was silent for a moment, trying to process the shock and strange sensation of dread that came with this news. "How?" he asked.

Finally, Jonas rasped out: "Your sorceress sister."

Magnus's breath caught in his chest. "Lucia? You've seen Lucia?"

Jonas nodded weakly. "The man she was with, he murdered Lys. She tried to protect me, so he blasted her with fire. And then she was . . . just . . . gone."

The pain in Jonas's voice was a living thing. Magnus felt its sharp claws dig deeply into his chest.

Lucia and the man who'd tried to kill him with fire magic had been haunting his dreams ever since her visit.

"He must be a powerful witch," Magnus said.

"I don't think he's a witch," said Nic, his earlier bravado all but disappeared. "I've seen him twice now and it . . . he seems much more powerful than that. Princess Lucia must have claimed the fire Kindred. And somehow she and Kyan figured out how use its magic. He's in control of it now."

Magnus remembered the elemental wildfire that had broken out during the rebel attack on the road camp in eastern Paelsia. Whenever the fire touched a person, its flames burned blue, then shattered its victim like an ice sculpture.

To think that this power was out there, controlled by someone traveling with his sister . . .

"Why did you go there?" Magnus asked when he'd found his voice. "What did Princess Cleo want you to find for her there?"

"Cleo had nothing to do with it," Nic insisted. "We were visiting a market to search for a gift, just like I said. That's all."

Magnus could have the boy tortured, beaten, put into isolation—but he knew his story would never change. As for Jonas, he was already half dead by the look of him.

If the rebel had truly been broken by this, he'd be of no use to Magnus at all.

"What about our deal?" Magnus asked, looking directly at Jonas.

He lifted his gaze. "You're choosing now, of all times, to ask me about that?"

"I am. And I demand an answer."

"I don't know. I don't know about anything anymore."

"I empathize with your pain, Agallon, I truly do. But this is a new day, which will be followed by another and then another after that. Your friend is dead, and that's a tragedy, but nothing else has changed. Do you remember what you agreed to?"

"Yes."

"And are we still in agreement?"

There was an extended silence, through which Magnus waited patiently.

"We are," Jonas finally said.

Magnus summoned the guards back into the tower. "Unchain these two, feed them, clean them up, and bring them to me in the throne room. We have an important matter to discuss."

Jonas and Nic were brought into the throne room, both wearing fresh clothes and no longer smelling like they'd been traveling for days without a wash.

"Sit," Magnus instructed.

Jonas took a seat, then Nic reluctantly did the same.

Magnus pushed aside a stack of papers and picked up a message he'd received by raven that very morning. He slid it toward Nic. "Read it. Out loud."

With a sullen look on his face, Nic picked up the message, squinting at it in the dim late afternoon light.

> *Your Highness, Prince Magnus Damora,*
> *Since I'm currently in Kraeshia, let me be as blunt as its people. I have been working as your father's bodyguard during his trip here. He has offered the air Kindred to Emperor Cortas in exchange for sharing power over all of Mytica and Kraeshia.*

Nic paused, then looked up. "The king has the air Kindred?"

Jonas had gone completely pale. "Keep reading," he said, and Nic went on.

> *Should the emperor refuse, believe me when I tell you that both you and your kingdom will be at great risk. I strongly*

advise you to respond to this message immediately, as well
as send a representative here to Kraeshia as soon as possible.
Mytica will need all the support it can get right now.
I've included a piece of evidence to prove that I'm no
longer loyal to King Gaius and his ruthless greed.
With great hope for the future under your rule,
Felix Gaebras

Nic unfolded the last length of the message and pulled out what looked like a small, dry piece of parchment. He held it up to the light. "What is this?"

Jonas moved toward Nic to get a closer look at it. His eyes widened with shock. "Flayed skin. With a tattoo on it."

Nic dropped the piece of skin onto the tabletop.

Magnus nodded. "That is the official Clan of the Cobra mark— a group of skilled assassins who work specifically for my father. Felix must have sliced it off his own arm."

Finally, a small spark of life returned to Jonas's gaze. "I know Felix."

"You know him?" Magnus's gaze snapped to the rebel's. "How?"

"I thought he was a friend before I learned about his ties to your father. We had a . . . falling-out, and then he took off, back to the king who gave him the assignment to infiltrate my group."

"Small world," Magnus said, now unsure of the true intentions behind this message. "And proof enough that he isn't trustworthy."

"Two weeks ago I might have agreed with you," said Jonas, eyeing the tattoo and shaking his head. "But not now. Felix had decided to leave the Clan when he joined me, seeking redemption for his past. He was a true friend, and all I did was let him down." He went silent for a moment. "I believe he's telling the truth."

Magnus sat down heavily in his chair and pressed his hands

flat atop the table. It seemed that he and Jonas agreed on something. What an odd development.

His father was in Kraeshia with the emperor, conducting secret negotiations. And to think that, in his mind, Magnus was the traitor.

To rule the world was exactly what Gaius Damora wanted. And now he had the air Kindred.

Lucia and Kyan had the fire Kindred.

Amara had stolen the water Kindred.

That left only the earth Kindred unaccounted for.

"Agallon, you will go to Kraeshia as my representative to speak with Felix and his new group of rebels," Magnus announced. "And then you'll find my father and put a dagger through his heart."

It was the only way this could end.

"Will you do this?" Magnus asked after all had gone utterly silent at the table.

Jonas nodded. "I will."

"Good. You'll leave tomorrow at dawn."

CHAPTER 21

CLEO

LIMEROS

Roused from slumber, Cleo opened her eyes to find her room in shadows, and the sky outside her window still dark save for the light of the moon.

"Princess," whispered an urgent voice. "I'm sorry to disturb you so early."

A lantern's blaze cut through the darkness, bringing the face of Cleo's confidante into view.

She wiped the sleep from her eyes and sat up in bed. "What is it, Nerissa? Is something wrong?"

"I'm not sure 'wrong' is quite the correct word . . . but there's something I knew you'd want to know, and it can't wait until morning."

"Tell me."

Nerissa sat on the edge of the bed. "Jonas and Nic returned yesterday."

"What? Why am I not hearing this until now?"

"The prince got to them first and didn't want you to know."

Oh, no. A thousand different scenarios of how their return might have played out burst into her head at once.

"Are they all right? What has Magnus done to them?"

"They're fine," Nerissa assured her. "I just saw them briefly. Jonas asked me to tell you he's leaving at dawn, boarding a ship at Black Harbor bound for Kraeshia."

"To Kraeshia? Why to Kraeshia? To go after Amara and the water Kindred?"

"No. The prince has learned that King Gaius is currently in Kraeshia. He's sent him over to . . . take care of that situation."

"Oh. I see." Cleo was beyond surprised. Why would Magnus trust the rebel with such an important mission, especially after his unexplained disappearance? How desperate and bereft of other options he must be.

"Where's Nic now?" she asked.

"He's back in his room, sleeping I assume."

Cleo felt a sudden thud of disappointment. "If their trip to Paelsia had been successful, they would have woken me immediately to deliver the news."

"I'm sure Nic will tell you all about their trip in the morning." Nerissa rose from the bed. "For now, go back to sleep. You'll need your rest tomorrow."

It didn't feel right to her, any of it.

"Why would Magnus make such a monumental decision without consulting me first? Why hide it from me?"

"I don't know," Nerissa said, shaking her head. "Do you usually expect him to consult with you?"

"I don't have any idea what I expect from him anymore," she muttered. "Thank you for telling me this, Nerissa."

"Try to sleep, princess." Nerissa doused the flame in the lantern and turned to go.

"Do you really think I'll be able to go back to sleep now?"

Nerissa glanced over her shoulder. "Princess?"

"Help me get ready," Cleo said, pushing off her blankets and climbing out of bed. "We need to get to Black Harbor before dawn."

Black Harbor was located at the bottom of the high cliffs, below the castle grounds. A snaking road allowed travel by cart and carriage, but that route would make for a long journey, so Cleo and Nerissa decided instead to take the steps chiseled into the side of the cliff.

The *treacherous, icy* steps chiseled into the side of the cliff.

Finally, they reached the docks.

"Perhaps this was a foolish idea," Cleo whispered, her cheeks stinging from the frigid wind.

"Not at all," Nerissa assured her. "I admire you. You're standing up for yourself. You're not letting others make decisions that affect you. However . . ."

"Yes?"

"I wish we were still in Auranos. This cold is unbearable, and I miss the warmth of home."

Cleo couldn't help but laugh. "Agreed."

The small harbor was used only for docking ships visiting the palace, and for import and export. Today there were three large ships docked: two bearing the Auranian crest that carried imported goods such as vegetables, fruits, grains, and live animals—crates of chickens, pigs, and sheep—and one black ship with red sails bearing the Limerian cobra signet. Painted on the side of the ship were the words *Strength, Faith,* and *Wisdom.*

Dozens of sailors, servants, and other crew were moving about the docks, which was laden down with supplies. Cleo and Nerissa stayed back, watching the organized chaos.

"Princess." Nerissa took her gloved hand and squeezed it to get her attention.

And then she saw it, a sight she never would have believed possible.

Jonas Agallon and Magnus Damora, walking side by side along the dock.

"All right," she whispered. "That proves it. I'm still asleep and dreaming."

Nerissa smiled. "Or it's proof that miracles are possible."

Cleo couldn't tear her gaze away from the prince and the rebel. "Is Magnus smiling or clenching his teeth? Did Jonas just tell him a joke?"

"He's definitely clenching his teeth. I have a feeling Jonas won't be telling any jokes for a while."

"What do you mean?"

Nerissa shook her head. "I thought it best that Nic tell you."

Now Cleo was worried. Something must have gone terribly wrong in Paelsia. "Nerissa, Nic's not here. Clearly there's something I need to know, and you need to tell me."

Nerissa met Cleo's gaze with dark, troubled eyes. "Lysandra's dead."

Cleo gasped. *"What?"*

"During their journey they came across Princess Lucia and another man and . . . it didn't go well. I don't know much more than that, princess. I'm sorry."

"No. Oh, no!" Cleo gasped.

Lucia and another man. It had to be the companion who came to the palace, looking for the stone wheel. This was his doing. She knew it to be true, without a single doubt.

"I didn't know Lysandra was a friend of yours," Nerissa said.

"She wasn't. But this is still a great loss to us all. Lysandra was a skilled and passionate fighter." Cleo forced herself to breathe deeply, to compose herself and focus on the task at hand. Lysandra had never said a kind word to Cleo, but she knew how close she'd been to Jonas. Cleo had admired Lysandra for her strength and her ability to blend in and fight as fiercely as one of the boys.

And Jonas had cared so very deeply for her.

Her heart broke for him. *Oh, Jonas.*

Cleo pulled away from Nerissa's side and walked toward Jonas and Magnus.

Magnus saw her first, his expression shifting to displeasure in an instant. "What are you doing here?"

"Why wasn't I informed about this?" Cleo snapped.

Magnus rolled his eyes. "You shouldn't be here. Return to the palace immediately."

"No."

He hissed out a breath of annoyance. "These docks are no place for a princess."

Ignoring the prince, she turned to Jonas. "I just heard about Lysandra."

Jonas met her gaze. "I didn't even know how much she meant to me until moments before she . . ." He scrubbed his hand over his face. "I was so blind."

"There are no words, Jonas. I'm so very sorry."

She wrapped her arms around him and hugged him tightly. It took a moment, but he returned her embrace.

"I'm going to kill the king. Not for the prince, not even for all the Mytican citizens he's tried to own and exploit. I'm going to do it for her."

She nodded. "I know you'll be successful."

He pressed his lips against her forehead, kissing her gently. "I'll see you again soon, your highness."

"You'd better mean that."

Jonas nodded and gave her a half smile before heading for the gangplank and boarding the ship.

Cleo risked a glance at Magnus. Not for one solitary moment did she forget he was standing only a few paces away.

His arms were crossed over his chest and he studied her, his expression blank apart from the tight line of his jaw.

"What a tender farewell," he said. "How romantic."

Yes, of course the prince was dense enough to believe their exchange had been one of romance rather than friendship born during a time of hardship and grief.

She decided to let him believe whatever he wanted about her and the rebel.

She forgot all about Magnus when she saw someone approaching her—Nic, taking her completely by surprise.

"What are you doing here?" she demanded.

He regarded her with curiosity, shifting the bulky satchel he held to his other shoulder. "I was about to ask you the very same question. Have you spoken with Nerissa?"

"Yes. She hasn't told me everything, but she's told me enough." She took hold of his coat sleeve. "I know about Lysandra. That's awful beyond words. But, Nic, you could have been killed too."

"But I wasn't."

"Perhaps next time," Magnus said, interrupting them. "Cassian, go back to the palace. You're not wanted here."

Nic glared at him. "I'm going to Kraeshia with Jonas."

"Nic, no," she said, her voice nothing more than a rasp. "Jonas is ready to put his life in danger by going on this trip. You might think you're ready to do the same, but I refuse to risk losing you, too."

"I have to do this, Cleo. I need to help. What good am I to anyone if I just sit around the palace all day like a useless lump?"

His jaw tensed. "And I need to find Princess Amara. I want to get the water Kindred back, and she needs to pay for what she did to Ashur." The grief he'd been trying so hard to keep hidden from her, from everyone, flared in his eyes. "Please understand that I need to go."

"Would you stay with me if I asked you to?"

He let out a long, shaky breath. "Yes. Of course I would."

She nodded, then grabbed him around his waist and held on tightly. "I know how much Ashur meant to you, so I won't ask you to stay. Go. But remember one thing: If you get yourself killed, I'm going to be furious with you."

"I'll be furious too." Nic snorted softly. "By the way, you should know I don't have a birthday gift for you. Our trip to Paelsia was unsuccessful in every way possible."

She fought the urge to look at Magnus and lowered her voice. "I'm sorry to hear that."

"Me too. The vendor we wanted to visit to purchase your present . . . unfortunately, she'd recently passed away."

Cleo bit her lip. "Oh."

"She was quite old, so we can't be overly surprised. But I really hoped she'd still be around to help us out."

"We'll have to find someone else. She couldn't have been the only one."

"Yes." He squeezed her hands. "I love you, Cleo. But I think you know that already."

"What love for the princess this morning. How absolutely delightful for you all." Magnus crossed his arms over his black jacket. "Now, if you really are going, Cassian, then get on your way."

"You're not going to try to stop me?" Nic asked warily.

"Why would I? You are free to go wherever you please—as you have already proven by your recent trip with the rebel. And know

275

that if you *do* get yourself killed," Magnus said, offering him an unpleasant smile, "I won't be furious with you at all."

Ignoring Magnus, Nic kissed Cleo's cheeks, gave her another squeeze, and then did the same to Nerissa. With one last, wistful look at each of them, he boarded the Limerian ship.

Cleo reached for Nerissa's hand, needing her support now more than ever before. But she wouldn't cry. This was what had to be done.

As the sun rose above the cliffs behind them, the black ship set sail across the dark sea.

CHAPTER 22

AMARA

KRAESHIA

Amara knew the perfect place to go when she wanted to be alone.

It was a courtyard off the east wing of the Emerald Spear, a garden given to her by her father so she could contribute to the beauty of the royal residence. After all, the only thing expected from Kraeshian girls was an interest in pretty flowers.

But instead of flowers, Amara had cultivated a garden of tens of thousands of rocks and shells and semiprecious stones, all gathered from around the world. Her father had proclaimed it ugly and disappointing; Amara couldn't disagree more.

Especially now, because it was here that she'd hidden the water Kindred.

And it was in this garden that she'd sit and think about her plan to control her own future without being under the thumbs of men whose goal it was to make her feel like less than a person. In her life, she'd met very few men who strayed from the Kraeshian misogyny she'd come to expect.

Felix was one of them.

He wanted nothing from her. He made no demands. She'd taken him to her bed because she liked the width of his shoulders and the crookedness of his nose and the fact that her father would never approve if he ever learned of the affair.

But then she'd begun to look forward to spending time with the Limerian, and not only at night. He amused her and challenged her with his opinions—the few that he'd openly shared with her, at least. Felix had proved himself to be far more than just the king's own personal shield. Without even trying, he had become special to her.

This had created complications for her at a time when everything needed to be simple.

Her grandmother entered the rock garden and came to sit by her side on the stone bench.

"You have many worries, *Dhosha*. I see them on your lovely face."

"Do you blame me?"

"Not a bit. The fact that you approach your life and your decisions with thoughtfulness and care is what makes me know I've taught you well."

"I wish all of it were easier."

"Nothing worth having is easy, *Dhosha*," her grandmother said, resting a hand on her shoulder. "I went to see my apothecary earlier today."

Amara stiffened. Neela spoke of a man with a great and secret talent for creating magical potions for her grandmother and, in the past, for her mother. "And?"

"He mentioned that another client from the palace paid him a visit, not so long ago."

"Someone from the palace? Who?"

"Your brother. Ashur."

Amara's gaze widened. "But . . . I didn't know Ashur even knew of your apothecary."

"Nor did I."

"What potion did he request?"

"I don't know. He only mentioned Ashur's visit in passing, when he asked after his well-being."

"And you didn't ask any further questions? Grandmother, I need to know."

"Why? What difference does it make now?"

"If it makes no difference to you, then why did you bother to mention it to me?"

"I see now that I shouldn't have." Neela took Amara's hand in hers. "Quiet your thoughts, *Dhosha*. You are strong and you will do what needs to be done. You're close now. Closer than ever before."

Amara let out a long, weary sigh, then nodded firmly. "Don't worry about me, *Madhosha*. I know what I have to do."

"Come sit next to me, Daughter."

The emperor rose from his chair as Amara entered the solarium, a private room he used to entertain his most important guests.

She hadn't known what to expect when he summoned her here, and she saw now that she wasn't the only one he'd called upon. She was the last to arrive. King Gaius, Felix, Milo, and her brothers were already there.

Then it became clear. She'd been invited to be present to hear the emperor declare his decision.

She'd never been invited to such an important event before.

Had she somehow proven her worth to her father? That her political opinion mattered? He would do well to take her under his wing as an advisor; she would be far more helpful than both Elan and Dastan combined.

"Princess," King Gaius said, standing as she took a seat. "You look beautiful today."

"Thank you, your grace." Why did men always find it necessary to comment on whether or not a woman's exterior pleased them? She knew she was beautiful. No need to constantly restate it, as if doing so would earn one points in a game.

The king did look confident today. Did he honestly believe her father was about to agree to his overly ambitious terms?

Felix and Milo stood behind the king, their hands clasped behind their backs. Felix nodded at her, and their eyes met for a brief moment. He, on the other hand, did not look entirely confident today. Was that a shadow of worry sliding behind his dark eyes?

My pretty beast, she thought. *Don't fret. You've more than proven your worth to me.*

Her attention shifted to her brothers, neither of whom had risen from their seats to greet her. They each drank from golden, jeweled goblets, and she saw that the center of the table was laden with a beautiful display of colorful, fragrant fruit.

The emperor waved his hand toward the guards stationed at the doors. "Leave us to discuss our important matters in private." Amara watched as they left, noting that Mikah was not among them, and suddenly realizing she hadn't seen him in several days. Perhaps he was ill.

The guards closed the heavy doors with a loud thud, and Amara's heart began to race. Today was an important day.

A brand-new day that would either foretell an uncertain future for the Kraeshian Empire . . .

. . . Or a day that would mark the end of the King of Blood's life.

This was how her father conducted his political negotiations: He either agreed to obviously favorable terms, or he made an annoying problem go away by killing it and everyone involved. In the end, Emperor Cortas always won.

"I have taken time to consider your interesting offer, Gaius." The emperor remained standing, his lined face somber and humorless. There would be no playfulness today.

King Gaius nodded. "And I'm ready to hear your decision."

"You wish to become the second emperor of the Kraeshian Empire, to share the power, equally, with me. For this, you will give me the air Kindred and teach me how to unlock its magic. And along with that magic, I will also have your daughter's abilities of sorcery at my disposal. Do I have this correct, Gaius?"

"You do," the king said, his tone even, almost as if he were bored.

Amara had to admire the king's confidence—or was it stupidity? After all, he was nothing but a scavenger, asking a lion to share his meat for free.

However, the king didn't strike her as stupid. Just the opposite.

He had to have another plan up his sleeve.

The emperor spoke up again. "And I am expected to take you at your word that what you've told me about your daughter, about the Kindred, is true."

"Yes."

"This is what troubles me, Gaius. You've shown me no proof of either."

"And you will see no proof until we've come to an agreement. With respect, your eminence, this is the greatest opportunity of your life. You're wise, very wise, and I'm sure you must see that." Gaius took a sip from his goblet, his gaze steady on the emperor's. "And if you discover me to be a liar, you can have me executed and take Mytica without resistance. With my blessing, in fact. Simple."

The emperor pursed his lips. "Mytica will be mine no matter how this plays out. It will become part of the Kraeshian Empire, not remain a sovereign kingdom."

The king blinked. "Very well."

"And I want another Kindred. If we are to share power equally, it's only fair that I possess more than just the moonstone orb."

A thin smiled stretched across the king's lips. "You ask a great deal, but I will agree to that as well."

There was a long, uncomfortable silence, and all Amara could hear was the sound of her heart drumming wildly against her chest.

"Fetch the document," the emperor instructed Dastan.

Dastan got up from the table and returned quickly with a scroll, which he placed in front of the king.

"I was hoping you'd agree to my requests," the emperor said. "So here is the official agreement. You'll want to note the caveat there, at the bottom. Essentially, it states that you consent to being killed if you lie to me now or in the future."

The king scanned the parchment, his expression revealing nothing.

Finally, he looked up. "I will need something to sign this with."

The emperor smiled. "I won't make you sign in your own blood, although I did consider it." He motioned to Elan, who brought over a quill and ink.

The king took the quill in hand and signed the bottom of the parchment below the emperor's signature.

Men never failed to amuse Amara. Did these two truly think a mere piece of paper equaled a binding agreement?

King Gaius handed the signed parchment back to the emperor, whose lips lifted up to a self-satisfied grin.

"Much gratitude, King Gaius. Now. There is one more matter that may prove troublesome," the emperor said.

King Gaius leaned back in his seat, his jaw tightening. "Is there?"

"In Kraeshia, power is passed down through the bloodline. This," he waved at the parchment, "is a legal document between you and me only. Any future rulers of my empire will belong to the Cortas family."

"That is a problem," the king said. "And quite frankly, I'm confused. You agreed to my terms, and I feel I've been extremely generous and patient with you. And now you're trying to tell me that my family's stake in this empire ends when I die?"

Amara would have had to be deaf not to hear the dark threats behind his words.

This was getting interesting.

The emperor nodded at Dastan again. "Send for the palace augur."

Amara frowned. The palace augur was a religious official who conducted Kraeshian rituals and ceremonies exclusively for the emperor.

"Are you bringing him here to have me swear a religious oath?" the king said evenly. "Your eminence, forgive me, but what does this have to do with discussing my bloodline?"

"This is not that kind of oath," the emperor said. "This will ease your mind greatly when it comes to the future."

"My blood is Damora blood—not even magic can change that. It seems we have a problem, your eminence."

"Not a problem that can't be fixed," the emperor said. "You will marry my daughter. Today."

Surely, Amara had heard him wrong.

She grappled to hold on to her composure, to not suddenly flee from the room. So this was why her father had wanted her here, and it had nothing to do with respect.

He wanted to use her as a bargaining chip.

She felt Felix's gaze on her, and chanced a glance at him. He studied her with a deep frown.

"This union," the emperor continued, "will symbolize the joining of our families and the sharing of power between you and me. Is this agreeable to you, Gaius? I know you've recently lost your queen and must be ready for a new one."

The king appeared to consider this turn of events calmly. "Yes, my beloved Althea," he said. "I have missed the company of a wife so very much. But with respect, your eminence, I would never wish to force such an arrangement upon anyone, least of all your lovely daughter."

"Perhaps that is where you and I differ."

"Perhaps," the king acknowledged with a nod. "But I could only agree to this if Princess Amara does as well."

All attention shifted to the princess.

She'd refused every other suitor her father had thrust her way, and the emperor had never forced her hand before. But that was then, when she was of so very little importance to him.

She'd be incredibly naive to think she had a choice here. And Amara was anything but naive. To make a fuss would only cause unnecessary conflict.

Today, of all days, she wanted her father to be pleased with her.

"It would be my honor to become your queen, King Gaius," she said, ignoring the tightness in her chest.

The king raised his brow. She'd surprised him.

Dastan returned, accompanied by an old man with white hair and dressed in green robes.

"Excellent," the emperor said. "Augur, please, let's not waste another moment in making this official."

The augur produced a long silk scarf that had been in Amara's family for countless generations, and gestured for Amara to come stand before the king. Holding to Kraeshian tradition, he wound the scarf around her and the king, from ankle to shoulders, finally binding their hands together.

Amara looked up into the king's eyes. He looked so very much like his son, Magnus. She hadn't fully realized it until now.

As was custom, the wedding ceremony was performed in the Kraeshian language, with the augur repeating the vows in the common language so the king could understand.

The augur spoke solemnly about the duties of husband and wife. He stated that the wife would always be truthful to her husband. She would give him her power. She would give him children. She would serve him.

If she displeased him, it was within his rights to beat her.

The king's fingers tightened against hers as the words sliced into her very being, as if cutting her throat.

If he ever dared lay a hand on her in anger, she would kill him.

The ceremony was over, and they were proclaimed husband and wife. The augur unwound the scarf, and the king drew Amara to him and kissed her when instructed, to seal their union symbolically. Despite all her inner strife and the heart-sinking knowledge that she'd just married someone old enough to be her father, the kiss was not entirely unpleasant.

And this marriage was only another opportunity for her.

Her father came to her, clasping her face between his hands and kissing her on both cheeks. "I've never been so proud of you, my dear daughter!"

It seemed that she'd finally won his approval. "Thank you, Father."

"This is an incredible day—the joining of two families, two nations. A future bright with magic and power."

She smiled. "I couldn't agree more. As a matter of fact, I have something that will be perfect for such a celebration. It's in my bedroom suite, if you'll let me go get it? It's a bottle of fine Paelsian wine."

His eyes widened with surprise and delight. "How wonderful!"

"Yes, I completely forgot until just now that I brought it back with me from my journey. I knew you'd want to try it. And if you like it, there are two more cases still on the ship."

"I've heard Paelsian wine tastes like magic itself," Elan said.

"Yes, it sounds like the perfect way to honor this occasion," the emperor said. "Go fetch it, Daughter. And we will toast to the future of Kraeshia."

She left the room, her head in a daze of worry, excitement, and fear.

You don't have to do this, a small part of her urged. *There is another choice for you. If you run away, you could make a life for yourself somewhere else, somewhere far away from here.*

This moment of doubt very nearly amused her.

There was no other way. She knew this. She accepted this.

Her destiny had been set in stone from the moment she'd been born.

She hurried to her room and returned to the solarium, the bottle of Paelsian wine in hand. The emperor snatched it from her, swiftly uncorked it, and poured the pale yellow wine into four goblets. Her brothers received one each, and the emperor handed the fourth to the king. "I'm afraid there isn't enough for you, Daughter."

"I'm afraid I must decline," King Gaius held up his hand. "It's against Limerian religion to indulge in inebriants."

"What an unfortunate policy," the emperor said. "Very well, this goblet is for you, then, Amara."

She took the glass from him and gave a small bow. "Thank you, Father."

The emperor held his chalice up in front of him. "To the future of the Kraeshian Empire. And to many more sons for you, Gaius. Many, many more sons! Amara, boys, drink."

Amara took a sip of its contents and watched as her father and brothers all drained their glasses.

"This is incredible," the emperor gasped, his eyes wide with pleasure. "As delicious as I've always heard. And now I've finally tasted it for myself. Gaius, I will need more cases delivered to the Jewel, an endless supply."

The king nodded. "I will arrange it myself, your eminence."

"It is quite good," Dastan allowed.

"There's no more?" Elan asked. "I want more."

"Amara, have the cases waiting on your ship brought to the palace so we can continue our celebrations. I've already made sure to have a feast ready in anticipation of our mutual agreement today. And once you've returned, daughter, you must change into another gown. What you're wearing is not appropriate for the wife of a . . ." He frowned. "Amara?"

Amara counted slowly to ten, then she began again at the start. Her heart pounded. She couldn't hold on, not for much longer.

Finally, when she couldn't stop herself, she spit the wine back out into the goblet.

The emperor frowned. "What is wrong with you?"

She wiped her mouth with a silk cloth. "I know you won't believe me, Father, but I am sorry. I wish there could have been another way."

His quizzical expression shifted quickly to distress. He clutched his throat. "Daughter . . . what have you done?"

"Only what I had to." She glanced at her brothers, who were also clawing at their throats and gasping.

The poison was supposed to act very quickly and not cause any pain.

"I'm sorry," she said again, her eyes stinging.

One by one, each of her family members dropped to the ground, twitching, their faces turning purple as they stared at her with confusion, and then hatred.

Just as Ashur had.

Finally, they were still.

Amara turned to face the four guards who'd reentered the solarium during the wedding ceremony. Their hands were ready on their weapons, eyeing each other with uncertainty.

"You will not say anything about this," she told them. "To anyone."

"They won't listen to you," the king said, his voice surprisingly calm. "Felix, Milo. Take care of this."

Felix and Milo were on the guards in seconds, flashes of steel in their grips.

The guards were dead by the time they each hit the ground.

Amara let out a slow, shaky breath, her wild gaze now meeting the king's.

He regarded her without any accusation or shock. "I had a feeling you were up to something. But I had no idea it would be this extreme."

"You call it extreme. I call it necessary." She swallowed, hard, eyeing his deadly bodyguards with new apprehension. Felix had followed the king's command. Would he kill her just as swiftly as he'd killed the guards if the king ordered him to?

"I was once given a prophecy that I would rule the universe with a goddess by my side," Gaius said. "I was beginning to think it was a lie. Now I'm not so sure." He bowed his head. "If you'll

have me, I would like to remain your husband and your servant . . .
Empress Cortas."

A violent roiling inside of her grew still as she suddenly realized that she'd succeeded.

Bloodlines ruled in Kraeshia, and she was the first infant
daughter to survive an emperor's—and all his male heirs'—death.

An infant daughter that had grown to become a woman.

And the first empress Kraeshia had ever seen.

Perhaps she and the king made a excellent match after all.

King Gaius and Amara notified the captain of the guard that rebels
had infiltrated the palace and poisoned the royal family. Amara
was the only Cortas to have survived this stealthy attack.

Of course she'd blame it on rebels. Who would ever believe
that Princess Amara poisoned her family?

Amara went to see her grandmother after the bodies were
removed from the solarium. Her smile and embrace made some of
her pain fade away.

"This is all for the greater good, *Dhosha*," she said. "I knew you'd
be victorious."

"Without your belief in me, I don't know if I could have been."

"Do you have doubts about what must come next?"

"Yes, *Madhosha*," Amara admitted. "Many. But I know it has to
be done."

Neela pressed her cool palm against Amara's flushed cheek.
"Then there's no reason to wait."

She finally saw Felix again in the halls near her chambers and went
to him immediately. He eyed her with uncertainty.

"So . . ." he began. "*That* was rather unexpected, wasn't it?"

"Perhaps for you. But not for me."

"You're a dangerous girl." He cocked his head. "But I think I already knew that. Perhaps that's what I like best about you."

"So you *do* like me."

He let out a nervous laugh. "Was that ever at question, princess? Haven't I shown you how much I like you on a nightly basis?"

"That's not what I meant."

"Apologies, I'm being crude. I rely on my roughness when I feel off balance. And that's exactly how you make me feel." He cleared his throat. "Congratulations on your marriage. Quite the match."

"It is, isn't it? For now, at least."

He frowned. "What do you mean?"

"I need the king so I can acquire the remaining Kindred and learn how to access their magic."

"So you're telling me the king isn't safe around you? Are you sure that's wise, princess? To be so open with me, his bodyguard? It's my job to protect him."

"You don't fool me, my pretty beast. The day he dies, you'll be cheering right alongside everyone. You really should have agreed to work for me when I gave you the chance."

"I suppose I do work for you, now that you're his wife."

Amara took his arm, making him flinch. "Apologies. You're still hurt?"

He rubbed his forearm, which she knew was bandaged underneath the sleeve of his shirt from an injury he'd recently obtained. "I'm healing."

"Good. Now come with me. I need you."

He glanced nervously up and down the hallway. "I'm not sure this is a good time, princess. You were, after all, *just* married to the King of Blood. I don't think he would approve of our arrangement. In fact, I'm quite sure he'd chop off certain parts of my body if he knew about it."

"How strange. I wouldn't have thought you to be a coward."

His eyes sparked with passion. "I'm not."

"So prove it." She went up on her tiptoes and kissed him. He grabbed her by her waist, pressed her up against the wall, and kissed her back. Hard.

"Careful. I'm getting addicted to you," he breathed. "Considering an addiction like this could lead me to my doom, I'm not sure I like that very much."

"The feeling's mutual. Now come with me. I have something important to show you."

"I'd follow you anywhere, princess."

She led him to the grand foyer before the main entrance to the Emerald Spear. They were surrounded by windows that sent sparkling green light down upon the glossy floor.

"Is this it?" he asked, eyeing their surroundings. "It's a bit too public for my tastes. How about we go somewhere more enclosed?"

Amara's smile faded. "Guards!" she shouted sharply. "Here he is!"

Felix went stiff as he looked around with confusion at the dozen guards who were quickly closing in on him, their weapons drawn.

"What is this?" he asked her. "What's going on?"

She took a deep breath and raised her chin to the guards. "Felix Gaebras has revealed himself to be a rebel conspirator. He poisoned my family—*he* killed the emperor and my brothers."

"Princess, what are you saying?"

"Arrest him," she said, her throat raw.

"Are you crazy? The king won't let this happen!"

"The king already knows what you did, and he also believes you deserve to pay for it with death."

Amara watched as clarity, then fury, slithered into Felix's gaze. "You soulless bitch," he growled.

He then made the error of fighting back against the guards in an attempt to escape. The scuffle lasted only a few moments before he was overcome, beaten bloody, and knocked unconscious.

The guards dragged him away, bound for the Kraeshian dungeon and a swift execution.

Amara had found that she was starting to fall in love with Felix—and love made one weak.

This necessary sacrifice would make her strong again.

CHAPTER 23

JONAS

KRAESHIA

Jonas had spent most of his life surrounded by dirt.

But for the better part of this past week, he'd been surrounded by nothing but water—miles upon miles of it. The peaceful cool of the waves and the breeze had given him a great deal of time to think. And to mourn.

Now his mind was clear again and he was ready to follow through with his promise to kill the king.

"For you, Lys," he whispered to himself as he stared out at the coastline of the Jewel of the Empire in the distance. "Everything I do from now on, it's all for you."

The ship finally docked. Jonas and Nic grabbed their satchels and headed down the gangplank.

"So this is Kraeshia," Nic said, staring out at the glimmering city before him.

"I hope so," Jonas replied. "If not, we took a wrong turn somewhere."

"See? There's that cheeky rebel I like."

"You like me? That's news to me, Cassian."

"You're growing on me. Slowly. Like a fungus."

Jonas managed a grin. "The feeling's mutual."

Magnus had returned a message to the Kraeshian rebels with their original raven, ordering them to meet Jonas and Nic upon their arrival.

"I don't see Felix," Jonas said under his breath as he surveyed their surroundings. "I thought he might be here."

There was one person waiting at the end of the docks, standing still next to a sparkling white beach. They walked toward the tall young man with dark skin and pale brown eyes, who nodded at their approach.

"Jonas Agallon?" he asked.

"That's right."

"My name is Mikah Kasro. Welcome to Kraeshia."

Jonas introduced Nic, then asked, "Where's Felix?"

"Come with me and I'll explain everything," Mikah said, scanning the docks. "Too many curious eyes out here."

"I'm not going anywhere until you tell me where Felix is. And then I want to know where King Gaius is."

"What's your business with the king?"

"That's none of your concern."

"Everything that happens in Kraeshia is my concern. But I suppose the king's whereabouts don't matter much to you now. King Gaius and his new bride left for Mytica several days ago."

Jonas stared at him. "What did you just say?"

"His new *bride*?" Nic asked, frowning. "He got married?"

Mikah nodded, his expression grim. "To Princess Amara."

Nic's jaw dropped.

This was impossible. Jonas had just arrived, ready to put a dagger in the king's heart, to die doing it, if necessary.

But the king was gone.

He swore under his breath. "Unbelievable. So Felix went with them, then. Is that why he isn't here?"

"Not exactly."

"Then what, exactly?"

"Felix is very likely dead by now."

Jonas's chest clenched into a painful fist, and he stared questioningly at Mikah.

"He was charged with a very serious crime and was taken to the underground dungeons. Once a prisoner is put down there, the only way they come out is in pieces."

"What was his crime?"

Again, Mikah glanced back at the happy crowd on the beach. Jonas followed his line of sight. The Kraeshians basked under the sunshine, all of them seemingly clueless as to the darkness of the Jewel that lay so very close by.

Mikah turned back to Jonas and Nic and, in hushed tones, told them the story of the poisoned wedding celebration—the story that was not yet public knowledge.

When he was finished, Mikah seemed even more certain that Felix was already dead.

But Mikah didn't know Felix nearly as well as Jonas did.

After their talk at the docks, Jonas and Nic were brought back to the rebel base, a collection of rooms on the top floor of a purple building painted on the side with a floral mural. Such a happy-looking place for such a serious and deadly discussion.

"She's back," Nic said as he exited the building to have a private chat with Jonas.

Jonas looked up at the hawk circling above them. "Yes, I noticed her earlier."

"She's not going to give up."

"She should."

"You should talk to her."

"I don't want to talk to her."

"She could help," Nic persisted.

"How? By getting someone else I care about killed?" He hissed out a breath. "Fine. Go back inside. I'll handle this."

"Don't be too hard on her, all right?"

"Can't promise anything."

Nic nodded grimly, then disappeared back into the building.

It was far too hot for cloaks in Kraeshia, so instead he pulled his cotton shirt off over his head and threw it on the grass in front of him for Olivia to put on. Then he turned his back.

And he waited.

Just as he'd suspected, it didn't take long for him to hear the sound of flapping wings. He felt a charge in the air that raised the hair on his arms, making him swallow a quick intake of breath. He waited several more moments before he turned around.

Olivia stood, barefoot, six paces away from him, wearing his shirt. He'd always known she was gorgeous, but her beauty seemed much more obvious now that he knew she was an immortal. Her hair wasn't ordinary black; it was obsidian, and her brown skin shimmered as if lightly coated in gold dust. And while before her eyes had been just green, now Jonas saw they held the shade and depth of dark, otherworldly emeralds.

"Figured you'd need some clothes," he said. "I don't know much about Watchers, but I do know that most girls are modest about that sort of thing."

Her expression was tense, her gaze fixed on him. "I'm sorry, Jonas."

"Yeah, that's what you said the last time I saw you."

"I couldn't tell you what I was before."

"Why not?"

"Would you have asked me to join you if you knew?" She exhaled shakily, then straightened her shoulders. "I know I made mistakes, but please remember that I did save your life by healing your wound."

"And then you let Lysandra die."

"I wasn't ready. I had no idea our paths would cross with his so soon. My magic is substantial, but it's no match for the fire Kindred. Timotheus warned me to avoid him at all costs, that it wasn't my job to fight him, only to protect you."

Jonas blinked. "What the hell are you talking about? The fire Kindred?"

Olivia nodded solemnly. "Kyan . . . he is the fire Kindred. An elemental god previously imprisoned in an amber orb."

Jonas now stared at her with undiluted shock. "And you chose to wait until now to tell me that?"

"I told you, it wasn't my job to explain. Only to—"

"Yeah, only to protect me. Got it. You've done a stellar job, by the way." He rubbed his eyes. "Tell me, Olivia, why would you need to protect me?"

"Because Timotheus told me to."

"I've no idea who Timotheus is. And yet, Kyan mentioned him too."

"He is my elder. My leader."

"Another Watcher."

"Yes. He has visions of the future. One of those visions included you. Somehow, in some way, you're important, Jonas. Phaedra knew it too. That's why she watched over you. That's why she sacrificed her life to save yours."

"What role could *I* have possibly played in this Timotheus's vision? I'm a poor vineyard worker from Paelsia, a failed rebel leader. I'm nobody."

"That's exactly what I told him," she said, nodding. "That you're a complete nobody. But still he insisted."

He gaped at her. She presented her insulting words as simple facts, without a sliver of belligerence.

"You can go now. I don't want you anywhere near me. Go, fly off to your Sanctuary. Or have you exiled yourself on my behalf, just like Phaedra did?"

"Hardly. The mystical walls that kept us locked inside our world fell away when the new sorceress's blood was spilled. If the others knew this, they might try to leave, thus putting themselves in danger with the fire Kindred on the loose. So Timotheus is keeping it a secret."

Jonas's jaw tightened. "Go away, Olivia."

"I know you're angry about Lysandra. I'm angry, too. But we can't change it. It's done. I couldn't have saved her anyway, even if I'd gone against Timotheus's orders."

"You could have damn well tried."

Her expression tightened. "You're right, I should have. But I was afraid. I'm not afraid anymore. I'm back, and I mean to uphold my duty to Timotheus—even if it means I must occasionally break the rules."

"So you're back to stay, to keep me safe for some unknown future event."

"Yes."

"I don't care about the future. All I want is for you to leave me alone right now."

"I can't do that." He shot her a look of outrage, and she shrugged. "I will redeem myself in your eyes."

"I highly doubt that."

"I will stay and protect you whether you like it or not, Jonas Agallon. But it will be much easier for us both if you don't try to fight this arrangement."

She was utterly exasperating. But now, standing right before her and staring into her determined eyes, he found he couldn't hate her for flying away when she had. If Kyan really was what she said . . .

. . . Then they were in worse trouble than Jonas already suspected.

And the fact that there were three others out there like Kyan made the wrath of King Gaius's evil seem no more serious than a stubbed toe.

If Olivia was telling the truth about the current state of the Sanctuary, that meant her magic was just as strong as ever, not fading the way an exiled Watcher's did. And that certainly seemed to be the case: she could shift into a hawk at will; she had healed Jonas's fatal wound with earth magic.

"If you stay, we do things my way," Jonas said. "This time you're not only protecting me. You're protecting me and all of my friends."

"You're asking for a promise I don't have the authority to make. You are the only one I'm assigned to protect."

"I never asked for a personal guardian. You can tell that to your precious elder if he makes a fuss. This isn't negotiable. If you want to stay, you will commit yourself to protecting everyone I care about."

"But how am I supposed to—?"

He held up his hand. "No. No arguing. Yes or no?"

Her eyes flashed. "You're lucky that I even came back to protect you, mortal! And you dare to act as if you have any say in this?"

"But don't I? You can watch me from above, flapping your pretty wings while I throw rocks at you and lead myself into danger, or you can stay down here on the ground and fight with us. What'll it be?"

Olivia glared at him, challenge in her eyes. "Fine."

He cocked his head and challenged her right back. "Good."

Then she flung off his shirt and, in a quick blur of gold, bare skin, and feathers, transformed into a hawk and took off into the air, squawking with displeasure.

Jonas watched as she perched on the edge of a neighboring rooftop.

Felix had wanted another chance at life, to redeem himself for his past mistakes and set forth toward a brighter future. Jonas was sorry he hadn't given his friend that chance.

He'd give it to Olivia instead.

CHAPTER 24

FELIX

KRAESHIA

He didn't scream at all during his first day in the Kraeshian dungeon, but that resolve didn't last long. He wasn't that surprised when the howls came forth. As a Cobra, he'd quickly learned that enough torture would break anybody. Even him.

Especially torture meted out by prison guards faced with a Limerian accused of killing their royal family.

After a week in the dungeon, his back had been lashed into raw meat. A hundred, five hundred, a thousand kisses from the whip. He didn't know anymore. He hung limply from the chains bolted to the ceiling as the blood oozed down his ruined back.

"Go on," a guard taunted him. "Cry out for your mama. It'll help."

Felix didn't know the guard's name, but in his head, he called him the demon.

"Hey, remember this?" The demon threw something onto the dirt floor right in front of Felix. "Now you're looking at yourself."

A filthy eyeball stared right up at Felix.

How much simpler things had been earlier today, when it had

been in his head, before the demon-guard took a dagger to his left eye socket.

"Why don't you get on with it and kill me," Felix sputtered.

"Where's the fun in that? I have to work here, with you stinking, disgusting murderers, day in and day out. Why would you deny me a little joy?"

"Your joy is wasted on me. I didn't kill Emperor Cortas and his sons."

The guard smiled thinly. "Of course you didn't. You're completely innocent—just like the rest of the scum in this prison."

"That bitch you call a princess framed me for her crimes!"

"Oh, not this again. Beautiful, sweet Princess Amara, killing her father and brothers? Why would she do something like that?"

"For power, of course. Trust me, there's nothing sweet about her."

The demon-guard snorted. "She's nothing but a woman, what use would she have for power?"

"You're so stupid, I almost feel sorry for you."

The demon-guard narrowed his eyes and rose to standing. He took his dagger out and used the tip of his blade to poke the wound where Felix's tattoo used to be.

Felix cried out at the sharp, sudden pain.

"Aw, does that hurt?" the guard asked, grinning.

"I'm going to kill you," Felix gritted out.

"No, you're not. You're going to hang there in chains and let me keep hurting you until it's time for you to die. And then I'm going to beat you some more before I finally eviscerate you." He scraped at the flayed patch of skin again. "Yeah, we know all about you and your Cobra Clan here. You lot think you're so tough, so elite. Well, you were right to slice your meaningless tattoo off. Because now you're nothing. Can you see that? Can you see you're nothing?"

"Go kiss a horse's arse."

The guard trailed his blade up Felix's arm, along his shoulder to his neck, and up over his chin and cheek until the sharp tip came to rest right beneath his right eye. "Maybe I'll take this one, too. Maybe I'll take your tongue and your ears, too, and leave you blind, mute, and deaf."

He thought about reminding the moronic guard that taking his ears wouldn't make him deaf—he'd witnessed someone in the Clan make this mistake before—but he said nothing.

There was a knock at the door of his cell. The demon-guard answered it, speaking to someone through a small window.

"Sorry to disappoint you," he said, turning back to Felix, "but I have to leave you for a bit. I promise I'll be back later. Rest up." He cranked a wheel that lowered Felix's chains, relieving him from standing on the tips of his toes and sending him slumping down to the floor. "Look at you, red with your own blood. Red is the color of Limeros, isn't it? I'm sure that King Gaius would be proud to see your patriotism now—that is, if he gave a damn about you anymore."

Laughing, the guard left him.

"Well, now," Felix mumbled to himself, "this is certainly an unfortunate situation, isn't it?"

He choked out a laugh, but it barely sounded human.

The walls of his cell were covered in foul-smelling slime; the floor was nothing more than a mixture of dirt and bodily waste. He'd been given nothing but filthy water since he'd woken up there, and not a single scrap of food. If it wasn't for the chains holding him up, he didn't think he'd be able to stand on his own.

"What do you think about all of this?" He posed his question to the large, hairy spider in the far corner of the ceiling. Felix had named his ugly cellmate Amara.

In his nineteen long years of life, Felix has never hated anyone as much as he did Amara.

"What was that, Jonas?" Felix had also given a name to the spider's most recent victim: a fly who'd haplessly wandered too close to the web and was now as trapped as Felix was.

He held a trembling hand to his ear. "'Don't lose hope?' 'Keep that chin up?' Sorry to say, friend, but it's far too late for that. For both of us, it seems."

The only thing that was keeping him conscious, that kept him fighting to live through this hell, was a hopeless dream of vengeance. Oh, how he would ruin her if he ever managed to escape. That deceptive, conniving, ruthless, cold-blooded, power-hungry monster.

Just the thought of her now made him tremble with rage, a wracking motion that quickly devolved into a mess of dry sobs.

Oh come now, Amara the spider said. *You've done more than your share of harm in your life. Wouldn't you say you've earned this kind of treatment?*

You're as bad as they come, squeaked Jonas the fly. *You're a killer, remember? You don't deserve a second chance.*

"I'm not saying you're wrong," he replied. "But you two aren't helping, you know that?"

He gingerly touched his face, feeling the thick, dried blood caked to his left cheek. His severed eye stared at him from the far side of the cell.

Amara had made him feel like he mattered to her—like he mattered at all—if only a little bit. And then she'd done *this.* Why? And why did the king so readily go along with it?

It didn't make any sense.

Felix thought he'd earned the king's forgiveness and trust, but perhaps that too had been a lie. Perhaps the king had only brought him along for this very reason—to have someone to blame, someone to punish.

He lay down on his side, shivering.

He'd felt lost and alone and hopeless before, plenty of times, whether or not he'd ever admitted it. But never like this.

"I'm going to die," he whispered. "And no one in the entire world will miss me."

Slowly, he faded into a semiconscious state—whether it was sleep or simply pure blackness, he wasn't sure. But time passed. And then the rattling of a key in the door jarred him awake.

The demon-guard peered at him through the small window. "Did you miss me?"

Felix sat up quickly, his body screaming with pain. He scooted backward, as far as he could get from the iron door.

He didn't think he could endure more torture. Any more and he was certain he'd lose his mind completely.

He was already naming insects and talking to them. What next?

The guard was about to open the door when, suddenly, a loud boom sounded out, roaring through the dungeon. The walls shook, dust falling from the ceiling in large clouds that made Felix cough and wheeze.

The guard turned around to look down the hallway, and then disappeared.

Felix pressed his head back against the slimy wall, momentarily relieved.

Another boom, even bigger than before, rocked the dungeon. A small crack started splintering along the wall and spread up to the ceiling, until a chunk of rock crashed to the ground only a few feet away from Felix.

This whole place was going to come crashing down on his head.

Felix supposed it was better to die this way than at the mercy of that sadistic guard.

He moistened his dry, cracked lips with the tip of his tongue, tasting sweat and his own coppery blood.

"I'm not afraid," he whispered. "I'm not afraid of death. But I want it to come quickly. Please, goddess. No more pain. If that request makes me a coward, then so be it, I'm a coward. But please . . . please. I've had enough."

He waited, straining his ears to hear anything out in the hallway. But after the second explosion, all had gone deadly silent.

Minutes passed, or was it hours? He didn't know how long he waited. Time had no meaning here.

Then, he heard it. Shouts. Screams. The clash of metal on metal, the crash of iron doors against stone walls. He strained to break apart his chains, but the cuffs only bit deeper into his wrists, rebreaking the wounds they'd already inflicted.

Someone was trying to escape. And someone else was helping him.

"Here—I'm in here." He tried to shout it, but he could barely manage more than a rasp.

He had no idea who might come to his door, if he were calling out to friend or foe. But he had to try.

"Please," he gritted out again. "Please help me."

Finally, the clash and clatter hushed, and the battle sounds faded away to silence.

Felix inhaled, his breath making a shaky, pitiful sound, and he felt the shameful sting of tears.

He'd been left behind to rot.

He closed his eye against the dust and nothingness, hoping he could just fade away in peace. But then a small scuffle from the hall made him look up again.

Footsteps. And they were growing louder, closer.

Finally, someone came to the door. All Felix could see was a pair of eyes, briefly glancing in at him through the window before they disappeared again.

He heard a key turn in the lock, and his whole body tensed. He waited, barely breathing, as the door squeaked open.

Afraid to look up, first he saw a pair of mud-crusted black boots. Leather trousers. A dirty, blood-spattered canvas tunic with ragged, crisscrossed ties.

The glint of a sharp sword.

Felix began to tremble as he forced his gaze upward. Dust filled the air and Felix's eyes burned from it as he tried to focus on the shape of this intruder.

Familiar. He seemed . . . so familiar.

The young man silhouetted in the doorway wore an expression filled with horror. "Damn it. What the hell did they do to you?"

"I'm dreaming. A dream, that's all this is. You're not really here. You can't be." Felix leaned back against the wall. "Oh, how funny. A dream about an old friend, just before dying."

The dream figure came to crouch in front of him. "This is what you get for trying to be one of the good guys, you arse," he said.

"Apparently so."

"Any regrets?"

"A million or two." Felix blinked up at him. "Is it . . . is it really you?"

Jonas nodded. "It's really me."

Felix shook his head, still too afraid to believe this could be real. He felt something hot and wet on his cheeks. Tears. "How?"

"You're not going to believe me, but you have Prince Magnus to thank for this. He and I are allies now. Sort of. He got your message, then sent me here to kill his father."

"Now I know I'm dreaming. You'd never stoop so low as to help the prince."

"A lot has changed since we saw each other last." Jonas held out a small key and fiddled with the cuffs, finally easing them off Felix's bloody wrists. "You think you can stand?"

"I can try."

Jonas helped him to his feet, and Felix saw the shock on his face as he took in the sight of his missing eye. He swore. "You've been through hell."

It hurt too much to laugh, but that was an understatement if ever Felix had heard one. "Yeah, to the darklands and back again. How did you find me here? Mikah's revolutionaries planned to break some of their people out of here today?"

"Not exactly. They were sure you were already dead, but—I don't know. I had this feeling you weren't."

"And this feeling was so strong that you risked busting into a Kraeshian prison to see if you were right?"

"Looks like it worked."

"You came here to help *me*." Felix stared at Jonas, and the tears began to fall again. "Damn it."

"If that's your way of saying thank you. . . ."

Another short, painful gasp of a laugh lurched out of Felix. "I should be begging for your forgiveness right about now."

"No, I should be begging for yours," Jonas said. "I'm sorry, Felix. I'm sorry I doubted you."

Felix drew in a ragged breath. "Let's put it in the past where dark things belong. Right now, I need an enormous favor."

"Anything."

"Get me the hell out of here."

The rebel grinned. "That I can do."

Jonas quickly explained that the dungeon was in shambles and the Kraeshian revolutionaries were working their way through it, freeing prisoners and killing any guard who tried to stop them.

Felix just stared at his friend, his words a comforting buzz in his ears as Jonas helped him to his feet, his body screaming in pain with every movement.

Jonas helped Felix through the cell door. As they gingerly traversed the hallway, Felix saw what was left of his torturer, slumped over against the wall, hacked into several pieces.

Felix nodded at him. "That's unfortunate."

"Why's that?"

"I wanted to kill him myself."

Jonas shot him a dark grin as they continued to navigate the ruined dungeon.

"We've got a lot to do," Jonas said as they began up the stairs. "And we need your help. Are you in?"

Felix nodded. "I'm definitely with you. Whatever you need."

"I have someone who can heal you quickly." Jonas looked him over again, grimacing. "I don't think she can help with your eye, though."

"Ah, thanks for the reminder. I knew I forgot something in my cell."

"Here, consider this a gift." He fished into his pocket and handed Felix a black eye patch. "I'm sure it'll look better on you than it did on me."

Felix looked up at him, puzzled. "I won't ask."

Jonas grinned. "So how's your redemption plan coming along?"

Felix laughed, and it hurt just a little less this time.

The eye patch was going to take some getting used to, but Olivia managed to heal all of Felix's other wounds.

As the Watcher worked on Felix, Jonas looked on, vocally annoyed that her healing recipe hadn't included cow dung this time.

"I *had* to use that on you back then. You still thought I was only a witch," she explained. "There are no witches powerful enough to heal serious wounds with touch alone."

"Whatever you're doing," Felix said, gritting his teeth through the pain of the miraculous earth magic, "don't stop."

The prison break had officially marked the start the Kraeshian revolution. Rebels, including those who'd just escaped from the prison, poured out into the streets ready to fight, itching to take over the Emerald Spear and the Jewel itself.

Still, after Mikah explained the current situation, Felix knew—with fewer than three hundred dedicated rebels currently on the island—they didn't have nearly enough revolutionaries to succeed in a takeover in a city this size.

Even with twenty ships of Kraeshian troops sailing to Mytica to help with the king's "peaceful occupation" the remaining guards in the city outnumbered the rebels ten to one.

Still, Felix was even more impressed with Mikah now than when he'd first learned of his ambitions. He'd never known anyone more determined to make a difference in the world, no matter how long it took.

"Where's Taran?" Felix asked him now.

"On the south side of the city. I put him in charge of the faction over there."

"Who's Taran?" asked Nicolo Cassian, whom Felix remembered as Jonas's redheaded friend who'd helped them rescue Lys from her execution.

He'd asked about Lysandra, but hadn't gotten a satisfying answer. Likely, she'd stayed behind in Mytica to keep an eye on Prince Magnus.

That, or perhaps she hadn't been as forgiving as Jonas,

and still blamed him for what happened that terrible night in Auranos.

He'd have to deal with her later.

"Taran's a rebel," Felix replied. "You might even know him already. He's from Auranos originally."

Nic shrugged. "It's a pretty big kingdom."

"Amara and the king should be nearing Mytican shores by now, right?" Jonas asked.

"They probably have two or three days left ahead of them," Mikah confirmed. "And the rest of the ships are only a half day behind them."

"We need to get a message to the prince," Felix said. "To warn him what's coming. If this so-called peaceful occupation has anything to do with Amara, then Mytica is in for a lot of violence. She's the one who's taking over, and if the king gives her any problems, she's going to kill him."

"I don't see anything wrong with that," Nic said.

"For all his greed and ruthlessness, the king values Mytica," Jonas said, pacing back and forth, his arms crossed. "What Amara must want most from him is to get her hands on the rest of the Kindred."

Felix had admitted his stupidity and confirmed that the king had the air Kindred, but Jonas assured him that that was the only one the king would have in his personal possession.

Amara, that wicked, deceitful black widow spider, had the water Kindred the whole time, and Felix had had absolutely no idea.

"A raven won't get there in time," Jonas said. "Olivia?"

She came to his side. "Yes?"

"How fast can you fly?"

"Very fast."

"I need you to take a message to the prince. You'll need to leave immediately."

She scanned the group, her expression pinched. "I can't leave. If I do, you'll be vulnerable to attack."

"And if you don't, many people in Mytica will be in terrible danger."

"And?" Her tone held an exasperated edge. "Am I to understand that you're counting every living soul in Mytica a friend, and that I need to protect them all?"

"That's exactly right." Jonas took her by her shoulders. "Please, Olivia. This is important. Please do this for me."

"Mortals," she said, shaking her head. Olivia studied Jonas for a moment of stony silence. "Very well," she finally said. "Compose your message. But if you die before I return, I refuse to be held responsible."

Jonas nodded. "Fair enough."

CHAPTER 25

LUCIA

PAELSIA

The deadly events in the Paelsian market had stayed with Lucia ever since, troubling her thoughts by day and stealing her sleep by night.

Kyan had grown increasingly irate ever since, his violence more easily triggered. Moments of calm and introspection were few and far between as they continued searching for a way to draw Timotheus out of the Sanctuary.

That search had brought them to two neighboring Paelsian villages—five miles apart.

Kyan had already turned one of these villages to ash.

Lucia stood with Kyan in the midst of the flames that continued to burn. In front of them was an old witch whom Kyan interrogated, believing her to know more than she was telling them.

"You're evil," the witch snarled. "And you need to be destroyed. You are bound for the darklands, both of you!"

Kyan regarded her with disdain. "If it weren't for the misplaced lusts of the immortals, you witches, with your weak, tainted magic, wouldn't even exist."

"Enough," Lucia growled. "She knows nothing that can help us."

It had been a long, disappointing day, and all she wanted to do was try to get some sleep.

"Make her talk, little sorceress," Kyan said. "Or she will die."

Lucia had grown tired of witnessing so much suffering. She didn't want anyone else to die tonight; just the thought made her ill. So she did what Kyan asked.

"Look at me," Lucia commanded with as much strength as she could summon.

When the witch finally met her gaze, Lucia focused all of her magic into making her tell the truth.

"Where is the stone wheel that still possesses its magical link to the Sanctuary?"

Unlike all the others who'd fallen under Lucia's spell, the witch neither flinched nor gasped. Instead, she cocked her head and narrowed her eyes. "I told you, girl. I don't know. And if I did, I wouldn't tell you."

Lucia hissed out a breath and tried again, now clenching her fists.

Again, the witch deflected the questions as easily as if Lucia were speaking a foreign language.

Her magic wasn't working—only more proof that she needed to rest.

"Try a simpler question," Kyan hissed.

Lucia nodded assent. The sooner she got him a satisfying answer, the sooner they could leave this horrible place. "What is your name, witch?"

The witch spat directly in Lucia's face. "My name will die with me before it leaves my lips tonight."

Lucia felt the heat of Kyan's fire. She turned to him angrily as the flames rippled down his arms. "There's no reason to kill her."

He extinguished his fire, now showing that his hands were curled into tight fists. "She's useless!"

"So we'll find someone else. Tomorrow, the next day. What does it matter?"

"It matters more than you realize," he snarled at her, then turned and stormed away from them, trailing fire in his wake.

Lucia drew in a shaky breath, then turned back to the woman. "I didn't mean for this to happen tonight. Your village—"

"Leave here," the witch said through clenched teeth. "And never return."

Lucia straightened her shoulders. "I spared your life."

"Do you really think you can ever be forgiven for the death and devastation you've caused here tonight?"

"I would never ask for—"

"*Leave*," the woman snarled, her eyes brimming with tears.

Flinching, Lucia finally turned away from the woman and then trudged out through the flames and destruction Kyan had caused behind her.

Kyan was waiting for her at the top of a nearby hill, looking down at the village he'd crushed so easily, as if it were an ant hill he'd decided to step on.

He gave her a sidelong look, his expression grim and unfriendly. "I'm disappointed in you," he said.

"Is that so?"

"Yes. I believed you to be the sorceress reborn."

Her jaw tightened. "That's exactly who I am."

"Perhaps my memory of Eva grows dim after all this time. But you—you've shown tonight that you're *nothing* compared to her. If she were still here, still alive, Timotheus would already be dead."

Kyan rarely turned his anger on her, and when he did she didn't like it one bit. She glared at him, defiant. "You said yourself I've accessed only a small portion of my magic so far."

"Perhaps I was wrong. Of course I was—how could any mere mortal ever help me in my plan?"

Lucia's indignation grew with every word he spoke, but she tried her best to calm herself. One of them had to think rationally. She took a deep breath. "We need to take a break," she said. "We'll find an inn in the other town and get rest, food. And we *will* find a wheel, Kyan. I promised I'd help you, and I meant it. I still mean it now. But you need to control yourself. This," she said, indicating the smoldering village, "is becoming a problem."

Kyan's eyes flashed fiercely, and Lucia braced herself. "All *this* is, Lucia, is more useless, disappointing mortals turned to dust. I don't see any problem with that."

Despite herself, Lucia scoffed. "I do."

"More proof that you've become useless to me."

His words wounded her, but she refused to let it show.

She forced herself to breathe, to not unleash any more of her temper or, worse, start to cry. "The moment I killed Melenia, everything about my life, my journey, became so clear to me. I wanted to destroy everything and everyone."

"And now?"

"I'm not so sure anymore. But that's what you want, isn't it? You want to lay waste to this entire kingdom. So go ahead." She waited for his reply, but none came. "No? I think I'm starting to understand. You may be free of that crystal, but you'll remain imprisoned until Timotheus is dead and your siblings are released, won't you? Which means you do need me, much more than I need you. Which means you better start behaving yourself."

A dark, cold shadow slid behind his amber eyes. "You don't know me nearly as well as you think you do, little sorceress."

"If you say so. Now, I'm going to make my journey—*alone*—to the other village so I can find an inn and get some sleep. Don't disturb me until morning."

Lucia turned her back to him and walked away.

Lucia tossed and turned for ages, her thoughts in turmoil. It was as if the vivid memories of all she'd witnessed and been party to with Kyan over these past weeks had been branded in her mind.

Though she spent nearly all her energy trying not to think of Alexius, the image of his face came to her now, along with his words of love, his promises for the future. They were like daggers to her heart.

She thought of Magnus, her best friend and the only brother she'd ever known, reaching for her, offering to help her despite all she'd done to taint their relationship over the past year.

She thought of her father, who, despite his cruelty toward others, had never been anything but kind and understanding with her—even before he became certain she was the sorceress he believed her to be.

She thought of Cleo, how Lucia had reluctantly befriended her, and for a while had felt like she'd met someone she might trust with her deepest, darkest secrets.

And then Jonas, a boy she'd known only by reputation until that day in the market, when she'd stood by and witnessed his stunned devastation after Kyan murdered his friend—a brave girl who'd only tried to protect him.

Wherever Lucia went, she brought pain with her. There was a time not so long ago when she might not have cared, but now . . .

She asked herself the same question everyone was always asking Kyan.

Who am I? What am I?

Honestly, she didn't really know anymore. All she knew for sure was that there was no turning back.

It took a small eternity before the darkness of sleep finally claimed her.

But soon that darkness brightened, transforming itself into a familiar meadow. Standing there before her was a handsome young man in shimmering white robes.

No, not tonight, she thought. She couldn't bear to face him tonight.

Lucia turned in a quick circle, frantically searching for an escape but already knowing she was trapped.

"It's been some time, Lucia," Timotheus said. "How have you been?"

"Go away. Let me wake up."

"Has the fire Kindred been behaving himself?"

She wondered what he knew, what he'd seen. What he might be able to read in her sleeping mind. His confident posturing here, in this place over which he had complete control, intimidated her.

Lucia forced a smile, but didn't try to make it look friendly. "Kyan's just wonderful, thank you for asking."

His lips stretched out to a thin smile. "I'm sure he is."

She let out a sigh of frustration. "This is the second dream you've pulled me into. What's your reason tonight? Other than wanting to annoy me."

"Have you forgiven Alexius for deceiving you?"

Once again, the sound of his name was a blow. "I'll never forgive him."

"He deserves better than for you to hate him for Melenia's choices."

Her eyes began to sting with tears, which only infuriated her further. "That's a matter of opinion."

"One day you'll forgive him for leaving you to make stupid, selfish decisions all by yourself."

"Oh, Timotheus, this verbal abuse only makes me hate you more."

"You have no reason to hate me."

"Kyan does."

"Perhaps. But you are not Kyan." Timotheus leaned against the apple tree and studied her with his ancient golden eyes. "So. Why have I brought you into another dream, you wonder? Especially after the poor impression you left me with the first time?"

"I'm not the only one who left a poor impression."

Timotheus ignored her jab and went on. "I brought you here again because I believe Alexius truly loved you—even before he knew you were the prophesied sorceress. I knew Alexius, better than anyone else, and he wouldn't have given his love to someone who didn't possess true worth. He died to save your life."

Timotheus's unexpected words were like a hand thrusting through her chest and tearing out her beating heart.

She opened her mouth to retort, but found herself unable to find the words. Instead, the burning sensation in her eyes intensified.

"Tell me, Lucia. Are you finding much joy in the death and destruction you leave in your wake? Do the screams of the innocents Kyan kills lighten your heart, give you strength? Make you feel powerful?"

His harsh words—words that resounded so strongly with the doubts within her heart—made her breath catch in her chest. But she wouldn't let him get to her. If she didn't stay strong, she knew she'd lose all remaining control over herself.

"Tell *me*, Timotheus," she said. "Do I frighten you?"

He raised a brow. "You? Frighten me?"

"Does the thought of what I did to Melenia keep you up at

night, knowing I might be out in the darkness, waiting to bring about an end to your offensively long existence?"

"Not nearly as much as you might wish to believe." Timotheus watched her for a very long time, his gaze steady on hers. "You should know that even when Eva was at her weakest, she never lost faith in our mission to protect the world. She's the only one of our kind I ever trusted completely. Even after she fell in love with a mortal."

The knowledge of Eva's waning magic had been troubling her ever since Timotheus first told Lucia about it. "I don't understand," she said. "If Eva was the first, the most powerful sorceress, how could she let herself be defeated and drained of her magic?"

Timotheus now had a faraway look on his face. "Her magic was weakened by the half-mortal child she carried within her. A secret she tried to conceal from everyone, including me. When Melenia discovered Eva's pregnancy, she took it as an opportunity to rise in power by killing her elder, and Eva could not properly defend herself."

"So Eva didn't have a vision of her own future."

"Neither have I of mine. But I've seen many versions of yours. And I advise you to choose your path wisely."

"Tell me these futures and perhaps I'll understand you better!" The words tore from her throat. "If you want me to do the right thing so desperately that you insist on pulling me into these dreams, then tell me what the consequences are!"

But Timotheus didn't reply. Instead, the meadow faded away to darkness.

Lucia opened her eyes and found herself tucked into her bed at the inn.

"Many versions of my future . . ." she whispered aloud.

Suddenly, a violent wave of nausea hit her. She ran to the

chamber pot, and barely made it there before she threw up. This was the third morning in a row that this had happened, and she knew this sickness had likely contributed to her weakening magic.

She hadn't felt this lousy in . . . well, *ever*.

And she hated feeling weak.

"Stupid Timotheus." She sat there, on the floor of her small room, and pulled her knees up against her chest, rocking herself back and forth. As she waited for the next wave of nausea to pass she remembered what the immortal had told her about the original sorceress.

Despite her vast power, despite her immortality, Eva's magic had faded when a half-mortal child grew within her.

Lucia thought her magic, too, appeared to be fading.

She drew in a sudden, sharp breath and held it for so long that she began to feel dizzy.

"Oh, goddess," she whispered. "I'm pregnant."

CHAPTER 26

CLEO

LIMEROS

Ever since Jonas and Nic had left for Kraeshia, Cleo had been paying extra attention in her archery lessons. But still her skills did not improve.

Between her disappointment in herself and Lord Kurtis's increasingly insufferable and constant need to malign Magnus and the sorry state of Limeros now that he was no longer in charge, her patience had finally worn out.

So this morning, after a particularly frustrating hour of missed targets and Lord Kurtis's whining, she quit.

Cleo returned to her chambers, flinging off her gloves and cloak, and sat down on the edge of her bed. From there she could see herself in the vanity mirror.

"What am I still doing here?" she asked her reflection.

Nerissa had gently asked her that very same question only yesterday.

She didn't have an acceptable answer then, and she found she still didn't have one today, not even for herself. What was her purpose in this cold, stark palace? It wasn't as if she would lose her royal position if she were to leave.

All she was doing here was wasting time, waiting and waiting. . . .

Enough waiting.

She was deeply saddened to learn that Eirene, the exiled Watcher, had died, but she was not at all surprised—Eirene had been very old when Cleo had seen her last.

And all it meant was that now Cleo would have to find another exiled Watcher, and get the answers for herself.

She went to the window and lifted up a loose stone on the sill, under which she'd hidden the obsidian orb.

But the nook beneath was empty.

She blinked, the sight of the shadowy hollow still not fully registering. Of course the Kindred should be there; she hadn't moved it. She turned in a circle, scanning the room, trying to see if something had changed.

"No. It was here." She looked under the sill again, but there was no black orb to be found.

Her heart began to race.

The Kindred had disappeared.

Someone had stolen it. But who?

Certainly not Nerissa, the only other person who was aware of the hiding spot. Cleo trusted Nerissa completely and refused to doubt her.

Perhaps a maid or servant had come across it by accident while tidying up? But if that was the case, why would they steal such a thing? To an uninformed commoner, the orb would seem nothing more than a very large marble.

"Who could have done this?" she whispered aloud. Who else

knew about the Kindred, would risk their lives by searching her private chambers to find it?

Then, in an icy flash, the answer came to her.

She approached the throne room at a brisk pace, the guards opening the doors for her before she even had to ask. Magnus was inside, waiting for her, seated upon his father's iron throne.

The prince wore black from head to toe, as he always did, as if in an attempt to blend in with the throne, the room, the entire palace. But despite all of this darkness, she spotted the earth Kindred immediately. Magnus held it in his right hand.

"Look what I found," he said, tossing it up and down as Cleo approached the throne. "Shockingly, it was in your quarters. Did you have any idea it was hiding there?"

"That belongs to me," she hissed.

"Actually, princess, it was in my palace, so that means it belongs to me." He held the orb up in front of this face and studied it. "Obsidian is such a beautiful color, isn't it? I'm going to assume that Agallon brought this to you."

She stayed silent and resolute, her jaw tense and her arms crossed in front of her.

"Oh, princess, silence will not do you any favors today."

"I find I have very little to say on the subject."

"That's all right. I have plenty to say; I'll do the talking for both of us. What I hold in my hand is solid proof that you're an unrelenting liar, that you're still aligned with rebels, and that you continue to keep essential information from me. You knew exactly why this Kindred was missing from the Temple of Cleiona when we arrived to claim it. Why didn't you tell me about this?"

A humorless grunt of laughter escaped her throat. "Why would I? Despite your pretty promises to me, and your verbal agreements with Jonas, you've always made it very clear that we're enemies—today, tomorrow, and always."

"And how, precisely, have I made that clear? Was it the time I spared your little rebel friend from execution? Or was it my offer to return your kingdom to you? Shall I go on?"

"Magnus, you can't honestly expect me to believe your promises. Restore my kingdom to me? After all the lies you've told in the past? All the betrayals?"

His gaze grew colder. "I meant every word of that offer. And if there's anyone who knows that I'm capable of being a man of my word, it's you. But now?" He indicated the orb. "I've changed my mind. Mytica—all of it—will be mine. All mine. Yes, that sounds much better to me. I've never really liked to share my toys."

She took a few steps closer to the dais and looked up at him, frowning. "You're right," she said. "Perhaps I should apologize."

He blinked. "What?"

"It's clear to me that I've hurt you."

He scoffed. "You could never hurt me, princess."

Cleo shook her head. "I think you're hurt by everybody. That's why you act like this. You try to be as cruel and cold and horrible as possible so no one will get close to you. Because when they do, when you let people in, you get hurt."

Magnus let out one harsh, cold laugh. "Much gratitude for your opinions, princess, but you're wrong."

"I'm not blind, Magnus. I saw what happened between you and Lucia when she came here. Your heart broke to see your sister like that, when all you wanted to do was help her."

"Lucia is different. Whatever she does, she's family. But she's made it clear she doesn't need or want my help, and I'll never make that mistake again."

"It doesn't change how you really feel."

Magnus stood up and descended the steps. "I've grown bored of this conversation. You can try to manipulate me all you want, but the facts of this situation remain. You are a deceitful wench, and the earth Kindred is now mine."

"Very well. I wish you the best of luck accessing its magic. It's impossible. I've tried everything."

"I assumed as much. Otherwise, I'd be dead and buried by now, wouldn't I?"

"You think I want you dead? Even now?"

Magnus sighed. "You really do need to make up your mind on that subject, princess. Your duplicity is dizzying."

"Fine. Yes. I kept the Kindred from you. I did—and do—plan to use its magic to get my kingdom back. There. That's the truth. I'm finished with lies—what good have they done me? So now that you know, why don't you throw me in the dungeon? Demand my head?"

"You love to try my patience," he gritted out.

"You won't have me killed for this. Because, despite all of our differences, we *are* aligned. And maybe it's time we started to trust each other."

The more she spoke, the more she realized she was actually telling the truth. Magnus wasn't evil like his father. He never had been. She'd heard him try to reason with the council. She'd seen how much he cared about this kingdom. And she was certain that he would never try to harm her, no matter what she said or did. All of this, this cold, seemingly impenetrable façade, was just that: a thin shell protecting the genuine soul that lay beneath.

"How curious that you've come to this monumental realization only *after* I found the orb."

But he truly was infuriating sometimes.

"Kurtis came to see me earlier," Magnus said, before Cleo could reply. "Do you know why?"

"To tell you I've quit archery?"

"No, but it's adorable that you think I'd care about something so trivial. Kurtis came to me because he wanted me to know he'd been discussing politics with you. He told me about all the issues you and he seem to agree upon, my being unfit to rule Limeros being one of them."

Cleo waved her hand dismissively. "He greatly exaggerates."

"Does he? Or is this another little partnership you've hidden from me?"

"Can't you see that I'm here today trying to right the wrongs between us, Magnus?" she said, her patience wearing thin and brittle. "But you refuse to let me."

"If I told you about the things Kurtis has done in the past, you wouldn't want to go anywhere near him."

If Magnus refused to play nice, neither would she. "I suppose that's something you two have in common, then."

Magnus furrowed his brow, as if confused. "When we were children, Kurtis used to enjoy murdering animals, watching them suffer."

The thought of having spent so much time with a deranged young man sickened her. But Magnus couldn't possibly be telling her the truth. She decided to send a jab right back at him. "And you, on the other hand, enjoy murdering people I love. Which pastime is worse?"

Magnus glared at her with sudden fury. "You pretend to know me? You spit out venom like that moments after trying to gain my confidence, and all it shows is that you don't know me at all. You want this orb so badly, do you? Perhaps we can split it."

He turned, a look of rage still fixed on his face, and threw the earth Kindred against the stone wall. All went silent as he looked down at his empty hand in shock.

A moment later, the ground began to rumble beneath their feet. "No," he whispered.

Cleo's heart leapt into her throat. Her memory shot back to their wedding day, and the elemental earthquake that had destroyed the Temple of Cleiona, killing so many.

Frozen with fear, she watched as a gaping crack snaked across the floor, creating a deep rift in the stone that separated her and Magnus, then traveling up to the spot on the wall where the orb had made contact.

Then, as suddenly as the quake had started, the earth ceased shaking.

Cleo covered her mouth as relief flowed over and through her.

Magnus darted toward the orb and picked it up, inspecting it closely. "It's not damaged at all."

Cleo drew closer to see for herself. He was right; though the room was now in chaotic disrepair, the Kindred itself had remained fully intact. The thread of magic within it now spun faster, more frantically, than she'd seen it before.

"I think you made it mad," she said, breathlessly.

"For a moment, I thought—" Magnus locked his gaze with hers and his brows drew together. "Cleo . . ."

A loud squawk startled them.

They turned to see a hawk come to perch on a windowsill. It looked in at them with a cocked head, then flapped its wings, flew up and in through the window, and swooped toward them, so close that they both had to duck. The hawk dropped something onto the council table and then, after one final squawk, flew back out the window.

Magnus stared after it, jaw slack. "That's never happened before."

He picked up the piece of parchment the hawk had left behind, unrolled it, and read the message.

When he finished, he swore loudly, then roughly handed the message to Cleo.

> *Prince Magnus—*
>
> *I write to warn you that the king will be arriving on Mytican shores very soon, followed by a Kraeshian armada of twenty ships. Your father believes he has entered into an agreement that will make Mytica a part of the Kraeshian Empire, with him ruling over all. But he's wrong. Amara has poisoned her family—the emperor and her brothers— and is now Empress of Kraeshia. She's interested in Mytica only for its magic. She will stop at nothing to possess it. The king will come to Mytica bearing news of a peaceful occupation, but because of Amara, we believe it will be anything but.*
>
> *We will return as soon as we can.—Jonas*

Cleo's hands trembled as she placed Jonas's message back on the table.

"I had no idea my father was this stupid," Magnus said.

"We need to warn everyone that we may soon be under attack," Cleo said.

"I agree with Agallon that my father has done nothing to earn a reputation as a peaceful ruler . . . but I don't believe that he would just stand by and let Amara have her way with Mytica. Perhaps he agreed to this under duress. Perhaps he has another plan, and he'll come straight to us with it when he arrives."

"No, Magnus. I'm sorry, but I think Jonas is right. The king is thinking only of himself, he's driven by nothing but his own greed. You and I know how dangerous Amara can be, but he probably he sees her as nothing more than a weak, young girl he can manipulate and control."

"A weak, young girl who apparently murdered her family in cold blood to take all the power for her own. We watched her kill Prince Ashur right in front of us, we should have known something like this would happen next. I wonder how long she's planned this."

Cleo wrung her hands. "What are we going to do?"

He began pacing back and forth alongside the table. "Cronus was always the expert on defensive strategy," he said. A mournful tone entered his voice as he mentioned the name of the captain of the guard who'd stood watch over Cleo as she awaited execution in the dungeon.

"How unfortunate, then, that you killed him," Cleo said unpleasantly.

"Yes, it is unfortunate. That was a mistake I've come to regret more and more with each passing day."

Her breath caught in her chest. "Do you mean to tell me that you regret saving my life?"

"That one, foolish choice marks the moment that has destroyed my entire life. This"—he gestured at the note—"is final evidence of that."

Even at his harshest, even when he was being unbearably hateful, at least Cleo had been able to hold on to the memory of that day when he'd chosen to save her life whenever she needed to convince herself Magnus wasn't the monster his father had tried to create. No matter the motivations he claimed were driving him on that day—he was worried about Lucia, he was mad at his father, it had nothing to do with Cleo herself—the end result remained. He, alone, had saved her life. He, alone, had defied the king and acted out of kindness.

But if he really did regret it, then that hope, that belief in his good heart . . . all of it was erased.

A stormy mixture of anger and pain swirled within her. "How dare you say that to me!"

He rubbed his forehead and let out a humorless laugh. "Don't you see? When it comes to you, I only make foolish decisions that put everyone and everything around me in danger. I can't believe I've been too stupid to see that until now. If I'd been strong enough to let you die that day, none of this would be happening. What is wrong with me? Why would I choose to protect a liar and traitor who tries to destroy me at every turn?"

Her throat had tightened, but so had her fists. "Whether you hate me or not, it changes nothing. You believe me to be a worthless liar who'd be better off dead? Fine. But don't waste my time crying about your decisions now. Amara is on her way here, and she will kill anyone that gets in the way of her claiming every piece of the Kindred."

"Every piece. Perhaps you have the others hidden away somewhere, too. For all I know, you've conspired with Amara as well."

"You won't believe me, no matter what I say. Clearly there's nothing I can do or say that will change your opinion of me."

"You want everything, take all that you can get, but you give nothing back in return," Magnus snarled through clenched teeth. "Leave me."

Cleo shook her head. "But the king . . . Amara . . ."

Magnus moved toward her, a menacing look on his face, forcing her to back up until she found herself on the other side of the throne room doors.

"I will deal with the king and the princess when they arrive. If doing so means that I die, then it's a death I've earned through my actions concerning you. If I never see you again, it will be too soon."

With that, he slammed the doors shut between them.

CHAPTER 27

AMARA

THE SILVER SEA

It was the familiar line of a jaw that caught her eye. A swath of dark hair. The shape of his shoulders.

Ashur?

Amara's heart lifted with happiness, but then immediately closed with dread.

This can't be possible.

She followed the young man across the deck of the ship, turning a corner and heading toward the bow. Finally, she managed to catch his arm.

"Ash—" she started, but the name fell away as the boy turned around. It was Milo, looking down at her with surprise.

"Your highness, is there something you need?"

She frowned, glancing frantically to her left and right, but there was no one else around.

"No, nothing," she said, then signaled for Milo to be on his way.

She went below deck to the room she shared with the king, and was relieved to find it vacant.

She looked out the porthole and saw nothing but sea—endless expanses of brilliant blue.

She sighed, anxious to get to Mytica. She needed to know just how dishonest the king was being when he claimed to possess all of the Kindred. At the very least she knew he was bluffing about the water orb, which was wrapped in a silk scarf and safely hidden amongst her clothing.

The only thing she knew was that, with or without Gaius's help, she would soon possess them all.

She would learn the secret to unlocking their magic, and she would ascend from empress to goddess.

"Everything is going perfectly," she reminded herself.

"Is that so?" A familiar voice rang out from the far corner of her quarters, drawing her gaze.

She drew in a sharp breath. "Ashur."

Standing in the shadows, smiling at her, was the brother she'd killed only weeks ago. "Greetings, sister."

Amara squeezed her eyes shut, certain she was imagining him.

Summoning her courage, she stood up and moved toward him. She reached out for him, and he disappeared. She flattened her hands against the wall where he'd stood, letting a cruel combination of disappointment and relief wash over her.

But when she turned around, there he was again, sitting in a chair by the bed, regarding her with amusement. "Oh Amara, don't tell me you've *missed* me."

"What is this? A vengeful spirit come to make pleasant conversation?"

"Is that what you think I am? And here I thought you believed in reincarnation, like all good Kraeshians."

"If you're not a demon, then you're only my imagination, which means I can make you go away and leave me alone."

"You've killed us all, you wicked, wicked girl," he snarled, but still smiled that familiar, warm grin of his. "You took us all by surprise with your ruthlessness. Was it worth it? Now you have no one to share your secrets with."

"I have Grandmother."

"Ah, yes, a bitter old woman as ancient as the hills. She won't be a companion to you for much longer."

The thought of losing Neela was far too painful to contemplate, so Amara shook it out of her head and balled her hands into fists. "I didn't want to kill you. But you shouldn't have deceived me."

"Is that what you think I did?"

"There was a time when you and I were inseparable," Amara went on. "The best of friends. Then you wanted to go off and explore faraway lands, chase treasures, and you left me behind all by myself."

His silvery-blue eyes flashed with sadness and anger. "Don't you dare blame me for your choices."

"You chose to stand with strangers rather than with your own sister!"

"And I suppose I learned my lesson. Anyone who stands with you, Amara, should know better than to ever turn their back. You've done unforgiveable things, all in the empty pursuit of power."

She turned toward the mirror, anything to not have to face him anymore, and began to vigorously brush her hair. "When men do the same," she huffed, "they're held up as champions."

"Do you fancy yourself a champion, Sister?"

This snide little ghost was not Amara's brother, was only a manifestation of her guilt. She knew she'd done only what she had to do, nothing more. "I will bring about change in this world that will benefit millions," she said to her own reflection.

"There are many ways to do that, Sister, But you chose murder. It seems as though you're more like our father than you'd ever want to admit."

When she turned to face him again, he was gone.

Amara took time to compose herself in her cabin, and when she went back up to the deck she saw that the ship was approaching the frozen shores of Limeros. Cuddling deeper into the thick fur wrap around her shoulders, she felt that the air seemed even colder than it was the last time she'd been here.

She gazed out at the snow-dusted city. This was where Felix had grown up. Her thoughts had drifted to him many times during this journey—to the ache she'd felt over casting him aside, making him take the blame for her crime.

Just as a stab of guilt begin to gnaw at her, King Gaius approached to her left and stood at the gunwale next to her, holding a piece of parchment.

She straightened her posture and went to his side.

"You look troubled," she said.

King Gaius looked up at her, surprised, as if he'd just woken from a dream. "I will admit I am a bit troubled." He indicated the parchment in his hand. "Just before we left the Jewel, I received this message. It's from an informant at the Limerian palace. I've read it many times, but still find its contents difficult to believe."

"Is it about Magnus? Is the prince enjoying his moment in the sun?"

"Apparently a little too much. If I'm to believe what's written here, it seems he has met with rebels on several occasions."

She placed her hand over his. "I'm very sorry to hear that. But I have to say, if it is true, it doesn't surprise me at all. Your son has already committed treason against you once."

"He claims good reasons for doing so."

"Is there ever a good reason to commit treason?"

"You tell me, Empress. Why was it that you poisoned your entire family?"

She'd almost forgotten how sensitive Myticans could be. If she wanted to turn Gaius's head without him realizing it, she had to remember to use a gentler hand to guide him. "I understand that you'd like to think the best of him," she said sweetly. "After all, he's your heir. But more than once he's made a public display of opposing you, of standing against everything you do. He needs to pay for his crimes."

"Are you suggesting that I have my only son executed?"

A sharpness sprang into the king's dark eyes, a warning that her hand had not been nearly gentle enough. "No, of course not. There's no easy answer here. I'm not suggesting there is. But what I care about most is you. Us. Our future. And if Magnus meets our arrival with force, my guards will not hesitate to fight back. I want a peaceful transition as much as you do, but if the Limerian palace rises up, blood will be spilled."

"Peaceful," he repeated, then gave her a dour smile. "There are many words your name brings to mind, Amara, but 'peaceful' isn't one of them."

"Why not?" she said, indignant. "Why would I want to damage the newest jewel in Kraeshia's crown?"

"Why did you call for twenty ships to follow us, to dock at every Mytican port—to ensure we're met with no resistance?"

"Because I'm careful, that's why. Besides, you already agreed to this."

He sighed. "Yes, I did. I know we need to account for and control insurgents."

The tension in Amara's neck dissipated, and she finally allowed herself to relax. "Perhaps your homecoming will make Magnus see that all of this is for the best. That being a part of Kraeshia can only make Mytica stronger."

"I used to have no doubt that my son would come around, that we would see eye to eye again, that he would one day take on his responsibilities as my heir with honor and pride. But one persistent problem has trampled that belief." Gaius paused, narrowing his eyes at the Limerian shore. "Cleiona Bellos. From the moment that scheming little creature came into our lives, it seems there's been an impassable rift between my son and me. I raised him to be great, but she has managed to corrupt him. I was blind not to see it before, but I'm not anymore. He loves her." His knuckles whitened on the railing.

"He may love her, but does she love him?" she reasoned. "After all that's happened to her former kingdom, how could she ever see him as anything but her enemy?"

"It doesn't matter whether or not she loves him in return. Unrequited love is still love." He shook his head. "As I grow older, I'm beginning to understand my mother's choices more and more. I don't forgive them, but I understand. My son doesn't realize how very much he is like me."

Now Amara's curiosity was sharply piqued. "In what ways?" she asked.

He didn't reply.

She frowned, still hoping to coax more information out of him. "Do you mean to say that . . . you once loved someone in the way you believe Magnus loves Cleo?"

The king mouth had fallen to a grim line. "Never mind. It was a very long time ago. Meaningless now."

"Was it . . . are you thinking of Althea?" Amara had never met the former queen, but she'd seen her stern portrait in the hallways of the Limerian palace.

"No. Not Althea." Gaius stared down again at the parchment. Just when Amara thought he was done opening up for the day, he started speaking again, an almost pitifully wistful tone in his voice. "When I was a young man, even younger than Magnus, I took a trip overseas. I met a girl. A beautiful, challenging, frustrating girl. We sparred, we argued, we discussed every topic imaginable, and she quickly became my entire world. I wanted to spend the rest of my life with her, I was sure of it. But my mother had other plans for me—plans that didn't take into account my utter devotion to another. 'Love is weakness,' she told me. 'And it must be destroyed, or else deceptive, dangerous creatures will exploit that weakness for their own gain.'"

"What happened?" Amara asked, drawing closer to Gaius to make him feel comforted.

"My mother intervened. She poisoned this love with words and threats and a darkness I didn't even know she possessed, and soon the girl's love for me turned into hatred. Eventually she married someone else and had beautiful children."

And in turn, Amara though, *you became the very monster she believed you to be*. "And where is she now?" she said aloud. "Do you know?"

His jaw grew tight. "She's dead," he gritted out.

"I'm sorry," she said, still in silent disbelief that this story of love and loss and pain had just been uttered by the King of Blood himself.

"I'm not," he said, his eyes growing cold again. "My mother was right about love. Without her meddling, I would not be the king I am today. And now I know exactly what needs to be done when it comes to ensuring my son's destiny. I will remove the temptation from him, permanently, just as my mother did for me."

He tore the message into pieces and cast it into the sea.

CHAPTER 28

MAGNUS

LIMEROS

Magnus lay awake the entire night, prepared to meet the king's ship the moment he heard the guards' call. But when the sun began to rise and there was still no sign of the Kraeshians, Magnus grew frustrated, cursing Jonas Agallon for needlessly agitating him.

He left his chambers and walked through the palace, grateful at least to be stretching his legs. Everything appeared to be as normal as on any other day. But of course it did. Other than the few overnight guards he'd ordered to keep watch for any approaching ships, Cleo was the only one who knew what lay on the horizon.

His father's return. Amara's occupation.

The end of Mytica—and life—as he knew it.

He exited the palace, bracing himself for the icy chill that had recently reigned in Limeros. But, as he entered the ice gardens, there were none of the harsh, painfully cold winds that usually sliced across his face. He looked up to see that the skies were cloudy but bright today, and a few snowflakes had started to fall.

He tilted his head back and closed his eyes, feeling the familiar sensation of soft white flakes melting on his skin.

He slowly walked through the gardens, alone, allowing himself to enjoy the sights and sounds of his home, for once not moving as quickly as possible from one point to another.

He would miss mornings like this.

At the edge of the cliffs, with the black palace rising up to his left, Magnus scanned the Silver Sea, searching for signs of the Kraeshian armada. Resistance would lead only to more death and pain than his citizens already had in store. Magnus stood no chance against Amara's forces, and the king knew it.

It would finally be time for him to answer for his crime of treason, and he would soon understand fully why his father was known as the King of Blood. Magnus didn't expect any mercy.

And he swore to himself that he wouldn't beg for it.

During his sleepless night, Magnus had given a great deal of thought to the messages he'd received from Kraeshia. Something about his current situation felt desperately wrong, had left him with a sour taste in his mouth that he couldn't get rid of.

Both of the messages had been written by and sent from rebels—rebels who knew one another, had worked together in the past.

Felix Gaebras had sent along a swatch of his own skin to prove he'd shifted loyalties from the Clan to the rebels. But why should Magnus believe that it really was his tattoo, his skin? And what kind of coincidence was it that Felix had sent his message just as his compatriot Jonas arrived at the palace?

And then there was the message from Jonas that arrived last night, warning of imminent danger, striking dark fear into Magnus's heart.

A stark realization stole his breath.

Even now Cleo was working against him, with both Felix and Jonas.

Despite all her pretty words, all her pleas for him to believe her—pleas he'd started to believe—Cleo still thought of him as her enemy, an obstacle she needed to eliminate.

Of course. King Gaius would never be so stupid as to align with someone like Amara. The king knew what a deceptive creature she could be, that she was a sly manipulator, almost as skilled as Cleiona Bellos herself.

The sick feeling that had settled in his stomach lurched once more as he stumbled over a possibility he'd tossed aside the night before: that Cleo might be aligned with Amara.

They could have been working together from the very beginning, from the second Amara first set foot on Mytican soil.

Head spinning and in a daze, Magnus made his way to the Ouroboros. The familiar owner raised his bushy eyebrows high as Magnus pushed through the door.

"Food," Magnus barked. "And a bottle of Paelsian wine. Now."

"Yes, your highness," he said, this time making no efforts to deny that he had alcohol on hand.

Magnus violently tucked into the eggs, fried *kaana* cakes, and fig preserves that the man brought him, and made a toast to Cleo with the bottle of wine. "Well played, princess," he growled.

He drained the first bottle and then a second before he decided it was time to leave. On his way out, he stopped and clutched the barkeep's shoulder. "When I'm officially king, wine will flow readily in Limeros again. Wine for everyone!"

Cowering, the barkeep gave him a small smile, and then Magnus left without waiting for a reply.

Though he walked a swerving line, Magnus managed to make

it back to the palace without too much delay. It wasn't until he had the nearest gate in sight that he realized he hadn't taken any guards with him when he'd left the palace grounds.

"Don't need them," he grumbled. "Anyone who dares to cross the Prince of Blood will regret it."

As he neared the palace gates, he spotted Lord Kurtis, conversing with a man in a black cloak. Kurtis glanced at him, and in response Magnus laughed and made a rude gesture, then carried on right past him.

Stupid arse. To think, Magnus's childhood memories had caused him to consider Kurtis a true threat all this time.

From now on, he would cut the throat of anyone who might become a threat. With no exceptions.

It was now mid-morning, and the activity at the palace had greatly increased since Magnus's early departure. Servants scurried about the halls, whispering to each other and eyeing the prince as he passed. He followed the bustle toward the palace square, where he saw dozens upon dozens of citizens beginning to gather, having entered through the wide-open gates.

Magnus caught the arm of a passing guard. "What's all this about?"

"Your highness, don't you know?"

"If I did I wouldn't have to ask, would I?"

"No, of course not, apologies your highness. The royal address is"—the guard cleared his throat nervously—"about to begin?"

"I've made no plans to address anyone today." The guard looked back at him, dumbstruck, uncertain, and fearful. Magnus waved him off. "Go," he snapped, and the uniformed boy scurried off.

The two bottles of wine had taken their toll. His vision blurry, Magnus wended his way through the crowd, studying faces that looked eager and flushed with excitement.

This was Cleo's doing. She was going warn to everyone about the Kraeshian attack, which she herself had orchestrated.

How long did she plan to play this game?

The crowd quickly swelled to several hundred. Magnus continued to scan the scene around him, noticing that not a single person present gave him even a second look. Surely none of them were expecting to see the crown prince milling about the commoners, especially not with breath that stank of wine.

Suddenly, the boisterous activity in the square quieted to a sudden collective hush. Magnus looked up, following the crowd's gazes, to see Cleo, standing on the balcony overlooking the square.

"Welcome, welcome to you all," she began, her voice strong and confident. "And please accept my sincerest gratitude for sacrificing your time and duties to come here and listen to this important announcement."

Magnus felt his head go hot, his blood begin to boil.

He watched her put on a calm smile as she waited for the crowd's cheers to cease. "The last time I stood here was during my wedding tour, a ceremony to introduce me to everyone across Mytica as the wife of Prince Magnus, heir to the throne of his father, King Gaius. I'm sure many of you were here that day to hear the prince's speech, his claim that our union was one of choice. That we began as enemies and ended up two people in love, who wanted to spend the rest of their lives together."

Cleo paused and looked out at her audience, who appeared to collectively lean forward breathlessly as they waited for her to continue.

"This was a lie." Gasps and chatter began to spread through the crowd like a plague, and Magnus gritted his teeth. Cleo went on, and once again the people grew quiet. "King Gaius murdered my father and stole his throne. He spared my life only because he saw me as a way to ease his way into his reign. By marrying me to his son, he would show the people that I had accepted the Damoras as my new family, just as the Auranian citizens were expected to accept King Gaius as their new leader.

"Ours is a marriage into which I was forced by threat of death, and all I could do was wait and hope for a chance to change my situation. And hold on to the hope that I could one day reclaim my throne."

Magnus stared up at her, utterly astonished. She meant to overthrow him right here and now.

"I know that Limerians have endured years of fear," Cleo said solemnly. "Ever since your kind and benevolent King Davidus died, and was replaced by his cruel and sadistic son, Gaius. You have lived under his dark shadow ever since, and now Paelsia and Auranos have had to endure the cruelties of this King of Blood as well.

"I've gathered you all here today to tell you that that the king is in collusion with Princess Amara of Kraeshia. He has given Mytica—and therefore, all of you—over to the empire. They are sailing to our shores as we speak. We are now at risk of imminent occupation by Kraeshian forces."

The crowd swelled with banter and shouts, heated conversation edged now with fear and anger.

Cleo held up her hands, and she had their attention again. "As your princess, I am calling upon you for your help. We must spread the news of the Kraeshian invasion as quickly and as far across Mytica as possible. Know that, as of today, our enemy is not only Princess Amara, but King Gaius as well. What kind of king would do such a thing, sell his country and his people as if they were cattle, all for his own gain?"

She leaned forward, clutching the railing and staring out at the people with the gaze of a warrior. "These are the actions of a man who is not fit to rule Mytica. King Gaius is worse than selfish; he is *evil*. He takes everything and gives nothing back. And nothing will change unless we rise up against him!"

Magnus clenched his fists, forcing himself out of his frozen state of shock. He had to get up to that balcony, drag her away, put a stop to this before it was too late.

And expose his dear wife as a liar and a rebel, a fraud bent on destroying Magnus—and all the Limerian people—from inside the palace.

"But I want you to know," Cleo continued, "that there is hope. And that I am living proof of that hope. Because, even though I was forced into this marriage against my will, I have come to know Prince Magnus Lukas Damora very well these last months. And one thing I've learned is that Prince Magnus is *nothing* like his father. Prince Magnus is brave and compassionate, and he truly wants what's just and best for this kingdom. Kindness is what makes a good king who will put the needs and rights of his people before his own desires."

Magnus stumbled back, pressing himself against a pillar to keep from crumpling to the ground. He couldn't speak, he could barely think, and all he could do was stare up at her, utterly stunned.

"I believe, with all my heart, that Magnus is a worthy and superior successor to your current king. Therefore, I ask today that you reject Gaius Damora as your leader and take Prince Magnus as your new king. He will right the wrongs that have overtaken Mytica. And he will make Gaius Damora pay for all he has destroyed."

Still looking up at her in amazement, Magnus suddenly realized that Cleo wasn't wearing blue, her favorite color.

Today she wore red.

Cleo raised her arms up and out, as if reaching for the people. "Will you stand with me on this fateful day?" Her voice rose to a shout. "People of Limeros! Join me and my husband on a journey toward a new and better Mytica! Say it with me: King Magnus!"

Excited murmuring rippled through the audience and, one by one, the people began to join Cleo in her chant. Soon the volume in the square had risen to a deafening level, everyone shouting the same two words together, over and over: "King Magnus! King Magnus! KING MAGNUS!"

A sharp cry tore Magnus's attention away from the balcony. He watched with horror as a stream of green-uniformed Kraeshian guards—on foot and on horseback—flooded the square.

The warnings had been true.

And he'd been utterly wrong to doubt Cleo, in so many ways. The realization bit into him painfully like shattered glass.

The citizens scattered, the square was gripped in chaos. Magnus watched as nearly every fleeing Limerian was captured and restrained by the Kraeshians.

A tall, broad-shouldered guard atop a massive and majestic black stallion called out to the crowd in a booming voice. "I am the commander of Empress Amara Cortas's royal guard. The Empire of Kraeshia is now in control of Mytica. Our intentions here are peaceful. No one has to die today, but anyone who resists this occupation will pay with their life. From this day forward, you will bow before Amara Cortas, your glorious new empress."

Magnus looked back to the balcony to see that Cleo had disappeared. With one last glance at the chaos around him, Magnus darted back to the palace unnoticed.

He needed weapons. He needed to find the captain of the palace guard. He needed to stop these Kraeshian vultures before it was too late.

But first, he had to find Cleo.

Magnus raced through the hallways toward a winding staircase to the balcony, taking it two steps at a time. He reached the top and scanned the length of the long, dark hallway.

A flash of long golden hair caught his eye and he ran toward it, but staggered to a halt when he turned the next corner.

There he saw Lord Kurtis, clutching Cleo by her arm. She fought against him like a beast from the Wildlands, scratching and clawing at his face.

"Let go of me!" she yelled.

Kurtis grabbed her by her throat, smashed her against the wall, and slapped her hard across her face. "Behave yourself."

"I will kill you!"

"Deal with her," Kurtis said, shoving her at a guard who then struck her in the head with the hilt of his sword, rendering her unconscious. The guard picked up her limp body and tossed her over his shoulder.

Magnus ran at them, but suddenly found himself flat on his face, the wind knocked from his lungs. Someone had tripped him. He looked up to see a Kraeshian guard looming over him, his sharp sword pressed to Magnus's chest.

Magnus raised his arms to his sides. "I surrender."

The Kraeshian eased back on the sword, and Magnus clasped his hands on either side of the blade and rammed the hilt into the guard's face, breaking his nose. As the guard reeled back in pain, Magnus leapt to his feet and slammed his fist into his face, knocking him to the ground.

Then, without any hesitation, Magnus yanked the sword from the guard's grip and drove the blade down into his chest.

Sword in hand, he rushed along the hallway, desperately searching for Cleo. She was nowhere to be seen, but he spotted Kurtis, alone, headed for an exit.

"You better have answers for me." Magnus pressed the tip of

the sword between Kurtis's shoulder blades, just as the kingsliege reached for the door handle. "Where is Cleo?" he hissed.

Kurtis froze in place. "I don't think that's quite the right question to ask right now."

"Oh? And what's the right question?"

"The right question is, who was it I was meeting with at the gates earlier today?"

"Well, you're a coward, so it had to have been a Kraeshian. One who bribed you, told you he'd spare your life if you did as he asked."

Kurtis let out a dry little laugh. "Close," he said, "and yet so far. It wasn't a Kraeshian. It was a king. Your father, to be specific."

Magnus's blood grew cold and his face went slack.

"Yes, Magnus. Your father has arrived."

"And he took the princess. Why?"

"Why do you think? Honestly, Magnus, use your head."

Magnus stiffened and pressed his sword harder against Kurtis's back.

"All right, no need for violence," Kurtis bit out. "Your father took Princess Cleo because he wishes to personally finish the job that should have been done in Auranos, had you not intervened."

"He's going to kill her."

"Of course he's going to kill her."

"Where has she been taken?"

Kurtis shrugged and gave Magnus a smirk over his shoulder.

"*Where?*" Magnus pressed the blade down even harder, until he saw a spot of blood bloom out on the kingsliege's tunic.

"Kill me and you'll never know," Kurtis growled.

"You and me, Kurtis, we're all alone up here. No councilmen, no guards are going stroll by and help you out." He sliced downward along Kurtis's spine, making him whimper in pain. "You will tell me what I need to know swiftly, or I promise I'll have you begging for death when I start carving off body parts." Magnus grabbed a handful of Kurtis's hair, yanked him backward, and brought the sword's edge to his cheek. "I think I'll start with your nose."

"No, don't! Please!" Kurtis shrieked. "If—if I tell you, you will promise to let me leave the palace, alive and unharmed."

"Very well. And if you lie, I will hunt you down and make you suffer like one of the stray cats you adored so much as a child."

Kurtis swallowed hard. "The princess has been taken to my father's castle, where Amara and your father are staying."

"Much gratitude for the information, Kurtis."

"Now let me go."

Magnus pulled his sword away. "A promise is a promise."

Kurtis reached for the door handle, but before he could turn it, Magnus interrupted him.

"That's the hand you used to strike her, isn't it?" Magnus said.

"What are you—?"

Magnus swung his sword, severing the kingsliege's right hand at the wrist. Kurtis screamed, his eyes wide and wild with shock and pain.

Magnus grabbed him by his shirtfront, turned him around to face him, and slammed him against the wall. "By the way? I lied about not killing you."

Just before he could plunge his sword into Kurtis's soft belly, a servant appeared in the hallway, shrieking, pursued by a Kraeshian guard. Magnus turned to look, and Kurtis slammed his head against Magnus's forehead before tearing off down the hallway, dripping blood in his wake.

Magnus roared with anger and immediately ran after him, but when he turned the next corner, Kurtis had disappeared.

He charged down the stairs and pushed through the palace

doors, frantically searching outside for his enemy. The light snow-fall of this morning had now become a storm, the skies thick with dark clouds, making it difficult to see more than twenty paces away.

The Limerian palace had been captured. Amara's army was in control, her guards swarming the grounds like ants. And Magnus was trapped.

He knew he had to fight for his people, to destroy his father and Amara, to take back his kingdom before it was too late.

But right now, at this very moment, all he could think of was Cleo.

CHAPTER 29

LUCIA

PAELSIA

Downstairs at the inn, Lucia forced herself to eat some bread and honey, chewing each piece slowly and methodically before swallowing.

"Rough night?" the server girl asked as she brought some cider to Lucia's table. "Had a bit too much to drink, did you? I know what that's like. Stick with Paelsian wine and you won't have to suffer the next day."

"I appreciate the advice," Lucia replied as the girl left to attend to another table of travelers crossing the barren plains of Paelsia.

She'd tried to deny it at first, but now she knew it to be true.

She was pregnant with Alexius's child.

And she had never felt more confused, terrified, and alone in her entire life.

Kyan slowly approached her table and took a seat across from her. She sipped her cider, not bothering to spare him a glance.

"I need to apologize to you, little sorceress."

Lucia dunked a piece of the dry bread into the honey and popped it in her mouth.

"My behavior last night . . ." Kyan continued. "My behavior during these past several days, has been inexcusable."

"I'm glad to hear you admit it," Lucia said drily.

"That you're still here this morning, that you haven't abandoned me, is a miracle."

Finally she looked up at him. "Do you think I have anywhere else to go?" she said, her tone wracked with accusation. Kyan's hands were clasped in front of him on the table, and he wore an extremely grave expression.

"I'm unbearable to be around, I know it. I've always been this way. It's . . . in my nature. Fire, you know."

"Oh, I know it. I know it very well by now." She let out a long sigh and leaned back in her chair. "So what do you propose we do?"

"You are important to me, little sorceress. You're the only living thing on earth that still connects me to my family. You *are* my family."

Her throat tightened. "Is this how you treat family? With cruelty and abuse?"

"You're right. You're absolutely right. I'm sorry." He leaned forward until she had no choice but to gaze right into his sincere amber eyes. "Here is what I propose. There's no sense in continuing on in vain with our search for a gateway to the Sanctuary. Instead, we need to find that boy again, the one from the village market. Are you certain he has the obsidian orb?"

She felt a pang in her belly as she thought back to Jonas Agallon and the girl Kyan had killed. "I can't be completely certain," she said solemnly. "I thought he did, but perhaps I was wrong. We can look for him. But if we find him, you'll let me handle him, understood? I won't let you get carried away again."

A smile tugged at his lips. "Lucia Damora, magical protector of unworthy mortals."

"Only because you've given me no other choice, oh fearsome fire god." She let out a sigh and fought a smile of her own. "I forgive you this time. But if you lose your temper again, if you do *anything* to make me feel like I'm not worthy of your company because I'm nothing but a filthy mortal, we will have a very big problem, you and I."

"Completely understood," said Kyan, placing his hands on top of hers. "So. Now that all ill will is healed between us, tell me, little sorceress, how do you feel on this"—he turned and glanced out the window at a sky full of dark storm clouds—"rather gloomy and unpleasant Paelsian day?"

She'd heard it was always gloomy and unpleasant near the Forbidden Mountains.

"How am I?" she repeated.

Pregnant, she thought. *I'm pregnant and my magic is weakening because of it.*

Lucia couldn't help but think about the warning Queen Althea had issued her when she was little more than twelve years old.

"Men will tell you lies to get you into their bed, to use you for their own pleasure, only to discard you right after. You must not let this happen. If you do, all you'll end up with is unwanted children, a wasted life, and squandered potential—all because of a stupid decision to share flesh before a proper marriage. And if your father were to get word of that kind of behavior, he wouldn't hesitate to kill you."

What helpful, motherly advice from the woman who'd resented Lucia's existence since the day Gaius brought her home.

Alexius had used her for plenty of deceitful reasons, but not for her body. She'd given herself to him freely because she thought she was in love with him.

Perhaps she really was.

"Little sorceress," Kyan said, leaning forward. "Are you still here with me?"

She pulled herself out of her thoughts. "Yes, I'm here. Where else would I be?"

Part of her wanted to share her concerns about what was growing within her, but she held her tongue. Better to keep this a secret for a while longer, especially from Kyan. She'd been able to hide so few secrets from the fire Kindred, she'd allow herself this one.

Lucia gazed out of the window at the mountains in the distance. How tall they were, all sharp, jagged black rocks spreading north to south along the western border of Paelsia. She had read books about this countryside, ancient texts proclaiming that the Sanctuary could be found if one ventured deep enough into those mountains.

"What do you know about the Forbidden Mountains?" she asked Kyan.

"Only that mortals have given them a silly name, and they're rather unpleasant to look at."

"You're an eternal, all-powerful elemental god. Is that really all you know about the storied mountains that many fools think lead directly to the Sanctuary?"

He shrugged. "Geography doesn't concern me—that's my brother's area of expertise. Mine is a bit more interesting." He held his hand out and produced a flame that danced a jig upon his palm.

She laughed, surprising herself. "Very impressive."

"It's possible I'm even more talented than the Goddess of Serpents, wouldn't you say?" He closed his fist to douse the fire as the server girl returned to their table.

"What can I bring you?" she asked him.

"Nothing except a bit of information." He nodded at the

window. "Tell me about the Forbidden Mountains. Why are they so foreboding?"

She grinned. "You really want to know?"

"Oh, yes, I *really* do."

"Well, who really knows what the *real* truth is, but my grandmother used to tell me stories about them. About how they're not mountains at all, but gigantic guardians that protect the Sanctuary from the rest of the world. And that any witch or exiled Watcher who ventures there will not only have their magic stripped away, they'll be blinded, too, so they won't see the dangers threatening them right before their own eyes. She had so many stories like that." The girl's eyes grew glossy. "I miss her so much."

"Where is she?" Lucia asked.

"She died only a short time ago. I lived with her further west, she took care of me after my parents died. Now I have to work here." She glared around at the inn. "I hate being stranded in the middle of this wasteland."

Lucia listened carefully, realizing only now that she hadn't needed to use even a small amount of her magic to draw the truth from this girl. "What's your name?" she asked.

"Sera," said the girl, then shook her head. "Apologies, I shouldn't burden you with my many problems."

"It's not a burden at all." Lucia captured the girl's gaze. She could be a wealth of information. There was no way Lucia could let her walk away without first magically wrenching every detail she could out of her. "Tell me, Sera, did your grandmother tell you stories about gateways to the immortal world? Stone wheels in various locations around Paelsia?"

Sera drew in a sharp breath, as if someone had wrapped a hand around her throat and squeezed. "No. No, she never said anything like that."

"Was your grandmother a witch?"

The girl hesitated, her expression growing tense and pained. "Y-yes." Her bottom lip began to tremble. "But there were rumors that she was much more than just a witch. There was gossip and whispering that she used to be an immortal, one who exiled herself to marry my grandfather. That sounds foolish, I know. And of course she never admitted that to me. People would talk, and Grandmother would just ignore them."

The witch from last night had been very strong and had fought back against Lucia's weakened magical influence. This girl, however, didn't resist, which would keep her discomfort to a minimum.

Lucia concentrated and drew that magical shroud tighter around Sera. "What else did your grandmother say about the mountains? About their magic?"

"She . . . she always made sure to remind us that mountains themselves aren't magic. They just protect something *else* that is magic. Right in the middle of them, that's where the magic can be found."

Kyan listened attentively, hanging on to every word Sera spoke.

"Thank you very much for your help, Sera," Lucia said. "You can go now."

Sera nodded, shook her head as if she'd just emerged from a disconcerting and unpleasant dream, then wandered away from their table.

"It wasn't all that far from here that I was awakened and able to take mortal form," Kyan said. "I believed Melenia was responsible for that, but now I'm not so sure." He stared out toward the mountains again, now with much more interest than before. "There's something out there, little sorceress. Something powerful enough to draw me forth from my cage, something that released me without your magic playing a part in it."

"Those might only be stories, like Sera said. The kinds of stories grandmothers tell their granddaughters to make sure they don't wander off alone into the mountains."

"Perhaps it's just a story. But perhaps it's the answer we've been searching for all this time." He looked back at her and frowned. "I know I said we should stop looking for the stone gateway . . ."

Lucia stood up from the table, emboldened by her experience with Sera and ready to dive back into Kyan's mission once more. "You're right. This could be it. That's what the Forbidden Mountains hold—the magic we need to draw Timotheus out of the Sanctuary, and to release your family from their prisons."

"So we're in agreement."

"We are. We're going to the center of the Forbidden Mountains."

CHAPTER 30

CLEO

LIMEROS

Cleo opened her eyes, slowly and painfully, and found that she was lying on a hard bed in a small, unfamiliar room with white plaster walls.

She groaned as she pushed herself up and pressed her hand against her head, feeling dried blood matted in her hair.

And then she remembered.

Lord Kurtis.

She'd grown to dislike him more and more over the weeks, realizing what a coward he was ever since he'd tried to get her to help him regain the power Magnus had taken from him. But she never would have expected him to be bold or decisive enough to drag her off of the palace balcony as if she were nothing more than a rag doll, and hand her over to a pair of Kraeshian guards.

He would pay dearly for that mistake.

Cleo stood and went to the door, trying the handle only to find it locked. A single window opposite the door showed her it was night, which meant she'd been unconscious for quite some time. She pushed the window open, then leaned over the sill as far as she could to see if she could spot anything familiar that might give her some clues as to her location.

She was inside a large stone building, sprawling and at least four stories tall. This was grander than a villa, more like a castle, and made of the same black granite as the Limerian palace.

The room was lit up with several lanterns, but all she could see beyond the grounds beneath her window was a thick line of trees—a forest. Heavy snow was falling, further obscuring her sight.

For a moment she thought about jumping to the snow-dusted ground below, but then quickly put it out of her mind. Even with a generous padding of snow, she knew that a leap from this height would mean a severe injury at best, instant death at worst. With a sinking heart, she pulled the windowpane shut.

"Think, Cleo," she muttered. There had to be a way out of there.

She wondered where Magnus was. She hadn't seen him since their horrible argument in the throne room.

She knew the prince would be angry with her for the stunt she pulled on the balcony, but she wasn't sorry about the message she'd delivered. And she hoped her speech succeeded in changing his mind about her, once and for all.

After receiving Jonas's message and spending a sleepless night trying to find a way to avoid getting trapped under Kraeshian rule, Cleo came to the realization that Magnus was the only person who could keep their country safe from King Gaius and Amara and their overwhelming greed.

But now, after witnessing the force and swiftness with which the Kraeshian army had taken over the palace, she saw that her final grasp at a hopeful future had been unforgivably optimistic.

Suddenly, Cleo heard a key slip into the lock and the door creaked open.

She squinted in the torchlight to see Amara Cortas herself step inside.

She offered Cleo a big smile. "Good evening, Cleo. It seems like a very long time since I last saw you."

"It has," Cleo answered, offering a small smile of her own. "And I can see you've been very busy. I suppose I should congratulate you on your victory."

Amara glanced at the guard standing at the doorway. "Fetch us something to drink," she ordered. "Some Paelsian wine. Since most Limerians seem to be hypocrites about their religious beliefs, I'm sure Lord Gareth keeps a stash of it somewhere in his home."

"Yes, Empress," the guard said, then exited the room.

Amara turned back to Cleo. "You're probably still angry about how we left things between you and me."

"Anger fades, Amara. Even the most intense anger."

"I ordered my guards to have you killed."

"I remember. But, clearly, they failed."

"Clearly. Truthfully, though, I'm rather glad for my guards' shortcomings. My emotions were running very high that night. Looking back on it now, I'm ashamed of how drastically I lost my composure."

"It's in the past now." Cleo held on to her smile, willing herself not to remind Amara that she'd lost more than her composure that night. She'd lost her brother—had murdered him in cold blood without any hesitation. "So, this is Lord Gareth's home?"

"Yes. A rather quaint castle, isn't it?"

"I wouldn't trust Lord Gareth if I were you. And I would especially not trust his son."

Amara laughed. "Don't worry, I don't trust any man."

The Kraeshian princess moved to the window and took a seat on the sill.

"It seems we have a problem, Cleo."

"Oh?"

"The king wants you dead. And he wants to perform the execution himself."

A shiver shot down Cleo's spine, but she fought to show anything but surprise on her face. "That's . . . I . . . but I don't understand. What kind of threat could *I* pose to someone as powerful as King Gaius?"

"You don't know?" Amara raised a brow. "I thought it was obvious. My new husband believes you are the one obstacle standing in between him and his son's loyalty. And I must say, Cleo, given your prince's recent actions, I don't think he's wrong."

"Apologies," said Cleo, her mind reeling, "but did you just refer to the king as 'your husband'? You're . . . you married King Gaius?"

Amara shrugged. "My father's idea. He thought our marriage would symbolically bind him into the Cortas bloodline, making him worthy of sharing his power." She regarded Cleo with amusement. "Don't look so appalled. It's not nearly as repulsive as it sounds."

"But he's . . ." Cleo faltered, grasping to comprehend this strange new situation. "King Gaius . . . even apart from all the things he's done, he's . . ."

"Exactly like Magnus, only twice as old? That reminds me, I hope you're not still upset about my brief dalliance with your husband. I can assure you that it meant nothing—to me, at least."

"I couldn't care less about such matters."

"Of course not."

Cleo remembered the sting she'd felt when she realized that Amara had spent the night with the prince. At the time, she'd been convinced that sting was one of annoyance, of disappointment that Magnus would so quickly jump into bed with a potential enemy.

Now she wasn't so sure.

The guard returned, holding a bottle of wine and two goblets. "As you requested, Empress."

"Excellent." She gestured toward the table in the corner. "Put it down over there and leave us."

Amara poured the wine and held a goblet out to Cleo.

She hesitated briefly, then took it.

"Don't worry," Amara said, "it's not poisoned. Besides, your death wouldn't serve me in any way. I like you much better alive."

"That sounded almost like a compliment." Cleo raised her glass. "To your new role as empress . . . and to you and the king."

Amara clinked her goblet against Cleo's and took a sip. "You would toast a man who wants you dead?"

Cleo tipped her head back and drained her glass in one gulp. "I'm toasting to the day you become a widow, to the moment you decide he's no longer useful to you."

Amara smiled. "You know me well."

"I admire you, Amara. You go after what you want, and you get it, no matter what it takes."

"My grandmother was determined to make sure I grew up believing that I was every bit as good as my brothers, even if all the men in Kraeshia thought of me as little more than a pretty bit of trimming. I am proud of my accomplishments, yes, but I'm not without regrets."

"None of us are."

"Tell me, Cleo," Amara said as she refilled their goblets. "If I were to convince the king to keep you alive, would you pledge your alliance to me in return? Would you promise to stay loyal to me, from this day forward?"

Cleo froze, the delicate edge of the goblet pressed to her lips. "You would . . . why would you do that?"

"I have many reasons. I've also recently come to learn something very surprising about Gaius: his most important decisions are made by his heart."

"And here I was certain he didn't possess one."

"It may be small and dark and cold, but it's there. He loves his son so much that he's willing to forgive him for even the gravest trespass of treason. He loves Lucia as well—for more than just her magic." Amara paused and took another sip of wine, her eyes sly and gleaming. "I also learned something very interesting about his distant past. Something to do with a girl. A girl he loved with a passion that surprised even me."

Cleo had to scoff. "Did he tell you that? He's lying."

"I'm not so sure," Amara said, a knowing smile playing at her lips. She leaned forward. "Cleo, we could put our pasts behind us. We could work together, secretly, to help prevent any man from trying to steal our power."

"*Our* power?"

"My grandmother is old, my father and brothers are dead. I have no friends, no allies I can trust. You've been through so much tragedy and loss that I know it's changed you. Like me, you are beautiful on the outside, but your soul is forged from steel."

Cleo frowned, feeling more skeptical with every compliment Amara spoke. "You'd put your trust in me so easily?"

"Absolutely not. That kind of trust needs to be earned—on both sides. I know that. But I see enough of me in you that I'm willing to take this risk." Amara extended her hand. "So what do you say?"

Cleo stared down at Amara's bejeweled hand for a long moment before she finally grasped it. "I'd say that the future looks much brighter than it did this morning."

"Excellent." Amara smiled, then turned to gaze out of the

window. "When Gaius wakes, I'll speak to him. I doubt very much that he'll put up much of an argument before he agrees to keep you alive. After all, he sees you the same way he sees me: as an object to possess and control."

"His mistake, isn't it?"

"It certainly is."

Cleo picked up the bottle, poured more wine into her goblet, and swallowed it down.

Then she smashed the bottle over the empress's head.

Align with the most devious, untrustworthy, murderous girl she'd ever met in her entire life?

Never.

Stunned, Amara crumpled to the floor.

Cleo rushed toward the door and pressed her ear against it. She heard nothing. The crash of glass and thump of Amara's body hadn't drawn the suspicion of any guards.

Still, she knew she didn't have much time, and if she tried to escape through the castle she'd surely be captured.

Sidestepping the fallen empress, Cleo unlatched and pushed the window open again. A draft of cold air and snow blew into the room.

Was she ready to take this risk?

"Think," she whispered.

She leaned over the windowsill and looked down at the side of the building and saw something she hadn't seen before: a frost-covered trellis, partially hidden under the snow.

A memory came to her, of a time not so long ago, when all was well in the City of Gold and Cleo's biggest problem was having an overprotective king for a father and an overachieving heiress for a sister. Cleo had always craved freedom, had hated being cooped up in the palace.

She was with Emilia in her chambers when she noticed the vine- and flower-covered trellis alongside her sister's balcony.

The trellis made her think of the fence Nic had once climbed in order to fetch her a perfect red rose, and she'd decided to try it for herself. All she'd succeeded in doing was ruining her new gown, which got her in very deep trouble with her nanny. But she'd enjoyed the climbing, had reveled in her ability to get somewhere through only her own strength and balance.

"I want to try something," little Cleo had told Emilia, and without waiting for a response, she began climbing over the railing.

Emilia had put her book down and raced to the balcony. "Cleo! You're going to get yourself killed!"

"No, I won't." Her foot found a sturdy hold and she grinned up at her sister. "Look at me! I think I've found a new way to escape from the palace."

But Emilia's trellis had not been nearly this slippery, and her chambers were much closer to the ground.

Cleo heard some commotion beyond the door. With no time to think, she crawled through the window and sat on the ledge. The cold air brushed against her bare legs beneath her gown. Blindly, she tried to find a foothold. She searched with the toe of her slipper until finally she found one.

Narrow, so narrow. And so icy.

She said a silent prayer to the goddess she'd long since stopped believing in, and finally let go of the sturdy windowsill, now clinging completely to the snow-covered trellis.

"I can do this," she whispered. "I can do this. I can do this."

She repeated the phrase with each new foothold she found.

Snow continued to fall, thick and heavy, which only made every movement more treacherous.

One step at a time. One foot lower. Again. And again.

Her heart pounded hard, her fingers began to go numb.

Suddenly, her foot slipped. She scrambled to hold on. A scream caught in her throat as she lost her grip and fell.

She landed, hard on her backside, and, stunned but uninjured, gaped at the side of the castle.

There was no time to rest. She stiffly pushed up to her feet and started moving.

She had to find shelter, a place to rest and hide. And tomorrow, when the sun rose, she would hasten to Ravencrest where she could try to send word to Jonas and Nic.

The sound of dogs barking startled her, and she scrambled to hide behind a pile of firewood. From there she watched two guards and three black dogs emerge from the thick woods. The dogs dragged behind them a sled carrying the carcass of a deer.

"Take the dogs to the kennel and have them fed," said the taller guard.

His companion nodded and unhooked the dogs' harnesses from the sled and led them off toward the far side of the castle.

The remaining guard took hold of the reins and continued to drag the sled toward the castle. He looked up at the stormy sky, at the snow falling and coating his cloak, then pulled the bow off his shoulder and threw it down on the ground, along with the quiver of arrows. Then he took a seat on a large log, pulled out a silver flask from his cloak, and took a swig.

"Damn long day," he muttered.

"It really has been," Cleo agreed as she swung a piece of firewood at his head.

The guard looked at her with surprise for a single second, before he fell over, unconscious.

She hit him one more time, just to be sure.

Quickly, Cleo removed his cloak and threw it over her shoulders.

Then she scanned the area, knowing she needed to go deeper in the forest if she wanted to stay hidden until dawn. Her gaze then fell upon the bow and arrows.

If magic really did exist in this world, then maybe it was possible that her archery skills would emerge when she needed them the most. Even if she hadn't hit a single target during her lessons.

That's what happens when you have a coward as a weapons instructor, she thought darkly.

Cleo grabbed the bow and arrows and ran as fast as she could through the deep snow and into the woods.

CHAPTER 31

MAGNUS

LIMEROS

Magnus had visited Lord Gareth's castle only once before, but he was certain he remembered the way. He couldn't access the palace stables, so he ran to the nearest village and stole the first horse he came across—a gray mare likely used only for short trips and errands.

She would do. She had to.

His destination was nearly a half-day's journey northeast, and the snow was only falling more steadily and thickly as the sun set behind the dark gray clouds and day became night.

Soon the storm grew so strong that the roads and pathways had become completely obliterated by the snow. Magnus had lost his way, couldn't recognize a single checkpoint, and now had to go by instinct alone.

After trudging through the snow for hours, the horse began to protest by shaking her head and baying with displeasure. She needed water, food, shelter, and rest. So did he.

But he couldn't stop.

Magnus leaned forward and stroked her mane. "Please keep going. You must. I need you."

In response, the mare let out a mighty neigh, then bucked and threw Magnus from the saddle. He fell hard to the ground, but immediately scrambled up to his feet. Quickly, he tried to catch her reins, but they slipped through his gloved fingers.

Finally free, the horse galloped off into the distance.

"No!" he yelled after her.

He stared after her bleakly for several long moments of disbelief.

"Yes, wonderful," he finally muttered. "Here I am, with nothing but a cloak and a thin, useless pair of gloves to keep me from freezing to death out here in the middle of bloody nowhere."

He started walking, noting the position of the half-moon, which he could occasionally see through sporadic breaks in the clouds. The snow had now risen to his knees, making it impossible to move quickly.

The moon moved behind a heavy cloud, and once more his world was plunged back into darkness. Yet, he continued to move forward.

Another hour. Two, maybe three more after that. He'd lost track of time long ago.

Finally, he slowed to a halt. He hadn't wanted to admit it, but now he was certain and there was no denying it: he was well and truly lost.

He wondered how the king would choose to end the princess's life.

Would he be gentle with her, a girl who'd already experienced so much pain? Or would he be cruel, take his time torturing her before finally letting her soul go free?

King Gaius was so afraid of a sixteen-year-old girl that he insisted on having her captured so he could kill her himself.

A girl loved by her people, not only for her beauty, but for her spirit and courage.

Magnus had been cruel to her. Dismissive. Rude, cold, and unsympathetic.

Last night was the cruelest he'd ever been. He'd ransacked her chambers and stolen the earth Kindred while she was out shooting arrows with Kurtis. And then the last thing he said to her was that he never wanted to see her again.

His behavior was unforgivable.

But even then she'd seen past it, had insisted that she saw something more in him.

Magnus wasn't any different than the king. He, too, was afraid of the princess. Her spirit was so bright, he'd been blinded by it.

And yet, he'd never wanted to close his eyes to block out that light.

"I will kill him if he touches her," he managed to choke out, his throat raw. "I will tear his heart out."

To think, not so long ago, Magnus longed to be like his father. Strong, ruthless, decisive. Immune to any form of remorse.

When he'd learned that it was the king who had ordered Queen Althea's death, Magnus had ached for vengeance. But instead of acting on it, he'd doubted himself at every turn.

He was through doubting himself.

Magnus forced himself back to his feet. Weakly, slowly, he trudged onward, until the cold became so great that, despite his thick winter boots, he couldn't feel his toes.

So this is how it ends, he thought.

Just as he'd been given perfect clarity about his life, it would be taken away. What a cruel joke.

He looked up at the black sky and started to laugh, snowflakes melting on his cheeks and sliding down to his chin.

"All right," he said, his laughter growing sharper and more pained. "I've lost. I've lost *and* I'm lost. If only Kurtis could see me now."

He should have taken out the boy's eyes as well as his hand.

So many regrets.

If these were indeed his final moments, he would much rather think about Cleo than this. She'd once accused him of having a cold heart. Soon that would be very literally true. He'd heard that freezing to death was a great deal like drifting off to sleep—peaceful, with no pain.

But he needed pain. He needed to feel something so he could keep fighting against it.

"Oh goddess," he said aloud. "I know I haven't been your most humble servant. Nor do I believe in your radiance, now that I know you were only a greedy Watcher with stolen magic. But, whatever you are, whatever is out there looking down at us stupid mortals, please hear my prayer."

He wrapped his arms across his chest, trying to harness what little warmth he had left for as long as possible. "Send me pain so I know I'm still alive. Help me continue to suffer. For if my father has already killed her, then I need to live so I can avenge her."

So dark, that night. He could see no stars through the clouds. Nothing to light his way. Only the cold press of snow all around him.

"Please, goddess," he implored again. "Give me a chance to make this right. I promise I won't ask for anything else, ever again. Please"—he lowered his head to the snow and closed his eyes— "*please* let me live so I can kill him. So I can stop him from ever hurting anyone else again."

Suddenly, Magnus heard something in the distance. An eerie howl.

His eyes snapped open and he scanned the endless darkness. The noise rang out again. It sounded like the howl of an ice wolf.

He glared up at the black sky. "I was trying to be sincere, and this is what I get in return? A hungry wolf to tear me apart on the worst night of my life? Much gratitude, goddess."

The clouds parted and, gradually, the moon became visible again.

"Better," he muttered, pushing against the snow and forcing himself to his feet. "Slightly better."

With the help of the dim moonlight, he scanned the area again, searching for something, anything, that might offer him help. There was a forest up ahead, past the snowy plain. It wasn't nearly as good as a village, but the trees might offer him enough warmth and shelter to survive the night.

Magnus trudged toward the forest, keeping one hand on the stolen sword at his side in case any hungry ice wolves decided to interrupt him.

He made it into the forest, and immediately set about searching for anything that might serve him well as shelter. But when he finally saw exactly what he was looking for, he was certain his eyes deceived him.

It was a small stone cottage, no larger than something that might belong to a Paelsian peasant, but to him it might as well have been a palace.

He approached cautiously and peered through a dirty, ice-encrusted window, but couldn't see anything inside. No smoke rose from the chimney. No candles were lit. Just barely, he was able to climb three chiseled stone steps that led up to the door.

He tried the handle. It was unlocked. The door swung open without effort.

If this turned out to be the work of the goddess, he promised to start praying much more often.

Magnus stepped inside and felt around in the darkness until he found an oil lantern and a piece of flint. He struck the flint and lit the wick.

He nearly sobbed when the room swelled with light.

Taking the lantern in hand, he inspected the cottage. It was a single room, with a straw bed in one corner, equipped with a few ragged, but dry, quilts. In the opposite corner, he saw a large hearth, and some cooking pots.

On top of the hearth, next to another lantern, he found an effigy of the Goddess Cleiona, emblazoned with the symbols for fire and air. That meant that this cottage had at one point been occupied by an Auranian—or a Limerian who was secretly loyal to the Auranian goddess.

He built a fire with wood from the cottage's modest supply. He sat in front of the fire, atop a thick rug embroidered with a hawk and the Auranian credo: OUR TRUE GOLD IS OUR PEOPLE.

Magnus decided that the former occupant had most likely been arrested and taken away to the dungeons for worshipping Cleiona. If Magnus lived through this, he swore he would find that man or woman and free them.

There wasn't enough firewood inside to last the night, so Magnus took the lantern and ventured back outside. He found an ax and a chopping block, along with some larger pieces of wood, leaning against the cottage. He set the lantern down and prepared to do something he'd never done before in his entire life: chop wood.

But before he could take a single swing of the ax, a shout from not far away caught his attention. Magnus pulled up the hood of his cloak, snatched up the lantern and the ax, and went to investigate. Fifty paces away, he came across a dead man lying in the snow. He wore the green uniform of a Kraeshian guard, and had an arrow sticking out of his left eye socket.

Another shout caught his attention, back in the direction of the cottage. He tightened his grip on the ax and made his way back, slowly and cautiously.

Another guard lay dead behind the cottage, an arrow lodged in his throat. Magnus knelt down and yanked the arrow out to see that it bore Kraeshian markings.

He needed to check inside, to see if someone lay in wait. As he cautiously neared the door to see that it was ajar, something from behind hit him, hard, knocking him over the threshold of the cottage and through the door. He lost his grip on the ax and landed with a deep thud on his back. A cloaked assailant clutched an arrow and tried to stab him with it, but Magnus grabbed his attacker and rolled him over, knocking the weapon from his hand.

The henchman was small and agile and managed to wriggle free, but Magnus grabbed him by the back of his cloak and threw him down on the floor. He shoved the hood back from his attacker's face, ready to crush his throat.

A silky lock of long blond hair swung free from the hood. Magnus gasped and scrambled backward.

Cleo.

She grabbed for her arrow, but her hands found the ax instead. She hefted it up and, with a war cry, stormed toward him.

Magnus caught the handle of the ax just beneath the blade and snatched it from her grip, throwing it to the floor.

He took her by her shoulders and pushed her back against the wall.

"Cleo! Cleo, enough . . . it's me!"

"Let go of me! I'll kill you!"

"It's me!" He pulled down his own hood so she could see his face.

Finally, recognition dawned in her cerulean eyes.

Cleo continued to stare at him as if he were the last person she expected to see here—or anywhere.

"I'm going to let go of you now." He held up his hands and took a step back from her.

She was alive. Somehow, she'd escaped her captors, escaped the king. And she'd just killed two Kraeshian guards with nothing more than her bare hands and a couple of arrows.

To think he'd doubted that she'd ever become proficient at archery.

Cleo remained silent, unmoving, as if in shock.

"Do you even hear me?" he said, in the most calming tone he could muster.

"You!" she suddenly snarled. "This was all your doing, wasn't it? Trying to win back your father's approval by delivering me to him! So, what now? Did you come here so you could kill me yourself? Or are you going to bring me back to that castle so you can sit back and let him have the honor?"

"Cleo—"

"Shut up! I nearly broke my neck getting away from Amara. And then I nearly froze to death out here! *Yes*, I had the earth Kindred. *Yes*, I lied to you. What did you expect? For me to suddenly start sharing everything with you? You, the son of my worst enemy?"

Magnus just stared at her, unsure if he was impressed or horrified by this poisonous tirade escaping the petite blonde.

No, he was impressed. Very impressed and very happy.

Her cheeks flushed bright red. "I know you didn't hear my speech this morning, but it was a damn good one. I'm sure you'll think I'm lying, but I asked everyone to accept you as their king."

"And why would you do something like that?" he asked, his voice hoarse.

"Because," she said, letting out an exhausted sigh. "I believe in you. Even when you're being cruel to me. Even when you make me want to run away and never come back. I believe in you, Magnus!"

Her chest heaved up and then down as she took a deep, choking breath.

Magnus struggled to find his voice. He desperately searched for it; he needed to reply.

"I thought you were dead," he finally managed to say. "I was certain I was too late and that my father . . . that my father had . . ."

Cleo blinked. "So you . . . you're here to rescue me?"

"That was the general plan, yes, but it seems you're perfectly capable of rescuing yourself."

And then he sank down to his knees, his attention fixed on the wooden floor.

"What's wrong with you?" she said, warily now. "Why won't you look at me?"

"I've been a monster to you. I've hurt you over and over, and yet you still continued to believe in me."

"Actually, it's not until recently that I started." Her tone had grown uncertain and tentative, her voice quieter.

"Forgive me, Cleo. Please . . . please forgive me for all that I've said. All that I've done."

"You . . . you really want my forgiveness?"

"I know I don't even deserve to ask for it. But, yes." It was true agony to realize how wrong he'd been about her. About everything.

Cleo lowered herself to the floor, peering up at his face with a concerned frown. "You're not acting like yourself at all. Are you in pain?"

"Yes. Horrible pain."

She reached out with a shaky hand and pushed his hair back from his forehead. He raised his eyes to meet hers. He couldn't speak, he couldn't put all that he was feeling into words. So instead of speaking, he just held on to her gaze, no mask in place, no protection, his heart open and raw and messy.

"I love you, Cleo," he said, the words finally coming to him, with no effort at all because of how true they were. "I love you so much it hurts."

Her eyes widened. "What did you just say?"

Magnus almost laughed. "I think you heard me right."

Cleo drew closer to him, continuing to stroke his hair, which was damp from the melting snow. He froze under her touch, unable to move or to breathe. No thoughts, no words, only the feel of her fingertips on his skin. She stroked his face, his jaw, her touch growing bolder as she traced the line of his scar.

And she drew closer still, close enough that he could feel her warm breath against his lips.

"I love you too," she whispered. "Now kiss me, Magnus. Please."

With a dark groan, Magnus crushed his mouth to hers, breathing her in, tasting the sweetness of her lips as her tongue slid against his. She kissed him back without restraint, deeper and sweeter and hotter even than the kiss they'd shared in Ravencrest.

This—this overpowering *need*—is what had been building between them ever since that night. He'd thought he could forget it, put it out of his mind, ignore his heart. But the memory of that kiss had been nightly haunting his dreams and daily sending him to distraction.

He needed her, longed for her, ached for her. Not for a single solitary moment had his desire for her ceased.

Cleo broke off the kiss. He immediately started to worry. Was she coming to her senses and now pushing him away? But instead, she just looked at him, her eyes wide and dark in the shadows of the cottage.

He gently took her face between his hands and kissed her again, and a small moan escaped from the back of her throat, a sound that nearly drove him insane.

Cleo slipped his cloak off his shoulders and then pulled at the ties of his shirt to bare his chest. She brushed her lips against his skin, and he grasped her shoulders.

"Cleo . . . please . . ."

"Shh." She pressed her fingertips to his lips. "Don't ruin this by talking. We might start arguing again."

When she smiled then, he knew he was already ruined.

Her lips met his again, and Magnus surrendered any small grasp of control he had left.

He didn't deserve her; he knew he didn't. He was the Prince of Blood, the son of a monster, who said and did cruel things. Who preemptively leapt to hurt anyone before they could hurt him first.

But he would show her that he could change.

Magnus could change for her.

She was his princess. No. She was his *goddess*. With her golden skin and golden hair. She was his light. His life. His everything.

He loved her more than anything else in this world.

Magnus worshipped his beautiful goddess that night, both her body and her soul, before the heat of the blazing hearth, upon the rug bearing the symbol of the kingdom his father had stolen from her.

CHAPTER 32

LUCIA

THE FORBIDDEN MOUNTAINS

The closer Lucia came to the Forbidden Mountains, the more they started to resemble to her an arsenal of obsidian daggers slicing up into the gray sky. But she was accustomed to living amidst intimidating structures. After all, she had grown up in the cold, black Limerian palace.

She refused to be intimidated by the foreboding landscape around her. It would take a lot more than these so-called guardians to scare her away.

But that momentary recollection of her past, of the castle perched atop the cliffs where she'd lived for sixteen years, summoned an unfamiliar—and completely unwelcome—sensation in her.

Homesickness.

After so much time away from her home—first during her time in Auranos, and now on the road with Kyan—she'd finally become so weary that she found herself missing familiarities so banal as her own bed. She missed her attendants and the kind cook who always gave her an extra biscuit, a special treat just for her, with her breakfasts. She missed books, the collection she had at home and the incredible selection she'd only started to discover in the Auranian palace library. She missed her tutors, even the ones who taught the subjects she dreaded, especially drawing, which in Limeros was treated as more of a practical life skill than a fine art. Magnus was the artist in the family, not her.

She missed Magnus.

And most surprisingly of all, she missed her father.

She had to put them, put everything besides the task at hand, out of her mind. There would be no returning to her old life. She'd made her choice long ago, and now she had to stand by it.

Lucia concentrated instead on her surroundings as she and Kyan moved deeper into the mountains. It wasn't all that cold here, but curiously, she still found herself shivering. She pulled her cloak tighter around her shoulders.

Nothing grew here, no grass, no trees. No animals. No life.

No birds flew in the sky. No insects crawled across the dirt.

This was truly a wasteland.

"I don't like it here," Kyan said. "I think that wench from the inn was wrong. This isn't a place of great elemental magic, this is a forgotten place of emptiness and death."

Yes, she felt that too, but there was something about that emptiness, that stillness and lack of life, that compelled her as much as it concerned her.

Paelsia had wasted away over the generations, had become barren, dry, no longer able to sustain life at a prosperous rate. Some people said it was a cursed land—the same people who claimed that Limeros, too, was cursed, with its seemingly endless snow and ice. But Lucia knew the truth, that these extreme environmental shifts were due to the missing Kindred.

The Kindred made life itself possible. She didn't understand exactly *how* they did this, especially now that she knew Kyan had been released from his crystal in the form of a young man who'd become part of her new family. But he wasn't just an extraordinary young man; he was fire *elementia*. Pure fire *elementia* that could speak, breathe, eat, hate, need, love, and hope. And his Kindred siblings were just like him. Earth magic, air magic, water magic—all real, living beings, trapped inside their crystal cages.

Without these four exceptional siblings, there would be no life.

The entire world would be just as it was here in the Forbidden Mountains.

They'd only been exploring for a short time, but this stark environment had already begun to affect her mood. When they first trekked into the mountain range, she'd felt optimistic, so sure they were on the brink of finding the answers they sought, so ready to help Kyan gain his ultimate freedom and vanquish the immortal trying to control his fate.

But now, completely surrounded by dark, jagged mountains, with no flat land or villages in sight, all she felt was sad and tired and very alone.

She rested her hand against her flat belly. If this barren bleakness were to spread further out into Mytica, vanquishing all the life it touched, her child wouldn't have a future.

Death would be all that awaited the living being within her.

Luckily, one of the Kindred had been awakened. Soon, his siblings would join him and walk the earth. It was only a matter of time before the balance that had been lost over the last millennium would be restored.

The sun began to set and, with the growing darkness, it became much cooler. She didn't relish spending the night in this place. She and Kyan conjured torchlike flames as they walked, to light their way but also to reassure themselves that their magic remained strong. Sera had mentioned that witches and exiled Watchers couldn't access their *elementia* here, but that didn't seem to be the case for a sorceress and a god.

Perhaps the Guardians—the name Lucia had adopted for the black mountains surrounding them, watching them—had the power to drain Watcher magic, just as Lucia had drained Melenia's.

"Lucia," Kyan said after a time. "I suddenly have a very good feeling that we've finally arrived exactly where we need to be."

They'd come upon a small valley of black rock and dirt, at the center of which lay what looked like a garden.

They rushed over to the garden, which had a circumference of perhaps thirty paces. Soft green grass, colorful daisies and roses, olive trees. In the center of the garden was a large moss-covered rock as tall and wide as two of the stone wheels they'd previously found stacked atop each other.

Lucia gasped, taking in this small patch of beauty. "Do you feel anything?" Lucia asked. "Any magic?"

"No," Kyan said, "but I do feel life here." He walked around the circumference of the rock, sliding his hand along the moss. "There has to be some sort of force at work to sustain this isolated oasis."

Lucia's melancholy had been chased away by this patch of life, flourishing in the midst of so much death. "Perhaps this is what made people believe that the Watchers lived in the mountains."

He nodded in agreement. "The Watchers managed to keep this secret very well. But why would they do that?"

She wracked her mind, but came up blank. "I have no idea."

In one blinding instant, a flood of fire poured down his arms. "Stand back, little sorceress."

Lucia started. "What are you going to do?"

"Watch and see." Kyan's eyes turned bright blue.

Before she could say another word, he turned to the moss-covered rock, flung the flames toward it, and wrapped his fire magic around it. The moss burned away in an instant; the grass surrounding the rock turned black. Deeply dismayed, Lucia watched the swift destruction of this beautiful place, but held her tongue.

Kyan's amber fire turned to blue, and then to a bright, blinding white.

Lucia had never seen this white fire before, but she quickly learned that it was scorching enough to transform solid rock into bubbling lava in seconds. The rock melted like an ice sculpture on a summer's day.

Kyan snuffed his fire out. The lava glowed like an orange moat protecting a strange object now revealed beneath the rock.

Lucia craned her neck to look, expecting to see another stone wheel. Instead, she saw a jagged crystal monolith—light violet at the top fading into a darker shade of purple at the bottom.

The monolith lit up their surroundings with its otherworldly glow, like a magical bonfire. Lucia felt the warmth of that magic, the pure and pulsing life, emanating from the crystal.

She looked down, stunned, to see that her amethyst ring had begun to glow with the exact same violet light.

"This is an original gateway," Kyan whispered, pressing his hand against the crystal's surface. "One so rare it might lead to places even more secret, more sacred, than the Sanctuary. They've hidden it because of its power. What a dangerous, dangerous secret we've uncovered." He grinned at Lucia. "And now it's even more dangerous because we're the ones who've found it. Tell me what you can do now, little sorceress."

Lucia cautiously touched the crystal, and gasped.

It was the same sensation she'd felt when she'd stolen Melenia's magic. A warmth, a glow, a hunger for more.

She knew instinctively that she could drain enough magic from this crystal monolith to draw Timotheus out of his safe Sanctuary in seconds.

And she could kill him just as quickly.

"I can access its magic," she said. "I can draw out Timotheus. This is exactly what we've been looking for."

Kyan lips stretched into a smile, and he laughed. "Oh, this is wonderful. You *are* a goddess, my little sorceress. And you will stand by my side, as I burn all of the weakness away from this world."

"Just like a forest fire," she said, remembering a lesson from her past. Despite the devastation they caused, forest fires made new life possible by forcing old life to run its course.

"Yes, just like a forest fire. Once the Sanctuary is gone, we will rebuild this world, reconstruct it just as it was in the beginning."

"What beginning?" she asked.

He clasped her chin. "The *very* beginning. It will take patience, but we'll get it right this time. We will create a perfect world."

She willed the smile to stay on her face, but suddenly she felt unsteady. "I thought all you wanted was for Timotheus to die so he couldn't imprison you again."

"That is just the first step in my grand, revolutionary plan."

She drew in a shaky breath. "So what you're saying is, you believe this world—my world—to be one big forest that needs to be burned away so new life can grow in its place?"

"Exactly. It's for the best." Kyan's smile faded a bit, and he watched her more carefully now. "There's nothing to worry about, little sorceress. With magic as strong and pure as this"—he gazed up at the monolith—"you can become immortal, just like those who think they control me."

"But don't you need your siblings to be present for this?"

"They'd be better off remaining where they are for now. It's best that I be the one in control in these beginning days. But very soon we'll be reunited." His kind, broad grin returned. "Summon Timotheus here now, little sorceress. I've waited an eternity for this moment."

Timotheus knew this already—Kyan's grand plan for the world. He had to. But he hadn't said a word to her about this in her dreams. Not that she would have believed him if he had. Which was exactly why he'd left her to discover this all on her own.

On the cliffs the night Alexius died, after she'd killed Melenia, Lucia had been left feeling so hurt, so betrayed, that she'd wanted nothing more than to hurt everyone else in return. She'd nothing left to live for, so she hadn't cared if everyone else died right along with her.

Lucia had wanted to watch the world burn.

And now, because of Kyan, it would.

"No," she said softly.

"Sorry? What did you say?"

"I said no."

"No? No to what? Do you feel ill? Do you need to rest before we begin?"

She looked up into his amber eyes. "I won't help you do this, Kyan."

Kyan frowned, his brow furrowing and his eyes glowing hot. "But you promised."

"Yes, I promised to help you reclaim your freedom, reunite you with your family, to go so far as to kill someone I considered an enemy to get you what you desired most. But this . . . destroying everything and everyone." She shook her head, gesturing to the mountains and barren forest around her. "I'll be no part of this."

"The world is tragically flawed, little sorceress. Even in our short time together we've seen countless examples of this—men and women obsessed with their own little lives, their greed, their lust, their vanity, every weakness compounding on the next."

"Mortals *are* weak—that's what makes them mortals. But they're also strong, resilient during crises that test their faith or threaten the people and things they love. There's no such thing as perfection, Kyan."

"There will be once I carry out my plan. I will create perfection in this world."

"You aren't meant to create it. You aren't meant to destroy it. You're only meant to sustain it."

His expression had turned from plaintive to downright unpleasant. "You would dare judge me—you, a mortal child who's barely even tasted life?"

It was rare for her to feel this certain about anything. Even rarer that she'd take a stand when another opposed her.

She had changed.

"It's over, Kyan. I've made my decision. And now, I'm leaving. Of course you don't have to come with me; you can stay here as long as you like."

With a small nod, she turned from him and began to walk away.

But only a short moment later, she felt the rising heat behind her.

"If you think I'll let you walk away from this so easily," he said, "you're stupider than I thought. You still don't realize exactly what I am, do you?"

Slowly, she turned to look at him.

Fire rolled over his skin, burning away his clothing, until he blazed from head to toe. His eyes burned blue within the sea of amber flames.

"Yes, I know what you are," she said, her throat tight. "You are the god of fire."

"Yes. But you have no concept of what that truly means. Allow me to educate you."

With narrowed eyes locked directly on her, he began to grow in size. Twice, three times . . . four times as tall and wide as his usual stature.

He towered above her, a monster created from fire.

A monster who *was* fire itself.

The fire Kindred in his truest form.

As she trembled at the sight of him, Lucia fought to stand her ground, to not cower before this creature she had dared defy.

She had come so very close to helping him destroy the world. And now she needed to get as far away from him as possible so she could have the chance to save it.

He lowered his blazing face to hers, coming close enough to singe her hair. "I am eternal. I am fire. And you will do as I say, or you will burn."

"Is this who you really are?" she asked, breathless. "Have you been lying to me all this time? Using me like all the others have? I thought we were family."

He roared, and more flames rose up all around Lucia. Her cloak caught fire, so she shrugged it off, quickly stepping away from it.

"You won't kill me!" she yelled at him. "If you kill me, your dream of destruction and re-creation is over."

"I can do plenty of damage without you."

"Not nearly as much as you need to."

"Do you really think you're so special? That you're the only one blessed with these gifts? I will wait until a new sorceress is born, and *she* will help me. As you like to remind me, I have time to wait. You, though, are fragile—even more fragile than Eva was."

With that, a gigantic blast of his fire hit her full on. She squeezed her eyes shut and raised her arms, as if that pathetic effort might shield her from his elemental rage. She screamed, expecting the whole of her body to be consumed by burning pain as her flesh melted from her bones.

But she felt nothing.

Tentatively, she opened her eyes.

A whirlwind of fire swirled violently around her, but didn't touch her. It had been stopped by a barrier of violet light, surrounding her like a cool, glowing halo.

She looked down at her ring, the amethyst now blazing like a tiny violet sun on her finger, its light bright enough to blind.

She saw the fire Kindred standing just beyond the blocked wall of flames. "What have you done?" he demanded.

The ring—this had been the key all along. It held far more secrets, more power, than she'd ever imagined. This is what had allowed Eva to safely handle the Kindred in their crystal forms, while all other Watchers, like Valoria and Cleiona, were corrupted by them. For Lucia, the ring brought balance to the eternal conflict brought by being a sorceress trapped within a mortal shell.

And today this ring had protected her—and the life growing inside her—from the wrath of an immortal god.

The firestorm grew smaller as the glow around her grew brighter, expanding outward until it touched Kyan.

The ethereal halo transformed into strands of glowing purple that moved over him like chains, restraining his fire, restraining his rage. They wrapped themselves around him until Lucia couldn't see any flames beneath them.

Kyan started to shrink, smaller and smaller, until he returned to his usual height. But then the light only grew brighter.

Brighter still, until Kyan screamed and the light exploded into a million violet shards.

And then the world around Lucia turned to cool, endless darkness.

She woke to the scent of warm, green grass and apple blossoms. Slowly, she opened her eyes to find that she lay in the middle of a meadow—the very same meadow where both Alexius and Timotheus had met her in her dreams.

"Am I dreaming?" she whispered.

No one answered her, no beautiful golden boy appeared before her. No hawk took perch in the apple tree. In her previous dreams, everything here had appeared jewel-like, the grass like strands of emeralds, the apples as red as rubies.

But now the meadow appeared to consist of only soft green grass, and though the trees were tall and beautiful, they were no different from what she might find in Auranos.

Beyond the meadow was a huge stone wheel she remembered from her dreams. And in the distance, across green hills and valleys, lay a crystal city that sparkled like diamonds under the sun.

She was in the Sanctuary. The *actual* Sanctuary.

How was this possible? Alexius had told her that mortals couldn't come here. Had he lied? Or had something happened to Lucia that made her an exception to that rule?

Lucia turned in a circle, as if the answer might magically appear to her.

And then she knew.

Her unborn child. A baby who was half mortal, half Watcher. And she, a sorceress with the power to vanquish the god of fire. These two extraordinary developments combined had given her the ability to be here.

She didn't know where Kyan had gone or if he'd return. But if he did, she knew he had to be imprisoned again. And his siblings—they could never be released from their crystal orbs. Kyan had been the most dangerous creature she'd ever seen. She could only imagine how much worse things would get once he reunited with his family.

Had Timotheus foreseen this? She would ask him as soon as she found him.

She had to make right what she'd helped go horribly wrong.

Lucia took a deep breath, summoned every last remaining scrap of her courage, and began to walk toward the crystal city.

CHAPTER 33

CLEO

LIMEROS

This time, when Cleo woke, she knew exactly where she was. And with whom.

For her first waking moment, all she could do was stare at him as he continued to sleep beside her.

The events of the night had unfolded very unexpectedly. He'd come after her, he'd risked his life to try to find her.

And he'd told her he loved her.

Magnus Damora loved her.

She couldn't help but smile then—a scared, nervous, but hopeful smile.

He looked so different when he slept. Younger. Peaceful. Beautiful. She tried to memorize every line and every angle of her dark prince's face.

He slowly opened his eyes, and in an instant his gaze was locked with hers. He furrowed his brow.

"Princess . . ."

"You know," she began, "I really think you should start calling me Cleo now, exclusively. Proper royal titles are so . . . *yesterday.*"

The serious look remained in his eyes, but his lips curved up to a cautious smile. "You think so, do you? Hmm. I'm not sure I like it. *Cleo.* So short, so . . . cheerful. And it's what Nic calls you."

"It is my name."

"No, your name is Cleiona. A goddess's name shouldn't ever be shortened."

"I'm not a goddess."

His smile grew, and he stroked the hair back from her face. "It is encouraging that you haven't run away from here yet, away from me."

"I haven't, have I?" She brushed her lips against his, dizzy from the knowledge—both sweet and scary—of how she felt about him. She hadn't even realized the truth of these feelings until she'd spoken them aloud last night. But this was real—realer than any emotion she'd ever felt.

"Wait," she gasped and sat up, pulling the blanket around her. "Magnus . . . it's light out."

He sought her mouth again, his fingers tangling in her hair. "Light, yes . . . much, much better than darkness. I adore light—it allows me to see you completely."

"No, Magnus . . ." She pointed at the window. "It's dawn. It's *tomorrow.*"

His expression tightened and tensed, then he swore under his breath. "How long were we asleep?"

"From the looks of it, far too long. Lord Gareth's castle is only a few miles from here, and if they've sent more guards out to search for me . . ." She turned a bleak look on him. "We need to get out of here."

"You're absolutely right. We'll have to put this very important discussion about what I shall call you now on hold."

"Yes, right after we discuss what to do about Amara and your father."

"One thing at a time." As soon as Cleo mentioned his father, his expression again grew strained. "We'll go to Ravencrest, find a ship bound for Auranos. Put distance between us and the king. Lord Gareth couldn't possibly agree with my father's latest decision."

"Knowing his sniveling, devious son, that's debatable."

"Excellent point."

"But I do know people in Auranos," Cleo said. "Nobles and diplomats still loyal to my father and to me. They could help us."

"Me, begging for help from Auranian nobles?" He raised a brow. "Shall we argue about this later?"

She couldn't help but smile. "Fine, later."

When they were dressed, Magnus touched her arm. "I want you to have something."

She turned to him and saw that he held the earth Kindred out to her. Her gaze snapped to his. "I was afraid to ask if you still had it."

"This belongs to you." He put it in her hand and closed her fingers over it. "I have no claim on it." He nodded firmly before she could say anything in reply. "Let's go."

She slipped the orb into the pocket of her cloak as he pushed open the door. . . .

To reveal King Gaius, standing, waiting, on the stone step.

Cleo's heart stopped in her chest.

"Good morning," the king said. "What a lovely abandoned cottage. I learned about this place, so close to Lord Gareth's residence, so I decided to bring some guards with me here to investigate. It struck me as a perfect place to take refuge during a cold, stormy night."

Standing behind the king were four guards in Limerian uniforms.

"It's been some time, Magnus," King Gaius said. "Have you missed me? More importantly, are you ready to answer for the crimes you've committed?"

"That depends. Are you?"

"I have nothing to answer for."

"The armed Kraeshians now flooding Limeros suggest otherwise."

The king sighed. "Why must you make everything a battle between us?"

"Because everything *is* a battle between us."

"I have given you endless chances to prove your worth to me, to show that you're strong and smart and capable of being my heir. And every single time you've disappointed me. Your escape to this little cottage retreat is just the most recent disappointment." An expression of pure harshness settled deep within the lines of the king's face. "Guards."

Three guards set upon Magnus, one on Cleo. Neither of them resisted as they were accompanied out of the cottage.

Cleo's escort was Enzo, the kind guard who had become involved with Nerissa.

"I'm truly sorry for this, princess," he said under his breath. "But I have my orders."

"I understand." She didn't expect any help from him, and she wouldn't debase herself enough to ask. Limerian guards were well-trained to do as the king commanded.

The snow-covered corpse of the Kraeshian guard whom Cleo had killed remained, could still be partially seen as they moved away from the cottage. Cleo eyed it as they passed by, trying to think, to find a way out of this. She had the earth Kindred, but it was useless to her if she couldn't access its magic.

"Where are you taking us?" she asked. "Back to the castle?"

"Are you speaking to me, princess?" the king asked.

"No, I'm speaking to the birds in the trees."

He sent her a smirk over his shoulder. "Just as charming as ever, I see. I have no idea how a girl as venomous as you succeeded in manipulating my son."

"You don't understand," Magnus gritted out. "You've never understood."

"What don't I understand? Love?" The king laughed. "Is that what you think this is? A love worth committing treason for? Worth giving up your throne? Worth dying for, perhaps?"

Magnus's lips stretched to a grimace. "So what's your plan?" he said, unwilling to dignify his father's remarks with a response. "To kill us both?"

"If it comes to that, I suppose I will have to. But I have something else in mind."

Magnus hadn't looked at Cleo, not once, since they'd left the cottage. She tried not to let that unnerve her. Now, more than ever before, she needed her courage. She needed her strength.

The king led them out of the forest, but instead of Lord Gareth's castle, they'd come to the sharp edge of an icy cliff that dropped fifty feet down to a frozen lake.

"When I was a boy," the king said, "my mother would bring me here every summer. There was a waterfall just over there." The king gestured to their left. "It's frozen now, just like everything else." He glanced at Magnus. "I haven't told you much about your grandmother, have I?"

"No, Father, but how exciting for me to learn more about my family history."

"It should be. Your grandmother was a witch."

Magnus blinked. "You're lying. It's impossible that I wouldn't have heard about that before."

"Yes, well, you know how gossip can be. Rumors spread like wildfire. Which is exactly why she kept her identity a secret. She didn't even tell your grandfather. She only told me."

"Quite the coincidence, then. My grandmother was a witch, and so was my real mother."

"Ah, yes. That. I admit, I was surprised when you chose to believe that Sabina Mallius was your true mother." Magnus shot his father a sharp look, and the king laughed. "You really can't blame me. You did have a blade to my throat and were threatening to kill me. I needed a distraction."

"So it was a lie. Only a lie."

"Of course it was. Althea was your mother, no one else."

Cleo saw a breath hitch in Magnus's chest, and his hands turned to fists at his sides. "Well done, Father. How foolish of me to have ever forgotten how ruthless you are."

"Yes, I suppose I am ruthless. If I weren't, I never would have survived this long." The king turned to Cleo, cocking his head. "You have caused me extraordinary misery in your short life-time—more than you will ever realize."

"Me?" she said, sternly incredulous, refusing to show this monster a glimmer of fear. "It has never been my intention to cause misery or difficulties. I only want to live the life I was meant for."

"Amara is very angry with you, you know. She's asked me to bring you back so she can deal with you herself, but I don't think I will. Grant that girl too many wishes and she might start to think she has some power over me. No woman will ever have power over me. Not ever again."

King Gaius stood before her now, glaring into her soul with eyes like two black bottomless pits of hatred.

Finally, he tore his gaze away from her and looked back at Magnus. "Amara believes I should have you executed for treason."

"And what do you believe?"

"I believe in family. And I believe in second chances for family—if they are earned."

"And, pray tell, how could I ever earn this second chance from you, Father?"

The king nodded, and a guard shoved Cleo to the ground, sending her to her knees, hard.

"You will earn it with a blood sacrifice. To the goddess Valoria, and to me. This girl is a threat—to both of us. She will lead you to your demise if you let her. I also had a choice once. To give my life for someone else or to sacrifice her and live in prosperity. When I made the wrong choice, your grandmother stepped in, vanquished my love, and saved my life. Should you make the wrong choice today, I will do you the same favor. But you will still not have earned your redemption. After all, falling in love is not the only crime you've committed for which you've yet to pay."

Cleo sought Magnus's gaze, but he remained focused on his father.

"You want me to kill her," he said.

"Quick, painless. A sword through the heart. Or perhaps a simple push off this cliff. But choose one, or I will choose for you."

Magnus stared at his father, his steely expression unreadable.

"I refuse to accept that this is the only way for me to redeem myself."

"But it is, son. I know this is difficult—the most difficult thing I've ever asked of you. But that's why it has so much value. Do this, and I will forgive you your past transgressions. You can rule the world at my side."

"I thought you meant to rule the world with Amara."

"That's what she thinks, too. And I'll let her keep thinking that for now. Do what's right, Magnus. Don't risk your life, your future, for one stupid girl. It's not worth it."

"I would have risked my life, my future, for Lucia."

After all that had happened, Cleo thought, all that his adopted sister had put him through, did Magnus still love her?

"Lucia is different," the king said. "She was worthy of your sacrifice. She was powerful. This Bellos girl"—he sent a venomous look at Cleo—"is only a pretty package containing nothing of value, a glimmering weight that will drag you down to the bottom of the sea."

"You're right. I know you're right, yet I still struggle. I know she's become the ruin of me."

Cleo couldn't find her next breath.

"A few unpleasant but necessary moments will fix all of that," the king said. "Whatever you think you might feel for her is only an illusion—*all* romantic love is only an illusion. And illusions fade. Power doesn't fade; power is eternal."

Magnus nodded solemnly, his brow furrowed. "I thought I'd destroyed my chance to rule. I'd tried to think of other ways to reclaim any power at all, but . . . you're right. There is no other way. I've risked everything, lost all of my potential because of my stupid decisions." He raised his gaze to meet the king's. "Yet you would still give me the chance to redeem myself for this."

The king nodded solemnly. "I would."

"Your capacity for forgiveness is both surprising and humbling." His jaw tensed, then he, too, nodded. "If this is what I must do to reclaim my power, my life, my future. Then so be it."

Cleo watched them both, stunned. This wasn't happening. It *couldn't* happen.

The king nodded at a guard, who handed Magnus his sword. The prince studied it in his hand, as if assessing its weight.

"Look out at the lake, princess," Magnus instructed her. "I promise this will be swift."

All she could see was the sword in Magnus's grip, light glinting off its sharp blade. A sword that, with one quick thrust, would end her.

"You . . . you honestly mean to d-do this?" she stammered. "To me? After—after everything we've survived together?"

"There's no other choice."

She grappled to maintain her composure, her grace, before dying, but it slipped through her fingers like sand. "And how will you do it?" she asked, breathless, heart fluttering like a flock of starlings. "Thrust a sword through my back when I'm not looking, like you did to Theon?"

"I was a boy then, I didn't know myself when I killed that guard. But I know myself now. You, too, know me now, Cleiona. Which means you can't be surprised by the choice I've made."

Tears stung her eyes and she faced the cliff's edge. "Everything is a surprise to me when it comes to you, Magnus."

She thought of her father, the good and noble king. She thought of Emilia, of Theon and Mira. Everyone she'd lost. Everyone she'd been fighting for.

"Then do it," she gritted out, glancing over her shoulder at him. "Do it now."

Magnus nodded, his expression grim. "Very well, my princess."

He turned and swung the sword. Cleo braced herself, and felt the gust of wind brought by the speed of Magnus's blade. But that was all she felt. Then, hearing a deep, primal roar, she turned with surprise to see Magnus striking at his father with a furious blow.

The king brought up his weapon just in time, and their swords clashed. Clearly, his father had been ready for him to strike.

"Oh, Magnus, don't look so surprised," the king said, their swords locked together, their faces uncomfortably close. "I know you, can predict your every move, because a long time ago I *was* you. But still I'd hoped, perhaps, that you would see reason much sooner than I did."

The guards took a step closer and the king flicked a look at them, halting them in place. "Stay where you are. It's time that my son and I had this out between the two of us. He likely thinks he has a chance to win."

"I'm younger," Magnus growled. "I'm stronger."

"Younger, yes. Perhaps stronger. But experience is the key to swordsmanship. And I am overflowing with experience in protecting myself, my son."

The king shoved him backward, then swung his sword. Magnus stopped it with his own, steel clashing.

"Experience, you say? It seems to me that your preferred method of protecting yourself these days is to hide away in your palace. Or perhaps go groveling overseas to more powerful men—or *women*—and offer up your kingdom like a shiny apple."

"Mytica is mine to do with as I wish."

"You could have fooled me. It seems to be Amara's now."

"Amara is my wife. Just another thing I own. When she's gone, I will be the Emperor of everything."

"No, Father. By the time she's gone, you'll already be dead."

Their blades crossed again, and there was such force from both sides that it seemed to Cleo that the two were equally matched.

"Is this really for her?" the king said with disdain. "You would oppose me like this, here and now, and throw away everything that could have been yours for the love of one girl?"

"No," Magnus replied, his teeth gritted together with the effort it took to fight his father. "I oppose you like this because you're a monster who needs to die. And when that monster is dead, I will fix the idiotic mistake you made by underestimating Amara, and reclaim Mytica as my own." He jabbed his blade, slicing his father's shoulder. "What happened to your experience? It seems to me that I've drawn first blood."

"And I will draw last." The king dodged the next strike with ease, clearly surprising Magnus. "Never show how strong you are from the very beginning. Save it for the end."

Gaius jabbed and flicked his wrist, and Magnus's sword flew out of his hand. Magnus stared at it, stunned, as it landed six paces away.

The king put the tip of his sword to the prince's throat.

"On the ground."

Magnus sent Cleo a pained look and sank to his knees before the king.

"I didn't want to have to do this," the king said, shaking his head. "But you've given me no choice. Perhaps you're not like me after all. You're too soft to do what needs to be done."

"You're wrong," Magnus gritted out.

"I saw potential when no one else could. And yet, here we are. Serves me right, I suppose."

Cleo was shaking her head, lost for words and feeling more hopeless than ever. "Please don't do this . . . don't kill him."

"It must be done. I can never trust him. I could lock him in the tower for months, years, but not a day would pass without the knowledge that he would be plotting to kill me again. However, my son, I will do you the honor of making this quick."

His arm tense, his expression without pity, the king raised his sword.

"King Gaius!" Cleo shouted. "Look over here!"

He froze, the sword stilled, but he didn't drop it. The king sent a glance over his shoulder at Cleo, who stood at the edge of the cliff, holding the earth Kindred out at a dangerous angle.

The king blinked. The guards reached for their weapons, but Gaius motioned for them to stay where they were.

"Do you know what this is?" she asked evenly.

"I do," he said past a tense, tight jaw.

"And do you know what happens if I drop it fifty feet onto a hard sheet of ice? It will shatter into a thousand pieces."

She was bluffing of course—she'd seen what had happened when Magnus had hurled the orb against the throne room wall. But she prayed he would believe her.

"I know you want this," she said. "I know you're obsessed with the Kindred, but that you haven't found a single one yet."

Finally, the king lowered his sword. "That's where you're wrong, princess. I have the moonstone orb."

Cleo tried to keep the shock from showing on her face.

"You're lying," she said.

"Wouldn't that be convenient for you? Unfortunately, I'm not." He nodded toward the closest guard, then to Magnus. "Watch him."

"Yes, your majesty."

Magnus stared at Cleo. "Drop it," he said. "Don't let him take it from you."

"Wonderful suggestion," she said. She shook her arm as the king drew closer to make him stop. "So. You have air and I have earth. But neither one is worth anything, as I'm sure you've discovered, with their magic locked away inside."

"Oh, my dear girl, how disappointing it must have been for you to have such a treasure in your possession and yet no clue how to access its power."

"And you do?"

He nodded. "My mother told me how. It was she who first told me stories about the Kindred. Somehow she knew I would be the one to claim them one day—all of them. And I would become a god more powerful than Valoria and Cleiona combined."

"How?" Magnus said, and his father gave him a withering look, which he ignored. "You may as well tell us. Even if she drops the orb, you'll still kill us both. Your secret will die with us."

Gaius cocked his heads and gestured at the guards.

"As if such information would benefit them," Magnus scoffed. "Come on, Father, humor us in our final moments. Share my grand-mother's secret. How do you release the magic of the Kindred? And if you do know how, why haven't you done it yet? Why not unleash the air magic and simply take the Kraeshian Empire for yourself without going through the hassle of negotiations and agreements?"

The king went silent then, shifting his gaze between Cleo and Magnus. Finally, a smile returned to his face.

"It's quite simple, really. The secret to the Kindred's magic is the secret to all powerful elemental magic."

Cleo's arm had begun to ache from holding out the orb for so long. "Blood," she said. "Blood enhances, strengthens *elementia*."

"Not just any blood," the king said.

Magnus's face went ashen. "Why wouldn't it have occurred to me until now? It's Lucia's blood—the blood of the prophesized sorceress."

The king only gave him a smug smile.

"How unfortunate it is, Father, that Lucia is off wandering the earth with her fiery new friend, nowhere to be found."

"I will find Lucia, I've no doubt about that. But there is another important component required to unleash the Kindred. Perhaps Eva's blood would have been enough on its own—she was created from pure elemental magic. But Lucia is mortal. Her blood must be mixed with an immortal's blood for it to properly work."

"According to Grandmother."

"Yes, according to her. Now," he said, turning to Cleo, "give me the Kindred."

"You'll kill us both if I do. You'll kill us both if I don't. It seems we've found ourselves with a big problem here, haven't we?"

"Do you think you can negotiate with me, princess? Are you that naive, even after all this time? No. Let me tell you what will happen. You will give me the earth Kindred, and then I will grant you the mercy of a swift death. If you give me a problem, if you flinch, if you sneeze, if you delay the inevitable, I will kill you slowly, so very slowly, and I will make Magnus watch you die before I do the same to him."

Cleo shared a last look with Magnus. "You've given me no choice, then."

She dropped the obsidian orb off the edge of the cliff.

The king stormed toward her, shoving her out of the way, and looked down toward the frozen lake far below, before he turned on her with a look of rage. "You stupid little bitch!"

As soon as the Kindred hit the hard surface below, an earthquake began to shake the ground, just as it had in the throne room when Magnus had thrown it at the wall.

A crack formed in the ice where the orb had first hit and, as fast as lightning, it snaked up the side of the cliff. A deafening sound of cracking, breaking, and splintering roared up and out across the land, and the edge of ice that Cleo and the king stood on broke away.

Cleo scrambled to catch hold of the rough edge of an icy rock as the very ground she stood on fell away beneath her feet. The king, too, scrambled for a handhold, but he failed.

With a roar, he fell backward into the abyss.

Just as Cleo's hand slipped, Magnus grabbed her wrist and hauled her up and over the side, crushing her against his chest as he pushed them backward and away from the damage.

"Are you hurt?" he demanded.

All she could do was shake her head.

The guards drew closer, but Magnus was on his feet, tugging Cleo up with him. He'd grabbed his father's fallen sword and now brandished it at them. "Stay back. I swear, I will kill each of you if you come any closer."

Enzo's brow was deeply furrowed, his expression confused and grim.

"We need to go after the king," Enzo said. "It's possible he survived the fall."

"I agree." Magnus nodded. "Just keep your distance from us."

"As you wish, your highness."

It took some time and care, but Cleo and Magnus made it down to the bottom of the cliff and the surface of the frozen lake where the king lay, his head resting in a shallow pool of blood that had already started to freeze.

Cleo picked up the black orb, which was clearly visible as it nestled within its stark white surroundings. Even though it had come to rest on a bed of ice and snow, it was hot to the touch, and the wisp of shadowy magic inside spun around and around furiously.

She slipped it into her pocket and looked down at the face of the King of Blood.

Magnus just stood there over his father, his arms crossed tightly over his chest.

"He damn well better be dead," he said. Despite the fierceness of his words, Cleo could hear a catch, a hoarseness to them.

"I'll check," she said, and sank down to her knees next to the king. She pressed her fingers to the side of his throat.

His hand shot up and grabbed her wrist, his eyes flying open.

She shrieked and tried to pull away, but his hold was too strong. Magnus had his sword to the king's throat in an instant.

"Release her," he snarled.

But the king paid him no attention. He only looked at Cleo, his brow drawn, pain in his dark brown eyes.

"I'm sorry," he whispered. "I'm so sorry, Elena. I never wanted to hurt you. Forgive me, please forgive me for all of this."

His eyes rolled back into his head and his hand dropped away.

Cleo was trembling now and she scooted back, away from the king's body.

Magnus now checked the king's pulse, and then swore under his breath. "He's still alive. I swear, he must have made a pact with a demon from the darklands to survive a fall like that." When Cleo didn't reply, he looked up at her. "What was that he said to you? Did he call you Elena? Who's Elena?"

She was certain she must have heard him wrong, but when Magnus repeated the name now, she knew she hadn't.

"Elena," she said, her throat raw. "Elena was my mother's name."

Magnus frowned. "Your mother?"

Enzo drew closer, but his weapon was not drawn. "Your high-ness, what do you want us to do?"

Magnus hesitated, uncertain. "You don't mean to arrest us?"

"You're the crown prince. Your father is badly injured, possibly near death. It's your command we must obey now."

"What about Amara's command?"

"We don't follow Kraeshian orders, even with an armada at the empress's command. We are Limerian. Mytican. And we will follow only you—all Limerian guards will follow only you."

Magnus nodded and rose to his feet. He met Cleo's gaze.

"Then it seems we have a war to plan," he said.

CHAPTER 34

JONAS

KRAESHIA

Jonas hadn't had his chance to assassinate the king, but saving his friend from certain death had made his trip to Kraeshia worthwhile.

His extremely *short* trip.

While part of him wanted to stay and help Mikah and his rebels with their revolution, he knew he had to get back to Mytica. The moment Olivia returned from delivering his message to the prince, they were ready to board the Limerian ship and set sail.

He clasped Mikah's hand. "Good luck to you."

"Thank you. I'm going to need it. You too."

Jonas turned to Nic and Olivia. "Is he here yet?"

"Not yet," Nic replied.

"We're not leaving without him."

"Agreed." Nic blinked and crossed his arms over his chest. "Exactly how long do you think we should wait?"

Jonas scanned the docks, looking for a sign of Felix, but he hadn't seen him since last night. Since right after he'd finally told him the truth about Lysandra. He'd wanted to wait until after they'd made safe passage back to Mytica, but Felix was relentless in his inquiries after her. So Jonas gave in, and relayed the tragic story of Lysandra's murder. Felix had disappeared shortly afterward, mumbling something about needing a drink, something to help him process this news until he passed out.

Jonas would have joined him, but he could tell Felix needed to be alone. Not only to find solace in his grief for Lysandra, but to recover from all the torture and trauma inflicted upon him in the Jewel.

The moment he'd opened the door to Felix's cell and saw him there, on the floor . . . broken, beaten, covered in blood, smelling like death itself. . . . It was all he could do to stay upright and standing, and help get his friend out of that dungeon.

Finally, Felix appeared on the docks, approaching with a slow, steady gait, and Jonas let out a deep sigh of relief.

"Ready?" Jonas asked him as he drew near.

There were dark circles under Felix's eyes, and his skin looked drawn and pale. "I'm so ready I'd be happy to swim all the way back just to get away from this rock." His brow drew together as Jonas clasped his shoulder. "I'm fine, don't bother worrying about me."

"I think I'll worry anyway, just to be safe."

"Promise me, Agallon, that when we get back, we're going to find this fire god, and we're going to tear him into small, smoldering pieces. Got me? He will pay for what he did to her."

Jonas nodded firmly. "Agreed. Now, let's get on our way."

"Wait!" Mikah called out to them just before they stepped aboard the ship. "Jonas, I told Taran to come here this morning to see you off—thought you'd want to meet my second in command before you leave."

"Ah, yes. Taran. The Auranian who broke my nose," Felix said, pointing at his face. "Luckily, Olivia took care of that too."

"I suppose we can wait a few more minutes," Jonas said. "I'd be honored to meet him."

A tall young man with bronze-colored hair walked down the dock and came to stand next to Mikah. "Jonas Agallon, this is Taran Ranus."

Jonas reached out to shake his hand. "Kick some Kraeshian arse for me, would you?"

"Gladly." Taran raised a brow as Nic tentatively approached them.

"Nicolo Cassian," Jonas said, now frowning at the way Nic seemed to be gawking at the rebel. "This is Taran—"

"Ranus," Nic finished. "Your family name is Ranus, isn't it?"

"How did you know that?"

"You have a brother named Theon."

Taran grinned. "Twin brother, actually."

"*Identical* twin."

"That's right. Theon was always the good one, the perfect son, following in our father's footsteps. I'm the . . . well, whatever I am. The troublemaker, I guess. When things quiet down here, I need to get back to Auranos for a visit. It's been so long since I've been in touch with my family. I take it you know Theon?"

Nic stared at Taran as if stunned, as if somehow frightened by the mention of Theon's name.

"Nic?" Jonas prompted when Nic continued to remain silent.

"I . . . I'm so sorry to be the one to deliver this news," Nic began. "But your father, your brother . . . they're both dead."

"What?" Taran stared at Nic in shock. "How?"

"You father, it was an accident. Terrible but unavoidable, and no one was at fault. But your brother . . ." Nic's eyes shifted back and forth with uncertainty before they narrowed in a solemn gaze. "He was murdered. By Prince Magnus Damora."

Taran took a step back, doubled over slightly at the waist. All was silent for several long, uncomfortable moments, save for the squawking of seabirds and the crashing of waves against the shore.

"Mikah . . ." Taran said, his face a shroud of stunned grief. "I have to go with them now. Today. I have to go to Mytica and avenge my brother's death. But I promise I'm not done with the revolution. I'll be back as soon as I can."

Mikah nodded. "Do what you have to do."

"So you're coming with us, are you?" Jonas asked. "Just like that?"

The friendly glint in Taran's eyes had transformed to a flash of fury. "Is that a problem for you?"

"Not if you don't make it one."

"I have no conflict with you, but I will find Prince Magnus. And when I do, he will pay for what he's done to my family. I know he sent you here. So does that mean you'll try to stop me?"

Jonas considered him for a long moment. He was currently allied with the prince, but that had nothing to do with this personal grievance. And as far as he could tell, Magnus deserved whatever Taran had in store for him. "No, I won't stop you."

"Good."

Taran left to fetch some belongings for the journey, and Jonas turned to Nic.

"I have a feeling that Taran's not the only troublemaker in our midst. You didn't have to tell him the truth about his brother. Trying to stir up old conflicts for the prince, are we?"

Nic shrugged lightly, but there was a hard edge to his expression now as he met Jonas's curious gaze. "All I did was tell the truth. Taran deserves to know what happened to Theon. And, what, you think Magnus shouldn't pay for his crimes?"

"That's not what I said, not at all. I just wonder about your motive."

"Pure, unadulterated hatred for Prince Magnus and his evil family. That's my motive. Cleo's gone completely blind when it comes to him. Whatever I have to do to protect her, I'll do it."

"Wonderful. We have a ship full of vengeance-seekers headed back with us."

"The more the merrier, I say."

Nic's gaze slid beyond Jonas and toward the docks behind him. In an instant, all the blood appeared to drain from his face, leaving him as white as snow.

"What's wrong now?" Jonas glanced over his shoulder to see someone—a stranger—approaching their ship. "Let me guess. Another ghost from your past?"

Nic stayed silent, his jaw gone slack.

Jonas turned and looked again at the man, still twenty paces away from them and drawing closer, a tall Kraeshian with shoulder-length black hair tied at the nape of his neck. "Who is it, then?" he asked.

"That," Nic said, his voice raw and barely audible, "is Prince Ashur Cortas."

ACKNOWLEDGMENTS

I want to start off by thanking my readers. You guys don't even know how amazing you are. Some of you do, I'm sure. But those who don't? You. Are. Amazing. And I thank each and every one of you for coming on this journey with me, spreading the FK word, and growing more enthusiastic with every single book that comes out.

Special shout-out to my online street team, the #RhodesRebels (special, special shout out to Lainey!), and the Kindred (which is what the small-but-mighty FK fandom is named), as well as everyone I've connected with on social media. I am so grateful for all of you!

Much love and gratitude to my family and friends . . . and pets . . . Mom and Dad, Cindy and Mike, Bonnie, Eve, Tara, Elly, Nicki, Maureen, Julie, Laura, Liza, Megan, Sammy and Spike. Also sending love to Seth, Rachel, Maggie, and Jessica: PToT 4ever!

A million thank-yous to my publishing family at Penguin, including the wonderful Ben Schrank, Casey McIntyre, and Vikki VanSickle.

To Liz Tingue, my fab editor—you make me look like a far better writer than I am, with a much larger and more robust vocabulary. I like that. FYI, Liz flags things in my first drafts like "whatever, losers!" and suggests more appropriate language for a high fantasy. And I usually agree to these changes. *Usually*.

To my kickass agent of more than a decade now, Jim McCarthy, just imagine a line of heart emojis **right here**. I so appreciate having you in my corner, and I look forward to many more years and many more books together!

The crystals have been discovered, but unleashing the magic of the Kindred could have disastrous consequences. The fate of Mytica has never been more uncertain.

Turn the page for an exclusive sneak peek of

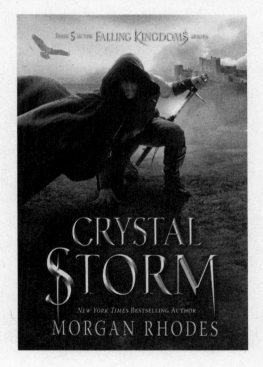

The thrilling fifth book in the Falling Kingdom series by *New York Times* bestselling author Morgan Rhodes.

CHAPTER 1

JONAS

KRAESHIA

Far across the sea in Mytica, there was a golden princess Jonas wanted to save.

And a god of fire he needed to destroy.

However, an obstacle now stood in Jonas's path on the Kraeshian docks, eating into time he didn't have to waste.

"I thought you said his sister killed him," Jonas said to Nic under his breath.

"She did." Nic's voice came out as barely more than a rasp as he raked both his hands through his messy, bright red hair. "I saw it with my own eyes."

"Then how is this possible?"

"I . . . I don't know."

Prince Ashur Cortas drew to a stop only a few paces away. He eyed both Jonas and Nic through narrowed, silvery-blue eyes that stood out against his dark tan complexion like the glinting edge of a blade at dusk.

The only sounds to be heard for a few long moments were the squawk of a nearby seabird as it plunged downward to catch a fish and the gentle, steady splash of the water against the waiting Limerian ship with its black and red sails.

"Nicolo," the raven-haired prince said with a nod. "I know you must be very confused to see me again."

"I . . . I . . . what . . . ?" was Nic's only reply. The scattering of freckles over his nose and cheeks contrasted boldly with his blanched complexion. He drew in a shaky breath. "This is impossible."

Ashur raised a dark brow at the boy, hesitating only briefly before he spoke. "In my twenty-one years of life I've come to realize that very little in this world is impossible."

"I watched you *die*." The last word sounded as if it had been dragged painfully from Nic's throat. "What was that? Just another lie? Another scheme? Another plan that you didn't feel the need to tell me about?"

Jonas was surprised that Nic dared to speak to a member of royalty with such insolence. Not that Jonas himself had much respect for royals, but Nic had spent enough time in the Auranian palace, side by side with its princess, to know it wasn't wise to be this openly rude.

"It was no lie. What happened at the temple was not a scheme." Ashur swept his gaze over the Limerian ship, which was ready for imminent departure from the Jewel of the Empire's crowded, busy docks. "I'll explain more once we're at sea."

Jonas's brows went up at the prince's commanding and confident tone. "Once *we're* at sea," he repeated.

"Yes. I'm coming with you."

"If that's what you're looking to do," Jonas said, crossing his arms. "Then you'll explain more *now*."

Ashur eyed him. "Who are you?"

Jonas eyed him back. "I'm the one who decides who gets on this ship—and who doesn't."

"Do you know who I am?" Ashur asked.

"Well aware. You're the brother of Amara Cortas, who just recently seems to have made herself the bloodthirsty empress of most of the damn world. And according to Nic, you're supposed to be dead."

A familiar form appeared behind Ashur, catching Jonas's eye.

Taran Ranus had left the docks only a few moments ago so that he might quickly prepare for an unplanned journey to Mytica. But he was already back. As the rebel drew closer, he swiftly pulled out a sword from the sheath at his waist.

"Well, well," Taran said as he raised the tip of the sword to Ashur's throat. "Prince Ashur. What a pleasant surprise to see that you've strolled into our midst this morning, just as my friends are working to topple your family's reign."

"The general chaos around the Jewel did give that much away," Ashur said, his tone and demeanor surprisingly serene.

"Why have you come back? Why not stay abroad, chasing after meaningless treasure as everyone says you're fond of doing?"

Chasing after treasure? Jonas shared an anxious look with Nic. It seemed that very few were aware that the prince had been presumed dead.

"The circumstances of my return are none of your business."

"Are you in Kraeshia because of . . ." Nic began, then hesitated. "Of . . . what happened to your family? You must know, don't you?"

"Yes, I know." Ashur's expression darkened. "But that's not why I'm here."

Taran smirked. "As the true heir to the throne, perhaps you'll make an excellent tool for negotiations with your grandmother now that your sister's married the enemy and sailed away."

Ashur scoffed. "If that's what you think, then you know nothing about her desire for power—or my sister's. It's easy to see that your rebels are vastly outnumbered. This current uprising will be as effective as the chirp of a baby bird in the shadow of a hungry wildcat. What you really need to do is get on this ship and leave while you still have the chance."

Taran's smirk disappeared. His brown eyes flashed with outrage. "You don't get to tell me what to do."

Jonas felt uneasy about Ashur's attitude. He seemed to be taking the recent news of most of his family's massacre in stride. He couldn't tell if Ashur grieved their loss or celebrated it. Or did he feel nothing at all?

"Lower your weapon, Taran," Jonas growled, then hissed out a breath. "Why are you back so soon anyway? Didn't you have belongings to gather?"

Taran didn't budge. He kept the sharp tip of his sword pressed to Ashur's throat, his biceps flexing. "The roads are blocked. Granny Cortas has decided that all rebels are to be slain on sight. Since we blew up the city dungeon yesterday, there's nowhere to put any prisoners."

"All the more reason for us to go now," Nic urged.

"I agree with Nicolo," Ashur said.

The angry squawk of a bird caught Jonas's attention. He shielded his eyes from the sun and looked up at the golden hawk swooping above the ship.

Olivia was getting impatient. That made two of them.

He willed himself to remain calm. He couldn't afford to make any rash decisions.

Just then, an image of Lysandra slid into his mind, along with the sound of her laughter. *"No rash decisions? Since when?"* she would have said.

Since you died and I couldn't save you.

Pushing his grief away, Jonas forced himself to focus on the prince.

"If you want any chance to board this ship," he said, "then explain how you've managed to rise from the dead only to walk right up to a group of rebels like you've only been out for a tankard of ale."

"Rise from the dead?" Taran repeated, his furious expression giving way to confusion.

Ignoring Taran, Jonas searched for any sign of intimidation in the prince's demeanor. A signal that he feared for his life, that he was desperate to escape his homeland. But only serenity filled his pale eyes.

It was unsettling, really.

"Have you ever heard of the legend of the phoenix?" Ashur asked smoothly.

"Of course," Nic replied. "It's a mythical bird that rose from the ashes of the flames that originally killed it. It's the symbol for Kraeshia, to show the empire's strength and ability to defy death itself."

Ashur nodded. "Yes."

Jonas raised his eyebrows. "Really?" he said.

Nic shrugged. "I took a class with Cleo on foreign myths once. I paid more attention than she did." He flicked a wary look at Ashur. "What about this legend?"

"There is also a legend of a mortal fated to one day do the same— return from death to unite the world. Grandmother always believed that my sister would be this phoenix. When Amara was a baby, she died for a brief moment but came back to life thanks to a resurrection potion our mother gave her. When I recently learned of this, I had the same potion created for me. I'm not sure I truly believed it would work, but it did. And as I rose at dawn in the temple where

I'd died the night before at my sister's hand, I realized the truth." "What truth?" Jonas demanded after Ashur fell silent.

Ashur met his gaze. "That *I* am the phoenix. And it's my destiny to save this world from its current fate, beginning with stopping my sister from her dark need to blindly follow in my father's footsteps."

The prince fell silent again as his audience of three stared at him. Taran was the first to laugh.

"Royals always think so damn highly of themselves," he sneered. "Legends of heroes who defy certain death are as old as legends about the Watchers themselves." Taran glanced at Jonas. "I'm going to cut off his head. If he gets up after that, consider me a believer."

Jonas didn't think Taran was being serious, but he didn't want to take any chances.

"Lower your weapon," Jonas growled. "I'm not going to tell you again."

Taran cocked his head. "I don't take orders from you."

"Do you want passage on this ship? Then yes, you *do* take orders from me."

But still Taran didn't budge, and his gaze grew only more challenging.

"You giving Jonas a problem, Ranus?" Felix's voice boomed out, just before he came to stand at Jonas's side.

Felix Gaebras—with all his height and muscles—was someone Jonas was grateful was on his side. A former member of the Clan of the Cobra, a group of assassins who worked for King Gaius, Felix's ability to cast a deadly and intimidating shadow was no accident.

But Taran was just as deadly and just as intimidating.

"You want to know about my problems?" Taran finally lowered his blade to his side, then nodded at the resurrected royal. "This is Prince Ashur Cortas."

Felix peered skeptically at the prince with his good eye. After spending the last week imprisoned and being mercilessly tortured for poisoning the Kraeshian royal family—a crime Amara had blamed on him—it was his *only* eye; the other was covered by a black eye patch. "Aren't you supposed to be dead?"

"He is." Nic had stayed very quiet, never taking his attention off of the prince, wearing an expression that was equal parts stunned and confused.

"I'm not." Ashur spoke patiently to Nic.

"It could be a trick." Nic's brow furrowed in concentration as he studied the prince carefully. "Perhaps you're a witch who possesses enough air magic to change your appearance."

Ashur raised a dark eyebrow, as if amused. "Hardly."

"Witches are female," Taran reasoned.

"Not always," Ashur replied. "There have been a few notable exceptions over the centuries."

"Are you trying to help your case or not?" Jonas asked sharply.

"He's Amara's brother," Felix growled. "Let's just go ahead and kill him and be done with it."

"Yes," Taran seconded. "On that, we agree."

Ashur sighed, and for the first time, there was an edge of impatience in the sound. Despite any threats, he kept his attention firmly on Nic. "I understand your hesitation in believing me, Nicolo. It reminds me of your hesitation that night in the City of Gold, when you left the tavern . . . the Beast, I believe it was called. You were drunk, lost, and you looked at me in that alleyway as if I might kill you with the two blades I carried. But I didn't, did I? Do you remember what I did instead?"

Nic's pale face flushed in an instant, and he cleared his throat. "It's him," he said quickly. "I don't know how, but . . . it's him. Let's go."

Jonas studied Nic's face, unsure whether to believe such a

promise, even from someone he'd very recently begun to trust. His gut told him Nic wasn't lying.

And if Ashur wanted to bring a halt to his sister's evil machinations, believing himself to be this legendary phoenix who'd risen from death, true or not, then he could possibly be an asset to their group.

He wondered what Lys would have to say about *this* situation.

No, he already knew. She very likely would have put an arrow through the prince the moment he'd appeared.

The glint of Taran's sword again caught his attention. "If you don't lower that weapon, I'm going to have Felix chop off your arm."

Taran laughed, an unpleasant crack of a sound that cut through the cool morning air. "I'd like to see him try."

"Would you?" Felix asked. "My eyesight's not as good as it was, but I think—actually, I *know*—I could do it real fast. It might not even hurt." He chuckled darkly as he drew his sword. "No, what am I thinking? It's going to hurt very badly. I'm no ally to any Cortas, but if Jonas wants the prince to keep breathing, he's going to keep breathing. Got it?"

The two young men glared at each other for several tense moments. Finally Taran sheathed his weapon.

"Fine," he said through clenched teeth. The tight smile on his face didn't match the cold fury in his eyes.

Without a word, he shoved past Felix and boarded the ship.

"Thanks," Jonas said to Felix under his breath.

Felix watched Taran's departure with a grim look. "You know he's going to be a problem, right?

"I do."

"Great." Felix glanced at the Limerian ship. "By the way, have I mentioned that I get really seasick, especially with the thought of

Amara's undead brother on board? So if our new friend Taran tries to cut my throat while I'm vomiting off the side of the ship, you're the one I blame."

"Understood." Jonas eyed Nic and Ashur warily. "Very well, whatever fate awaits us on the other side, let's set sail for Mytica. All of us."

"Thought you didn't believe in fate?" Nic muttered as they made their way up the gangplank.

"I don't," Jonas said.

But, to be honest, only a small part of him believed that anymore.